EXCLUSIVE

LYN ANDREWS

The storyteller to generations
returns on 9th March 2006 with
her spellbinding new novel

-- ✂

Get £2 off
your copy at

5 019388 227294

A Mother's Love

Lyn Andrews

headline

First published in 2004
by HEADLINE BOOK PUBLISHING

First published in paperback in 2005
by HEADLINE BOOK

4

ISBN 0 7553 0838 7

Typeset in Janson by Avon DataSet Ltd,
Bidford-on-Avon, Warwickshire

Printed and bound in Great Britain by
Mackays of Chatham plc, Chatham, Kent

Headline's policy is to use papers that are natural, renewable
and recyclable products and made from wood grown in
sustainable forests. The logging and manufacturing processes
are expected to conform to the environmental regulations
of the country of origin.

HEADLINE BOOK PUBLISHING
A division of Hodder Headline
338 Euston Road
London NW1 3BH

www.headline.co.uk
www.hodderheadline.com

For my son-in-law, Luis Andrade, my future daughter-in-law, Joanne Robinson and last, but certainly not least, my treasured grandson Joseph Robert Andrews, who is possibly the brightest, most sweet-natured, adorable three-year-old in the world – but then I'm biased!

My grateful thanks to and sincere admiration for Mr Poonawalla, the radiologists and all the staff of the Linda McCartney Unit of the Royal Liverpool Hospital and the staff of the Liverpool Women's Hospital who were all so marvellous to me during what was a very worrying and stressful experience.

Lyn Andrews
Tullamore, 2004

Chapter One

Liverpool 1933

'EVE, WHERE'S ME COLLAR studs?' Eddie Dobson's voice, irritated and full of belligerence, came from the kitchen.

Eve raised her eyes to the yellow smoke-stained ceiling of the lounge bar and pursed her lips in annoyance. Could he never find anything himself? Did she always have to place everything right under his nose? The trouble with Eddie was that he was lazy and impatient. He just *wouldn't* look for things.

'They're on the mantelpiece in that little china bowl thing!' she shouted. 'Where they always are,' she added *sotto voce*.

Gathering up the two remaining dirty beer glasses she placed them at the end of the bar counter and attacked the brass handles of the beer pumps with a cloth. They should have been done hours ago, she thought with growing

1

annoyance, as should all the chores that still awaited her attention. They were of course part of Doreen's job but there was always some excuse from that little madam as to why she had failed to do them. It was half past ten and there was no sign of the girl. A fine barmaid *that* one was – and now Eddie was off to see Mr Harrison at the brewery about the state of business, leaving her to cope with the dinnertime trade alone.

Turning, she caught sight of herself in the rather ornate mirror she'd insisted they put up behind the bar 'to give the place a bit of class'. She'd had a serious argument with Eddie over that mirror. He'd said loudly and disparagingly that he wasn't having the parlour of the George looking like 'a tart's bedroom'! She smiled to herself. Well, she'd won that argument.

'Do I look like a tart? Do I?' she'd demanded and of course he'd backed down.

She peered more closely at her reflection. She'd taken great care never to look remotely flashy or common but was she beginning to look her age? she wondered, smoothing down the short, neat dark curls and searching for telltale grey hairs. Her large, dark brown eyes had always been her most attractive feature – so everyone told her – and her nose was straight, her lips full and her complexion wasn't bad. A bit pale perhaps, but wasn't that only to be expected, being stuck behind this bar morning, noon and night? She certainly wasn't going to resort to rouge or even a dab of lipstick rubbed into her cheeks. Lipstick and a dusting of face powder on special occasions were the only cosmetics she used.

She turned sideways, her hands on her hips. Not a bad figure even after three children. She hadn't run to fat like so many did nor had she let herself go. She was petite and always took care with her clothes and appearance, as much as time and money would allow. 'No, not bad for thirty-seven, girl!' she said aloud, though the thought depressed her a little. She was fast approaching middle age.

Eddie came through the door fumbling with the stiff collar, his face red with the effort. 'I can't do this blasted thing up, I'm all thumbs. I hate these bloody meetings with Harrison, all bloody doom and gloom!'

Eve turned to her husband of over twenty years and grimaced. 'You're worse than a kid at dressing yourself! Come here, you'll have that collar like a grubby rag at the rate you're going.'

He shifted impatiently from foot to foot. 'Why don't you get me those shirts that have soft collars attached? Then there wouldn't be this performance and I wouldn't be half choked.'

Eve's small fingers worked deftly on the fiddly stud. 'Because they cost a small fortune for one thing and for another you'd have to have a clean shirt every day and I've enough to do without spending hours ironing dozens of your shirts! There! I don't know what all the fuss was about.'

Eddie ran his finger around the collar and then turned and straightened his tie with the aid of the disputed mirror.

Eve leaned against the bar and watched him shrug on his best jacket. She had to admit that he was still quite a good-looking man, even though he'd turned forty on his last birthday – a fact that had seemed to add to the constant state of disgruntlement that possessed him these days. There were a few strands of silver now in his fair hair and fine lines radiated from around his blue-grey eyes, but not too many. He was tall, nearly six foot two, and he'd been slim when they'd first been married. Years of standing behind the bar and joining his customers in a 'swift half' had thickened his girth; he had a definite paunch although she wouldn't exactly call it a beer belly.

'Right, I'm off,' he announced, patting his pockets to make sure he had his keys and wallet.

'And what time can I expect you back then?'

'How the hell should I know, Eve! You know what old Harrison is like when he gets going.'

Eve sighed heavily. 'Never having met him, I don't know. Oh, take your time, I'll manage.'

'Well, there's hardly likely to be a stampede, is there? Takings are down, that's what this blasted meeting's about, although just what I'm supposed to do about it I don't know. I can't drag them in, can I?'

You could try to stop drinking the profits and stay clear of the bookies, she thought, but said nothing. He was in a bad enough mood as it was.

After the door had closed behind him she glanced around and sighed again. The George wasn't a big fancy pub like some in this city where competition for business was fierce. There seemed to be a pub on every single street corner. It was just a small hostelry on the corner of Upper Dawson

Street which opened out on to Williamson Square. There was the saloon bar, the lounge bar – which despite her efforts most people still called the parlour – and a small snug. The living accommodation comprised a large kitchen cum sitting room, three bedrooms, a storeroom and the privy in the yard. Not exactly palatial but she had to admit it was a damned sight better than the slum houses most of their customers were forced to live in, some of them packed five and six to a single room.

Taking a damp cloth, she began to wipe the tops of the small tables that were dotted around the room. Pale rays of spring sunlight filtered through the window panes, showing up the dust and glass marks. The whole place needed a good clean, to say nothing of a fresh coat of paint. Well, there was nothing she could do about the paint, no one was going to spend money on redecorating when there were so many people out of work, but at least she could give the place a clean – when that lazy little madam Doreen deigned to put in an appearance.

The room was stuffy and heavy with the odours of stale beer and tobacco smoke and she pulled open the door, wedging it wide with a folded beer mat. Upper Dawson Street was much quieter than either Williamson Square or Queens Square, both of which were busy all day long with the carts and wagons pulled by the huge, patient shire horses, delivering to the hotels, shops and warehouses. Peering down the narrow street, she caught sight of the girl making her way slowly along, frequently glancing at her reflection in the shop windows.

Eve glared at her. You'd think it was eight o'clock in the morning instead of nearly a quarter to eleven. Well, Miss Doreen Travis would be looking for another job if she didn't buck her ideas up.

'What time do you call this, miss?' she demanded when the girl was within earshot.

Fiddling with a blonde curl, Doreen hurried her steps slightly and shrugged. 'Me mam needed a few things from Cooper's.'

Eve was openly derisive. 'And when have the likes of you ever shopped at Cooper's?' she demanded. It was Liverpool's most exclusive and expensive grocer's, situated in Church Street and specialising in imported and exotic foods.

'Since me da got home from sea and won't drink nothing but coffee with his breakfast,' the girl shot back.

'Hasn't he got all high and mighty since he signed on with Cunard! And since when do bedroom stewards get to drink coffee?'

'He's not a steward no more. Got promoted to waiter in first class on the *Franconia*. He gets to eat all kinds of fancy food now.'

'Nice for him,' Eve said cuttingly. 'Now, get inside and give me a hand to give the lounge a bit of a spring clean. It's a living disgrace.'

Doreen flounced in. 'I'm a barmaid not a flaming cleaner,' she muttered sullenly. She'd spent an hour painting her nails with the new varnish she'd bought in Woolworths yesterday, now it would be ruined.

6

'And you won't be either if business doesn't pick up soon!' Eve snapped. She was beginning to detest the girl. Not only was she lazy, she was hardfaced. God alone knew why Eddie had taken her on. To encourage trade, was the reason he'd given. Well, in her opinion a plainer, more hard-working and willing girl would have suited them better. Doreen Travis, with her peroxide blonde hair, painted nails and over-bright lipstick (to say nothing of the far too low-cut blouses she was so fond of wearing) was not much of an asset, in her opinion.

Handing Doreen a dishcloth and a bowl of hot soapy water, Eve instructed her to start stripping the shelves of the bottles behind the bar.

'What's the point in starting now? It's nearly dinnertime – the fellers will be in soon,' Doreen complained.

'I *know* it's nearly dinnertime, miss, and not a flaming thing done yet!'

'Where's Eddie?'

'Gone to the brewery for a meeting, if it's any of your business.' Eve began to pull out all the chairs.

Doreen pulled a face at Eve's back and began half-heartedly to wipe the bottles of spirits. If Eddie had been here she wouldn't have to be doing this. Oh, no! She could twist him around her little finger. He liked her a lot, she knew that only too well. He was always finding excuses to flatter her and put his arm around her; once or twice he had kissed her: only on the cheek, mind, but it just showed you! It was why she got away with murder. He wouldn't get rid of her. He was always telling her that she livened the place up.

She didn't mind the work, actually. It was far better than many jobs. The hours were long but they were in other jobs too and here she could dress herself up and chat and flirt to her heart's content – when Eve wasn't around. She knew her presence had brought quite a few young fellers into the George who would have taken their custom elsewhere had she not been there to amuse them. And she was no fool either. She was twenty-four, for God's sake, not a kid of seventeen. She knew what she wanted out of life and it wasn't being stuck in a couple of dingy rooms with a gang of kids hanging on to her skirts, with not enough money or time to herself and a husband wanting to be waited on hand and foot. Oh, no! Doreen Travis wasn't going to be a bloody skivvy to anyone!

They worked in hostile silence until a shout from the saloon bar interrupted their limited progress.

Doreen threw down her cloth thankfully. 'I told you it was a waste of time starting this now, there's Uncle Uk looking for his pint!'

'You finish what you're doing, I'll go and see to him,' Eve replied sharply, determined the girl wasn't going to shirk the task she'd been set. Drying her hands, she went briskly into the other room.

The old carter was leaning on the bar, his cap pushed back revealing a face so weather-beaten it resembled old leather. 'It's like a bloody graveyard in 'ere, girl. Where's everyone gone?'

Taking down a clean glass Eve began to pull a pint of Higson's Best Bitter. 'Eddie's down the brewery and Doreen and I are doing a bit of cleaning. Have you finished for the day then?'

Edward Bevington shook his head. Eve's oldest daughter Sarah had been unable to pronounce his name as a child so she had christened him 'Uncle Ukward'. Now he was known to all as 'Uncle Uk'. He watched Eve carefully and licked his lips in anticipation. 'Got one more load this afternoon but I'll be puttin' the poor auld horse out to grass at the end of the week at this rate. Them ships is coming in half empty an' goin' out the same way too. It's the Depression in America, it's affecting trade the whole world over!'

Eve nodded and placed the glass down in front of him. 'That'll be sevenpence, please.'

' 'Ave the brewery put the prices up again?' he demanded.

'Don't start that! You know they went up last month.'

He grinned. 'Worth a try, girl!'

Eve grinned back. 'You never miss a trick, do you?'

'Put it on the slate, luv. Yer know I'm good for it cum Friday.'

'You'll have me in the bankruptcy court yet!'

The man's good humour deserted him and he stared gloomily into his pint. 'You an' me both, Eve, if things don't look up soon. This city's going to the dogs.'

Before she had time to reply the door opened and a group of men crowded in, all wearing rough jackets, moleskin trousers, mufflers, caps and heavy boots: the uniform of the poor working class.

'No more work then, lads?' Uncle Uk asked of them collectively.

'Not a bloody ship in sight! Over a thousand fellers on the stands this mornin' and only two 'alf-empty bloody freighters in eight miles of docks. I tell yer, it's gettin' bad, really bad.'

'What's up with yer face, Jacko? 'Ad an argument with a lamppost?' Uncle Uk demanded of a thickset man who had a cut on his cheek and the beginnings of a black eye.

'No, with some 'ard case from the south end,' Jacko answered sullenly.

'It's gettin' desperate, Uk. Yer've ter fight fer work and I mean fight! The blockerman threatened ter bring in the scuffers if there was any more trouble between the lads this mornin',' another said grimly.

'A crowd of bloody youngsters started it, sayin' they never get no work, it always goes ter the older fellers and it's not fair. They've got kids ter feed too.'

Uncle Uk took a swig of his pint. 'Reckon they've got a point.'

'There's not enough work fer us all when the docks are full, never mind 'alf empty. I'll be goin' on the Parish meself at this rate,' Jacko added morosely.

Eve bit her lip. Things really were getting worse and she couldn't put all these drinks on the slate, Eddie would have a fit. Yet she sympathised with them. It was humiliating to say the least to have to stand in pens like cattle, twice a day, and wait to be picked for a few hours' work, if you were lucky. Even more degrading was the fact that they literally had to fight their fellow workers for the chance to earn a few shillings. Still, she had to make the position clear.

10

'I've heard the brewery are going to insist we put a "No Credit" sign up over the bar,' she said, grimacing apologetically.

'It's all right, girl, we've the price of a pint! We're not lookin' fer charity,' the battered docker informed her.

She nodded with some relief but wondered just how they did manage to find the price of a pint when their wives were half demented trying to make ends meet. She'd begun to serve them when Jim Stokes from the newsagent's and Alf Casey from the cobbler's came in, followed, to her dismay, by Dick Taggart. He was one who'd start a row in an empty house.

'Doreen! Come in here, I need you to serve!' she called with some annoyance. The girl would have that smug, self-righteous grin on her face and be only too pleased to leave the cleaning.

'Aren't you a sight for sore eyes!' Dick Taggart grinned, his gaze taking in the tight-fitting pink floral blouse that dipped to a low V at the front.

Doreen basked in the attention as all eyes focused on her. She smiled archly and fluttered her eyelashes at Taggart. 'What can I do for you, Dick? Dare I ask what's your pleasure?'

The bar erupted in loud, raucous laughter and a few highly questionable comments.

Eve's temper rose. 'That's enough of that! This is a respectable pub not a bawdy house on Lime Street!' she snapped.

'Just a bit of fun, girl!' Taggart retorted, smirking.

'Come in for a quiet pint and a bit of decent conversation and what do you get? A bloody bear pit!' Jim Stokes muttered peevishly. He'd not had a good morning. Mary had been on top note for hours.

'What's up with yer gob? The missus been at yer all mornin' then?' Taggart snapped aggressively. Mary Stokes was a shrew of a woman.

Eve lost her temper. 'Don't you start, Dick Taggart! I've enough to do without having to call the scuffers in here to sort you out at just after twelve in the afternoon. Doreen, when you've served this lot you can get back to your cleaning!'

Doreen had had enough of Eve's belittling comments. 'Eddie took me on as a barmaid not a cleaner and—'

Eve cut her short. She had no intention of having a yelling match with the girl in front of this lot. 'Well, Eddie's not here, is he, so you'll do as you're damned well told!'

Doreen's face went scarlet and she slammed down a glass of mild on the counter. 'I won't be treated like a flaming skivvy and Eddie's the boss, not you! I'm not taking orders from you!'

Eve's hand tightened on the pump and her cheeks burned. The girl had never openly defied her before. 'You'll keep a civil tongue in your head, lady, or there's the door!'

There was complete silence in the room. Pints were ignored, conversation and newspapers abandoned at this fascinating turn of events.

The two women faced each other, both seething with rage. Finally Doreen turned away and snatched her bag from under the counter. 'Right then, I'm off! Tell Eddie I'll call round later to see him and collect my wages!' Ignoring the startled looks of the customers and Eve's outrage, she strode to the door, yanked it open and let it slam shut behind her.

'Looks like yer're on yer own, girl!' Uncle Uk commented drily, draining the last of his pint. 'Fill it up again.' He settled down to wait. It was going to be an interesting couple of hours until Eddie returned to sort out this little cat fight.

Conversation resumed. Eve was consumed with anger and run off her feet until young Harry Dempsey came round behind the bar to give her a hand.

'She asked for that, Eve,' he murmured when things had quietened down.

She smiled at him. He was a decent lad who lodged with Ma Flanagan and got work when he could at whatever he could. He was a good-looking young man too, with dark curly hair and dark brown eyes. He wasn't as tall as Eddie but he was certainly slimmer. 'She *has* been asking for that for a long time, the hardfaced little madam! Over an hour late this morning she was and me on my own.'

'What'll Eddie say?'

'I don't care what Eddie says! Anyway, after his meeting with the brewery we might not be able to afford a barmaid.'

'Oh, I didn't think things were that bad. I was sort of hoping that, well . . . you might take me on to replace her. I'm a hard worker, but not as . . . er . . . attractive.' He laughed.

'Do you think that one is attractive?'

He shrugged. 'In an obvious sort of way. Some fellers like that kind, though.'

'But not you?'

'Not my type, Eve. Brassy, a bit of a gold-digger too, so I've heard.'

'Good riddance, is what I say. What time is it?'

Harry consulted the clock on the far wall. 'Nearly half past two, rush over. Just the stragglers left now. No hope of any work for them today.'

'Then perhaps they'll go home to their long-suffering wives, my feet are killing me.'

'Why don't you go and have a bit of a rest? I'll see to things.'

Thankfully Eve nodded. Not only were her feet aching but her head was too and she knew there would be cross words with Eddie when he finally got home.

It was nearly half past three when she heard the kitchen door open. She sat up. She must have dozed off: her head felt muzzy.

'What's Harry Dempsey doing behind the bar?' Eddie demanded. He'd got little satisfaction from the lad when he'd asked where Eve and Doreen were.

Wearily Eve got to her feet and put the kettle on. 'He's been helping out. There was a bit of a rush, then I got a headache so he said he would cope.'

Eddie took off his jacket and hung it on the back of a chair. 'Where's Doreen? Didn't she turn up?'

Eve faced him squarely. 'Oh, she turned up – late as usual – then there was a row and . . . and I sacked her!'

14

Eddie stared at her. 'You did *what*?'

'You heard. She was downright rude and refused point blank to do as she was told, so I said if she didn't do what I asked, there's the door. She left.'

'Eve! She was the best barmaid we've ever had! Why the hell did you do that?'

Eve was stung. 'The *best barmaid*? She was lazy, insolent, always late and she was just too . . . brazen! You should have heard what she said to Dick Taggart. Far too suggestive for a young girl. I won't have *staff* making a show of me in my own pub and she was!'

'God Almighty! I can't leave you alone for a few hours without you start fighting with everyone.'

'Not *everyone*, just that little madam.'

'You never liked her, did you? What was it you really didn't like, Eve?'

'I've just told you, or are you deaf?'

'I know she could be a bit temperamental, like, but you just didn't know how to get the best out of her.'

'Was there even a *best* to get out?'

'There was! Face it, Eve, you just didn't like her because she was young and attractive, the fellers flocked around her and spent money. She was an asset we needed.'

'Oh, don't be such a bloody fool, Eddie Dobson! She's tarty! She's a peroxide blonde with a painted face and the morals of an alley cat. Why else isn't she married? Most decent girls of her age are. We're well rid of her. Harry's a far better worker and he gets on well with the men and he can handle the troublemakers. I'd sooner pay him.'

15

'Well, we can't afford to pay *anyone*!'

Eve placed the teapot on the table and bit back the comment that they would have had to get rid of Doreen anyway. 'So the meeting went badly?'

'The takings are down, there's to be no more credit allowed, we've to tighten our belts from now on. And a load of facts and figures that mean nothing to me.'

Eddie didn't listen half the time, Eve thought impatiently. She was certain that had Mr Harrison explained everything to her she would have understood. She *did* understand figures, far better than Eddie did; in fact she often wondered if Eddie thought she was totally ignorant of business matters? To her they were relatively simple, there didn't seem to be anything complicated about running a pub.

'Then we'll just have to do as he says. Tighten our belts. No more swift halves and no more bets on the horses.'

'And no more new hats,' he shot back, stung by her implications.

'And when was the last time I even had a new hat?' she retorted.

They stared at each other until Eve at last sighed. 'Well, at least all the girls are working, thank God, and talking of girls, here's our Sarah now. She must have finished early.'

Eddie sat down and sipped his tea. It had been a far from satisfactory day so far. Harrison's droning, half-whining voice had given him a headache. He'd lost half a crown on a horse he'd been certain would win, he'd missed his tram and now he had the matter of Doreen to sort out. He had to get to the bottom of this – and he owed the girl money. He'd go round to her house later on, when he could get a few minutes away from Eve and his three daughters, the eldest of whom was coming up the yard. By the look on her face, she too was far from happy.

Chapter Two

SARAH DOBSON WASN'T IN the best of moods. She hadn't been too upset when she'd been told that she was to finish early, because it had been a trying day. Business was slack at the Stork Hotel where she worked as a waitress. She seemed to have spent most of the day just looking for things to do. There had been few people for breakfast and even fewer for lunch and Mr Stevens, the head waiter, had been impossible to please.

'You're home early, luv,' Eve greeted her, handing her a cup of tea.

'The place is almost empty so he sent me home. I didn't mind that but I'll be short in my wages,' Sarah said wearily. 'I have to admit I'd sooner be rushed off my feet – at least the time doesn't drag – but we've only been a quarter full for weeks now.'

'Oh, don't you start too! I'm sick of hearing just how bad business is for everyone,' Eddie said sharply.

Sarah raised her eyebrows questioningly.

'He's been to see Mr Harrison – we're on an economy drive,' Eve said by way of an explanation, while grimacing apologetically at her eldest daughter for Eddie's bad humour. Sarah was like Eddie in looks, she mused. Tall and slim with blue eyes and thick straight fair hair that was the bane of her life. She too was pale, Eve thought. Not enough time spent in the fresh air. When she wasn't working she helped out a lot in the house and, when required, in the pub.

'It's a pleasant evening, why don't you and our Lily go for a bit of a sail after tea? Go over to Seacombe or New Brighton on the ferry. It'll do you good – both of you.' And it will keep Lily out of mischief for once, Eve thought to herself.

'I promised Maggie I'd help her with that dress she's making,' Sarah replied a little regretfully. She wouldn't have minded a ferry trip and Maggie was such a misery at times.

'And where did our Maggie get the money for new dresses?' Eddie demanded. This was the first he'd heard of this extravagance.

Eve was losing patience. 'Not from me! She bought the material herself from Blackler's last week. She's been saving up.'

Eddie wouldn't let the subject go. 'So, what's the big occasion then?'

'I told you the other day. She's going to Billy's granny's for tea with his mam and dad.'

'And what's so special about Billy Wainwright's granny?' Eddie demanded.

'She's got a few bob, that's what.'

'And he's hoping to get his hands on some of it!' Sarah put in a little derisively. She didn't have a very high opinion of her sister's young man.

Not wishing to hear Eddie's opinion on this matter, Eve began to clear the tea things. 'You'd better get yourself behind the bar while I make a start on the meal. I'll have the other two in soon and not a thing done.'

Both Sarah and her father reluctantly got to their feet. At least the bar would be fairly quiet and he'd get a bit of peace, Eddie thought. There was a horse he fancied in tomorrow's three o'clock at Haydock, he'd have a look at the odds. Despite Eve's comments he had no intention of cutting out his betting. A man had to have a bit of an interest. He was often lucky and he never bet more than he could afford to lose – unlike some fools he knew. Unknown to Eve he had a few pounds put away, for a 'rainy day'.

Sarah went upstairs to take off her uniform and have a quick wash. Sitting on the edge of the bed in the room that, because of being the eldest, she had to herself, she studied her reflection in the dressing-table mirror. Mam was right, she did look pale. She frowned. It didn't help that her eyebrows and eyelashes were so fair. Sometimes she thought she looked like a white rabbit. The frown deepened. Thinking like that wouldn't improve her mood. She pinched her cheeks and then swept up her hair. If she were to wear it up, would it make her look too old? She sighed as she let the heavy locks fall down over her shoulders. 'Oh, for heaven's sake, stop depressing yourself into the ground, Sarah Dobson!' she said sternly to her reflection. Maybe she should cut her hair short; she'd ask Mam's advice later on. Now she'd better get a move on.

When she returned to the kitchen, Sarah began to set the table. Eve smiled gratefully at her.

'You know you really should get out more. You're a great help but you need a life of your own, luv.'

'I'm fine, Mam, honestly I am. You know I've never been one for running off to the Grafton or the Rialto.'

'Maybe you should go dancing. You never seem to bother with lads. There's our Maggie almost about to get engaged, I'm certain of it—'

'Mam, if I couldn't do better than Billy Wainwright I'd not bother at all!' Sarah interrupted scornfully.

Eve grinned conspiratorially. 'Don't for God's sake say I said so, but I agree! He's a right wet week.'

'And he does exactly as our Maggie tells him. I don't think he's got a mind of his own at all!'

'Still, I suppose she could do worse. Look at our Lily, she seems to have the knack of picking the most unsuitable lads in the neighbourhood.'

'Oh, leave her, Mam, she's only a bit of a kid.'

'That's what worries me.'

'She's not a fool, Mam. I know she's a bit scatty at times but she's got her head screwed on the right way.'

'I just hope so. I live in fear of her turning out like . . . well, like that brazen little madam that I sacked this morning.'

Sarah put down the plates she was laying out. 'Doreen? Doreen Travis? You sacked her?'

Eve nodded. 'I'd just about had enough of her. It's good riddance!'

Sarah grinned. 'Good for you, Mam.' She'd never liked the girl.

'Good riddance to who?'

They both looked up to see Maggie standing in the kitchen doorway, a deeply suspicious look on her face.

'Oh, don't worry, we weren't talking about your precious Billy,' Sarah replied, shooting an amused glance at her mother.

'Doreen Travis. I sacked her this morning.'

'Not before time either! She's so undesirable, so Billy says.'

Sarah raised her eyes to the ceiling.

'Oh, there's many who would disagree with that! There's quite a few who think her very *desirable*!' Eve retorted.

Maggie sniffed. Some fellers were blind. In her opinion Doreen Travis was little better than a common tart, the only difference was she didn't charge. She'd said as much to Billy, who'd been quite horrified at her bluntness, but it was true. She'd seen the carry-on of her with at least three different fellers in the back entry.

'Mam, can we get the tea over early tonight? I've so much to do.'

Eve smiled at her middle daughter. Maggie was so serious and earnest. Eve didn't know where she got it from. Not from herself and certainly not from Eddie. Oh, Sarah could be very down to earth but not as intense as Maggie, and as for Lily, well, she was just as Sarah had described her – scatty. Maggie did look like her mother. She was small with the same dark curly hair and large brown eyes but there the similarity ended. She was strong-willed and determined and ambitious in her own unimaginative way. True, she was a hard worker and never complained about her job in McMillan's Greengrocer's, which meant she was up and out early and had to stand long hours on her feet in often cold and damp conditions. She complained only that her hands were a disgrace and her clothes got filthy. Sarah interrupted her thoughts.

'So, I take it we're not going to have the pleasure of Billy's company tonight?'

'You know he's not coming round tonight. I'd never get my dress finished with him fussing.'

'What's she like, his granny?' Sarah probed.

'I don't know, I've never met her. That's why we're going on Sunday.' Maggie wouldn't admit it but she was very apprehensive about this visit. According to Billy old Mrs Wainwright was a bit of a tartar and he'd stressed how important it was that she approved of Maggie. All their plans depended on it. Maggie got on well enough with Billy's mam and dad but the old lady was a different kettle of fish.

'You'll look just great, Maggie. She'll be delighted with you.' Eve had noticed the look of apprehension on Maggie's face.

'Of course she'll like you. Who wouldn't?' Sarah added.

'Is there any sign yet of a meal on that table? All I can hear is you three nattering fifteen to the dozen. My belly thinks my throat's been cut!' Eddie asked impatiently, sticking his head around the door.

24

'Is it quiet in there, Da?' Sarah asked.

'As the grave!'

'Maybe word's got round already that there's to be no more credit given,' Eve said quietly.

'A right Job's comforter, isn't she?' Eddie said gloomily before disappearing back into the saloon bar in the hope that soon there would be someone to air his grievances to and put a few coppers in the till.

Eve was just dishing out the meal when Lily, breathless and laughing, burst into the kitchen.

'God, those Molloy lads are the end!'

'Now what have you been up to?' Eve demanded.

'They had a dead rat and they chased me with it all the way up the street!' Lily laughed.

'It's about time they all grew up. The age of them!' Maggie said, full of disapproval.

'They have poor Agnes half out of her mind with the carry-on of them,' Eve added, thinking of her neighbour's often repeated cry that her four youngest would end up in a reformatory.

'Oh, it's only a bit of fun, Mam.' Lily was unrepentant.

'Well, you can just calm yourself down and after tea you can give these two a hand, you're the apprentice seamstress,' Eve instructed.

Lily was instantly up in arms. 'Oh, Mam, do I have to? I spend all day flaming well sewing and I was going to go to the Royal Court, there's a good variety show on and it's cheaper mid-week!'

Eve shook her head. It hadn't been easy to get Lily an

apprenticeship. They were harder and harder to come by now that ready-to-wear clothes were so popular. The number of dressmaking establishments had dwindled considerably but it was still a much-sought-after trade. She sighed to herself as she thought of her youngest daughter. At seventeen Lily was the prettiest of her girls. She had Eddie's height and his best features, including his blue eyes, but her hair was thick, dark and curly and worn long. She was also strong-willed, inclined to be flighty, rather impatient and possessed of a burning desire to be 'famous', although just exactly what she meant by that Eve couldn't fathom. She doubted Lily even knew herself. The girl was full of the exuberance of the young who hadn't yet experienced the hardships and disappointments of life. Everything was exciting to Lily, everything except her job.

'Oh, Lily! That show is on all week and I've only got four days to finish my dress!' Maggie cried. She'd banked on her sister helping with the more awkward bits.

'And don't go saying anything to Da about going to the theatre,' Sarah warned.

'I'm only going in the gods! It's all I can afford. What's up with him anyway?'

'He's not had a good day,' Eve said.

'He had to go to the brewery and Mam sacked Doreen,' Sarah added.

Lily giggled.

'What's funny about that?' Maggie asked.

'Davie Todd told me he interrupted *that one* giving their Frank a knee-trembler in the Stokeses' doorway last night!'

'Lily Dobson, wash your mouth out!' Maggie cried, horrified.

'Don't you let your da hear you saying things like that, miss! You're too forward for my liking and you shouldn't be discussing things like that with Davie Todd. What must he think of you?' Eve reprimanded.

Lily pulled a face. 'I only told you so you'd know what kind of a girl she is.'

'We already *know* that. That's why Mam got rid of her,' Sarah said flatly.

'Shut up all of you, here's your da. And, Lily, don't you dare repeat that!' Eve hissed. 'Right, Eddie, it's on the table. Leave that door open so if anyone does come in we'll hear them.'

Only one person came into the bar and Eve went through to serve. It didn't help Eddie's mood and he sat wondering what excuse he could give to get out to see Doreen for an hour. Did he need one? he asked himself. Was he or was he not master in his own house? Eve usually said where she was going but he never demanded that she tell him. Well, if she wanted to know he would just say he was going out, and that was it! Besides, the thought of standing all night listening to the woes of the handful of customers who might come in depressed him.

When the meal was over all three girls cleared away, Eve went back into the bar and he sat in the corner with his copy of the *Echo*, but his bit of peace was short-lived. Within minutes the room was filled with paper patterns, yards of material, reels of cotton and three rather noisy and impatient

27

girls. After he'd been asked to move his feet for the third time, he folded the newspaper and got up. It was just the excuse he needed.

'Right, I'm off out for an hour or two. It's like a bloody circus in here.'

'Da, it's no use carrying on, I *told* you we needed the kitchen tonight. I've got to get this finished by Sunday!' Maggie said.

'I don't know why you and Billy Wainwright don't go and take up residence with his flaming granny, then I might get some peace!'

Maggie ignored him.

'Hadn't you better tell Mam where you're going?' Sarah asked.

'What the hell for? Am I not allowed out on my own now? Do I have to ask permission?' he snapped.

'I'll go and give her a hand if she needs it,' Lily said, raising her eyes to the ceiling.

'No, you won't. I need you here,' Maggie reminded her.

'I'll go if needs be,' Sarah intervened as Eddie slammed out.

Still annoyed that her visit to the theatre had had to be postponed, Lily held up the yellow and white sprigged cotton her sister had bought. 'I still don't think this colour will suit you, Maggie.'

'Oh, for heaven's sake, Lily, don't start her off again. Give me that pattern and let's get started or we'll be up all night!' Sarah admonished.

* * *

Eddie took a deep breath of evening air as he closed the yard door behind him. It was good to get out. He was fed up with the pub. He'd been in the business for most of his life. He'd virtually grown up in the place. His father had been the licensee before him and his mam had always impressed upon him how lucky he was to be allowed to take over after his da had died suddenly of a heart attack. Three months later his mam had announced that she was going to live in Chester with her sister Florrie, who had never got over losing her husband in the Great War. Eve had been delighted at that. At last they'd be on their own, running the pub without any interference, she'd said. He pulled the collar of his jacket up around his ears, for the wind was cold. She'd been so different then, had Eve. She'd never snapped at him, never nagged, never challenged any of his decisions, never belittled him. When had she changed? When she'd had Lily? And when had he stopped loving her? He shrugged. What did it matter now, he was out of the place for an hour. Sometimes he felt as though the women were stifling him. The house always seemed to be full of them and all the noise and clutter that went with them. He felt depressed. He was fed up with worrying about the state of trade. Fed up with listening to Eve worrying over her girls. Fed up with this poverty-stricken, depression-hit city. Life seemed to be passing him by. He was forty, a middle-aged man and the fact that his daughters were fast becoming young women served only to emphasise that fact. And, to cap it all, it had been very high-handed of Eve to sack Doreen as soon as his back had been turned.

Doreen had certainly brightened up his life recently. She'd always been a flirtatious girl, and not only with him, but he'd been surprised and very flattered when a couple of weeks ago, after Eve had gone to bed and he and Doreen had been clearing up the bar, she had made a deliberate pass at him. A pass that had turned into something far more serious. They weren't exactly having an affair: they had only managed to make love hastily and furtively in the cellar three times, but she made him feel young, virile and desirable. He'd even gone so far as to boast that he wasn't totally tied to Eve's apron strings, he had a fair bit of money put by and could give a girl a good time, which wasn't exactly true. He didn't have *that* much money and his time usually had to be accounted for – or did it? Whatever, he wasn't going to let her go. All the long hours behind the bar would be unbearable without her.

It wasn't far to the house where Mr and Mrs Travis lived with their two youngest kids. The others were all grown up and married.

'Evening, Mrs Travis, is Doreen in?' he asked when the door was opened to him.

'You come to pay her what you owe her, seeing as how that snotty wife of yours give her the push?' the woman demanded argumentatively.

'Yes. That's what I've come to see her about.'

She was slightly mollified. 'You'd best come in then.'

He followed her along the dark narrow lobby towards the kitchen.

'Eddie Dobson's here to see you, girl,' she called.

Doreen came to the kitchen door and shot a warning look at her mother. 'We'll go in the parlour.'

Mrs Travis sniffed and closed the kitchen door.

Doreen wasn't really surprised to see Eddie, although he'd never been to her house before. She'd known he would be furious with Eve. He'd often complained about his wife's high-handed ways and she'd always been sympathetic and had supported his views.

'I was going to come down and see you later, Eddie. Sit down.'

Eddie glanced around, surprised to see that the room was quite well furnished, and sat down on the edge of the overstuffed, shiny hide sofa. 'Look, Doreen, luv, I'm sorry about that . . . misunderstanding this morning. Eve had no right to sack you. No right at all!'

Doreen sat down beside him and looked upset. This was promising. 'She doesn't like me, Eddie, I don't know why. I mean I try, I really do, but she started bossing me around, treating me like a skivvy and then showing me up in front of all those fellers!' Her bottom lip trembled and she dabbed at her eyes.

Eddie was perturbed. 'Come on, luv, don't upset yourself. You know if I'd been there it wouldn't have happened. I won't have you treated like that!'

Doreen sniffed and pressed the handkerchief to her eyes. 'Oh, Eddie, I *know* that, but you weren't there and I'd . . . well, I'd just had enough! I'm so upset, I really am!'

He put his arm around her comfortingly. He felt very protective of her and somehow more powerful. After all, *he*

31

made the decisions, not Eve. 'I know, luv, and I'm so sorry. Don't cry, you know I hate to see you like this. I won't have it!'

Doreen glanced at him from beneath her tear-stained lashes. This was going to be so easy. She knew he was fed up with Eve: she was so dour and always seemed to be carping and nagging at him. Doreen nestled closer to him. An idea had been forming in her mind for quite a while that appealed to her greatly, and the events of the morning had made her determined to put it into action. She'd had all afternoon to think about her position. She was twenty-four and going nowhere, as her father had reminded her scathingly when she'd come home and told them the tale of her dismissal, suitably edited, of course. There wasn't a man she even half fancied in the entire neighbourhood, let alone wanted to marry. She had quickly deduced that it would be impossible for her to replace Eve as landlady of the George. Eve would never stand for that, she'd fight her every inch of the way. So, why not extract Eddie from his family? He'd told her he had quite a bit of money and could give a girl a good time. He wasn't young, but was that a disadvantage? He was putty in her hands, he'd treat her well and she was sick of working and sick of living with her mam and da and, come to think of it, she was sick of living in this city with its increasing misery and unemployment. She wanted to see places, do things, *live*!

'You will come back? The place isn't the same without you,' he begged. Her closeness was having a very strange effect on him.

'Can you afford me? She said you'd gone to the brewery. What did they say?'

'Don't you worry about that. I'll find your wages.'

'Oh, I don't know, Eddie. I'm getting so sick of everything! I feel as though I'm being stifled!'

He sighed. 'I know what you mean.'

'No, you don't! You've got the pub and . . . everything. What have I got? Nothing!' She dabbed her eyes again.

'You're young! You've got your whole life ahead of you. I haven't, and believe me I'm pretty sick of my life at the moment!'

'Are you really?' she breathed. This was very promising.

'You've no idea what it's like living with that lot!'

'It must be terrible,' she murmured as she slid her hand up his chest and around his neck. 'Don't you wish sometimes that you could just . . . *go*? Do all the things *you* want to do? Go where *you* want to go without worrying about anyone else? I know I do.'

Eddie felt the room growing warmer – or was it just him? Her fingers were stroking the back of his neck and his insides were churning. He felt excitement stir in him. 'Do you?' he at last managed to say.

'Oh, I *do*, Eddie! But . . . but it would depend on . . . who I was with.' She was so sure of herself now. She could feel him trembling. He wanted her, she was experienced enough to be certain of it. 'And you know how much I like you. I really do, Eddie.' She raised her head and kissed him full on the mouth.

Eddie was lost. He couldn't help himself. He surrendered

entirely to the force of the passion that was consuming him. He kissed her hungrily and slid his hand down to her breast. She uttered a cry of pleasure and arched her back, pressing herself against him, urging him on.

As he became more demanding she pulled away. 'Eddie! Eddie, stop!'

He reached for her again, his senses inflamed. 'Oh, God, Doreen, I need you!'

'I know you do and I . . . I want you, Eddie, I *really* want you, but not here! Mam could come barging in at any minute.' She wasn't fool enough to give in so easily.

'Come back to work, please? We could find . . . time?' he begged.

'Much as I want to, much as I want *you*, I don't think I can come back.' She softened the blow by kissing him.

'What do you want?' he begged, beside himself at the knowledge that she was willing to fulfil all his desires. Oh, she was so young and pretty, so mysterious and tempting and *exciting*.

Doreen smiled to herself. All she had to do now was reel him in. She pressed herself close to him and let her hand move slowly to the waistband of his trousers. 'Eddie, you know I adore you, but I want you with me . . . always. I don't want just a quick tumble in the cellar when no one's around. I don't want the fellers making snide comments about the way you look at me.' And they were already noticing just how he did look at her and couldn't keep his hands off her, she thought.

A quick flash of reason pierced Eddie's befogged mind. 'What are you saying?' he gasped.

Her eyes hardened. 'You know what I'm saying! I want us to go away together. I want to *be* with you! Just the two of us, away from here. Don't you want me, Eddie?' Her hand moved lower.

He groaned. 'What will I tell Eve?'

'You don't have to tell her anything. We'll just go! Now, come here and let me spoil you a little. You need spoiling, Eddie, it's what you've been missing and when we're together I can spoil you day and night!'

He pushed all thoughts of Eve and his daughters out of his mind. He wouldn't think of them now. All he could think of was Doreen and the way she was making him feel.

Chapter Three

————✦————

BUSINESS HAD BEEN SLOW and Eve took it in turns with Sarah to go through to serve the few customers who came in. After her initial annoyance with Eddie for slamming out had died down, she watched with interest as Lily supervised the cutting-out of the new dress for Maggie.

'Come on, Mam, get a needle and some cotton and you can give us a hand with the tacking,' Maggie urged, eager to get on with the task.

Eve laughed. 'You know I'm not much of a one with the needle and cotton! I'm all thumbs.'

'Oh, honestly, Mam! It's so simple!' Lily exclaimed.

'Why do you think I sent you to be a seamstress?' Eve rejoined.

'Look, you do the tailor's tacks. You can't go wrong with them, I'll show you.'

Sarah sighed, peering at the instructions. 'Maggie, why did you have to pick such a complicated style? There seem to be a dozen pieces to this skirt.'

'I liked it and, besides, I want to make an impression.' Maggie was struggling with a piece that said 'cut on a bias'. 'Lily, what *is* a "bias"?'

'It means cut it on the cross, like this. You really would have been better with something easier and I'm still not sure about this material. It looks sort of prissy and washed out. I suppose we could trim it with something a bit brighter.'

'I don't want to look flashy or cheap!' Maggie cried in alarm. Lily's taste in clothes was far more colourful and adventurous than her own.

'You could never look cheap, luv! You're far too *conservative* in your taste,' Eve consoled, shooting a warning glance at Lily.

Lily was not to be diverted. 'Boring, you mean, Mam. She's so dark she suits bright colours, but she insists on wearing such dull things!'

'Will we have a cup of tea?' Sarah intervened, seeing an argument brewing.

Maggie was fearful. 'Only if you promise to be careful of my dress. I don't want it ruined before it's even started.'

'Oh, damn, there's the door of the snug,' Eve interrupted with some impatience.

'I'll wait until you come back, Mam,' Sarah smiled, then turned to her sisters. 'Providing there's no arguments between these two.'

Maggie shrugged and Lily, her mouth full of pins, nodded.

Eve was startled to see a stricken and shaking Agnes Molloy clutching the counter.

'Mother of God, Agnes, what's the matter? Is it those lads again? What have they done now?'

Her neighbour, who was without a coat or shawl and whose normally tidy hair was hanging in loose strands around her face, was in such a state that she couldn't speak. There was something very wrong indeed. Eve had known Agnes Molloy for twenty years and had never seen her like this. Quickly she lifted the counter flap and drew her neighbour towards her. Agnes was shaking like a leaf.

'Come into the kitchen, luv. Come in and tell me what's wrong,' Eve urged gently.

Tears were pouring down the woman's thin cheeks. 'Oh, God! Oh, Eve! I can't believe it!'

'What? For God's sake, what's happened, Agnes?'

'It's . . . it's . . . Ted!'

'Ted?' Eve echoed. Ted Molloy was a hard-working, mild-mannered man who spent little time in the George or any other pub. He'd been out of work for nearly two months now and she knew things were hard in the Molloy household, but there were thousands like them all over the city.

Agnes swayed and Eve put her arm around her.

'Eve, Eddie's . . . Eddie's got to come! I can't . . .'

'Eddie's not here. He's out. Come on in, luv. Calm down and tell me what's wrong with Ted. Is he ill?'

Agnes clung to her, sobbing uncontrollably as Eve guided her into the kitchen.

'Mam, what's the matter with Mrs Molloy?' Lily cried in alarm.

Eve shook her head as she eased Agnes into the chair Maggie quickly vacated.

'I'll put the kettle on,' Sarah offered.

'No. Go into the bar and get a drop of brandy. I think this is serious, too serious for tea.'

After a few sips of brandy Agnes pulled herself together a little, although she was still shaking and her face was ashen.

'Now, luv, in the name of heaven what's wrong?' Eve pressed.

'He . . . he's . . . hanged himself!' Agnes croaked, clutching the glass tightly.

Eve stared at her in horror. 'Holy Mother of God!'

Lily screamed and Sarah blanched; Maggie automatically crossed herself, the new dress utterly forgotten.

'How? Why? Oh, Agnes! Agnes!' Eve gathered her neighbour into her arms and held her while she sobbed. Dear God! Poor Agnes! What a terrible shock! What could she say? What could she do? Where the hell was Eddie when she needed him? She had to force herself to stay calm and to think rationally. They couldn't all fall into hysterics.

'Lily, go down and bring those young lads up here at once, they can't stay in there. Sarah, did your da say where he was going or how long he'd be?'

'No, Mam.'

'Mam, I . . . I can't go!' Lily cried in terror. She just couldn't face seeing Ted Molloy hanging there!

'I'll go and get them, Mam,' Maggie offered, taking her cue from her mother.

'Will I go for the doctor?' Sarah asked.

Eve shook her head. 'No, and say nothing to anyone – not yet.' Suicide was a crime. She poured another stiff measure of brandy and held the glass to Agnes's lips. 'Drink this up and then . . . then we'll have to sort this out.'

As Agnes tried to calm down, Eve's mind was working feverishly. He would have to be cut down, the authorities would have to be informed, and arrangements would have to be made.

'Agnes, luv, where is he?' she asked gently.

'On . . . on the landing. I thought he'd gone to bed early; he's been doing that lately. He's been so depressed, so worried about having no job and no money coming in, and that lot on the Board of Guardians wanting to know *everything* when he went to see if he could get Parish Relief . . . The rent's not been paid for weeks and the landlord's threatening to evict us and I've pawned everything and . . .' Her shoulders heaved and Eve pressed the glass to her lips again. 'I . . . I was going to take him a cup of tea and I . . . I . . . found him . . . hanging . . . by his belt. Oh, God, I'll see him there like that for the rest of my life! What'll I do, Eve! What'll I do now?'

Eve shuddered involuntarily, her heart going out to the hysterical woman. She hadn't known things were so bad.

'Oh, Agnes, why didn't you say something? I could have helped, you know we wouldn't have let this happen for the world.'

Agnes couldn't reply.

Sarah touched Eve's arm. 'Mam, what . . . what are we going to do about him?'

Eve's mind was working quickly. 'Go down to Ma Flanagan's and ask Harry Dempsey to come up here now, but don't breathe a word of what's happened. The whole neighbourhood will know soon enough. Lily, pull yourself together and put the kettle on. Maggie will be back with those lads in a minute and they're going to be in a right state.'

She said nothing more but continued to try to soothe Agnes while a distressed Lily started to make a pot of tea.

Maggie and the four young Molloy lads arrived a little ahead of a worried-looking Harry Dempsey and Sarah.

The two youngest lads were sobbing and clinging to each other and the others were white, shaken and desperately trying to hold back the tears.

Harry looked around the kitchen mystified and ran his fingers through his shock of dark hair. 'Eve, what's up? Sarah wouldn't tell me.'

Eve disentangled herself from Agnes and led him into the snug.

'Ted Molloy's hanged himself. Poor Agnes found him and came up to me. Eddie's out, God knows where . . .' She gripped the counter for support.

'Oh, God help her!' Harry was profoundly shocked but seeing Eve so upset immediately became practical. 'He'll have to be cut down and the police informed. And he'll need to be laid out before she can go back there.'

Eve nodded. 'Harry, I didn't know who else to send for.'

'Don't worry, Eve, you can rely on me. I'll see to it all and I'll get Mrs Moreton to call in and lay him out.'

'Thanks, Harry. I can't send her back there, not tonight, they'll all have to stay here. I just wish she'd said something! I didn't know he was so desperate, but you know how quiet he was. He never complained, bottled it all up inside. Oh, God help him! God help them all!'

Harry's dark eyes were serious. 'He's not the first and he won't be the last, Eve, if things don't pick up soon,' he said grimly. He'd liked Ted Molloy. Ted had been a conscientious worker and a good family man. He'd had his pride too. It must have all become too much for him to bear. Harry had little stomach for the tasks that now lay ahead of him, but they had to be done.

When Eve went back into the kitchen things had quietened down. All the paraphernalia of dressmaking had been hastily cleared away, and all three girls were trying their best to put the shock and horror behind them and comfort the four distraught and now fatherless lads. Eve took Agnes up to her bedroom and sent for Father Delaney, the parish priest. Of course he would be horrified by what Ted Molloy had done, she thought, suicide was a mortal sin, but he would at least show compassion for poor Agnes and she hoped he would show some practicality too.

When the priest had gone Eve got the boys upstairs, assisted by Harry. The girls tidied up again and did the dishes. Eve had settled Agnes in Sarah's room and on her return downstairs told the girls to go to bed themselves.

'Will you be all right, Mam?' Sarah asked. Her mother looked pale and drawn.

Eve nodded. 'I'll be fine, luv.'

'I'll stay with her until Eddie gets in,' Harry offered.

With some relief Sarah went upstairs.

'Will I get you a glass of something, Eve? You've had a pretty rotten night.'

She smiled tiredly at him. He was a good lad, thoughtful, considerate and practical. 'A drop of sherry would be nice, Harry, and get yourself something, it's been pretty terrible for you too.'

She took the glass he offered and sipped the sweet liquid. 'Thank God I could rely on you. That's twice today you've been a godsend.'

He smiled at her. 'It's no trouble. I don't want to criticise, Eve, but . . . well . . . Eddie does seem to be leaving you in the lurch today.'

'You can say that again! I don't know what's the matter with him lately, he's so *restless*. And he bites my head off every time I open my mouth.'

'What did he have to say about Doreen Travis?' Harry asked, trying to take her mind off the tragedy.

Eve rolled her eyes expressively. 'Plenty. He seems to think she's the best barmaid that ever drew breath! I ask you! Well, the brewery said we have to economise so she'd have had to go anyway. You saw how bad business was tonight.'

'It's not just you who's suffering, Eve. All the pubs are the same, although I bet trade picks up at the weekend. They always manage to find the money for their beer on Friday and Saturday.'

'I hope they do or we'll be shutting up shop completely and then *we'll* be on the Parish.'

'Things will look up soon, I'm sure. The government can't let it get any worse.'

'Oh, there's still plenty of money in some quarters. You've only got to look at the shops in Bold Street and the fancy cars up and down Dale Street. Not everyone's broke.'

He nodded his agreement. 'But there's not as many people sailing on the liners, except for those who are emigrating.'

'Then if I were Mrs Travis I wouldn't be worrying about my husband demanding coffee and the like. He won't be waiting on first class for much longer,' Eve said tartly, remembering Doreen's excuse for her lateness that morning.

Harry managed a grin. 'He might even have to stay home and take his daughter in hand!'

'Well, someone needs to!' Eve replied with some spirit.

Eddie felt as though he were walking on air. He'd never felt so elated in years. Doreen loved him! She had actually said she loved him! More than that, she *adored* him! She'd made him feel as though he were twenty years old again. She'd opened up a whole new world to him. She'd made him feel carefree, capable of doing anything, *anything* he wanted. She'd made him feel alive. She'd brought him alive. In fact the things she'd done had driven him wild with desire and afterwards they'd made plans – and such plans. They were going to travel to London. They were really going to live life to the full. They were going to go to restaurants, shows, dances, and race meetings. Of course he was fully aware that the money they had wouldn't last for ever, but when it did run out they could get a pub of their own. What an asset she would be to him as landlady! They would still have a good life. She could still have all the clothes she wanted; if they found a decent reliable barman they could still have their nights out, and there would be plenty of people coming in for her to chat to. Oh, yes, London was the place to be. Tomorrow he was going to Lime Street Station to get their tickets and she was going to find them a nice place to stay. Her da was a great man for that kind of information; he knew all kinds of people. Not that she would tell him exactly why she needed somewhere to stay in London. She would say it was for a friend. He was later than he intended to be but he didn't care any more. He wasn't even perturbed at the thought of facing an irate Eve. Oh, no, those days were over. He had Doreen's adoration now and he felt ten feet tall.

He was surprised to see the place closed up and in darkness. That was all to the good, he realised, but there was at least half an hour yet to closing time. It irritated him but then he shrugged. What did it matter now? As he went around the back he saw there was a light on in the kitchen.

'Was business so bad that you put the towel on early?' he asked, trying to appear matter of fact as he threw his hat on the dresser. Then he noticed that Harry Dempsey was sitting at the table, a glass of whiskey in his hand.

'Just where have you been until this hour?' Eve snapped.

'Out. Does it matter where? Can't a man have a bit of time to himself?'

'You can have all the time in the world to yourself for all I care, I just wish you were here when you were needed.'

'So, who *needed* me?' he blustered.

'Ted Molloy hanged himself tonight,' Harry said quietly.

Eddie went pale and sat down. 'Jesus Christ!'

'Agnes is upstairs and so are the lads. It's . . . it's terrible! Harry went and cut him down and I've had the police here and . . . where were you?'

Eddie was profoundly shocked. Ted Molloy was the last person he would have expected to have committed suicide. 'What the hell made him do that? Does she have any idea?'

'You know he's been out of work. Things were bad, really bad. They were going to be evicted, she'd pawned everything, and they were at their wits' end. I wish she'd said something. I would have helped her out if I'd known it was that bad, but you know how proud he was.'

'I expect it all just got too much for him,' Harry added.

Eddie got up and poured himself a drink from the bottle Harry had brought into the kitchen. What a waste. Ted Molloy had slaved all his life and for what? To end up facing destitution and misery. Out on the street without even a roof over his head, no wonder he'd been driven to . . . that!

Eve's voice cut across his thoughts. 'You still haven't said where you've been while I've been half demented trying to cope with it all!'

'Just out. Walking. Wandering around. I did call in for a drink in a couple of pubs – just to see how they were doing for customers,' he lied, tossing back the whiskey and refilling his glass.

47

Harry got to his feet. 'Well, I'll be off, Eve. If there's anything else I can do . . .'

Eve smiled at him. 'You've done more than enough tonight, Harry. I really don't know how I would have managed without you or the girls. Thanks.'

'Goodnight then. 'Night, Eddie.'

Eddie just nodded and stared into his drink.

'You could at least have thanked him, Eddie. I really wouldn't have known where to turn without him,' Eve snapped.

Eddie shook himself. 'Has anyone told those two girls of Ted's?'

'The police will notify them.'

'And I suppose they'll be down here then.'

'There's nothing they can do tonight. I told the police to tell them that Agnes and the lads would be staying here. She's in our Sarah's room. The lads are in Lily and Maggie's room.'

'Where are they?'

'In our room.'

'Where the hell are we going to sleep?'

'I'm sleeping with them; you'll have to make do with the sofa. I've brought a pillow and a blanket down for you.'

Despite everything, Eddie was annoyed. He was tired; he had things on his mind. The last thing he wanted was to have to spend the night on the cramped and lumpy sofa in the kitchen. 'Oh, that's bloody great!'

Eve was furious. Not only had there been no satisfactory explanation of his absence but he didn't seem to be at all bothered about the traumatic experiences the evening had brought her. 'Don't be so damned selfish! I couldn't send the poor woman back there tonight, nor those lads either. It won't hurt you for once; no doubt Agnes's daughters will sort things out in the morning. I'm going to bed, it's been a long and harrowing day and tomorrow isn't going to be much better!'

Eddie glared at her retreating back and tried to settle himself comfortably on the sofa. He was sorry for Agnes, he was, but he was sorrier for Ted. If that wasn't an example of a total waste of forty years, he didn't know what was. Well, he wasn't going to let life grind him down. He had a chance of happiness – real happiness – excitement and something to look forward to and he was going to take it. He was going to grab it with both hands!

Chapter Four

N O ONE SLEPT WELL that night and the Dobson girls
went off to work heavy-eyed and with equally heavy
hearts. Eve coped as best she could with Agnes and her sons,
while Eddie went about the usual mundane tasks in silence
but with his mind elsewhere.

It hadn't taken long for the news to get out and it seemed
to Eve that all morning long people were in and out,
shocked, shaking their heads and muttering condolences.
Later on both Agnes's daughters arrived with their
husbands and it was with some relief that Eve agreed with
Vi, the eldest, that Agnes and the lads should go and stay
with her in Walton.

'I had no idea that things were so bad, Vi, really I didn't,
or I would have helped out, I *would*!' Eve impressed on the
shaken and grieving young woman.

'I know you would, Eve. So would our Lizzie and me, but
you know what my da was like. He never said much; he had
his pride, though much good it did him. It just made things

worse. I didn't even know he'd been to the Parish. He'd have *hated* that! He really must have been desperate.'

'He was, luv,' Eve said sadly.

'She somehow managed to keep up the payments to the Burial Club. It was only a couple of pennies a week but it will give him a bit of a funeral. Oh, me poor da!'

Eve patted her shoulder. Ted couldn't be buried in sanctified ground and there would be no Funeral Mass. It could be no more than 'a bit of a funeral'.

'We'll all go to whatever kind of a service there can be. I'm sure Eddie will say a few words and Harry Dempsey said he'd come and so will a lot of the neighbours. Your da was well liked. Oh, it's such a tragedy.'

The girl sniffed and dabbed her swollen eyes. 'Our Lizzie and me will put on a bit of a tea, like. It won't be much, but you've got to try, haven't you? Me poor mam's in no state and I'm not having her shamed even more than she is by not giving him a proper do.'

'You're both good girls and I know he was proud of you.'

'We've only got a little house but my Alfred says he doesn't mind taking Mam and the lads in.'

'That's good of him. There's not many who would do that.'

'I know but I can't just leave her to try to cope, can I? We'll manage somehow. I'm still working so that will help. Just as long as those four don't start acting up! If they do Alfred will sort them out – and there's a police station at the bottom of the street.'

'Well, that should be enough of a threat to keep them in

order. But they're not bad lads, and they're very upset. I know your mam's always saying they have her heart broken but they're only full of mischief, there's no real harm in them.'

'If it were left to our Lizzie's husband they would end up in a reformatory. He's useless, that feller!' Vi said disparagingly.

'Well, maybe you and Lizzie could take turns in having them?'

Vi shrugged and Eve decided not to pursue the matter. 'I can let you have a few shillings towards the do, Vi, and Eddie will give you a couple of bottles.'

'A couple of bottles of what?' Eddie asked, catching the end of the conversation.

'Spirits, for the funeral tea. And I said we'd all go and that you'll say a few words because Father Delaney can't,' Eve informed him.

Eddie stared at her, aghast. He'd been trying all morning to find an excuse to get out to go to Lime Street to get the train tickets and now she'd sprung this on him! He felt trapped, frustrated and angry. He didn't want to be here at all, never mind have to go to a hole-in-the-corner funeral and 'say a few words', not even for Ted Molloy! After all, *he* was past his suffering now. 'When . . . when's it likely to be?' he managed to splutter.

'Saturday morning,' Vi said, becoming practical

On Saturday morning he planned to be on the train with Doreen, heading for a new life. He had to get out, now, before any more plans were made and questions asked. 'I . . .

I can't! Not on Saturday! Look, Eve, I . . . I've got to go out.' He didn't wait for her reply but grabbed his jacket and cap and, barging past the two astonished women, went out.

'What's the matter with him?' Vi cried.

Eve was just as taken aback. 'I don't know, Vi, that's the truth. But I intend to find out,' she said grimly. Just what had got into him lately? Why on earth was he acting like this? He'd liked Ted Molloy and now he was refusing to go to his funeral. 'Don't worry though, he'll be there,' she finished firmly.

She'd seen Agnes and her family off and opened up with still no sign of Eddie when, at ten past twelve, Harry put his head round the door of the saloon bar.

'Need any help, Eve?'

'Am I glad to see you! The bitter's off, I haven't tidied up, I need a couple of crates of stout – there's bound to be a crowd in to drown their sorrows over poor Ted – and God knows where Eddie's got to!' She ran her hands distractedly through her dark curls.

'I didn't call earlier because I knew you'd have a houseful. You go and see to the tidying, I'll see to the beer and any customers.'

Eve nodded thankfully and did a quick tidy-up of the lounge bar and the snug, put on a bit of lipstick, brushed her hair and rejoined Harry, who was talking quietly to Uncle Uk and a few of the regulars.

'We was just saying, Eve, it's a bad business! Poor Ted. As steady a feller as yer'd ever meet. It's a bloody disgrace, driven to *that*!'

A Mother's Love

Eve nodded sympathetically.

'There should be some sort of 'elp from the government, like, when a feller can't get work through no fault of 'is own. The bloody Assistance Board is no use! Yer'd think it was their own bloody money they were givin' yer! Out of their own pockets! They think yer don't want ter work! That yer're bone bloody idle an' 'appy ter see yer family starvin'!' Fred Hunter added bitterly, having had plenty of experiences in that field.

'Vi said they are going to bury him on Saturday morning.'

'Well, let us know where and exactly when and we'll be there. He was a good feller, God rest 'im!' Uncle Uk stated, shoving his empty glass towards Harry to be refilled.

'Where's Eddie?' Fred asked.

'Out! And don't ask where. Your guess is as good as mine!' Eve snapped, glancing warningly at Harry.

Harry said nothing. There was something very wrong between those two and he was sure it wasn't Eve's fault. She deserved better in his opinion. He admired her a lot, especially the way she had coped last night. She was always cheerful, generous and loyal to friends and family. She worked hard and provided a happy and comfortable home for Eddie and her girls. He often wished he'd been as lucky. Both his parents had died when he'd been young and he'd ended up in an austere orphanage. Since he'd left he'd had to work damned hard to pay for a bed and board; there had been times when he'd been hungry and without shelter. Eve had shown him many kindnesses in the few years he'd known her; indeed she had persuaded Ma Flanagan to take him in when he'd admitted his lodgings were no better than a doss house.

'At least the place is clean and once she gets used to the idea she'll be glad of the company,' she'd said and so it had proved.

'The girls all gone to work?' he asked.

Eve nodded. 'They're pretty shaken up but they've been a big help. I know I can rely on *them*.'

'I suppose it's just as well,' he said, thinking of Eddie's strange, irresponsible behaviour.

They were both just clearing up when Eddie at last appeared.

'I'll just go and check that that pump is working, Eve, then I'll be off,' Harry said, seeing the light of battle come into her dark eyes.

'Thanks, Harry. Come in later and have some tea with us and Eddie will give you something for your trouble,' Eve called after him.

'You're very free with the money lately!' Eddie snapped.

'It's the least you can do! I couldn't have managed without that lad what with you waltzing off out by the minutes! What was so damned important that you had to go dashing off like that? And why can't you go on Saturday morning?'

Eddie had had enough. He'd been to Lime Street, bought the tickets and on the way back had called to see Doreen. She had been full of sympathy but determined that Ted Molloy's demise wasn't going to interfere with their plans and had said so.

'No, of course nothing has changed, luv!' he'd protested,

equally determined to break free of the web that Eve seemed hell bent on entangling him in. Doreen had been in on her own. Her mam and dad wouldn't be back for hours, she'd told him, and she'd taken his arm and led him up the stairs to her room. After that he'd needed no more encouragement to stand up to Eve. He was determined to get away.

'I'm not going to get into an argument, Eve. I'm just not going to discuss it. It's *my* business, nothing to do with you. End of matter!' he said firmly and walked into the kitchen, leaving her staring after him in astonishment.

Eve spent the afternoon getting the bedrooms back to normal and quietly seething. Well, if that was the way he intended carrying on she would just let him stew! He needn't think she was going to be all sweetness and light. She'd had more than enough to cope with in the last twenty-four hours so he could just do what the brewery expected him to do: stand behind the bar and serve drinks and with no help from her! She didn't know what was the matter with him and quite honestly she was beginning not to care. He could just get it out of his system. She was going to ask no further questions, but come hell or high water he was going to put in an appearance at Ted's funeral. Nothing could be more important than that.

'You look tired, Mam,' Sarah said when she arrived home to find Eve cooking the tea.

'I am, luv. It's not been an easy day.'

'Did Mrs Molloy go off with Vi?'

'She did, and your da went off on some wild-goose chase but Harry came in to give me a hand.'

Sarah looked anxious. 'Is everything all right, Mam?'

'Yes, luv. He's just a bit . . . unsettled. Probably over poor Ted.'

Sarah nodded as Maggie and Lily appeared together.

'I was just saying to our Lily, we'll have to work extra hard tonight on that dress, we didn't get much done last night.'

'Honestly, Maggie, can't you think of anything else?' Sarah said sharply. 'It's a bit insensitive of you. Mam's worn out and the last thing she needs tonight is all that fuss and mess.'

'I'm not asking Mam to do anything! *I'll* stay up all night if I have to, but I've got to get it done. I've told Billy he's not to come round until Saturday,' Maggie said earnestly. It was very sad about poor Mr Molloy but Sunday was very important to both her and Billy. Their future depended on it. At some stage over the next few days she was going to tell Mam all their plans.

'Well, don't expect me to stay up until all hours! I hardly slept at all last night with you poking me with your elbows!' Lily retorted irritably.

Eve lost her temper. 'Oh, for heaven's sake, stop it, all of you! Your da's got a right cob on and I've got a headache! And Maggie, I wish you'd stop being so dogmatic about this bloody dress!'

Maggie was unperturbed. 'Mam, you know I have to make a good impression on Sunday. It's *important*. It really is!'

Eve sighed and stared at her determined daughter. 'I know it is. I know that you and Billy want to get engaged.'

'How? I never said.'

'It's as plain as the nose on your face. Don't worry, you'll have your dress and you can borrow my good hat and bag. I won't have old Mrs Wainwright looking down her nose at you and not giving you a few bob. You'll need every penny you can get your hands on, marriage is no picnic at the best of times.'

'Oh, Mam, don't say things like that!' Maggie cried.

'Well, it's not, luv. Just look at poor Agnes Molloy.'

'When's the funeral, Mam?' Sarah asked.

'Saturday morning and I expect you all to be there. And, Maggie, if Billy Wainwright is going to be part of this family he can put in an appearance too.'

Maggie wasn't too happy with this but said nothing. Mam was in a strange mood, she thought, but then she shrugged. She was probably just tired.

The meal was a somewhat silent and strained affair. Eddie said virtually nothing to anyone and Eve only brightened up when Harry Dempsey appeared, although he, sensing the atmosphere, didn't stay long – just time enough for a cup of tea and to receive a few shillings, handed over rather reluctantly by Eddie, in payment for his bar work.

Sarah cleared up while Maggie and Lily once more got out the sewing.

'Mam, why don't you have an early night, you really do look worn out. We'll clear up, we promise,' Sarah urged.

Eve, whose headache had grown worse, agreed. Eddie could cope in the bar and she was in no mood for the sewing party so, relieved, she went upstairs after taking two aspirin.

'What's up with those two?' Lily asked when they had all settled down.

'I don't know. I expect they get fed up like everyone else,' Sarah replied, frowning as she threaded a needle with tacking cotton.

'Do you think it will look awful if I go to the Royal Court on Saturday night? It's supposed to be a really good show.' Lily was quickly tacking the pieces of bias-cut skirt together.

'I don't suppose anyone will mind much. The funeral will be over and Mrs Molloy will have gone to their Vi's. Things should have calmed down,' Sarah said thoughtfully.

'Who are you going with?' Maggie asked.

'Terry Farraday. You know him, his mam has a barrow in Clayton Square.'

'His mam's a *Mary Ellen*?' Maggie cried.

Lily was stung. 'And what's the matter with being a Mary Ellen? They sell fruit and veg from a barrow. You work in a greengrocer's. You sell fruit and vegetables too!'

'It's different! You know what they're like, those barrow women, they're so loud and common!'

Lily rounded on her. 'Maggie Dobson, you snob! You out and out snob! This is all Billy Wainwright's doing. I can just hear him now: "Maggie, you don't want to let your Lily associate with the likes of *them*, my granny won't approve!" '

Maggie glared at her. 'It's got nothing to do with Billy! Anyway, I bet Mam won't approve either.'

'She won't mind!' Lily shot back.

'You do seem to pick the most unsuitable lads, Lily. I know Terry Farraday and he's a bit of a tearaway,' Sarah said.

'He's not! He just likes a bit of a laugh and what's wrong with that?'

'All I'm saying is that Mam's got enough on her plate without you making a show of yourself with Terry Farraday. Just make sure you behave yourself on Saturday.'

'Well, Mam's always got Harry Dempsey around here and he isn't exactly high society.'

'There's nothing wrong with Harry Dempsey,' Sarah said sharply.

'Oh, I *see*!' Lily cried.

'No, you don't *see* anything. He's been a big help to Mam and just because he was dragged up in a God-awful orphanage and has been knocked from pillar to post all his life is no reason to look down your nose at him, Lily! You calling Maggie a snob is like the pot calling the kettle black.' Sarah was annoyed. She did like Harry Dempsey and she didn't like Lily's tone. Secretly she thought Harry was the nicest boy she'd ever met. She flushed a little. Did she have a crush on him? Did she think she was even a bit in love with him? She pushed the thoughts away. Well, she certainly didn't want either of her sisters to think such things!

'Oh, will the pair of you give it a rest!' Maggie intervened. 'Harry Dempsey only comes in now and then, he's not going to take up residence and, Lily, if you have to go with Terry Farraday just you make sure there's no nonsense out of you!'

Lily grimaced. Sometimes both her sisters were pains in the neck. 'Right, that's all the tacking done. Who's going to give me a hand to get the sewing machine out and who's going to set up the iron and ironing board? If we can get the skirt and bodice together tonight we won't have done badly.'

Eddie had chatted half-heartedly with the few customers who had come in during the evening but his mind had been on just how he was going to get away on Saturday without raising a hue and cry. He'd decided to leave packing his few things until as late on Friday night as possible and then to hide the case in the cellar behind the beer kegs. He'd also decided that he would leave Eve a note; he realised he owed her that much and he didn't want her to have the entire Liverpool City Police force out looking for him, thinking he'd come to some harm. The funeral presented a problem. If he continued to refuse to go an explanation would be demanded by them all. No, it would be better to say he would go along but might be a bit late arriving and if they demanded to know why, well . . . well, he'd just stick to his guns and refuse to tell them. Or tell them he'd explain later – after the funeral.

He poured himself a large whiskey to steady his nerves. It was a huge decision he was making but he knew it was the right one. He *had* to have this last chance at doing something with the rest of his life. Eve would manage, she always did, and the girls didn't need him – they had their own lives to lead. Sarah was twenty and look at Maggie, already thinking of settling down with that po-faced, spineless little runt Billy Wainwright, who would do exactly what Maggie told him to do. No, he had to get away. It was his last chance. And of course Doreen was so *wonderful*. There was no other word for her.

He poured another drink.

'You're hitting the bottle hard tonight, Eddie!' Fred commented.

Eddie pulled himself together. 'Got a lot on my mind, Fred.'

'Who hasn't these days? There's some talk of a march, about the unemployment.'

Eddie tried to look interested. 'Oh, aye.'

'Like the Jarrow Crusade. Marching to London to take our cause to the government. Things can't go on like this. Half this city's unemployed.'

'London? When?' Eddie demanded.

'It'll take a bit to get organised. You thinking of coming with us?'

Eddie breathed a sigh of relief. For a horrible moment he'd thought it might be Saturday and that would be all he'd need, getting caught up in a protest march. 'I might, Fred, you never know,' he replied.

Chapter Five

THE ATMOSPHERE OVER THE next few days had been very strained. Eve, despite many attempts, had been unable to glean any further information from Eddie as to where he'd been and all he would say on the matter of the funeral was that he had some important business to attend to but that he would come along as soon as he was able. She was mystified and angry and maintained a cold silence, except with the girls and Harry Dempsey.

Maggie had taken a couple of hours off from the sewing and had asked Eve to sit with her in the snug.

'I really want to talk to you, Mam.'

Eve smiled fondly at her earnest little face. 'I know, luv. You're going to tell me all your plans.'

'How did you know?'

'Maggie, I'm not stupid! Well, out with it.'

'Mrs McMillan is going to sell the shop and Billy and I want to buy it.'

'*Buy* it? Maggie, it will cost a fortune! Can't you just rent it?'

'No, Mam. Billy says his granny will lend us the money, he says she's got pots.' Maggie looked furtively around and lowered her voice. 'No one knows this but she used to be a moneylender. You're not to say a word to anyone, not even our Sarah and Lily, promise?'

Eve smiled. Well, that was a turn-up for the book! The oh-so-respectable Wainwrights having a moneylender in the family!

'Promise, Mam!'

'I promise. Won't she charge you a shocking rate of interest? They do, you know.'

'She won't charge Billy anything. He's her favourite.'

'I see.'

'We want our own business. We don't want to work ourselves into the ground for someone else,' Maggie continued earnestly. It was a wonderful opportunity for them.

'Like your da and I do?' Eve reminded her.

'Oh, Mam, I didn't mean it to sound like that!' Maggie wailed apologetically.

Eve was unperturbed. 'I don't blame you one bit, Maggie. I just wish your da had had a mam who'd had "pots of money".'

Maggie was mollified. 'Eventually, we want to have our own house too.'

'How much money does old Ma Wainwright have, for God's sake?' Eve laughed. They certainly had very big plans.

'Enough, and Billy's mam says she's going to leave it all to Billy when she dies.'

Eve shook her head doubtfully. 'I wouldn't bank on it.

She does have other grandchildren. Mr Wainwright has sisters, wills can be and are contested and sometimes they're even overturned. Don't count your chickens before they're hatched, Maggie.'

'Well, anyway, that's all in the future. There are a couple of rooms over the shop; we'll live in them. So, you do see, Mam, how important it is that she likes me. Really approves of me.'

'I do indeed but I'm sure she will, there's nothing to dislike or disapprove of, Maggie.'

'Oh, Mam, I just don't know!'

'Now don't go getting yourself into a state about it. You're a lovely, well-brought-up, hard-working girl and you come from a decent, hard-working family – one that doesn't have any skeletons in the cupboard! No moneylenders or the like!'

'Hush!'

Eve laughed and squeezed Maggie's hand. 'Your secret is safe with me. Now, back to the sewing or you'll be going in your petticoat!'

'Will you tell Da? He's . . . he's a bit odd at the moment.'

'Oh, he's *that* all right! Of course I'll tell him. When I get the right opportunity.' Though God alone knew when that would be, she thought irritably.

After two nights of frantic work Maggie's dress was finally finished.

'I've never worked so hard!' Sarah declared, sitting back on her heels and admiring their handiwork as Maggie twisted and turned to get the desired effect from the skirt.

'I know! Honestly, I'll be glad to go to work for a rest on Monday!' Lily added. 'But it does look great, Maggie.'

'You see, I told you the colour would be all right,' Maggie said a little smugly.

'And I told you that that yellow bias binding around the collar and sleeves would make all the difference.'

Maggie smiled. 'You did and you were right, Lily. I wonder if I'll have enough time to go into Blackler's on Saturday after the funeral to get a pair of white cotton gloves? I've got to work in the afternoon.'

'Don't you think that's taking the dressing up a bit *too* far?' Sarah asked.

'No! For one thing all decent girls wear gloves and for another it will hide my hands, they really are a mess.'

'At least it shows you work hard. His flaming granny should be impressed with that!' Lily was full of scorn.

'You'll look very respectable, Maggie, with Mam's good hat and bag, and perhaps the gloves are a good idea,' Sarah conceded as she began to tidy up. 'Is Billy coming tomorrow morning?'

Maggie nodded. 'He wasn't very keen but I told him that it would look bad if he didn't.'

'I'm not very keen myself. In fact I'm not looking forward to it at all. It's only because we're so slack that I've got the morning off,' Lily added.

'Do you think Da will go?'

Sarah looked anxious. They were slack at the Stork too and not only was she worried about her job but she couldn't help being concerned about her mam and da, also. 'Maggie,

I don't honestly know. I just don't understand what's got into him. Mam is furious and she's upset. All he'll say is he'll be late.'

'I think she's got every right to be! I certainly wouldn't stand for Billy carrying on like that. All this dashing off and not saying where he's been or where he's going. It's . . . it's not *right*!'

Sarah sighed. 'I suppose we'll find out eventually.'

'Well, it's between him and Mam, but I just wish they'd sort it out. I hate this atmosphere,' Lily muttered.

'Sarah, do you think it's got anything to do with Mam and Doreen Travis?' Maggie probed.

'I don't think so. Oh, he was annoyed that Mam sacked her but, well, the brewery told him he had to economise and I don't think she's really *that* important. He's probably got some hare-brained scheme in mind to make money that he knows Mam won't approve of so he's not telling her. It'll all blow over in a day or two. Lily, give me a hand with the sewing machine, then I'm off to bed.'

'Would you listen to that wind! It sounds as if there's going to be a storm. So much for the lovely spring weather,' Lily said scathingly as a shower of hail rattled against the window.

'That's all we'll need in the morning: gale-force winds and rain!'

'Oh, Sarah, don't say that. If it doesn't pass by Sunday my outfit will be ruined!' Maggie wailed.

'God! I'll be glad when the whole weekend is over,' Lily muttered to herself. Then she remembered her proposed

69

visit to the theatre. At least that was something to look forward to.

March was proving very predictable, Eve thought as she dressed next morning. After a spell of fine weather earlier in the week, the sky was grey and leaden and the wind was blustery and chilly. At least it wasn't raining – yet. She'd slept badly, only falling into a deep sleep in the small hours. By the time she'd woken, to her annoyance Eddie had already got up and gone out, but she tried to console herself with the fact that the sooner he went out and did whatever it was that was so important, the sooner he would get back.

She wasn't looking forward to the morning; it would be an ordeal for everyone.

She had the breakfast cooked when the girls came down and shortly afterwards Harry Dempsey knocked on the kitchen door.

'Come in, Harry, and have a bit of something to eat. It's going to be a long, hard morning.'

'I'll just have a cup of tea thanks, Eve. Ma did me a bit of a fry-up. It's not very warm out there and it looks like rain.'

'Do you have to be so cheerful?' Lily said grumpily.

'Did you see any sign of Billy on your way?' Maggie asked.

'No, what time did you tell him to be here?'

Maggie glanced at the clock on the mantelpiece. 'Now! If Mrs McMillan is good enough to give me the time off today on one of our busiest days, then the least he can do is to be on time. He doesn't have to work on Saturdays.'

'Maggie, for heaven's sake don't start on the lad the minute

70

he walks in the door!' Eve snapped irritably. Sometimes Maggie was very hard on Billy.

Sarah and Lily exchanged glances. This didn't bode well. Da had obviously gone out already. They hoped there hadn't been a row.

'That'll be him now. Harry, let him in,' Eve instructed on hearing a quiet rapping on the door.

Maggie forestalled him and, taking her mother's words to heart, kissed Billy on the cheek. 'I thought you had been delayed.'

'Mam was fussing a bit, that's all. You know what she's like,' he said apologetically.

Eve smiled at him. He was an inoffensive lad of twenty-one, slight and not very tall, with sandy hair and grey eyes. He would never set the world on fire or many hearts aflutter, but he seemed to be what Maggie wanted and Eve had to admit they suited each other. She had been surprised, in fact, that they had both shown such ambition in wanting to take over the shop.

'Have you had your breakfast, Billy?'

'Yes thanks, Mrs Dobson.'

'Well, we've nearly finished. We'll leave the clearing up until we get back. If we don't get a move on we'll be late.'

'Has Mr Dobson, er, gone out?' the lad asked hesitantly.

Maggie glared at him.

'He has, but don't worry, he'll be along later,' Eve said firmly, anchoring her black felt hat with a long, dangerous-looking pin.

They walked the short distance to the small piece of land

beyond the cemetery wall and Eve was surprised and touched to see how many of the neighbours had turned up. Her heart went out to poor Agnes; she was bowed down with grief and the shame of not being able to bury her husband decently, her swollen, streaming eyes often straying to the wall beyond which were the headstones and monuments of those who had been given a Christian burial.

Jim Stokes from the newsagent's led them in the Lord's Prayer and Alf Casey recited as much as he knew of the De Profundis and then Mary Stokes started them off with the first decade of the Rosary.

As the simple service progressed, with two or three of Eve's customers reflecting on Ted Molloy's life and tragic death, Eve herself quietly seethed with anger and humiliation for there was no sign of Eddie. At last the men started to fill in the grave and everyone began to move away. Eve felt she was about to explode. She was grateful that everyone was being very tactful about Eddie's absence but it didn't help. He had let her down. He had let them *all* down – badly!

'Don't say a single word to me about your da!' she hissed to Sarah as they walked back towards the road, following Agnes and her family.

'I wasn't going to, Mam.'

'Oh, what's everyone going to think of us now? I could swing for him, I really could!' she fumed. 'Just *what* is so flaming important?'

'Well, let's just hope no one sticks their twopenn'orth in once they've had a few drinks!' Lily muttered.

'I've no intention of staying that long! I've a pub to open up!'

'We'll just have a cup of tea and then we'll all go home, Mam. I think it will be best,' Maggie said grimly as they headed for Agnes's poor, bare and comfortless house for the last time. She was just as furious with her da. How would this sound when Billy's mam and da got to hear of it – and they undoubtedly would!

They didn't linger and, after kissing Agnes and telling her that when she felt more settled, she must come back and visit regularly, Eve shepherded her little flock back to the George.

'Well, at least it's over!' Lily commented thankfully, casting a wary eye at her mother who was taking off her hat and coat.

'Yes it is and now I'm going up to get changed and then I'll have to open up! Lily, you and Maggie tidy up this kitchen. Sarah, will you go and make a start on the saloon bar, luv? Billy, you can go and give her a hand. No, on second thoughts go and ask Harry Dempsey if he can spare me an hour or two later. I think I'm going to need him!'

Without waiting for any complaints Eve went upstairs. She sat down on the bed and looked around. What the hell was Eddie up to? Where was he? Well, it would have to wait. Quickly she took off her black skirt and jumper and pulled on a beige and brown knitted two-piece. She'd brush her hair, put a bit of lipstick on and go down to face the Saturday lunchtime drinkers.

The folded piece of paper was lying beside her hairbrush on the dressing table and she was puzzled as to why she hadn't noticed it earlier. She'd probably been in too much of a rush. She frowned as she picked it up. It just said 'EVE' and it was in Eddie's handwriting. Now what was he up to? Was this some kind of explanation for his hurried departure and absence? She sat down again on the bed and unfolded it. She read it and then let it drop to the floor. She felt as though someone had hit her hard in the stomach, knocking all the breath from her. He *couldn't* have! It *couldn't* be true! She stared unseeing at her reflection. He'd gone to London, with . . . with . . . *that* one and he wasn't coming back! Now everything became crystal clear. How long had this affair been going on – and right under her nose? Oh, no wonder he'd been so restless and edgy and secretive and no wonder that little *bitch* had been so insolent and arrogant and downright *smug*!

Waves of humiliation and hurt washed over her. She'd given him twenty-one years of her life. The best years. She'd worked hard for him, kept a clean and comfortable home, kept herself looking as attractive as she could, given him three beautiful daughters and – what hurt most of all – she'd loved him. And now everything, *everything* had been thrown back in her face. It was as if she'd done nothing at all for him. Absolutely nothing.

She never knew just how long she sat there. Utter disbelief, shock and a feeling of unreality paralysed her mind and her limbs. She felt cold. Cold and numb and slightly sick. She just stared down at the innocuous-looking piece of paper, so white, so flimsy yet so devastatingly dark in its purpose. Those few lines of sprawled black ink effectively signalled the end of her marriage.

'Mam? Mam, what's wrong? You've been up here ages and I . . .' Sarah's voice trailed off as she caught sight of her mother's stricken face. She grasped her hand. 'Mam, you're freezing! What is it?'

Eve turned huge, dazed eyes towards her. 'Your da . . . He's gone . . . The note . . .' she stammered.

Sarah picked it up and scanned it, then uttered a cry of disbelief and horror. 'No! No, he can't have! Not . . . not with *her*!'

Her words seemed to break the spell that held Eve in its grip and she started to tremble. Tears filled her eyes and slid down her pale, cold cheeks. 'Oh, Sarah, luv! He has! He's deserted us for her! Oh, God, why did I ever let that one set foot in this place?'

The two women clung together, crying, still unable fully to take in the reality of the situation, until at last Sarah pulled herself together.

'Mam, I'm going to get our Maggie and Lily. They'll have to know right away. Will you be all right? I won't be long.'

Eve dashed away her tears with the back of her hand and nodded. Then, wrapping her arms around herself, she began to rock slowly back and forth as if the movement would somehow alleviate the pain and shock.

Sarah was back within seconds, white-faced and still shaking and pushing her two sisters into the room ahead of her.

'Mam, what's wrong? She won't tell us. She just grabbed us and shoved us up here!' Lily cried indignantly.

Sarah stuffed the note into her hand. 'Read it. Both of you.'

There was silence as the two girls scanned the lines and then Maggie, stunned, sank on to the bed beside Eve and put her arms around her. Lily stood holding the note as though it was something strange and foreign and incomprehensible.

'Why, Mam? Why has he done this to us?' Maggie groaned. Her face was a mask of misery.

'I . . . I . . . don't know how to answer you, luv!' Eve choked.

Lily was crying noisily. 'He loves that little *tart*. He says he *loves* her. Doesn't he love us? Doesn't he love you, Mam?'

Sarah's anger was beginning to overcome her shock. 'He says he does love Mam, he does love us, but he's *in love* with her – whatever the difference is. Oh, that scheming, conniving, brazen little bitch! She's nothing but a common bloody whore!'

'It's not Da's fault! It's her! She's . . . she's . . . enticed him away!' Lily was sobbing hard now. She loved her da and she'd always been his favourite, he'd loved *her* until Doreen bloody Travis had got her claws into him.

Eve looked at her three heart-broken daughters and knew that no matter how devastated she felt, she had to try to be strong. She had to try to take this situation in hand.

'He does love you all! He does! He's not . . . himself. He's not in his right mind! He must be besotted with her.'

'He's off his bloody head, that's what's the matter with him!' Maggie cried, hurt and betrayal giving way to fury.

Eve was struggling hard for composure. 'Just give me a bit more time to . . . to pull myself together, then I'll be able to talk to you.'

'Mam, we won't leave you!' Sarah cried vehemently.

'Then sit down all of you, here beside me, while we try to think what we have to do.'

'Go after him, Mam! Make him come back! Tell him she's no good! Please, Mam?' Lily begged.

Eve shook her head. 'No, Lily! I . . . I can't. I *won't*!'

'Mam, *please*?' Lily sobbed.

'No! You can't ask Mam to humiliate herself like that, Lily!' Sarah cried.

'Do you want that one to stand there laughing while Mam . . . Oh, Lily, for God's sake, have some sense!' Maggie stormed.

Eve gathered her distraught daughter in her arms. 'If he wants her, then let him go. We're better off without him, Lily.' The words cut her like a knife but she couldn't, wouldn't think about their implications – not now. She took a few deep breaths. There would be time to think about all that later. So much time. 'Who is in the bar?'

'Harry and Billy,' Sarah said quietly. Mam was trying so hard to be brave and she in turn drew strength from that.

'Go and ask them to stay. Just say there has been a . . . crisis. A domestic crisis and I . . . I won't be down until later.'

'What if they ask about Da?'

'Just say he's been called away. I'll have to explain. Oh, God . . .'

'It's all right, Mam. I'll deal with them,' Sarah said. She was the eldest; it was up to her to give Mam all the support she possibly could.

'Billy will have to know, Mam!' Maggie cried.

'Later, luv, not just now. Give me time to . . . to calm down.'

'Wouldn't it be better to put the towel on? Close up?' Maggie demanded.

'No! Not on a Saturday. That would cause more speculation.'

'But, Mam, we can't face everyone on a Saturday night!'

Eve squared her small shoulders. 'Yes, we can. We have to, Maggie! Oh, not you, Lily, but I'll need Maggie and Sarah in there to help me. Harry will stay but Billy's not a lot of use, Maggie, you know he isn't.'

'Mam, none of us will be much use,' Maggie groaned, shrinking in horror at the thought of facing the Saturday-evening customers.

'We'll have to get through it, Maggie. We'll *have* to! I won't have them sniggering and jeering at us.'

'We'll manage, Mam, we *will*,' Sarah said with grim determination.

They were the longest, darkest hours Eve had ever spent as she tried hard to comfort Lily, to answer the unanswerable questions and to calm Maggie's growing outrage. Sarah, despite her own heartbreak and anger, was a tower of strength. When finally Eve had managed to bring a measure of stability to their turbulent emotions, both she and Sarah felt drained.

Somehow they all got through the evening. Eve nailed a smile to her face and was as cheerful as she possibly could be, although it was like being in a dream – a nightmare – with long, painful, heart-searching hours stretching ahead of her.

Sarah and Maggie worked alongside her, just as determined to try to make things appear normal and fielding questions about the whereabouts of their father with shrugs and half-answers. Sarah was sustained by a cold fury but Maggie's seething emotions were troubled further by a deep and worrying fear about how Billy and his family would take the news.

Harry was aware that something was very wrong but he said nothing. He was certain that he would be told before the night was over.

Maggie had told Billy nothing but promised that they would have a long talk after the pub closed.

'Mam won't be very happy with me being out so late, Maggie,' he'd said.

'For God's sake, Billy, you're twenty-one and for once I don't care what your mam thinks! This is important. I can't talk to you now, but I will later. I . . . I need you here, Billy!'

Concerned by the sob in her voice and the incipient tears in her dark eyes, he kissed her on the cheek.

'Oh, Mam, what a day! I thought it would never end!' Sarah cried when they finally switched off the lights and went through into the kitchen.

Lily was sitting huddled up in the armchair, a hand-kerchief clutched in her hand. She still couldn't believe it. Still couldn't understand why he'd gone and left them all.

'What did you say to Terry Farraday?' Maggie asked her.

'I told him I wasn't going, I wasn't well. He got all narky so I told him to go to hell!'

Eve sat down at the table and dropped her head in her hands. Her face actually ached from the effort of smiling and she felt as though someone was beating her skull with a hammer. 'Harry, would you do me a favour? Get us all a drop of brandy, we all need it.'

He nodded and went back into the saloon bar.

'What are you going to tell him?' Maggie asked.

'The truth. I'm going to need him and he can keep his mouth shut,' Eve said wearily.

'Mam, can I take Billy somewhere a bit . . . private?'

'Go into the snug, luv. I know you want to tell him in your own way.'

'Tell me what, Mrs Dobson? What's wrong?' Billy was totally confused.

Maggie grabbed his hand and dragged him out. The others all sat in silence until Harry came back with the bottle and glasses and looked expectantly at them.

'Oh God, Mam, it doesn't get any better, does it?'

'No, Sarah, and I don't expect it ever will. You and Lily go to bed. You're exhausted.'

'I don't want to leave you on your own,' Sarah protested.

'I won't be, luv, and I prefer to tell Harry without you having to listen to it again. Lily, will you be all right?'

Lily nodded, but she was fighting back yet more tears. She'd never forgive him – *never*!

Eve took the glass from Harry and gulped back the liquid, shuddered, then refilled the glass. She felt a little better but not much.

They sat in silence until Sarah got to her feet. 'Come on, Lily, let's go up.'

'I won't sleep, I know I won't,' Lily protested, feeling as though she were being excluded.

'You can try. It's not going to be easy, for any of us.'

Reluctantly Lily got to her feet. The last thing she wanted was to be left alone with her thoughts.

'Sarah, will you sleep with me tonight? Maggie can sleep in your room, it'll be ages before she comes to bed.'

Sarah managed a weak smile. Poor Lily, she seemed to be taking it harder even than Mam. 'Of course.' She bent and kissed Eve's cheek. 'Mam, if you need us, just call.'

'I will, luv. Go and try to get some sleep.'

'Eve, what the hell is going on? What's happened?' Harry urged when the two girls had gone.

Eve took another sip of the brandy and swallowed hard. 'Eddie's gone.'

'Gone?' He looked bewildered.

'He left a note. Oh, Harry, this is so hard. I still can't believe it.' She picked distractedly at the cuff of her jumper. 'He went this morning.'

'Where's he gone?' he demanded.

'To London. He . . . *they* went this morning, that's why he didn't show up for the funeral. That's why there's been all

81

this secrecy. He's gone off with Doreen Travis.' There. It was out and somehow she felt relieved.

He stared at her in disbelief. The man must be mad, stark raving mad! 'He's left you for *her*? He's gone off with that *tart*? In the name of God, why, Eve?'

'He says he loves her. No, he's "in love" with her.'

Harry jumped to his feet and slammed his fist down on the table. 'Then he's a bloody fool. She loves no one but herself. She's a gold-digger; all she's after is a good time! He'll be back, Eve.'

Eve shook her head. 'I've had all day to think about it, Harry, and I . . . I don't want him back. Even if he came crawling on his hands and knees I wouldn't have him back, not after being with *her*! I just couldn't! I might not have much else right now, but I've got my pride.'

'Oh, Eve, I'm so sorry.' He meant it. It was inconceivable that Eddie could prefer Doreen Travis to Eve.

The pity in his voice and in his eyes broke down Eve's restraint and she began to cry. 'Twenty-one years down the drain, Harry! Oh, what did I do wrong? Why? Why did he do it?' she sobbed.

He didn't know what to do or say to comfort her. She looked so broken that anger consumed him. She didn't deserve this. She didn't deserve to be humiliated and cast aside for that little trollop.

'Because he's a fool, Eve. He must really have taken leave of his senses, or that one's enticed him.' He couldn't just stand here and do nothing. He went and put his arm around her. 'Don't upset yourself. I'll help out as much as I can, I promise. You've always been good to me.'

Eve pulled herself together a little. 'I know you will. I know I can rely on you.'

'Have another drink.' He didn't know what else to say.

Eve wiped her eyes. 'I'll be tipsy.'

'That might not be such a bad thing. In fact, no one would blame you if you got blind drunk!'

She shook her head. 'No, Harry, there's not just me to think of, there's the girls. Lily's taking it really hard. She was his favourite.'

'How could he do it to them? Doesn't he care about them?' He'd never had a family but if he had he was certain he'd never treat them like this.

'Oh, I don't know. I just don't know! Who knows what he's thinking?'

Harry became practical. 'What will you tell people?'

'The truth, I suppose. I can't hide it for ever and it will get out, you know it will.'

'I hate to see you humiliated like this. It's so unfair and you know what some of the women are like round here. Tongues like bloody vipers!'

Eve sighed wearily. 'It will be a nine-day wonder, Harry. I'll manage. And people aren't *that* bad!'

'There'll be a lot of sympathy for you, Eve.'

'I know.'

'How will you manage?'

'I haven't thought that far ahead.'

Harry was remorseful. 'I'm sorry, I shouldn't have been so thoughtless.'

'You're right. It's something I have to think about. Life doesn't stop.'

'But not tonight, Eve.'

'Why not? The sooner I face it, the better it will be.'

He nodded slowly. Tomorrow had to be faced up to and she was being so brave. 'Will the brewery let you keep the pub on? You could run it just as well as him and I'd help, if they'd let you take on a barman.'

'I think I could do it, I've had plenty of experience and, let's face it, there's not much else I can do. It's all I've ever known.'

'Sarah would help too.'

Eve nodded. 'She's a great help to me, she's so steady.'

'Will you open tomorrow?'

'I don't know. I feel so exhausted and yet . . .'

He smiled. 'Why don't you have a day off? I'll manage, they'll just have to be patient.'

It was very, very tempting but was it fair? 'I don't know. It doesn't seem right to leave you to cope.'

'I don't mind, Eve. What he's done to you isn't bloody *right*!'

'What will you say?'

He'd already made that decision. He felt it was the least he could do. 'I'll make the announcement. I'll tell them about him.'

Tears welled up in Eve's eyes. 'Oh, Harry, would you? I'd be so grateful and yet I really feel it's my place, that I should be the one to . . . explain.'

'You've been through enough, all of you. He's not going

to put you through that, Eve, not if I can help it.'

Eve grasped his hand. 'What would I do without you? You're so good, so understanding!' Relief was surging through her. She couldn't have faced them all.

'Then that's settled. You have a day off tomorrow and then on Monday maybe you'll feel up to facing them. They'll all know and it won't be as bad.'

Eve nodded. 'There'll always be a welcome in my home for you, Harry.'

He smiled at her. 'You'd better try and get some rest now. Will your Maggie be all right on her own with Billy? She's bound to be very upset.'

'Yes. She's not a fool, far from it. She won't be letting him take advantage of her. She's more angry than anything else – furious, in fact.'

'She's had a shock, Eve.'

'I trust her. I trust them both. He's a bit of a wet week but he's a good lad.'

Harry patted her awkwardly on the shoulder. 'Then I'll let myself out. I'll be here to open up in the morning. Goodnight, and try and sleep.'

'Maybe I will have just one more small drink.'

'Finish the bottle if you feel like it!'

She managed a smile. 'And give them something else to talk about?'

Chapter Six

MAGGIE TOLD BILLY AS simply and as briefly as she could and then her resolve deserted her and she broke down in tears.

'I can't understand him, Billy, I just can't! He's cast us aside like a pile of old clothes!'

'Hush, Maggie, luv. Hush now,' he soothed ineffectually, reeling from the news himself. He had never expected this. People like themselves – respectable people – never did things like that!

'I can't hush. Oh, it's not just that he's left us; he's left us for *her*! The shame of it! I . . . I don't know how we're going to face people.' She raised a tear-stained face and swallowed hard, screwing up her courage. 'I wouldn't blame you if you . . . if you don't want to marry me now.'

He was horrified. 'Maggie! Don't say that! It's not *your* fault!'

'But your mam and your granny? What will they say? What will they think?'

Billy pulled himself together. 'If I left you now I'd be no better than him. I love you, Maggie!'

She clung to him in relief and gratitude. He really did love her. How could she have doubted it? 'But we'd made such plans, Billy! We were going to make something of ourselves, our life. We were going to be so respectable!'

'None of that has changed.'

'It has! People will *talk*! How can we hold up our heads? How could he do this to us? She's a trollop and she's years and years younger than him. Your granny will never lend us the money now. What will she think of me? She'll say I'm no bargain with a da like that. "Like father, like daughter", is what she'll say!'

'Stop it! You're getting yourself into a state. It's not your fault. You're not like that. Mam likes you and so does Da, they'll speak up for you. She'll lend us the money.'

'Oh, Billy, do you really think so? All we ever wanted was something of our own and a nice house in a nice area, is that too much to ask for?'

'Of course it's not. We'll both work hard and we'll have all that, you see if we don't, and no one is going to look down their noses at us!'

Maggie felt much better but she was still worried and upset. 'I don't think I can go tomorrow. Can we put it off?'

'Of course we can. Mam will explain. You need time, you all need time.' He paused as a thought struck him. 'Do you think that maybe he'll come to his senses and come back?'

She looked at him in horror. 'I don't want him to come back! Not after this! It would rake it all up again and how could I feel the same about him after he'd been with *her*? I've got no respect for him at all now. And what's more, Mam says she wouldn't have him back. She wouldn't, would she?'

'It's very early days, Maggie, and you don't know just how she'll feel.'

Maggie was horrified. 'She can't!'

'All I'm saying is, everyone is still shocked. Things may . . . change.'

'I'll ask her! I'll ask her now!'

Billy wished he'd kept his mouth shut. 'No. No, leave her alone.'

Maggie collapsed against him. 'Oh, Billy, everything is such a mess. I don't know what to think or do, really I don't!'

'Of course you don't. I don't know how you've all got through the day. I just wish you'd told me earlier.'

'So do I. Oh, my head is pounding!'

'Why don't you go to bed, luv? You're worn out with it all. Things will look a bit better in the morning. And don't worry, I'm going to stand by you – all of you.'

Maggie did feel a bit better. She hadn't expected him to be so strong, so comforting, and it really was a great relief to her. 'I think you're right, Billy. Perhaps if I get some sleep . . .'

'That's my girl – and you are *my* girl and always will be!'

Despite the brandy and the sheer exhaustion Eve couldn't sleep. She lay in the bed she had shared with Eddie for so long and stared at the ceiling. Everything felt so unreal. She could still hear Lily's sobs through the thin wall and she had heard Maggie come up and then the quiet conversation between the girls before silence had descended again. What was she going to do? What did life have in store for her now?

As the hours passed she had tossed restlessly. Where was he? What was he doing? Fury and pain shot through her yet again. Oh, she knew damned well what he'd be doing! She was filled with revulsion. How could he? Well, she wasn't going to lie here thinking of them! She had to make some plans. Why shouldn't she keep on the pub? She'd put as much into it as he had. She'd go and see Mr Harrison and persuade him that she could do just as well, if not better. He wasn't going to ruin her life – what was left of it – nor that of her girls either. No, they'd get over this, put it all behind them. Forget him! Let him stew! She was certain that Doreen Travis would get tired of him before very long: he was middle-aged, for God's sake. What would a young girl want with him? She wouldn't want to settle down and play happy families, not that one. She was just out for a good time. Nor did she think Eddie himself wanted to play happy families either. No, when Doreen Travis realised just how little money Eddie had to spend on her she wouldn't be sticking around. She'd be off looking for someone younger and wealthier. Well, let them get on with it! And when she did get fed up with him, he needn't come crawling back here. Oh, no! It was over. This was the end. Tomorrow she would start to make plans for the future, her future and that of her girls, and it was a future that had no place in it for Eddie Dobson!

Her anger at last gave way to exhaustion and she slept.

* * *

Sarah lay awake for a long time, patting Lily's shoulder until at last, worn out by the events of the day, Lily had dropped off. Lily was still very young and was very hurt and confused, she thought. But what about herself? Would she ever come to terms with it? Could she ever trust any man? You were at least supposed to be able to trust your father! And what about Mam: would she ever get over the hurt and humiliation? Would she ever be happy again? Oh, suddenly life was such a mess, with nothing safe and secure any more. Their whole world had been rocked. Would it ever recover? Would they?

Well, Maggie might. Sarah'd been relieved when her sister had told her of Billy's supportive attitude. It had crossed her mind that Billy Wainwright's profound sense of respectability might make him think twice about marrying Maggie now. Yes, Maggie had Billy but she, Lily and Mam had no one. No, that wasn't entirely true, they had Harry Dempsey. He'd been a tower of strength. She liked Harry, she always had, and she admired him too. He hadn't had the best start in life and many other lads in his position went to the bad but he hadn't.

Unlike Maggie and even Lily with her daft ideas of being 'famous', Sarah had no clear plans for her future. When she thought about it, which wasn't often, she'd thought that she might one day like a decent job, nursing maybe, something useful, but she needed a decent education for that. She'd occasionally thought about going away to sea, as a steward-ess. It would be hard work but at least you got to see the world, although now wasn't a good time to be thinking of that. Not when Mam would need her. Had her da thought like that? Had he wanted something else? Something different? Something more *exciting* than standing behind a bar day after day? Oh, she didn't know what he really wanted but whatever it was it wasn't them – any of them. She knew with infinite sadness that she would never forgive him for what he'd done and she doubted Mam would either.

Eve awoke heavy-eyed and muzzy-headed and for a few minutes wondered what it was that was lying so leadenly on her heart. She stretched out her hand and, feeling the emptiness beside her where Eddie's hunched-up form usually lay, she remembered. She raised herself on one elbow and looked at the unrumpled side of the bed. This was how it was going to be from now on. Every morning she would wake up alone.

She shook herself mentally. All the resolutions she had made last night, the half-formed plans: now was the time to start to carry them out. She had to be strong and not just for herself, for her girls. She looked at herself closely in the mirror as she dressed. She was pale and had dark circles under her eyes but wasn't that only to be expected? There was still this feeling of heaviness and unreality about everything. But this was reality. He had gone and, as far as she was concerned, he'd gone for good. There was no looking back. A thought came into her mind. It shocked her and she guiltily tried to push it away. Would life be so bad? If she could manage, financially, did she really need him? Would it actually be a bit of a relief that he'd gone? He had been so hard to live with lately with his rapidly changing moods. It had been like walking on eggshells, never knowing if, whenever she opened her mouth, he would bite her head off or make some nasty remark or even just ignore her. Life would be different without him but would it really be worse? It was up to her now to make a go of things, to make a life for them all, starting this minute.

All three girls were surprised to find their mother up, dressed and laying the table when they came down.

'Did you get any sleep, Mam?' Sarah asked with concern.

'A little. How about you?'

'A little. I think Lily got the most sleep.'

Eve gave her youngest daughter a quick hug. 'Things will be better today, Lily. I had a lot of time to think last night and, well, I've decided to ask the brewery if I can take over the pub.'

'Was that Harry's idea?' Sarah asked.

'It was and he's going to open up today and he's going to tell everyone about . . . about your da.'

'He's taking a lot on himself for a stranger,' Lily said peevishly. How could Mam be so calm and sensible? How could she even start to think of the future?

'He's not a stranger, Lily, and I for one am very grateful for his help. We're having a day off. Maggie, you're going to Billy's granny's as planned.'

Maggie looked horrified. 'Oh, I can't, Mam! I told Billy to put it off. I can't face that. Not today.'

Eve stared at her steadily. 'You can! And you are! There's

no reason to give old Mrs Wainwright anything more to disapprove of. We have to show that we will cope, that we've all got some strength of character, that this isn't going to destroy us. You get yourself ready and go as planned. As you've been saying for weeks, this is important to you, Maggie – to both of you. Don't let him ruin your chances in life!'

Maggie looked apprehensive. She hadn't expected this. But maybe Mam was right.

'You get yourself dressed up and go, Maggie. You show them what you're made of. You hold your head up, girl, you've nothing to be ashamed of!'

Maggie smiled. 'I will, Mam!'

'What are we going to do?' Lily asked, still mutinous.

'We're going out. It's not a bad day so we'll go over to New Brighton on the ferry. It's years since I've been for a day out. We're going to get ourselves dressed up and go out, put on a brave face and, who knows, we might even enjoy it a bit.'

'How can you talk about enjoying ourselves? How can you, Mam?'

'Lily, for God's sake, try and pull yourself together. Haven't you understood a single word Mam's been saying? We'll put a brave face on it; after all, you can bet he's not moping around worrying about us!' Sarah cried bitterly.

Lily's lip trembled and her eyes filled with tears. 'That's cruel.'

Eve nipped the situation in the bud. 'Right, that's enough. I don't want to hear another word about him! Let's get some breakfast down us.'

94

'I can't eat anything!'

'Lily, you've got to eat. Do you think it's easy for me? It's going to be hard for us all, very hard, but it will get better, I promise you. Let's get this week over and then I'm sure we'll all feel better, but we've got to make an effort. I've got to keep this family together.'

'And we'll all help you, Mam, won't we? Won't we, Lily?' Sarah urged more kindly, sorry she'd vented her anger on Lily.

Lily nodded. She could see what Mam was trying to do and knew it couldn't be easy for her.

By twelve o'clock they were all ready. Harry had kept his promise and opened up and Eve's heart had turned over when she heard him call for a few minutes' quiet as he had an important announcement to make. She hadn't been able to bring herself to listen; she had shut the kitchen door firmly. She didn't want to hear their reactions.

Billy had been surprised to receive Maggie's message but duly turned up in his best suit.

'Well, off you go,' Eve pressed. 'And I hope it all goes well.'

'You have told your mam and da?' Maggie asked Billy worriedly.

Billy nodded but refrained from repeating the comments his parents had made on Eddie Dobson's morals and character.

'And?' Maggie asked warily.

He looked helplessly at Eve and shrugged. 'Da said something about there being no fool like an old fool,' he muttered.

'He's right! Now, we're off to the Pier Head for the ferry.'

'At least you shouldn't see anyone you know, not today,' Billy said consolingly.

'In this city you just never know. Lily, make sure you've that hat pinned on firmly, it's bound to be breezy.'

Sarah handed Eve her bag. 'Come on, Mam, let's get out of here and get some fresh air. We could do with some.' She didn't really feel much like the ferry trip but anything was better than sitting around here trying to make sense of it all.

Maggie felt very nervous as the tram moved slowly out to the suburbs. It was a lovely spring day after the stormy weather of yesterday. Was it really only a day since they'd discovered that Da had left them? It seemed like ages, she thought. She really hadn't wanted to come, despite Mam's encouragement, but Billy's mam and da had been kindness itself and that had helped. They'd said how sorry they were and hoped that her mam wasn't thinking it was any fault of hers.

'When some men get to that age, Maggie, they do stupid things that they live to regret; you have to keep your eye on them. It's a dangerous age and there's always some flighty piece ready to lead them astray!' Billy's mam had said quietly when her husband and son were out of earshot.

'Well, he can regret it all he likes, Mam's not having him back and neither are we!' she'd hissed in reply.

'I don't blame any of you,' Billy's mam had agreed fervently.

As the little group walked down the quiet street of

well-kept terraced houses, Maggie clutched Billy's arm
tightly. Mam had taken her aside privately and told her she
was just as good as they were, if not better, and that if
Billy's granny started to get high-handed she was to
remember that the old rip wasn't all that respectable herself:
moneylenders could never be classed as that, not even
retired ones.

'It's all right, Maggie, she won't eat you! Her bark is worse
than her bite,' Billy whispered.

Maggie bit her lip. She wished he hadn't said that.

The door of number ten Claudia Street was opened by a
small, stout woman dressed in a plain black dress with a gold
brooch pinned to the collar. Her hair was taken straight
back in a neat bun and a pair of spectacles was perched on
her nose. She looked formidable.

'Hello, Ma! I hope you're well. This is Maggie, Billy's
intended,' Mr Wainwright announced, smiling encouragingly at Maggie.

Maggie held out her hand tentatively. 'How do you do,
Mrs Wainwright. I . . . I'm very pleased to meet you.'

'Are you indeed, girl? Well, I'll reserve my judgement for
now. Come in, all of you. Hilda, put the kettle on. I want to
talk to these two before we have tea.'

Maggie's heart sank at the brusque reception but she
remembered Eve's advice and followed Billy into the small
parlour, which was crammed with furniture and ornaments.

'Sit down and let's have a look at you, girl. Billy's been
singing your praises but then he's biased.'

Maggie sat gingerly on the edge of the sofa, which sported

half a dozen brocade cushions in rather garish colours, and clutched her bag on her knee.

Mrs Wainwright peered at her closely and came straight to the point. 'So, you plan to get married?'

'Yes, ma'am.'

'I told you our plans, Gran,' Billy interrupted.

'Indeed you did! You want to borrow the money to buy the greengrocer's shop where you work, Maggie? It's a very ambitious plan and you're very young.'

Maggie took a deep breath. 'I know it is, ma'am, but . . . but you see we want something of our own. Something steady for the future. We intend to work very hard and we'll pay you back.'

'You will indeed, if I agree! I have to say it's very farsighted of you and you so young. His father never had any such notions, more's the pity!' The old lady sniffed. The girl was an attractive little thing but she appeared steady and earnest, and she was well turned out, but you never could tell.

'Well, I don't want to work all my life for someone else, Gran. We want to get on, have a nice house and a bit of money in the bank in our later years, like you.'

'Don't be impertinent, lad!'

'I'm not, Gran! What's wrong in wanting to be like you?' Billy was all innocence but Maggie shot him a fearful glance.

The old lady turned her attention back to Maggie. 'And just what do your parents think of it all?' Hilda had told her Maggie's parents ran a pub but that her mother worked hard and wasn't in the least bit common or flashy.

This was what Maggie had dreaded all morning but she

squared her small shoulders. 'Mam's all for it. She approves of Billy. She likes him.'

'And your father?'

Billy took her hand. 'Maggie's had a bit of a shock, Gran.'

Maggie went cold and panic rose in her. He was going to tell her! Now, this minute. She'd thought his mam would have done that later.

The spectacles were adjusted. 'What kind of a shock?'

Maggie's grip on Billy's hand tightened until her knuckles were white and he winced.

'He . . . he's left them, Gran. Gone off to London. Yesterday, with someone else.'

The old lady peered hard at Maggie and then leaned back in her chair, nodding slowly.

'Mam said . . . she said I still had to come and see you. That I shouldn't let him ruin my future.' Maggie looked down at the polished lino.

'And what about you?'

'I agree with her.'

'A shock indeed.'

'She was the barmaid,' Billy informed her.

Maggie's humiliation was complete.

'I see.'

Maggie was near to tears but felt she had to say *something*. 'Mam . . . Mam's coping as best she can,' she stammered. 'It was a terrible shock and . . . oh, the shame of it! Mrs Wainwright, I don't know what to say. Mam always worked hard and kept the place nice and . . . *she*'s terrible! Mam's been so strong. It's not fair. It's just not fair!'

'Life is never fair, child, and some men are complete fools. She's probably better off without him if that's the way he wants to carry on, though no doubt he'll live to regret it. They usually do.'

'She won't have him back!'

'Sensible woman. And she insisted that you still come here today?'

Maggie could only nod.

The old lady regarded her thoughtfully. 'She shows great strength of character; I'd like to meet her. And so do you, child, it can't have been easy.' No doubt she would get the whole sordid story from Hilda after tea.

Billy was delighted. His gran could be very contrary at times but she seemed to approve of Maggie and her mam. 'So . . . so, you'll lend us the money, Gran?'

'I will. You deserve a chance and it's nice to see some ambition in the family. We'll sort it all out later, now I think we could all do with a cup of tea. Maggie, go and see what's keeping Hilda and later on we'll have a talk. Just you and me.'

Maggie could have cried with relief. Mam had been right to insist that she come. She was so glad that it was all out in the open.

Chapter Seven

———◆———

E VE COULD HARDLY BELIEVE a whole week had passed as she sat waiting in the reception area of Higson's Brewery for her appointment with Mr Harrison.

Somehow they'd got through it but there were times when everything still felt so unreal. When she would walk into the bar and be surprised not to see Eddie standing there, or look up when the kitchen door opened expecting him to walk in, or, worse still, wake in the morning and find only an empty space beside her. And it still hurt terribly. The sense of loss, betrayal and humiliation were always with her but so too was her anger and bitterness.

Having to make her first appearance in the bar had filled her with dread, but she'd been determined to be 'professional'. She'd dressed with care and rehearsed her little speech.

There had been a moment's awkward silence when she'd joined Harry; no one had quite known where to look.

'Good evening, lads. You've all come here for a pleasant

drink and a chat with your mates, so there'll be no long faces, no complaints and no mention of "certain people". There's no need to treat me as though I'm ill – I'm not. I won't say I'm fine but I'm managing and I'll go on managing so let's have no awkwardness. What's done is done. Now, Uncle Uk, your usual?'

Conversation had resumed and she'd noticed during the evening quite a few approving glances. Uncle Uk had muttered that some fellers didn't know when they were well off and hadn't the sense to stop chasing floozies.

'That wasn't too bad, was it?' Harry had smiled as they finally closed the door.

'No, but it would have been terrible but for you being so good yesterday,' she'd replied.

The girls too seemed to be settling down; even Lily didn't spend quite as much time in tears, although Eve had caught her daughter looking at her with something akin to suspicion in her eyes and that worried her. Sarah was very bitter and refused even to mention her father. Maggie seemed to be coping the best. This Eve put down to the fact that she was wrapped up in her plans for the future with Billy.

Eve glanced around her at the neat and very official-looking room and the smartly turned-out woman who sat typing away at the desk. Oh, she hoped this wasn't going to be hard! If he wouldn't agree to her request she didn't know what she would do. As well as being a place of business, the George was her home. At the end of the afternoon would she be without work and a roof over her head? What would she do then? Sink gradually into the terrible poverty and despair and degradation that had claimed so many? Would she finish up in a single room in a falling-down slum hovel, dressed in rags, with no food, no fire – nothing? She could only pray hard she wouldn't.

She jumped a little nervously as a buzzer sounded and the receptionist looked across at her.

'Mr Harrison will see you now, Mrs Dobson. It's the first door on the right.'

'Thank you,' Eve replied, standing up and smoothing down her best skirt. She'd worn her one good dark grey tweed costume and the pale pink blouse with the embroidery on the collar. Her shoes and bag had been polished up and she wore the hat Maggie had borrowed the week before for the successful visit to Billy's granny's. All the girls had assured her she looked very smart, neat and professional, but now she wondered if the blouse was a bit too fancy. Well, it was too late now to do anything about it.

Mr Harrison was a tall thin man with sparse grey hair and a drooping moustache. He looked as if he'd never had a decent meal in his life, Eve thought as he stood up to greet her. Nor did he look very approachable. This wasn't going to be easy. Yet again she would have to explain Eddie's desertion, without resorting to self-pity.

'And what can I do for you, Mrs Dobson? We haven't met before, have we?'

Eve shook the proffered hand. 'No. No, we haven't. It's usually my . . . husband you see but, well, this is a rather delicate and personal matter, Mr Harrison.'

He looked a little surprised as he indicated she should sit.

She'd better get it over with. 'My husband has left me. He's gone to London. I don't know where exactly he is, I have no address. It . . . it was a terrible shock.' She smoothed an imaginary crease from her skirt with a hand that shook slightly.

Mr Harrison looked very shocked. 'He's absconded? When was this?'

'A week last Saturday. I had no idea . . .'

He tapped his pen on the desk, a habit he had when annoyed or disconcerted. 'And how has the business been faring? Have you had to close? This really is most serious! Most unusual and, I may say, very unprofessional and irresponsible!'

Eve sat bolt upright in the chair. 'Don't you think I *know* all that, sir? But we haven't closed. I've kept the pub going with the help of my two eldest daughters and a very good young barman. It's been business as usual *and* we've remained cheerful for our customers. We've tried very hard to be professional. Business hasn't suffered.'

He leaned back in his chair and scrutinised her. 'Well, I'm certainly relieved to hear that, Mrs Dobson. As you know, it's not a rosy prospect for us to face, the way things are at present. All this unemployment, you understand.'

Eve wondered if he realised that it was a far from rosy prospect for her too, but she didn't dwell on it. 'I understand only too well, sir. My husband came to see you the week before last.'

'He did indeed and I impressed upon him the need for hard work and economy.'

'What I've come to see you for, sir, is to ask you to transfer the licence to me. I've worked at the George all my married life. I know the business. I know the customers and I know that I can make a go of it. I'm prepared to work very hard indeed and I can assure you that I will be far more economical than he was. I'm just asking for a chance, sir, please? The George is also my home and has been for twenty-one years,' she finished simply.

Again he tapped his pen on the polished surface of the desk and looked thoughtful. Considering the strain she must be under she seemed to be very calm and self-assured and she had coped remarkably well under the circumstances. And Eddie Dobson's flight had left him in an awkward position. He had no wish at all to close the pub, not when the brewery's financial position was suffering in these troubled economic times. Once customers went elsewhere they seldom came back. Nor did he want to have to pay a relief manager to take charge, but he was very unsure about turning the business over to a woman. It went against everything he believed in.

'Your daughters have other employment, Mrs Dobson?'

Eve saw what he was getting at. 'Yes, they do. My three daughters all have jobs, they will be no burden to the brewery.'

'And you said you have a good barman. A young man?'

'Yes. Very reliable and trustworthy. I couldn't have managed this week without him. Harry Dempsey is his name.'

'Indeed,' he mused. So, the lad wouldn't expect too much in the way of a wage. He shuffled the papers on the desk in front of him, his mind working rapidly.

Eve held her breath. Please? Oh, please, let him just give her a chance. That's all she was asking for: a chance.

He straightened up. 'Well, Mrs Dobson, even though I have grave misgivings about turning the business over to a woman, I will give you a trial, say two months, and if business remains steady or hopefully improves, then we will consider giving you the licence permanently. We will allow you to keep on this Mr Dempsey on a similar trial basis.'

Eve could have kissed him. It wasn't exactly what she wanted but it was a start and she would make sure that business did improve, even if it was only slightly. She already had a few ideas – or at least Maggie had come up with a few.

'Oh, thank you, sir. You really won't regret it!'

'I sincerely hope I won't, Mrs Dobson.'

'Can I ask you, sir, what the brewery's . . . er . . . policy is on food?'

He looked surprised. 'Food?'

'Sandwiches and maybe pies? You see, I've heard a lot of the men saying it would be great if they could have a bite to eat, particularly at dinnertime, with their pints, and I thought that maybe some sandwiches or bread and a wedge of cheese with some pickle and home-made pies might be called for?'

He was taken aback. 'I hope you don't envisage turning the place into some kind of café, Mrs Dobson?'

'No, of course not. Selling beer would be my first concern, but I just thought it might help to bring in some more trade?'

'Just as long as that *is* your first priority. We don't want public houses turned into eating establishments.'

'Oh, it will be. The food will be an extra.'

He nodded. She could give it a try but in his opinion men went into pubs for beer and company. Food they could and *should* get at home.

'We'll see how it goes. We can review it later.'

Eve leaned forward. 'Well, Mr Harrison, if I'm to prove I can run this business successfully, even as a woman, we'd better go over all the figures you discussed with my husband recently so I can see for myself just what we're up against. I can assure you that I do understand accounts and facts and figures – unlike my husband!'

'I sincerely hope so, Mrs Dobson,' he replied, opening a large ledger.

At the end of half an hour, Eve stood up and held out her hand. 'Thank you again, Mr Harrison. You really won't regret it.'

He shook it firmly this time. 'Thank you for coming, Mrs Dobson, and I really am very sorry for your . . . er . . . position.'

Eve managed a smile. 'Life has to go on, sir. I'll manage,' she said with determination.

Harry was waiting for Eve in the saloon bar. There had been a few customers at dinnertime but now he was alone. He looked up anxiously when she came in. He knew just how much the licence meant to her.

'How did it go? What did he say?'

Eve took off her hat. 'He's going to give me a two-month trial and he says I can employ you as a full-time barman!'

Harry grinned at her. 'That's really great, Eve! I'm so

pleased for you and it's the first time I've ever had what I could call a permanent job.'

'It's not all that permanent, Harry. You're on a two-month trial as well and I have the feeling that if business doesn't improve we'll both be out on our ears.'

'We'll make it improve.'

'We'll have a damned good try! At least we won't have Eddie eating or should I say drinking into the profits. Get two glasses and we'll have a drink to celebrate.'

'What about the profits?'

Eve laughed. 'I don't think that one small sherry and one small whiskey will break us! And I've got plans.'

'What for?' Harry asked as he poured the drinks. He'd not seen her looking so animated since Eddie had left.

'I asked him about having some food at dinnertimes. It was Maggie's idea.'

'Food?'

'Pies and ploughman's lunches. It won't cost me much; I'll bake the pies myself and sell them at a reasonable price. I told him I'd heard the fellers asking for them.'

'I've never heard them.'

'Neither have I but I bet once they've tasted them they will. Just to smell them will be enough. You know what they're like, especially once they've had a few pints.'

He looked doubtful. 'I don't know, Eve.'

'Harry, I have to do something to boost business. I've got to do something to hang on to this place! It's my home! We'll try them tomorrow and see how it goes.'

He nodded. He could see her point and he admired her for trying.

Sarah thought it was a great idea and offered to give Eve a hand and Maggie said she knew where good cheese could be bought wholesale. She'd thought of adding cheese and even butter to the things she and Billy would sell when they took over the shop from Mrs McMillan. They intended to extend the range of fruit and vegetables they sold too, she added.

'Billy said why don't you put up a sort of noticeboard in the bar. We can put things on it, like any odd jobs that are on offer. They've got one up in their place.'

Eve looked at her admiringly. 'You two are full of ideas! I'm beginning to think I've seriously misjudged that lad.'

'And where will we hear about jobs? Haven't they got the *Echo* and the Labour Exchange?' Sarah asked her.

'You hear about all kinds of things in a pub and we can all keep our ears open,' Maggie replied.

Eve smiled at Maggie. 'Right, we'll do that. One of the first jobs can be putting the board up.'

'Harry can do that, Mam,' Sarah said.

'Harry will have enough to do, and they say the Lord helps those who help themselves. I'll stand whoever volunteers a drink for their trouble.'

Sarah gave her a hug. 'We'll all help, Mam. We'll all pull together.'

'I know. We'll make a go of it, luv, you'll see. I'm sure there are plenty of other little things we can do to bring in the customers.' But Eve noticed with concern that Lily had said nothing at all.

To Eve's delight her pies and ploughman's were a great success. After some initial mistrust and a few scathing comments, she found she had to increase her baking. She also added soup and a cob and hotpot to her list. There were enterprising women all over the city who were turning their kitchens into 'canteens' providing hot meals for twopence or threepence, and she found that soon there were women coming to her door with jugs for soup and bowls for hotpot. Because she could buy in much larger quantities she could buy cheaper and make it go further than many housewives could. Each evening the three girls helped her as much as they could, although she was getting increasingly worried about Lily who was withdrawn and sullen.

Lily wasn't the only worry. Her sleep was often disturbed by her fears as to what would happen to them all if she wasn't given the licence. What else could she do to earn a living? Where would they all live? It cost money to rent a decent house, buying was completely out of the question, and she had a hard enough time making ends meet now. If she didn't get the licence they would all be out on the street.

She did think about trying out special offers on drinks between five and six o'clock in the evening on weekdays, as this was often a slack time. Harry had agreed that it was worth a go. He had suggested employing a barmaid for Saturday and Sunday nights, someone young and attractive but respectable. Eve had been very doubtful about this but had agreed to give it some thought. She had definitely decided to expand her menu to fish and chips and agreed with Sarah that they'd try it out one lunchtime. This was much to Harry's disapproval; he thought the idea of a barmaid far more sensible.

'Eve, if they want fish and chips they can go to any number of chip shops. You know what Mr Harrison said about turning the place into an eating house,' he'd protested.

'I know, but I've got to try things. I've *got* to make a success of this place.'

'Next thing you know you'll have a bookie's runner permanently hanging around the back door so if anyone feels like putting on a bet they can do so without any inconvenience!'

'I will not! I had enough of that with Eddie and besides it's against the law. Serving fish and chips isn't,' she'd retorted.

It had been with great foreboding that Harry had watched her serve cod and home-made chips to a couple of hungry dockers she'd sat down at a table at the far end of the saloon bar.

'There's knives and forks, salt and vinegar and a round of bread and butter each. Isn't that better than standing in the street eating them with your fingers out of newspaper?'

'That looks dead posh, girl!'

'Well, I'm not looking for it to be posh, just a decent meal at a fair price in some comfort and with your pint of beer on the table too.'

'Better than we gets at 'ome!' the man replied, tucking in.

'You'll have a queue of wives beating at the door

complaining that you're encouraging them to spend even more money and not go home for their meals either!' Harry warned.

Eve was stung. 'I won't! I don't expect hordes of men in here demanding fish and chips every day!'

Harry shrugged. He still wasn't convinced.

'That's unusual, being able to get a meal in a pub?'

Eve looked up to see a man in a shabby suit, well-worn overcoat and rather shiny bowler hat standing at the bar. She hadn't seen him in here before and assumed he must be a blockerman, as foremen on the docks were known because they always wore bowler hats.

'I'm just trying it out. I do ploughman's and pies, soup and a cob and hotpot too, but if the fish and chips are successful I'll add them to the menu. Can I interest you in something? It's all home-cooked on the premises and it won't take me a minute to lay another table.' She smiled encouragingly but was dismayed to see he didn't look very interested or very pleased.

'I don't think so, Mrs Dobson. Mr Harrison asked me to drop in, unannounced, to see how things were going. I don't think he had valuable space being used to serve full dinners or an extensive choice of menu in mind when he agreed to allow you to serve food. I might remind you that pubs are for the consumption of alcohol.'

Eve stared at him in horror. She had never dreamed that Mr Harrison would check up on her. 'Oh, it . . . it was really only an experiment! The fish and chips, I mean! Of course, I'll go back to just pies and ploughman's and really concentrate on beer and spirits. You see, I really do want to make a go of this place. I do!'

'Then I'd strongly advise you to stick to what you outlined to Mr Harrison. I'll be calling again, Mrs Dobson.'

'When?'

'Oh, it will be unannounced. These visits always are.'

When he'd gone Eve turned to Harry. 'Don't you dare say "I told you so!" '

'Would I?'

'How could they be so sneaky? I thought he was just a blockerman.'

Harry remained silent.

'Oh, well, that's the end of that. I'll worry myself stupid now over the licence.'

Harry was concerned. 'Don't, Eve. Worrying about it won't help and you never know, he might not even report it to old Harrison. Besides, haven't you enough on your plate? You're already worried half to death about Lily.'

The following week Lily came home from work in tears.

'What's the matter, luv?' Eve cried, seeing her daughter's blotched and tear-stained face.

'I . . . I've got the sack, Mam.'

'What? Why?'

'I'm eighteen next week!'

'What's that got to do with it?'

'They said I'm too expensive now. They've got another girl starting on Monday, who's only fourteen.'

'They can't do that!'

'Oh, Mam, they can! I remember just after Christmas

they told Joan Parker the same thing, she was in a terrible state.'

Eve put her arm around Lily's shoulder. 'Oh, Lily, luv, come and sit down. It's not fair! It's just not fair!'

'I never wanted to be a seamstress anyway. I hated it but . . . but . . . we need the money.'

'We don't need it that badly, Lily. And you'll get something else.'

Eve sounded far more confident than she felt. Takings were fairly low and the future was still uncertain; she did need Lily's wage even though it wasn't much. Every penny counted but she couldn't say so. She couldn't, *wouldn't* upset Lily further.

'What, Mam? There are hundreds of girls like me. They only want someone really young that they don't have to pay a half-decent wage to,' Lily sobbed. It was true she had hated it but it was so unjust and so humiliating. On top of everything else it was just too much.

'Don't you upset yourself, luv. Perhaps when our Maggie and Billy get themselves organised properly you can give them a hand.'

Lily didn't want to work in a cold, dirty greengrocer's, and she certainly didn't want to work for Maggie. 'I don't want to, Mam.'

'Then maybe our Sarah can get you something at the Stork.'

'I don't want to do that either.'

Eve sighed. 'Well, we'll think of something.'

'Mam, I want to do something different! Something . . . exciting for a change!'

'Like what?'

'Maybe I could do something at a theatre.'

'A *theatre*?'

'I wouldn't mind what! It would be wonderful! Being able to watch all those shows, speak to real actors and actresses, maybe even meet some famous ones!'

Eve's heart sank and she looked worried. 'I thought you'd got over all that wanting to be famous nonsense. I thought you'd settled down a bit. Grow up! People like us never get to be famous. It's just a dream.'

'No, it's not, Mam! Look at . . . well, Marie Lloyd for one.'

Eve was becoming exasperated. 'Lily, that was the music hall not the theatre and it was years ago. What can you do? You'll finish up sweeping the floor, that's what!'

Lily glared at her. 'I don't care. I could learn things! I could learn to . . . to act!'

'Lily, I won't hear any more of this rubbish. You can't act. You can't sing or dance or play an instrument. It's just a dream and the likes of us don't have the time nor the energy for such things. It's hard enough keeping a roof over our heads and food in our bellies.'

Lily thumped the cushion. 'I knew you wouldn't understand. I just knew it.'

'I don't! I don't know where you get these ideas from.'

'Maybe I'm like Da. Maybe that's why he left: he wanted something more exciting from life than standing behind a flaming bar all day listening to a crowd of old bores moaning!'

Eve was shocked at her outburst. 'Lily! How can you even think like that? How can you try to justify what he's done?'

'You won't even try to understand *him*! You could have gone after him, Mam, you could have tried to get him back. He would have listened, I know he would, if you'd told him how much I miss him, how much we all miss him. Oh, I didn't mean to hurt you but . . . but you don't understand! You just don't understand!'

Eve stared at her, speechless. She'd never realised how Lily really felt. Sarah and Maggie had been so supportive, so furious with their father. 'No, Lily, I don't understand how you can think I could possibly humiliate myself further by running after him and begging him to come back. Don't you realise how desperately hurt I am?'

'But you don't seem to *care*! You've put him out of your mind. You've just carried on as if things were normal with the pub and everything.'

Eve reached for her hand. 'Oh, Lily! I do care, I care very much. I'd given him most of my life, luv, but I had to carry on for Sarah, Maggie and you. I couldn't just let everything fall apart because he didn't want us any more. Lily, you have to understand that he didn't want to be *with* us any more. He wants to be with *her*. It was his choice, no one forced him to go.'

'*She* did! Mam, you could have changed his mind, I know you could!'

'Lily, stop it. Stop it this minute. You have to accept it and the sooner you do the easier it will become to look at

116

the future with hope. Now, go upstairs and wash your face.'

Lily burst into tears and stormed upstairs and Eve collapsed in the armchair. Oh, what was she going to do with Lily? How could she make her understand the awful truth that Eddie *had* made his choice? He *didn't* want them and that included Lily. And now the poor child had lost her job. Yet another rejection. Should she let her pursue this crazy idea of working in a theatre? It might get it out of her system. Was there some truth in what Lily said? Perhaps these mad ideas did indeed come from Eddie. Was that what he had really wanted from life? Excitement – in the form of Doreen Travis and the bright lights of London? What *was* she going to do about Lily?

Chapter Eight

THE MATTER OCCUPIED HER thoughts until Sarah and Maggie arrived home from work when she decided to confide her worries to them.

'Lily's very upset. She's had some bad news,' she announced tentatively.

'What's wrong with her?' Maggie asked irritably. She'd had a hard day and she was tired. There had been no pleasing most of the customers. There had been complaints that Mrs McMillan was buying inferior produce and charging far too much for it. That hadn't improved her employer's temper and Maggie had had to listen to a tirade of caustic comments from Mrs McMillan on the characters of her regular clients. Since they would soon become Maggie's source of income, Mrs McMillan had insisted she take advantage of her experience and had gone on and on for what seemed like hours. Added to that, her employer had had to go out on a matter of business so Maggie had had no lunch.

Eve wiped her hands on her apron and sighed. 'I'm afraid she got the sack.'

'What did she do?' Sarah asked with some resignation. Lily had always been inclined to have too much to say for herself, which didn't go down too well with employers.

'Nothing. She's just too old.'

Sarah put down the kettle she'd begun to fill. 'Too old? She's not eighteen until next week!'

'Oh, you know what it's like now, they want the cheapest labour they can get. They've sacked her and taken on a fourteen-year-old to replace her.'

'It's not fair, Mam, but there's nothing anyone can do about it. It's happened in our place. I've only kept my job because Mr Stevens says he won't have cheeky, inefficient kids straight out of school in his dining room.'

'I know, Sarah.'

'Well, thank goodness Billy and I will be working for ourselves in the near future. That's if she leaves us with any customers at all. They've all been complaining and she's been like a bear with a sore head all day!'

Eve found Maggie's unsympathetic attitude disturbing. 'Oh, Maggie, is that all you can say? Lily's really cut up about it, and about your da, too.'

Maggie shrugged and began to set the table. 'We're all cut up about him!'

'But she's taking it really badly. She actually said I could have tried to talk to him. That I really don't understand him.'

Sarah became irritated. 'Mam, we've been through all this!'

'I know, but she just doesn't seem to understand—'

'Doesn't want to understand, more like. It's about time our Lily grew up and faced the fact that life isn't always easy. Sometimes it's flaming hard,' Maggie interrupted.

'Maggie, she is still only a kid and she's hurt.'

'And so are we, Mam!' Sarah reminded her quietly. 'But if you like I'll talk to her. Sometimes she'll listen to me.'

Eve sighed. 'There's more.'

'Now what?' Maggie demanded.

'She said she wants to go and work in a theatre.'

Maggie was thoroughly exasperated. Honestly, Lily was the living end. 'It really is time she grew up and stopped all this nonsense about being famous! What in the name of God can she do in a *theatre*?' she exploded.

'That's what I said, but she said she doesn't mind what she does, she just wants something more exciting.'

Sarah shook her head and poured the tea while Maggie poked the fire with more than usual vigour.

'She'll be doing nothing more exciting than making tea, sweeping up or running errands!'

'I pointed all that out to her, Maggie.'

'Mam, we all want a bit more excitement out of life, but life's not like that. Not for us,' Sarah said flatly.

'She said that maybe your da had wanted something more exciting from life and that's why he left.'

'That's not fair! Are you supposed to be a mind reader? How were any of us expected to know what he wanted or thought he wanted?'

121

Eve didn't want to get into a discussion about this. 'Sarah, maybe I should let her try it. It might help to take her mind off things and if she's disappointed then at least she can't blame me. She can't say I didn't give her a chance.'

Maggie was astounded. 'Mam, are you mad? She'll get all kinds of silly ideas and no doubt get into all kinds of trouble too. You know what she's like. She's so irresponsible and easily led and what will people say? It's not exactly the kind of life people like us live. There's always some kind of scandal in the newspapers about theatrical people.'

'You mean what will Billy's granny say?' Sarah said cuttingly.

'All right, maybe that is what I mean but I do have to consider her and it doesn't make us look very responsible, allowing Lily to run around with the likes of them.'

'Maggie, they're not that bad. You're such a snob!'

'I'm thinking of my – our – future, Sarah. And of Mam. She'll get no peace of mind worrying about what Lily is up to.'

Eve felt weary. This was solving nothing, in fact it was fast degenerating into a full-blown argument and she began to wish she'd never even mentioned the matter to them. 'Oh, stop it, both of you! This is getting us nowhere. Maggie, you worry far too much about what people will think, especially old Mrs Wainwright. You don't have to tell her anything yet. Lily's not just going to walk into a job or become famous overnight. Just get married, and then if Lily does make a go of it and if Mrs Wainwright doesn't like it she can go to hell! You'll be part of the family and she'll have lent you the money by then. I have to think of Lily and she's desperately unhappy.'

Maggie said nothing but she was far from happy. She'd at least have to tell Billy about this. Oh, why did Lily have to be so difficult? She just didn't understand her sister at all.

'I agree with Mam. Let her try it and you don't have to tell Mrs Wainwright or anyone else for that matter. Now, can we have a cup of tea in peace?'

Before she went through to the bar to help Harry open up Eve went up to talk to Lily who had stubbornly remained upstairs.

Lily was sitting on the bed with her scrapbooks strewn around her. Her cheeks were streaked with newsprint and tears. She felt utterly miserable. It was true that she'd hated her job but it was sickening, really sickening to be told she was no longer required. No longer needed. No one seemed to need her any more. Even Mam seemed to be coping very well. It had taken quite a bit of courage to tell Mam about wanting to do something so utterly different from what was expected of girls like her, but it hadn't done any good.

Eve moved aside a scrapbook dedicated to cuttings of scenes from recent productions at the Liverpool Empire and sat down beside her dejected daughter. 'Lily, I want to talk to you.'

'I don't want another lecture,' Lily muttered sullenly.

'I'm not here to lecture you, luv. I just want to say that I've been thinking about what you said about working in a theatre and I think that maybe you should give it a try.' Eve smiled and gently pushed Lily's tangled dark curls away from her cheeks. 'You're only young and if you can't follow your dreams when you're young it's a sad state of affairs.'

Lily's face lit up. 'Mam! Do you mean it? Can I really?'

'I do. I don't think Sarah agrees with me, Maggie isn't a bit happy about it, but go ahead. Just remember what I said though. It might not be that easy.'

'I don't care, Mam! I'll take anything and I don't care what those two think. It's my life!'

Eve became serious. 'It is, Lily, and you have to make the most of it, but you have to be sensible about it and realistic too. It might not work out.'

'But at least I can try!'

'Come down and get something to eat. You must be cold – it's not very warm up here.'

Eve went through to join Harry behind the bar and Sarah poured Lily a cup of tea and took her dinner from the oven where it had been placed to keep warm. She decided it was time to talk to her sister about her proposed career.

'You know, Mam's being very patient with you, Lily. I'm really sorry about you losing your job—'

'I'm not, not now!' Lily interrupted with spirit.

Sarah shot a warning look at Maggie whose brows had rushed together in a frown. Maggie bit back the sharp words that sprang to her lips.

'It might not be as easy as you think, Lily. There's not much money around. If we're not getting much custom then people aren't going to have the money for the theatre either.'

'I know that, but I don't mind what I do. I *hated* sewing all day!'

'You might hate sweeping the floor all day,' Maggie said tersely.

Lily shrugged.

'Just what do you want to do – eventually? And don't just say "be famous"!'

Lily thought for a few minutes. 'I want to be an actress, I really do, and yes, I would like to be famous – eventually. Is that so bad?'

Maggie raised her eyes to the ceiling but Sarah shook her head. 'I don't suppose it is but how do you learn to act?'

Lily frowned. 'I don't really know but I suppose you just sort of pick it up. You watch and learn and then hope that someone gives you a chance – and that if they do, they think you're good enough to do more. Then you get bigger parts and people will take notice of you.'

Sarah smiled at her fondly. 'You always were what Sister Mary Francis called "a notice box" when we were at school. And you'll be really happy doing that?'

'I *know* I will! I just want a chance.'

'Well, Mam's giving you the chance so promise me you'll give *her* a chance and stop blaming her for what's happened. It's not her fault, Lily!'

Lily nodded. She felt so much better now but it was still hard to understand why Mam hadn't tried harder to get Da away from Doreen Travis.

'When you've had your meal, I'll get the *Echo* and we'll look and see if there's anything in the jobs section. Or we can make a list of all the theatres you can try?' Sarah suggested helpfully.

Maggie compressed her lips tightly. It was one thing for Mam to say Lily could try to find a job but she wasn't going to encourage her the way Sarah was doing. It was a ridiculous idea.

It had been quiet all night until half an hour before closing time when there was a sudden rush.

'You're all cutting it fine. I'll be putting the towel on soon,' Eve quipped, reaching for a pint glass.

'There was a meeting,' Arthur Lethbridge, a usually taciturn docker, informed them.

'About what?' Harry asked, deftly opening a bottle of stout and pulling a pint more or less at the same time.

'About this march ter London,' Jacko answered.

'That again. Was anything at all decided this time?' Eve asked, turning to the till.

'Well might yer ask, Eve! Harry, lad, hurry up with that pint. I'm spittin' feathers, I've been arguing fer hours about actually getting somethin' done!'

'And did you?' Harry demanded, putting a pint of mild on the counter in front of him.

Jacko took a deep swig and licked his lips. 'I did, finally! We're all goin' two weeks on Saturday. We've got ter do *somethin*'!'

'Well, I admire you for trying,' Eve said.

Dick Taggart pushed forward and slumped against the bar. He'd had more than a few drinks during the evening, thanks to a mate who had managed to 'liberate' a couple of bottles of whiskey from a damaged box on the back of a cart that had been bound for 'imprisonment' in a bonded warehouse on the dock estate. 'Might even pay a call on Eddie when we get there,' he slurred.

Eve froze and the colour drained from her cheeks but before she had time to gather her wits Harry had grabbed Taggart by the collar of his jacket.

'You're barred! Get out now and don't show your face in here again!' he roared.

Jacko grabbed Taggart and hurled him bodily towards the door which Uncle Uk obligingly held open.

'Yer stupid bloody gobshite! Sling yer 'ook or yer'll feel me boot up yer arse!'

The door slammed and Eve passed a shaking hand over her eyes.

'I'll bloody kill him!' Harry fumed.

'You'll have to wait in line, lad! I'm so sorry, Eve! He's always had a gob like a parish oven and no bloody sense!' Jim Stokes snapped.

'He always fancied *her* and all,' Arthur muttered before he was silenced by a sharp jab in the ribs by one of his neighbours.

Harry glared at him. 'You looking to follow him?'

Eve pulled herself together. 'All right, that's enough. It's over. I suppose I'll have to expect remarks like that from drunken fools like him!'

'No you won't, not while I'm here!' Harry said grimly. He carried on serving and conversation resumed but the incident had shaken Eve more than she would like to admit.

When they had closed up and Harry had gone Eve was surprised to find Maggie still sitting in the kitchen.

'You're up late?'

'I wanted to talk to you. Is something the matter, Mam?'

'Oh, there was a bit of trouble earlier on. Harry barred Dick Taggart for . . . some remark he made and Jacko threw him out.'

'Good for them, he's no loss! Deadbeats like that we can do without!'

'Put the kettle on, luv.' Eve determinedly pushed the incident from her mind but wondered what it was that was worrying Maggie now. She hoped it wasn't Lily. She felt in no mood for an argument.

'You know you were saying earlier about me not saying anything about our Lily?'

'Oh, Maggie, please don't start on that again!'

'I'm not! I've been thinking about it and I wanted to discuss our plans. My plans, that is.'

Eve nodded. 'So?'

'So, I think it would be a good idea if we all got together. You, me, Billy and his mam and dad and maybe even his granny.'

Eve's eyebrows rose. 'Why his flaming granny?'

'Well, she *is* lending us the money and it's quite a lot.'

'She doesn't have to stick her oar in about everything!'

'She said she'd like to meet you, Mam.'

'Did she? To see if I meet with approval too?'

'No! I think she . . . admired you.'

Eve sighed. 'Oh, ask her if you want to.'

'Thanks, Mam. Will it be better one evening or at the weekend?'

'You know it's always busier at weekends, Maggie.'

'Then say next Tuesday night? I want to get things sorted out.'

'Hadn't you better start to get things sorted out with Billy first?'

'Oh, Billy will go along with whatever I think.'

Eve nodded. He very probably would.

Chapter Nine

'MAM, IS ALL THIS fuss really necessary?' Sarah complained as the following Tuesday evening they were all busy putting the finishing touches to the supper Maggie had insisted on providing. The kitchen had been scrubbed and polished to within an inch of its life. A freshly washed and ironed cloth covered the table and Eve's one cherished china tea set, bought piece by piece over the years, was set out in all its rose-strewn glory. Maggie had bought ham and tongue for sandwiches and Eve had baked an apple pie and a Victoria sponge cake.

'You'd think it was the flaming queen coming to tea instead of just Billy and his mam and dad and that auld one!' Lily muttered.

'Lily, don't call her that! I don't want her thinking we've got nothing or that we don't know how to behave properly,' Maggie said heatedly, wishing that the furniture was a bit more presentable or that they had a decent parlour to use for occasions like this.

Lily ignored her. 'I wouldn't mind but we've had to do all this work and we won't even get a bite to eat *and* this is a really great way to spend my birthday!'

'I'll make sure there's something left for you and I've given you the money for a new blouse,' Eve said firmly. She too was tired of all the fuss.

'And you've had cards and presents from us too,' Maggie put in.

'Well, I'm glad I'll be in the bar with Harry,' Sarah said thankfully.

'I wish I was!'

'Lily, light that Tilley stove in your room. It's still chilly up there at night,' Eve instructed.

Lily nodded gloomily. She had promised to stay upstairs and out of the way until the discussion was over in case she accidentally let anything slip about her plans for the future and her efforts so far, or was asked any awkward questions.

At a quarter past seven the Wainwrights arrived en masse and Sarah and Lily, after being introduced to the old lady, thankfully disappeared.

'Won't you sit down, Mrs Wainwright?' Eve said, thinking she was going to have to call Billy's mam 'Hilda' to avoid confusion, although she didn't know the woman all that well.

'It was good of you to include me, Mrs Dobson,' the old lady said, settling herself in the armchair.

Eve was determined not to take the credit for this. 'Actually, it was Maggie's idea.'

'Really? That was thoughtful. So, how are you managing?' Billy's da coughed nervously.

Eve was a little taken aback at such forthrightness. 'I'm doing well. I have plenty to keep me busy.'

'That's the best way! Don't give yourself time to dwell on things, it does no good.'

'I don't. Now, shall we listen to what these two have got to say for themselves?' Eve's tone was businesslike. She had no intention of discussing her situation further.

Maggie was slightly relieved as Hilda was looking decidedly edgy. 'Billy and I have decided that, if it's not too much of a rush, Mam, we'd like to get married at the beginning of next month. May is usually nice, weatherwise. Mrs McMillan's accepted our offer for the shop, she can't wait to get it off her hands and go and live with her daughter in Wales and she hasn't had any other offers. We'd like to do up those rooms before we move in—'

'I've told Billy I'll give him a hand with them,' Mr Wainwright interrupted.

Maggie smiled at him.

'And I've promised to sort out some curtains and other stuff for them.'

'That's good of you, Hilda,' Eve thanked her.

'You should think of giving the shop a coat of paint, inside and out, and get some new fittings. I was passing there the other day and it looked very shabby,' old Mrs Wainwright put in.

'She's not done much to it since Mr McMillan died,' Maggie informed them.

'You have to speculate to accumulate,' Mrs Wainwright said sagely.

'I suppose you would know about that,' Eve said meaningfully, ignoring Maggie's startled expression.

The old lady stared hard at Eve and then gave a little chuckle. 'Oh, indeed I would. You're no fool, are you?'

Eve grinned back. 'I hope not. Well, I suppose the beginning of next month is all right. It will be a bit of a rush but we'll manage.'

'How are you for money? I don't want it to be a hole-in-the-corner affair. He's my eldest grandson and I'm investing a good bit in his . . . their future.'

'Ma-in-law!' Hilda gasped but Eve held up her hand.

'It's all right, I can manage to give her a decent do, although it will have to be here. I can't run to fancy hotels or the like. We can have it in the lounge bar; I can't close the pub, I have a living to earn.'

'Of course you can't, girl! Business is business and I hear the brewery is giving you a trial as licensee.'

Eve could have killed Maggie for divulging this information. 'They are, and I'm confident they'll give me the licence permanently.'

'And so they should!' Mrs Wainwright agreed.

Maggie decided to steer the conversation away from such matters. 'I'll have our Sarah and Lily as bridesmaids. Do you think our Lily will give me a hand to make my dress? I don't want anything too fancy or expensive.'

'I'm sure she'll be delighted to, Maggie.'

'She can sew then?' Mrs Wainwright demanded.

'She trained as a steamstress at Elliot's,' Eve said quickly.

'And who will give her away?'

Hilda bit her lip. She knew it was something that had to be discussed but she just wished her mother-in-law were a little more tactful.

Maggie had already come to a decision about this. 'Well, if Mam has no objection I thought – and Billy agrees – that I'd ask Harry Dempsey.'

Eve was surprised but pleased. 'I've no objections at all, Maggie.' She turned to Mrs Wainwright. 'You see, I've no brothers and neither has . . . her da. And Harry has been a tower of strength.'

'It's a bit odd asking the barman but I don't suppose it's any odder than our Billy not wanting our Effie's lad Charlie as his best man,' the old lady sniffed.

'I told you, Gran, I'm not having our Charlie, he's a right hooligan!' Billy said firmly.

'He is, Ma! You know how many times our Effie's had the law on her doorstep over him!' Mr Wainwright agreed.

So, there was a black sheep in the family! Eve thought with some amusement. Maggie had kept that quiet. 'Right then, I think that's all settled. I'll provide the reception and the flowers too and I think I can manage something in the way of a wedding present.'

'I'll pay for my own dress, Mam, and there won't be any need for a carriage – we can walk to church, give the neighbours a chance to see me in my finery.'

'You'd better get yourselves down to see Father Delaney pretty soon,' Eve advised.

'Well,' said old Mrs Wainwright, 'I've agreed to lend them two hundred and fifty pounds for the shop and the goodwill

Lyn Andrews

and I'll give them thirty pounds as a wedding present.'

'That's very good of you, Gran!' Billy was delighted.

'It's very generous of you!' Maggie added. She hadn't expected anything. The loan for the business would have been enough.

Hilda and her husband exchanged looks, which said clearly that Billy and Maggie were getting far more than they'd ever got.

Eve was in shock at the amount of money Billy and Maggie would be borrowing. It would take a lifetime to pay back, but then she doubted it ever would be fully paid. The old lady didn't have a lifetime to wait although she looked robust enough to last a good few years yet.

Eve and Maggie served the tea and sandwiches, pie and cake and they all chatted comfortably for a while longer, but Eve was relieved when the Wainwrights took their leave. Old Mrs Wainwright invited both Maggie and Eve to call on her whenever they liked.

'Didn't that go well, Mam?' Maggie was delighted with herself.

'It did. You've obviously made an impression on her! Thirty pounds for a wedding present!'

'I know! I didn't expect that, I really didn't.'

'What will you do with it? You could furnish those rooms really well, Maggie. You can get a good quality bedroom suite for seven or eight guineas in walnut or mahogany.'

Maggie was thoughtful. 'I think we'll save most of it. I don't want to put really good stuff above the shop. I'll wait until I get a nice house.'

'You might have a long wait, especially having to pay back two hundred and fifty pounds! It's a fortune, Maggie! I wouldn't sleep in my bed at night if I owed that much money,' Eve said fearfully.

Maggie smiled knowingly. 'Mam, can you honestly see her living *that* long? She'd have to be about a hundred and twenty!'

Eve grinned. 'Oh, you scheming little madam! But she must realise that, she's no fool.'

'I know, so she really must like me.'

'And have a soft spot for Billy. No wonder: it doesn't sound as if she's much to be proud of in that Charlie!'

'She'll leave everything to Billy when she does die, he knows that.'

Eve looked amazed. 'You mean she's got more?'

'Billy reckons she's got a *thousand pounds*!'

'God Almighty! I've never even *heard* of anyone – let alone *met* anyone – who's got that much money, and she's been here in my kitchen drinking tea!'

Maggie looked smug. 'Didn't I do well?'

Eve was concerned. 'Didn't you just, but I hope it's not just Billy's inheritance you're after.'

'Of course it's not, Mam! I love him!' Maggie protested vehemently although admitting to herself that she would never have married anyone who had no prospects at all.

Lily poked her head tentatively around the door. 'Can I come down now? Have they gone? The fumes from that stove are making me feel sick!'

Eve smiled. 'Then you won't want any cake, will you?'

'They haven't eaten everything, have they?' Lily demanded.

'Of course not, there's plenty left. Will I go and get our Sarah?'

'You'd better get Harry too, if the bar's quiet, and tell him the good news, Maggie.'

'What good news?' Lily asked, pouring herself some tea and helping herself to a piece of cake and two ham sandwiches.

'You'd better let Maggie tell you herself. Such plans!'

Maggie returned with both Sarah and Harry.

'There's only four of them in and Jim Stokes said he'd keep his eye on the bar for me,' Harry informed Eve.

'Then make the most of it. Help yourselves,' Eve instructed.

Maggie perched on the arm of the sofa and, after everyone had got settled, ran through the plans.

'It's a bit quick, isn't it?' Sarah said when she'd finished.

'Well, there's no point waiting. It won't take long to get things sorted out with the shop and Billy and his dad will spruce those rooms up in no time. I'll help Mam with the food for the reception. As we're having it here it will only need to be a buffet, not a sit-down meal.'

'What colours will we have?' Lily asked.

'What colours would you like? Nothing too bright!'

'You don't have bright colours for bridesmaids' dresses. I wouldn't mind pale blue or pink or peach,' Sarah mused.

'Peach would be better; the others are a bit wishy-washy. Or apple green? That's nice—' Lily suggested.

'Some people say green is unlucky for a wedding,' Eve interrupted.

'Then green is definitely out. I'm not tempting fate,' Maggie said firmly.

'I look a bit washed out in blue, unless it's a dark blue.'

'Not dark blue, Sarah.'

'I thought you asked us, Maggie?'

'You can decide definitely later,' Eve put in quickly, not wanting an argument at this early stage.

'Do we have to pay for them ourselves? I haven't got much money.'

Sarah smiled at Lily. 'I think I can manage to pay for the material for both.'

'I said you'd help me make my dress, Lily. I don't want anything too fancy.'

Lily looked sceptical. 'God, Maggie, there's not a lot of time to make three dresses!'

'Well, what else have you got to do?' Maggie demanded, hoping Lily wasn't going to be awkward.

Lily was indignant. 'I've got to find myself a job and it's taking time! I can't expect just to walk into something.'

'Look, you can all go to Blackler's on Friday night and get the material and patterns and I'll help. I can at least tack,' Eve offered.

'You'll have enough to do, Mam, and you'll need something for yourself,' Sarah reminded her.

'It's quiet enough in the pub, Eve, I can always manage. You're going to have a lot to do,' Harry offered.

'You're going to have to get yourself along to the fifty-shilling tailors, Harry,' Eve informed him.

'Me? What do I need a suit for?' He hadn't expected to be

139

invited; he'd thought he would be needed to run the pub that day.

Maggie grinned at him. 'Because you're not going to give me away in that old jacket and flannel trousers, Harry Dempsey!'

Harry was taken aback. 'Me? You want me . . . ?'

'Well, who else is there?' Maggie asked.

Lily jumped to her feet, upsetting her teacup, her face scarlet. 'It's not *his* place! It's . . . it's Da's! Maggie, how can you ask him, he's . . . he's not even family!' She'd assumed her da would give Maggie away. She'd hoped so. It was the perfect opportunity for him to come home to them.

'Lily! Haven't you forgotten something?' Eve said sharply.

'No, Mam! It's not . . . *right*!'

Harry looked embarrassed but Maggie was on her feet, her eyes blazing. 'Lily, Da knew Billy and I were going to get married sometime but he didn't care! He didn't care! He didn't want to stay around long enough to give me away so I don't want him to. I want Harry to give me away and it's my wedding and you're not going to spoil it by behaving like this!'

Lily turned on her outraged. 'You all *hate* Da! He should at least be given the chance to come home!'

Maggie really lost her temper. Things had been going so well, despite what her da had done and what Lily intended to make of her life. 'Lily, I don't want him, can't you get that into your head? He doesn't deserve any kind of a chance! How would it look if he turned up? How would Mam feel? I don't know how you expect her to act. To welcome him with open arms, as though nothing had happened? Just what would people think of her then? And what if he turned up with *her*? Oh, could you imagine it? I'd *die*! We'd all *die* of mortification, except you! Stop behaving like a stupid, spoiled brat. It's bad enough that you want to go making a holy show of yourself on the stage – if you ever get that far – without carrying on like this. I'm having Harry and there's an end to it.'

'Look, both of you, if it's going to cause this much trouble, I'd sooner Mr Wainwright gave Maggie away,' Harry intervened grimly. He was angry with Lily too. How could she expect Eve to agree to Eddie being asked? Was she totally insensitive to her mother's feelings? And what if Eddie did turn up? With or without Doreen Travis, Harry knew it would totally ruin the day for Eve and he himself couldn't be certain that he wouldn't take a swipe at the man.

'I don't want him, I want you!' Maggie cried furiously.

'Lily, Maggie's right. Da didn't think about us – any of us, and that includes you. I know it sounds cruel but it's true. You *can't* expect Mam to have to face that!' Sarah interrupted. She, too, was livid with Lily, having seen the colour drain from her mother's face at her sister's outburst.

Lily gazed around in desperation. They were all against her. 'Then I . . . I'm not going. I won't be your bridesmaid and I won't help with your stupid dress!'

Eve was on her feet. 'Lily, stop it. Stop this at once! I won't have it. You *are* acting like a spoiled brat. I won't have you ruining Maggie's wedding. We've all been through enough and it's your da's fault, no one else's. I'm giving you the chance to do what you want, it's not what I want for you, so don't you be so selfish. This is Maggie's life, it's what she wants, it's her day and you're not going to spoil it. We're going to act like a family – a united family. I'm not having you missing as well. Now, there's an end to it!'

Lily burst into tears and fled, slamming the door behind her.

'I'll go after her, Mam.'

'No, Sarah, leave her. She knows I mean it and I do! She'll get over it.'

Harry turned to Eve. 'Eve, I meant it too, about Mr Wainwright. Better to have him than not have Lily.'

'And *I* meant it, Harry! I want you. I'm sick of our Lily and her tantrums,' Maggie cried, close to tears.

'There won't be any more tantrums, Maggie, I promise you that, because if there are then that's the end of her career in the theatre,' Eve said determinedly. This time Lily had gone too far.

Chapter Ten

———————

N O MORE WAS SAID on the subject by Sarah or Maggie but Maggie and Lily hardly exchanged two words over the next few days. Eve was struggling hard to understand her youngest daughter. She had tried to make allowances for her, telling herself that Lily was still very young; she had bent over backwards to boost her self-confidence and soothe her troubled emotions, but nothing she said or did seemed to get through. However, she was determined that Maggie's wedding day was not going to be ruined.

On Friday morning, when Sarah broached the subject of the dress materials, Lily shrugged and so Eve told the two older girls to go to Blackler's by themselves.

'Don't worry, she'll help, Maggie,' she said grimly, seeing her middle daughter biting her lip and looking uncertain.

When they returned, laden down with parcels, Eve suggested brightly that they spend the evening cutting out the paper patterns.

'Then you can all make a start tomorrow morning, bright and early. This is really lovely, Maggie!' she finished, studying the simple but elegant design on the front of the packet and fingering the plain white satin gently.

'Well, I didn't want anything too fancy; I'm too small to carry off frills and flounces. Anyway, they're not all that fashionable.'

Sarah passed over the other pattern. 'I thought Lily and I could get away with the frill around the neck and sleeves.'

'You can, you're both taller. This is a lovely shade. What colour flowers will you have?' Eve was determined to be enthusiastic, despite Lily's sullen mood and uninterested silence.

'I thought peach and cream, with enough greenery so it doesn't look insipid.'

'Maybe a little bit of blue too?' Eve suggested.

'What colour will you have, Mam? Billy's mam is thinking of navy and white. I think it's a bit plain, but she says it's serviceable.' Privately Maggie thought it was downright dull.

Eve hadn't really thought about it. 'It is more serviceable, I suppose. Maybe I'll have brown and beige.'

'Oh, Mam! Why not pale blue or pink or even lilac? The weather will be warmer so they'd look lovely – and suitable.' Maggie wanted Eve to look really nice. She wanted her to buy something that would cheer her up. Make a statement that said: 'I don't care if he has left me for a young girl, I'm still attractive.'

'Maggie, I'm not the Lady Mayoress! Where will I ever

go to wear lilac again? Be practical. I can't afford to buy something I'll not get any wear out of.'

Maggie sighed. Mam was right. 'Well, why not go for a sort of cornflower blue with navy accessories?'

'Billy's mam might not be too pleased about the navy,' Eve said doubtfully.

'It's only shoes and bag, you could get a blue hat,' Maggie suggested.

Eve was thoughtful. 'I suppose I could. I'd at least get some wear out of a darker blue.'

Lily said nothing but dutifully began to cut around the edges of the pattern. She wasn't going to get enthusiastic about any of this. She'd decided she would have to help: she'd never seen Eve so angry and she knew her mother meant what she'd said. Nevertheless, she'd made up her mind about one thing.

Her initial efforts at finding a job, any job, in a theatre hadn't been very successful. She'd tried the Empire, the Royal Court, the Shakespeare, the Hippodrome, the Rotunda and the Playhouse. Only at the much smaller Playhouse had she been given any encouragement. There might be a job in the wardrobe department, doing odd bits of sewing, at the end of the month but they couldn't promise anything. It did help that she had been training as a seamstress, but it didn't help that she was eighteen and had no experience and a definitely untheatrical background. Times were hard, and getting harder, and the cinemas weren't helping, that was what she'd been told. It wasn't encouraging. Spurred on by her outrage over Maggie's decision and her initial disappointment in her chosen career, she'd thought long and hard and had formed a plan that she was determined to carry out.

The following morning, early, she slipped out the back way and walked quickly to the Travises' house, avoiding the streets where she was bound to be recognised.

Mr Travis opened the door to her.

'I've come to see if you know where my da and your Doreen are. In London, I mean.'

Mr Travis peered hard at her and looked annoyed. 'A fine bloody carry-on that! Yer'd best step inside, girl. Which one are yer?'

'Lily. I'm the youngest and Mam would kill me if she knew I was here,' she answered stepping into the lobby.

'I could kill the pair of them! I don't know which is the worst: 'im or 'er. Ada's still in a right state over it all. I'll be glad ter sail again, I'm sick of 'earin' about it! It's all I get, twenty bloody times a day, an' she blames me! What the 'ell am I supposed ter do about the carry-on out of 'er? A man's got ter earn a bloody livin' and goin' away ter sea is the only one I've ever known and she's never complained about the bloody allotment I've always left her and—'

'Look, I can't stay long, have you got any idea?' Lily interrupted, impatient to put an end to the tirade.

'Oh, aye! Didn't that brazen little madam ask me fer an address? For a friend, she said it was! Friend, I ask you, and me, like a bloody fool—'

'Can you give it to me, please?' Lily again interrupted,

thinking the man must have been vaccinated with a gramophone needle.

He searched his waistcoat pocket and brought out a stub of a pencil and a small scrap of paper on one side of which was written a bet.

'This'll do. That bloody 'orse is still runnin'!' he muttered, scribbling down a few lines.

'Thanks. I'd best be going.'

Mrs Travis's voice floated out of the kitchen, enquiring who was at the door. He quickly opened it and shoved Lily out.

'Don't come 'ere again, girl!' he hissed.

'I won't,' Lily replied ungraciously, tucking the piece of paper into her pocket.

From there she went to Lime Street Station and made enquiries as to train times and prices. If she borrowed five shillings from Sarah she'd just about have enough for a single third-class ticket. Well, that would do; if everything went well she wouldn't need a return. Da could find her somewhere to live and there were plenty of theatres in London, big ones too. There was bound to be more work there and people would have more money. Also, in her opinion Da ought to know Maggie was getting married. He had a right to give her away, no matter what Maggie said. It might even make him come home for good and then wouldn't they all be delighted that she'd gone and found him? Yes, she was definitely doing the right thing for everyone concerned.

'Where've you been?' Sarah demanded when she arrived home.

'I went to see someone about a job. I had to go early as it was the only time they could see me,' Lily lied.

'And?' Eve demanded.

'There might be something next week. I have to go back on Tuesday morning, quite early.'

'I wouldn't have thought anyone started early in the morning in theatres, seeing as how they all work at night.'

'They have matinées!' Lily reminded her mother.

'Now you're here, I think we'd better make a start on Maggie's dress. It's the most important.' Eve was giving Lily no chance to back out. At least the girl did seem happier in herself and for that Eve was thankful.

Lily nodded. 'If we're going to get it cut out you'd better get some sheets to put down, or it'll get dirty.'

'Sheets?'

'We always covered everything with sheets at work,' Lily replied, thinking how glad she was that those days were over.

'You can use the ones off my bed. I don't mind and it is my dress after all,' Maggie said with resignation, knowing her mother had none to spare.

By Monday Maggie's dress had been cut out, tacked, fitted and part machined and they had made a start on cutting out both Sarah and Lily's dresses. Lily felt she had done more than her fair share. She'd shown Sarah how to set in sleeves, attach facings and do the frills. Maggie and Sarah could finish the dresses themselves and she wouldn't need hers at all so it didn't matter if it never got finished. She'd packed a few clothes and hidden her grip bag in an outhouse in the yard; she'd managed to borrow the five shillings from Sarah, saying she was completely broke but needed a pair of stockings and some other bits and pieces if she was to have any chance of getting a job.

'Good luck, Lily!' Eve called from the bar where she was cleaning on Tuesday morning as Lily put on her hat and her jacket.

'Thanks!' Lily called back, feeling a pang of guilt. Maybe she should leave a note? She really didn't want to worry her mother but . . . no, Mam wouldn't understand and might even come after her if she found the note too soon. It would be disastrous to be dragged off the train!

The carriage was crowded and smoky but she squeezed into a corner seat, thankful she had managed to get a seat at all. It was a long way and she certainly didn't want to spend it standing in the corridor or trying to sit on her bag. She studied the scrap of paper. London was a huge place and she had no idea where this place was, but she had a tongue in her head, hadn't she? She could ask for directions and there were buses and the tube. Her heart sank. She only had about fourpence in her pocket. Just enough to get a cup of tea and maybe a bun but she was determined not to get depressed. Everything would be sorted out by tonight. Well, almost everything.

By half past three Eve was getting worried. She'd expected Lily home at lunchtime if not before. She told herself that maybe Lily had been lucky and they had wanted her to stay on and start right away, especially if there was a matinée. Then she realised that she didn't even know which theatre Lily had gone to.

When Sarah and Maggie arrived home and there was still no sign of Lily, Eve became seriously worried.

'Mam, she's not a child! Maybe she stayed on, matinées don't finish until five o'clock sometimes and she might have jobs to do afterwards,' Maggie reminded her.

'You know what she's like if she's excited: she forgets the time. If they've given her a job she'll be more than excited.'

'Oh, I know!'

'Which one was it?' Maggie demanded, thinking that with any luck when Lily returned her mood would have improved considerably.

'I don't know. She never said. I should have asked her.'

'Don't worry, Mam. She'll bounce in here full of the joys of spring, you see if she doesn't.'

Eve smiled. 'Oh, I expect you're right, Sarah.'

'I hope she'll have enough energy to give us a hand. There's still a lot to be done. Billy's coming round later to see what colour I want those rooms painting. They're going to make a start tomorrow after work.'

'You're really getting organised, luv. Now, put the kettle on. We'd all better have something to eat before we start and I promised Harry I'd give him a hand tonight. It will be busier later on, there's another meeting about the march.'

By ten o'clock Sarah was as worried as Eve, although Eve had little time to dwell on the matter as the bar was full of thirsty men, a good many of whom also declared they were starving hungry and did Eve have any pies or ploughman's left over from lunchtime. Business was picking up, thanks to the schemes Eve had introduced to bring in more custom.

'Maggie, there's something wrong. I know it!' Sarah bit her lip anxiously. 'She should have been home hours ago.'

'Maybe she's stayed on for the evening performance.' Maggie wasn't really perturbed, her mind was on paint colours and plans for more shelving and the wisdom of getting a new gas cooker.

'We don't even know if she got the job! We don't even know what theatre it is! Mam's going to be out of her mind when she realises.'

'Give her another hour.'

'And then what? Go and look for her? There are dozens of theatres in this city.'

'Where else could she have gone?'

'She's got no money to speak of, she said she was broke. She cadged five shillings off me.'

'Oh, you know Lily, she's probably thought up some madcap idea or met someone.'

'Maggie, I wish you'd take this more seriously! Anything could have happened to her.'

'Give her another hour. By that time Mam and Harry will be closing up and we can think what to do,' Maggie advised calmly, though she was beginning to think Sarah was right.

When the bar was closed and Harry and Eve had tidied up and brought the takings through to the kitchen, they were confronted by two worried girls.

'Oh, God! She's not in?' Eve cried.

'No, Mam.'

'Where did she go?' Harry asked.

'That's just it, we don't know. I should have asked her!'

'Was it one of the big places?'

'No, she's tried all of them. It could be anywhere.'

Eve was biting her lip. 'Should I go to the police?'

'Let's just think first,' Harry advised. 'She was upset, right?'

'I had thought she'd sort of settled down over the week-end. She was helping out with no complaints.'

'What did she have on? Did she take anything with her?'

'Her hat and best jacket, I think. I didn't see her actually go out.'

'I'll go and see if her things are still in the drawers,' Sarah offered, following Harry's line of thinking.

Eve uttered a cry. 'You don't think she's . . . she's run away?'

'Where to?' Maggie demanded angrily.

'I don't know! Who knows what she was thinking, you know how she's been.'

Sarah returned with a very anxious look on her face. 'She has taken some clothes, Mam, and her grip bag has gone, but she's got no money. All she had was five shillings she borrowed from me.'

Eve was distraught. 'Oh, God! Where has she gone? And why?'

Maggie flung the scissors down. 'She's got that damned bee in her bonnet about Da, that's why! She's just doing this to punish us, to punish me!'

'Could she have gone to him?' Harry asked tentatively. It was possible. Lily had been very upset and she was very headstrong.

'How, with no money?' Eve demanded.

'Oh, she *couldn't* have!' Maggie cried.

Harry ignored the outburst. 'She might have had something. Just enough to buy a ticket.'

'But she has no idea where he is! None of us does,' Sarah reminded him.

'She could have gone to see the Travises, to ask if they knew.'

'She wouldn't do that, surely?'

'She might have, Eve. I'll go round and ask them if they've seen her and if they haven't, well . . .'

'If they haven't I'm going to the police station! She could be lying . . . hurt somewhere!' Eve was fighting back tears. This was a dangerous city for a young girl alone at night.

'Mam, don't upset yourself, please,' Sarah begged, but she couldn't hide her own concern about Lily.

Maggie made a pot of tea and before long Harry returned looking grim.

'What did they say?' Eve demanded, jumping to her feet.

'She was there, Eve. Mr Travis gave her the address.'

'They knew where those two had gone?' Maggie was outraged.

'I got a long rigmarole from him about that, but you can bet that's where she's gone. She must have got the train fare from somewhere. She'll be there by now if she went first thing this morning.'

Eve dropped her head in her hands. 'Oh, Holy Mother of God, what possessed her?'

'Mam, it's a good hiding our Lily wants and if she shows her face back here then I'll give it to her!'

Eve, like Harry earlier, ignored Maggie's interjection. 'Harry, what am I going to do?' She was seriously worried about Lily. She was so young and so trusting and there were all kinds of men who hung around train stations waiting to lure naive girls into all manner of trouble.

'I've got the address, Eve, do you want me to go after her?'

'No, Mam! Let her stew!' Maggie raged.

'He might well send her back, Mam. I can't see him being exactly overjoyed to see her. It might just be what will bring Lily to her senses.'

'I agree with Sarah, Eve, but if you want me to go, I will.'

Eve shook her head. 'No, not yet. You might miss her.' It was torture sitting doing nothing, but it was the right decision. She too thought Eddie would send Lily packing – but how would that make the poor girl feel?

Chapter Eleven

———◆◆◆———

LILY WAS VERY TIRED and she was hungry. It had been a long and tedious journey and when she'd arrived at Euston Station the first thing she'd done was get a cup of tea and a large, sticky bun. Then she'd shown a porter the now grubby piece of paper and had been told to get a number eighty-six bus and ask the driver to put her off on the corner of Stockton Road. It wasn't far from there. When she'd explained that she didn't have any money, he'd given her some complicated directions and told her it was quite a long walk.

She'd soon realised he was right and regretted spending her last pennies. She'd got lost more than once and as it was now dark she was getting worried. The streets all seemed to look the same: rows and rows of houses, some quite big, others much smaller and seedier-looking. There were plenty of pubs too and all of them seemed to be full. She had passed through areas where there were big shops and theatres and that had given her hope, but now she wished she'd borrowed a bit more money from Sarah, at least enough for her bus fare.

She was standing under a streetlamp, deciding whether to go into the next pub she came to and ask if someone would take pity on her and show her the way, when she saw a man approaching her. He was quite well dressed in a sharp sort of way.

'You lost, girlie?' he asked, grinning and raising his hat in an overly polite manner, revealing dark oily hair.

Lily didn't like the look of him. 'No. Just waiting for someone,' she snapped.

'Strange place to be meeting someone! A feller is it, love? Has he stood you up?'

'No! And anyway, it's none of your business.' She sounded more confident than she felt.

'That's an accent I don't recognise. You don't come from around here, do you?'

Lily looked quickly up the street but there was no one in sight. She wondered if she should take refuge in the pub. 'I'm from Liverpool, which is quite a big city and one full of hard-case seafarers, so if you think I was born yesterday you're wrong!' She wished he would go away.

'Right little hard case yourself, aren't you, girl?'

'Oh, go to hell!' Lily cried.

To her surprise he shrugged and turned away and disappeared into the pub. She looked around and saw the reason why. A policeman had turned the corner.

'Oh, excuse me, sir, can you help me?'

He looked at her a little sternly. 'Now, miss, what's a young girl like you doing wandering the streets at this time of night?'

'I'm lost. I'm looking for this address. My da lives there. I came down from Liverpool on the train this morning to find him.'

He took the piece of paper and scrutinised it by the light of his flash lamp. Then he beamed at her with amusement and a little pity. 'It's just around the corner, luv. Come on, I'll walk you there, see you safely in.'

Lily could have cried with relief. 'Oh, I'm such a fool! I've probably walked right past it; I seem to have been wandering around here for ages!'

'It's a bit confusing all right. Is he expecting you?'

'No, it's a . . . surprise.'

'Then I'd better wait and see you in,' he replied, thinking that, judging from past experience, it might not turn out to be such a welcome surprise for her father. 'Does your mother know you've come?'

'Oh, yes,' Lily lied stoutly.

When they stopped outside the door Lily realised that she had indeed walked past the house. It didn't look much like a hotel, more like an ordinary house, but on closer inspection you could just make out the faded lettering that said there were vacant rooms available for rent. She'd been looking for something a bit grander.

'I somehow thought it would be, well, bigger. It does say the Westmoreland Hotel.'

'I know and I agree it's a bit too pretentious; it's really a boarding house. There are a lot of them in this area. What's his name?'

'Eddie. Eddie Dobson.'

The policeman hammered loudly on the door and eventually an old man in a misshapen woollen cardigan, old trousers and carpet slippers opened it.

'Have you got a Mr Eddie Dobson here?'

'What's he done?' came the suspicious reply.

'Nothing that I know of. Should he have done something?'

'In this business you never know!'

'This is his daughter. Is he in?'

'They both are, it's the first floor, second door along.'

'I'll come up with you,' the constable offered.

'I'll be all right now, honestly I will, thanks.'

The man looked a little doubtful. 'I'll just make sure. I don't want you wandering the streets all night if—'

'I won't be!'

'I have to be certain of that, miss. I'd be failing in my duty if I didn't make sure you were safe.'

Lily didn't argue but, a little thankfully, let him lead the way. She looked around with distaste. The place smelled musty, the banister rail was rickety and the scuffed lino on the floor was sticky. The dark brown paint on the door in front of which the policeman had finally stopped was scarred and peeling.

'Well, shall I knock or will you?' The constable had noticed the look of apprehension and distaste on her face.

'I will,' Lily decided. She rapped on the door, rather timidly. There was silence, and then the door was finally opened.

Eddie was astounded. He looked wide-eyed from the burly policeman to his youngest daughter. 'Lily! What the hell are you doing here? How did you find me?'

'Nice way to greet anyone!' the constable muttered. He'd been right in his assumption that the girl's appearance wasn't the delightful surprise she'd envisaged.

Lily threw her arms around his neck.

'Da! Oh, Da! I've missed you! I came to find you!'

'I take it she *is* your daughter?'

Eddie was trying to compose himself and disentangle himself from Lily's embrace. 'Yes! Yes, she's my girl.'

'Then you'd better take her in, hadn't you? She's been wandering around for God knows how long. She's come down from Liverpool and I'd say she's exhausted.'

There was nothing else Eddie could say faced with such obvious censure. 'Yes, yes. Come on in, Lily.'

'Right then, I'll be on my way. I couldn't rest easy if I'd left her out there alone.'

Rather sheepishly Eddie ushered Lily inside and closed the door.

Doreen was sitting in front of the cheap little dressing table, applying her lipstick. When she caught sight of Lily in the mirror she swivelled around on the stool. 'What the hell is *she* doing here?'

Lily glared at her defiantly but didn't reply. She turned to her da. 'Can I talk to you?' She hadn't really known what to expect but she had hoped Da would be a bit more pleased to see her. She'd assumed too that there would have been somewhere she could talk to him privately. 'I have to talk to you, Da,' she pleaded, her gaze fixed on his face.

Eddie ran his hands through his hair distractedly. This was a fine kettle of fish! She was the last person he'd expected to see here. 'Lily, what did you come for?'

'To see you! I had to see you!'

Eddie was in a dilemma. He felt sorry for Lily, but he was annoyed that she'd followed him. Had it been her own idea? he wondered. He'd heard nothing from Liverpool and the occasional pangs of guilt he'd experienced in the first few days had quickly faded. He'd been enjoying himself. It had been one long round of pleasure with Doreen. No work, no nagging, no worries or responsibilities. He felt young and carefree, and London was a great place. He'd been disappointed in the 'hotel' but, as Doreen had said, it suited their needs and wasn't expensive. If they'd been staying in a fancy place they would soon be having to watch every penny and they didn't want to do that, nor did they want to have to find work yet. They wanted time together and that time was the best of all. But now he was faced with an obviously upset, tired and hungry daughter he just couldn't turn away.

Doreen stood up and snatched her jacket from the bed. 'We're going out!' she snapped. 'Eddie, get your jacket!'

Lily was taken aback. 'You can't be going out now, it's too late! Da, I've *got* to talk to you.'

Doreen laughed. 'It's never too late to go out in London! Come on, Eddie, you promised,' she wheedled, a smile masking her annoyance.

Lily wanted to smack her. 'Da, I'm worn out and I've had

nothing to eat all day except a cup of tea and a bun. You can't go out and leave me!'

Eddie made up his mind. 'Look, Lily, I'll go and get you some fish and chips. We . . . We're just going for a drink, but I'll take Doreen to the pub and get her settled then I'll nip back with the chips and we'll talk.'

'Oh, that's nice, I must say, Eddie. Dumping me in the pub and then running back here!' Doreen protested. 'You can't expect me to sit on my own for hours.' She cast him a long meaningful look. 'But maybe I won't be on my own for long?'

'Look, luv, it won't be for long. Just until I get this sorted out,' Eddie pleaded with her, putting his arm around her shoulders, a dart of fear entering his heart at the implications of her words.

Lily's cheeks burned and a cry of disgust sprang to her lips but Eddie pushed her down into the one small armchair, and then shrugged on his jacket.

'I'll be back in a few minutes, Lily, I promise.'

When they'd gone Lily looked around the room and wrinkled her nose in distaste. It stank of stale cheap perfume. Clothes were scattered on almost every available surface, the bed was unmade and the top of the dressing table was littered with bottles and spilt face powder. It was disgusting. How could Da live like this? Mam had always been so clean and tidy and although they didn't have much it was considerably better than this hovel! She was tired and cold and miserable but she hadn't given up. When her da returned she would make him help her get settled. Even if she could only afford a room like this, she would certainly keep it cleaner and tidier! But she couldn't bear to see the way Da treated *her*! It made her cringe to see how he looked at her – how he touched her! What did he see in her? She was brassy and cheap. Lily picked up a grubby camisole top from the floor at her feet and shuddered. She wasn't even very clean! Oh, she'd make him see all that. She'd *make* him go home!

Eddie was as good as his word and returned five minutes later clutching a greasy parcel.

'Here, Lily, eat these while they're hot.' He took off his jacket and sat on the end of the bed while she began to wolf down the chips. 'Now, luv, what possessed you to come here? If your Mam sent you then—'

'No, she didn't,' Lily interrupted.

Eddie tried again. 'I know you won't understand why I left—'

'But I think I do, Da. You wanted something more exciting than standing in the pub all day and I can understand that.'

'It was more than that. Doreen and I—' Eddie began.

Lily didn't want to hear anything about Doreen Travis. She plunged into her plans. 'I want something more exciting too! I want to work in a theatre; Mam said I could, but I can't get anything in Liverpool. There are hundreds of theatres in London: I'm certain to get a job in one of them, and you could help me get settled, find a room or something—'

'Lily, I *can't*!' Eddie protested, horrified by her plans and knowing all too well what Doreen would say about them.

'Oh, Da, you can! I won't be any trouble. I wouldn't come *here*, I could meet you anywhere.'

Eddie was seriously worried now. Lily would certainly be trouble. Even if she got a job – which he doubted as she had no experience and was in no way talented – she would always be running to him for help and advice. He would be responsible for her and he didn't want that. And Doreen – well, Doreen might even leave him!

'No, Lily. It's not that simple,' he said emphatically.

'It is! I just want a chance,' Lily cried.

Eddie tried again. 'Lily, it's just a daydream! A fantasy! You can't stay.'

Lily was desperate. She could see her dream slipping away from her. 'Please? Please, help me?'

Eddie shook his head vehemently. 'Go home to your mam and your sisters, Lily.'

Lily tried a different approach. 'Our Maggie's getting married to Billy Wainwright at the beginning of next month and it's your place to give her away. You should be there. She wants Harry Dempsey but I said it should be you!'

Eddie was becoming desperate too now and he didn't want to know about any of this. 'Lily, stop it. Stop it! Let Maggie have who she wants. I . . . I made my decision. I don't want to go back – ever. All that's behind me now.'

Lily stared at him in misery, tears welling up in her eyes. 'Don't you want – us? Our Sarah, me, Maggie?'

'Oh, Lily, it's not that I don't want you! But . . . but you're grown up now; you don't need me – any of you. Maggie's getting married, our Sarah will too and soon you'll meet a nice lad. I've got my own life to lead.'

'But you can't want to stay here with *her*. Look at the mess she's got this place in.'

Eddie got up and thrust his hands deep inside his trouser pockets. He had to be firm. 'I *do* want to stay here with Doreen. That's just it, Lily. I love her. I'm happy, we have fun! You can't understand, luv, and you *won't* understand until you love someone. I've made my choice.'

Lily stared at him in utter disbelief. 'You don't care about us? It's true, you don't . . .'

'I do in my way but I want her and there's an end to it. Your mam should have explained it to you.'

'She did her best, but . . .' Lily's voice trailed off. She had never felt so small or so humiliated.

Eddie suddenly remembered that Lily had said Eve hadn't sent her. He seized on it. 'Does your mam know where you are?'

'No. I told no one,' Lily muttered.

'She'll be worried sick! You should have told someone, she'll have the police out looking for you. Look, you can stay here tonight then first thing in the morning you can get the train back. I'll give you your fare.'

'I don't want to go back! I told you I want to work here.'

Eddie was losing patience. 'You'll have to, Lily. Have some sense, you've got a good job, you'll have a trade in your fingers.'

'I got the sack. They didn't want to pay me, they got someone cheaper,' Lily cried brokenly.

A Mother's Love

'Well, you can't stay here. Doreen would leave, she *would*, and I'm not having that! Go home, Lily. Go back to your mam. You're too young to stay down here on your own and I can't be responsible for you and that's my final word. I have to get back to Doreen now but we'll sort things out later.'

Lily just stared at him dumbly as he turned and left, then she curled up in the chair feeling utterly desolate. He didn't care what happened to her, he really didn't! Oh, they'd all tried to tell her but she wouldn't listen. She'd believed, deep in her heart, that if she could just talk to him . . . now all her hopes and dreams were shattered. Her gaze fell on a creased pale blue satin nightdress that lay across the arm of the chair. She snatched it up and began to tear it to shreds as rage surged through her. This was all Doreen Travis's fault. She had turned her da against them all. She'd made him as hard and uncaring and selfish as she was! Oh, how she hated her! Methodically she ripped every piece of clothing she could find into shreds and then smashed every bottle on the dressing table, emptied out the face powder and ground the cardboard pots of rouge into the lino with her heel. Then, utterly exhausted, she sank down on the floor amidst the mess and sobbed brokenly.

She had cried herself to sleep but was wrenched awake by Doreen's screams of rage.

'You bitch! You little bitch! I'll kill you! I'll bloody kill you!' Doreen was beside herself. She grabbed Lily by her hair, yanking her to her feet.

Eddie looked around in horror at the destruction.

Lily was screaming and Doreen, crying with temper, was shouting abuse and shaking her.

Eddie dragged them apart. 'Stop it! Stop it the pair of you! Do you want us thrown out?'

'Look what she's done – she's ruined everything. Everything! The spiteful little cow!'

'I'm glad! I'm glad! I hate her!' Lily yelled defiantly, lashing out suddenly and catching Doreen a hefty swipe across the face.

'Eddie, get her out of here *now*!' Doreen shrieked, then began to sob.

'For God's sake, shut up, Lily!' Eddie pushed his daughter down into the chair and pulled Doreen away, holding her tightly. 'Doreen, luv, calm down. I'll buy you more things. I'll replace everything. Stop crying now, luv!'

Doreen clung to him. 'Oh, Eddie, what did she have to come for? We were happy, we were doing just great . . .'

'She's not staying. She's going back on the first train in the morning, I promise.'

'I don't want her here another minute,' Doreen cried.

'I can't throw her out on the street, although she deserves it carrying on like this! Lily, I don't want to hear another sound out of you! I *knew* you'd be trouble. You don't think, you just don't *think*. I'll get this mess cleaned up and then we'll all try and get some sleep and then you're going home first thing in the morning!'

Lily slumped in the chair, shocked and spent. She didn't want to stay here now. She just wanted her mam.

Chapter Twelve

A<small>FTER A RESTLESS NIGHT</small>, Eve was up early. She had made up her mind to meet every train from London. She was certain that Eddie would send Lily home: he wouldn't want her there and neither would Doreen Travis, and she could imagine how devastated Lily would be. It was Sarah who had stopped her from going down to Lime Street Station at half past eight.

'Mam, she couldn't possibly be on such an early train. He wouldn't throw her out to walk the streets.'

'He might not but *she* would!'

'He wouldn't allow it, Mam. It would have been too late for her to catch the overnight sleeper; it will be at least dinnertime before she arrives back, if not this afternoon. You can't spend the entire day down at Lime Street.'

'She's going to be in a terrible state, Sarah!' Eve pleaded.

'*You're* in a terrible state, Mam!'

'I have to be there,' Eve insisted.

'Go down about one o'clock. Harry will manage.

Promise me you won't go running off before that?'

Eve finally nodded. 'But promise me that you won't go giving out to her, nor our Maggie either? She's been through enough, poor kid.'

'Well, I can't speak for Maggie but I won't, even though she deserves it. What possessed her I don't know.'

'She wouldn't accept it. I suppose she thought if she went to see him . . .'

'That's the whole trouble with Lily, she just doesn't think. She just goes tearing off at a tangent,' Sarah said, unknowingly echoing Eddie's words.

Eve stood anxiously just beyond the barrier as the first train drew in. She scrutinised the crowds closely but to her dismay there was no sign of Lily. There wasn't another train due until four o'clock so she went to the buffet and got a cup of tea. Then she went into the ladies' waiting room and sat for what seemed like a day and a night until at last she went out and looked at the huge clock on the station wall. Then she walked back to the barrier.

With much clanking and grinding of brakes and great clouds of steam hissing and spiralling up to the glass-domed roof the train at last pulled in and people started to alight. Porters, their trolleys piled with luggage, pushed past Eve as her eyes darted over the faces of the travellers. When the crowds had thinned and she was again despairing she caught sight of a woebegone and dishevelled Lily slowly walking up the platform. Tears of relief sprang to her eyes and she rushed forward.

'Lily! Oh, Lily!'

Lily started to run, tears pouring down her cheeks, and flung herself into Eve's outstretched arms.

Eve hugged her. 'I was so worried! I was nearly going to the police!'

'I'm sorry!' Lily choked.

'It's all right, luv. You're back now, it's all over. Come on home and we'll talk about it.'

'Oh, Mam, I don't want to talk about it. It was awful!'

Eve's heart went out to her. 'It must have been! And you don't have to tell me everything if you don't want to.' She could only imagine Lily's hurt and chagrin. 'Have you had anything to eat?'

'Not much. I didn't feel like eating.'

'Then we'll go and get a cup of tea and you can calm down a bit, then we'll go home.'

Lily smiled weakly, thankful there were going to be no recriminations, nor demands for explicit explanations. During the journey she'd tried to find the words but her mind had just been numb.

When they finally arrived back Eve sent Lily upstairs to wash, get changed and unpack her things, and then went through to the bar.

Harry was opening up. 'She's back then?'

'Worn out and very upset but I'm not going to press her on anything just yet.'

He nodded slowly. 'Do you think she's accepted it now?'

'Dear God, I hope so. I can't go through all that again.'

'What about the other two? Maggie was really furious,' Harry reminded her.

'I know. Sarah promised she'd go easy on her but I don't know about Maggie. I think Lily's been through enough.'

'Then you'd better go and see if you can catch Maggie before she starts on her,' he advised.

Sarah was already in. 'You found her?'

Eve nodded. 'She's upstairs. Would you do me a favour, luv? Go out and watch for Maggie and ask her not to start on Lily until I've had a chance to at least try to talk to her? I'm exhausted and I don't want a screaming match now.'

Sarah grimaced. 'She's not going to be happy.'

'I know that, luv, and I suppose she's right.'

Eve went upstairs and found Lily sitting on the bed with her knees drawn up to her chin, her head resting on them. Eve sat down beside her and put an arm around her. 'I know you felt very strongly about your da, Lily,' she began tentatively.

'It wasn't just that. I thought, well, I thought I'd stand a better chance of getting a job in London. I thought he would help me to get settled somewhere but . . . Oh, Mam! He didn't want to know! He didn't care. He just sent me home. He put me on the train and he even waited to make sure I didn't get off again.'

Eve sighed sadly; poor girl, she thought. But she was angry too. Did he have to be so callous? But then what could you expect? It must have been quite a shock to find Lily on the doorstep of his little love nest.

'Maybe it's for the best. You'll get something here soon, I'm sure. Didn't you say there might be something at the Playhouse?'

'I have to wait until next month and it's only bits of sewing and you know how boring that is.'

'It's a start. Who knows, you could end up in charge of the wardrobe department.'

'I don't want that! I want to be an actress!'

Eve decided not to push the matter. 'You've years ahead of you, Lily. Come on down now, we'll have tea.'

'What about the other two?' Lily sniffed.

'Don't worry about them, they won't start on you, they know what you've been through.'

Lily looked very contrite. 'Mam, now I . . . I do understand how you feel. How terrible it's been for you. I'm sorry for . . . everything.'

Eve hugged her. 'I know you are. I do know it's been very hard for you but you've got to let him go. It's his choice and he's chosen *her*.'

Suddenly the floodgates burst and Lily sat down and told her mother about her ordeal.

Eve closed her eyes and tried to shut out the images Lily's words conjured up in her mind. She didn't want to know all the lurid details.

'And I smashed and tore everything, Mam! She didn't have a single thing left!' Lily finished.

Eve managed a grim smile. 'I would have liked to have seen that.'

'And I belted her!'

'Good for you, Lily. I wish I had but at least *I* got rid of *her*! Now dry your eyes and let's go down.' In one way Eve was glad to hear that Eddie wasn't living in the lap of luxury, yet it worried her. At some time in the future would he come back, penniless, and expect her to take him in? Well, she wouldn't think about that now. She had enough on her plate.

Maggie said nothing when they appeared. She compressed her lips tightly and carried on spooning the tea into the teapot.

'Are you all right?' Sarah asked.

Lily nodded.

'So, can we get back to the dressmaking? Not tonight, if you don't feel like it,' Maggie finished in a kinder tone.

'Tomorrow, if you don't mind? Sarah, I can give you back the money I borrowed. He gave me some.'

'Keep it. I want nothing from him and you'll need it. You're probably broke now. You did pay your fare down there, didn't you?'

'Yes. I just had enough. I'm sorry I lied to you, Sarah.'

'That's all right. Just let's forget it now! We've got a few busy weeks ahead.'

Maggie put the pot on the table and set out the cups. 'We have indeed. Dresses to finish, head-dresses to make, Mam's outfit to sort out and a hundred other things.'

Seeing that Maggie wasn't going to be difficult Lily felt much better. 'And I've got to find a job.'

* * *

The next few weeks seemed to fly, Eve thought as she ordered food and flowers, made lists and wrote out invitations, helped make the head-dresses of artificial flowers and bought her own outfit. Maggie and Sarah went with her to Frisby Dyke's in Lord Street where she chose a rayon two-piece in a beautiful deep cornflower blue, with a neat fitted jacket with a stand-up collar and a straight skirt with two box pleats in the front. She bought navy blue court shoes, a bag and navy cotton gloves. The outfit was completed by a large blue picture hat that sported a navy bow at the back and two huge blue flowers attached to the left side of the crown.

'Mam, you look really posh!' had been Sarah's verdict.

Maggie had approved too. 'You'll look far nicer than Billy's mam. Much smarter.'

'And so I should for what it's cost,' Eve had replied, although she was very happy with the outfit.

Harry had gone to the fifty-shilling tailor's and had bought a dark navy serge suit and a new shirt and tie. Persuaded by Eve to try them on, he was pronounced 'the height of style' by Maggie. He'd grinned, embarrassed by the fuss.

Lily had applied herself diligently to finishing all the dresses and to helping Eve as much as she possibly could. She had plenty of time, she told herself a little dispiritedly. She'd been back to the Playhouse but there was still no sign of anything definite, although while she was there she'd taken up a hem that was too long and her neat stitching and willingness had been favourably remarked upon. That had given her cause for optimism.

Lyn Andrews

Maggie felt there weren't enough hours in the day. The shop was coming along nicely. It had been given a fresh coat of paint, which made it look brighter. Some new shelves had been put up to hold the jars of jam, honey and lemon curd that she intended to stock, purchased from the woman in the market who sold eggs and what she termed 'Fresh Country Produce'. New wooden bins for potatoes had been installed to replace the wicker baskets, which leaked dry soil and dust on to the floor, and a new low display counter had been added.

The rooms above it were looking clean and Billy and his da had brought home and laid the rolls of new linoleum they'd bought in Great Homer Street Market. Hilda had hung curtains and relined the kitchen shelves with fresh paper and Maggie had bought dishes and pans, also from the market, and some good pieces of second-hand furniture from the auction rooms. She was hoping to get some bedding and towels as wedding presents but was quite satisfied with the way her new home and business were shaping up. And she had managed to hang on to most of the money Billy's granny had given them.

Almost before she could believe it, it was the night before her wedding day and she was sitting with Mam in the kitchen, both their heads full of curling papers.

'We both look like clowns! I just hope the results are worth it!' Eve laughed.

Maggie looked anxiously into the mirror above the fireplace. 'I hope it doesn't turn out a frizzy mess.'

Eve smiled affectionately at her anxious daughter.

'It won't. You'll look beautiful, Maggie. Billy will be delighted with you.'

'The dress is lovely, isn't it? I'm glad I chose a simple style and a short veil.'

'It is and you've all worked so hard.'

'So have you, Mam. The lounge bar looks lovely.'

'I wish we could have given it a coat of paint but with those streamers and those few flowers on the window sills it does look better.'

'And there's plenty of food so there should be no complaints in that department.'

'Are you happy, Maggie?'

'I'm more than happy; I've got so much! Much more than I ever dreamed of!'

'You're both very lucky and Billy is a good lad. You have a great life to look forward to.'

'I'm a bit nervous,' Maggie admitted.

'Every bride is. I was.' Eve smiled sadly. She'd been nervous but happy as well. How fortunate it was that no one knew what the future really held, she thought, but she didn't have any real worries about Maggie and Billy. They were well suited and were getting the best possible start to their married life.

'I'll miss you, Maggie.'

'Mam, I'm not moving miles away! I'll still see a lot of you and you know that if there's anything, *anything* at all you need, you only have to ask.'

Eve patted her hand. 'You're a good girl and I'm really thankful for all the support you've given me since—'

'Oh, don't let's spoil things by mentioning *him*! I'm not even going to let myself think of him tomorrow.' Maggie's voice was full of determination but inside she didn't feel quite as confident as she sounded. In her heart of hearts she admitted that she would have liked her da to give her away. Even though she was so angry with him and felt so bitterly hurt by what he'd done – especially to Mam, which was why she was so infuriated by Lily's behaviour – she still missed him. However, she wasn't going to dwell on that or Lily's carry-on. Her sister had worked really hard since her ill-fated trip to London.

'I'm so sorry he won't be here, Maggie. Oh, I know you're still furious with him and so am I, but I would have liked him to be present – under different circumstances of course. You're the first of our girls to go.'

'Well, I'm quite happy with Harry,' Maggie said firmly.

Eve smiled. 'It's going to be a great day. Now, I think we'd better go and try to get some sleep, despite these damned curling papers, which I have the feeling are going to turn into lumps as hard as iron as soon as our heads touch the pillow!'

Maggie hugged her. 'I love you, Mam! I'll never do anything to make you ashamed of me.'

'I know. And I'm proud of you, Maggie, I really am. I never thought a daughter of mine would end up owning a business. God's been good to you, Maggie. Be a good wife and mother, that's all I ask.'

'If I'm as good as you, I'll have done well,' Maggie said sincerely.

Eve kissed her cheek and smiled but she wondered had she indeed been a good wife? She must have misunderstood something about Eddie, otherwise he would still be here and looking forward to walking Maggie up the aisle tomorrow.

Her early married life hadn't been perfect. They'd lived with Eddie's parents and at times that hadn't been easy but she'd thought they were happy enough. When had Eddie started to change? Had he changed, actually? Perhaps in those early days she had mistaken his charm and tall, fair good looks for strength of character, generosity and loyalty. Had he ever been the man she thought he was? Had she loved the *idea* of him and not the reality of the man himself? She sighed. It was too late now to ask herself these difficult questions.

She found it impossible to sleep. For one thing the curling papers dug unmercifully into her head no matter which way she lay and for another she couldn't banish the memories of her own wedding day and the contented years that had followed. And then the future stretched ahead of her: bleak and lonely and full of worries. Would the brewery give her the licence permanently? Could she make the pub pay? Maggie's rosy future only made her think of Sarah's dead-end job and the fact that her eldest daughter seemed destined, at the moment, for spinsterhood. And then there was Lily. All she could see in prospect for Lily was disappointment unless some miraculous stroke of luck came her way, and that didn't seem likely. Lily had already been badly wounded and let down; what was she going to do with her?

Eve went on tossing and turning, nothing resolved in her mind, when to her dismay she found she was watching the first fingers of dawn penetrate the crack in the bedroom curtains.

Chapter Thirteen

EVE FOUND MAGGIE ALREADY up and with the kettle boiling when she got down to the kitchen.

'I was going to bring you a cup of tea in bed this morning! It's a bride's privilege.'

'I couldn't sleep. I don't think I got a wink all night with these flaming curling papers!'

Eve laughed. 'Neither did I. We must have been mad to let our Sarah talk us into putting them in. We'll both be worn out before we start and it's going to be a long day.'

Maggie grinned. 'We *must* be mad – we've both got curly hair already!'

'Well, we'll have a cup of tea and then you'd better start to get ready. Use my room and take your time.'

'Thanks, Mam. Oh, I'm so glad it's a lovely day. It would have spoiled it if it had been raining.'

'It *is* a lovely day and it's going to be the happiest of your life so far, now off you go.'

* * *

Sarah stared at herself in the mirror. She looked so pale and tired: it was a good thing she wasn't the bride today. She was so glad for Maggie and relieved that Lily seemed to have got over Da's desertion at last; even Mam was looking better, but what about herself and her future? She leaned her elbows on the dressing table. Good, sensible, reliable Sarah! she thought. Dull and boring more like! Oh, she didn't want the excitement in life that Lily craved or even the rather grand ambitions of Maggie. Just . . . just something *different*! Did she want a husband and a home of her own? Of course she did, she told herself. Did she want Harry? Oh, if she was truthful she really didn't know. What exactly *was* love? She knew what everyone said it was but look at Mam and Da. They must have thought they were in love once. She did like Harry but was it enough? More to the point, did he love her? He *liked* her, she knew that, but it wasn't the same thing at all. She leaned back and straightened her shoulders. There really wasn't time for all this heart searching, not now, there were a million and one things waiting to be done.

She got dressed and went downstairs, followed by Lily, and then there was a knock on the back door and the flowers arrived and things began to get a little chaotic.

Eve and Sarah, helped by two of the neighbours, laid out the buffet on the long trestle tables Harry had set up in the lounge bar and which had been covered by clean white sheets. The two-tier iced wedding cake stood in the centre in pride of place and Sarah had draped some trailing green smilax artistically around its base.

Jim Stokes and Alf Casey had volunteered to serve in the

saloon bar, although their wives would be amongst the guests, and Agnes Molloy and her daughter Violet were coming from Walton just for the afternoon. Eve had been delighted when she'd heard this, for despite all her troubles she'd managed to keep in touch with poor Agnes.

'Mam, Maggie's getting into a state about her hair. She says it's going to frizz,' Lily informed her, appearing in her long petticoat and camisole top.

'Lily, put something on, for heaven's sake! Harry's in and out with bottles and glasses. Tell her to smooth it down with some of that Amami setting lotion, that should do the trick.'

Lily disappeared but then Sarah walked in holding up the long peach taffeta skirt of her dress and looking grimly at her feet. 'I think I'm going to be persecuted in these shoes, Mam!'

'Didn't you try them on?' Eve demanded.

'I did and I said then they were tight but they didn't have a bigger size and Maggie said they'd be fine, that they'd give a bit.'

'Well, you'll just have to grin and bear it. You can't wear your black shoes with that dress.'

Sarah sighed with resignation. 'Isn't it about time you started to get ready yourself?'

Eve looked startled. 'Why? What time is it?'

'Half past ten.'

'Oh, my God! We're due at the church in half an hour!'

'That's what I mean and you're still in your old dress and apron.'

Eve made a dash for the stairs but when she flung open

the bedroom door she stopped and tears started in her eyes.

'Oh, Maggie! You look . . . like an angel!'

Lily was carefully arranging the train of Maggie's dress but she smiled up at her mother. 'She does, doesn't she?'

Eve sat down on the bed, a lump in her throat. If only Eddie could see Maggie! The gleaming white satin dress suited Maggie perfectly. Its fitted bodice emphasised her slim waist and the high collar set off her small, oval-shaped face. It had long tight sleeves that ended in a point and the train was draped elegantly behind her. The simple wreath of artificial orange blossom confined her dark curls and the white tulle veil formed a diaphanous cloud around her shoulders. On Eve's dressing table lay the bouquet of white lilies and trailing green smilax.

'I want to hug you but I'm afraid I'll mess everything up,' Eve said in a tight little voice.

'Oh, Mam! I don't care about a few little creases!' Maggie cried, holding her arms wide.

'You'll take the sight from the eyes of everyone today—' Eve choked, overcome with pride.

'Mam, you'd better get a move on or you'll be taking the sight from everyone's eyes for the wrong reason,' Lily interrupted.

Eve dashed away her tears. 'You look lovely too, Lily. That colour really suits you.' Lily did indeed look pretty in the peach taffeta. The deep frill around the scooped neckline and around the short puffed sleeves really set the dress off. Lily's long dark hair had been swept up and was crowned with a circlet of peach and cream wax flowers.

Lily smiled. 'Thanks, Mam. It suits our Sarah too. It makes her look younger.'

Eve tutted. 'Honestly, you'd think she was thirty, listening to you!'

'Harry wants to know will everyone be ready in time?' Sarah asked, looking down with annoyance at the white court shoes that were already pinching mercilessly.

'Just give me five minutes!' Eve cried, snatching her suit from its hanger.

To Harry's intense relief, ten minutes later the wedding party was ready to leave and they stepped out into the street into bright sunshine and cries of admiration from the neighbours and customers who had come to see Maggie off on her journey to the church.

When Father Delaney pronounced the words which made Maggie the third Mrs Wainwright present in the church that morning, Eve again wiped away her tears of joy and pride and determinedly pushed all thoughts of her absent husband from her mind. She was going to enjoy today; they all were and Eddie Dobson could go to hell! It was his loss.

The wedding breakfast was going well, Eve thought. Everyone had said what a wonderful spread it was, how nice the room looked and wasn't the wedding cake gorgeous. As the drink was flowing well too the atmosphere was decidedly festive.

Ernie Foster had brought along his accordion and Maurie O'Driscoll his banjo and Mr Wainwright's brother-in-law,

Jack, produced a harmonica: soon a space had been cleared and quite a few people were dancing.

'Come on, Eve, I'm no Fred Astaire but I promise I'll try not to trample on your toes too much!' Harry laughed, pulling Eve to her feet.

'Oh, all right, but only if you ask our Sarah for a dance afterwards. She's looking a bit of a wallflower.' Eve had noticed Sarah sitting at the back of the room on her own. Eve thought how really attractive Sarah looked today. The colour of the dress seemed to add warmth to her complexion and the style suited her. Her fair hair had been swept up but the artificial flowers of her head-dress softened the effect. Excitement had also added colour to her cheeks and a sparkle to her blue eyes. In her own way, Eve's eldest daughter was a very lovely girl.

'It's a deal but Lily said she's happy sitting down as her shoes are too tight.'

'You can take her mind off them,' Eve laughed as Harry guided her quickly around the floor.

'Everything is going very well and they all seem to be getting along together,' he said affably.

'Why shouldn't they?' Eve demanded.

'Sometimes at weddings it's a bit "them and us", if you know what I mean?'

'I do. At mine my da's relations wouldn't sit at the same end of the room as Eddie's lot and then they all went off to the football match, including my da. Mam was furious!'

Harry laughed. 'Thank God the football season is over then! You look great, Eve, I've been meaning to tell you that all day. Very stylish.'

She smiled at him. 'And so do you, Harry. Maggie made a good choice.'

She was breathless and quite worn out, she told him as the musicians took a break for a pint of beer, and he rather reluctantly returned her to her seat and went off towards Sarah.

'You've done her proud, Eve. I give credit where it's due.'

Eve turned to find that old Mrs Wainwright had sat down beside her.

'It's gone very well, I have to agree, but they're very lucky. You've been extremely generous.'

'They've got that place done up very nicely. I went round to see it. They've worked hard and Maggie told me they're putting most of the money in the Post Office Savings Bank. I don't think you've anything to worry about with those two.'

Eve relaxed a little. 'No, I don't think I have. If they work hard and pull together they'll do very well indeed.'

'They're starting out with more than Tom and I had. Two rented rooms and hardly a stick of furniture, but they were good days,' the old lady mused a little sadly.

'The early ones usually are.'

'Don't dwell on the past, Eve, it doesn't help.'

'I know and I'm not. Not today at least. And with Maggie settled all I have to worry about now is the other two.'

'Sarah seems a sensible girl; I was talking to her earlier. But she's not much of an idea of what she wants to do with her life – unlike the other one!'

Eve sighed. She was too tired to remind the rather blunt

old lady that it really was none of her business what either of her girls did with their lives, and she didn't want to start an argument.

'You've been talking to our Lily then?'

'No, but I overheard her telling our Effie's lad, Charlie, what she wants to do. Sounds a bit airy fairy to me.'

'It does to me too, but I don't know what to do with Lily. She . . . she's been badly hurt and disappointed by her da.'

'She isn't the only one!'

'I know, but she went after him and was sent packing and if she's let down again . . .' Eve frowned. 'Oh, I really am worried about her!'

'You've every reason to be. You meet all kinds of unsuitable people in that profession. Have you ever thought of sending her away? Away from Liverpool?'

Eve looked at her with horror. 'No! I couldn't do that!'

'It might be the making of her. Get these ridiculous ideas out of her head. Mind you, it would have to be somewhere quiet, where there are no music halls or the like.'

'Theatres,' Eve corrected.

'Call them what you like, you'll have no peace of mind while she's living in this city – or any city for that matter.'

'But where could she go? If she would agree, which she won't.' Eve had never even contemplated this.

'Haven't you got any relatives who don't live here?'

Eve thought hard. 'I've got cousins in Ireland but I haven't seen them for years. I get the occasional letter and Christmas card.'

'In Dublin?'

'No. Down in the country.'

'The perfect place. Couldn't she go to one of them? You'd at least know she was safe and well supervised. I have relations myself down in County Cork and I can tell you over there they don't stand for all these "modern" notions young girls here get into their heads! No, decent young girls meet suitable husbands and settle down and have families, which keeps them out of trouble.'

'I couldn't send her away! She's only just eighteen.'

'Many girls of that age are married with young children. You think about it long and hard, Eve. It might be the making of her. If you keep her here you're storing up trouble and heartache for yourself.'

Eve nodded. She really was too tired to argue but she felt sure Lily would be horrified. At the moment she wouldn't have the strength to suggest it.

'I promised Eve I'd ask you to dance but Lily said your shoes are hurting.'

Sarah looked up at Harry and smiled wryly. 'They are, so sit down and talk to me instead. Anyway, the "band" are having a break.' He looked very smart, she thought.

'Are you enjoying yourself?'

Sarah shrugged. 'I suppose so, it's all gone very well.'

'You look lovely, Sarah. I mean that.'

She smiled at him. 'Thanks. I suppose it will be "always the bridesmaid" in my case.'

'Why? Don't you want to get married?'

'Chance would be a fine thing! Oh, Harry, I just don't know what I want to do with my life.'

'You'll feel very different when Mr Right comes along.' He had no idea she felt so unsettled. He wished she were happy; he liked Sarah, he liked her a lot.

'That's just it. How are you supposed to know just who Mr Right is? Look at Mam. She must have thought Da was her Mr Right.'

'Maybe she did at the time. People change their minds.'

Sarah studied her hands, feeling a little foolish. 'Harry, can I . . . ask you something?'

'You know you can!'

'Do you. . . . do you . . . like me?' She felt the blood rush to her cheeks. Was she mad?

Harry was startled. 'Of course I like you, Sarah!'

'Just *like*?'

Harry was uneasy at where this was leading but he didn't want to upset her. 'You're a great girl, Sarah.'

Sarah pulled herself together. For heaven's sake, have some pride, she told herself firmly. She wasn't going to humiliate herself by asking him if he loved her when he obviously didn't or he would have said something other than: 'You're a great girl, Sarah!' She just had a stupid crush on him, that's all, and she wasn't going to let him see that.

'Oh, take no notice of me, Harry! I'm getting all daft and soppy in my old age, it must be what happens at weddings!'

He smiled in relief. 'Well, your mam and old Mrs Wainwright don't seem to be getting all daft and soppy, they look decidedly grim.'

Sarah looked across to where her mother and the old lady sat deep in serious conversation and wondered what on earth Mrs Wainwright had said to Mam. The band had now resumed its position. 'Well, go and ask her to dance, take her mind off whatever it is!'

'I daren't until I've done a turn around the floor with you.'

Sarah grimaced. 'Oh, all right, if it will keep you quiet, but just don't step on my poor feet!'

Eve was utterly exhausted by the time everyone had gone home and Maggie and Billy had gone off to start their life together in the newly refurbished rooms over the shop, which now bore the freshly painted legend 'W. & M. WAINWRIGHT. QUALITY GREENGROCERS' above the door in smart red lettering.

Lily had gone to bed and Sarah was soaking her aching feet in a bowl of hot water and Epsom salts in her bedroom when Harry, minus his suit jacket and new tie, brought Eve a glass of sparkling white wine.

'To drink to the end of a perfect day, Eve.'

Eve smiled at him. 'It *has* been perfect, Harry, and I couldn't have managed it without you. You've done more than your fair share of the work, besides giving her away.'

'That was a pleasure, Eve. I . . . I felt quite proud myself, as though she were really family, like a sister.'

Eve's smile was sympathetic. 'You miss that, don't you?'

Harry nodded. Today he had felt like part of the family and he had really enjoyed it.

Eve sipped her drink thoughtfully. 'Sometimes family life can be a worry.'

'You mean Lily?'

'I worry about Sarah too.'

'Sarah will be all right.' Harry sounded confident.

'I just wish she could meet someone . . . like you.'

Harry smiled a little wryly. 'Matchmaking? I'm sorry to disappoint you but Sarah doesn't think of me like that.'

'How do you know?' Eve demanded. She would have been quite happy to see Sarah and Harry 'walking out'.

'She's more or less told me so.'

'Oh.' Eve was surprised. 'I thought you two got on well?'

'We do. We're great friends, that's all. Besides . . .'

'Besides *what*? Have you got someone in mind? Are you already spoken for? Is that it?'

'No! I meant . . . well . . . you know I'm . . . fond of you . . .'

Eve was jolted out of her amused curiosity by the earnestness of his tone. 'And I'm fond of you, you know how much I rely on you. You're like a son to me. In fact you're better than a lot of sons are!'

Harry looked down at his hands. 'You're not old enough to have a son my age, Eve. I'm only twelve years younger than you are.'

Eve didn't want to go along this path. 'You know what I mean! I come to you with all my problems, you even offered to go after Lily, and I didn't have to *ask*. And talking of Lily, old Mrs Wainwright says I should send her away.'

'Why?' Harry asked, half-heartedly. He didn't want to talk about Lily, not after he'd finally plucked up the courage to try to tell Eve that it was she who filled his thoughts.

'For peace of mind. She's all for me burying her in the wilds of Ireland, where she assures me they won't stand for airy fairy ideas!'

'Ireland? You don't know anyone there!'

'I have cousins there, but could you imagine the outcry that suggestion would be greeted with?'

Harry reluctantly gave up on his planned conversation for the moment. 'She wouldn't be happy, certainly, but what do you think about it?'

'Oh, if I thought it would be good for her, if she'd be happy, if she could settle down there, then I'd seriously think about it.'

'But she wouldn't?'

Eve smiled wryly. 'It's definitely not exciting, is it?'

'No, but then maybe Lily's had enough excitement for a while. She thought London was going to be exciting and look how that turned out.'

Eve sighed. 'I'll just have to see how things go. She might get that bit of a job at the Playhouse.'

'And she might find that that doesn't live up to expectations either.'

'Let's cross that bridge when we come to it,' Eve said with resignation. 'Now, I'm going to bed and you'd better get off home.'

Harry got to his feet. Maybe if Lily did go away Eve

would be less harassed and might even agree to their having the occasional afternoon out. Then perhaps they could have that conversation. It was his dearest wish, but he didn't want to add to her burdens in any way.

Chapter Fourteen

L ILY WENT BACK TO the Playhouse full of optimism and came home thoroughly demoralised.

'What happened?' Eve asked, seeing the naked disappointment in her eyes.

Lily took off her hat and threw it on the table. 'They're having to close, Mam, for a while at least. They said business is so bad that it's just not worth their while even finishing the run they're doing now.'

'Oh, Lily! I'm so sorry, I really am.' Eve hated to see her let down once more. 'Did they say when they might be opening again?'

'They couldn't be sure. They blamed the cinema again. People are going there instead – when they've got the money.'

'Could they suggest somewhere else you could perhaps try?'

Lily sat down and dropped her head in her hands, praying Mam wasn't going to say 'I told you so'. 'I've tried everywhere! It's useless, just liked you warned me. Now what am I going to do?'

Eve tried to cheer her up. 'We'll think of something, Lily. Just give me a bit of time. You could keep looking in the *Echo*, just in case something does come up. You never know.'

Lily didn't look convinced. She went upstairs without another word.

Eve thought again of the conversation she'd had with Mrs Wainwright and Harry. She just didn't know what to do. Perhaps she'd talk it over with Sarah. That might help.

She'd given Lily some money and told her to go out to the cinema to take her mind off things, and she and Sarah discussed the subject at length. Sarah suggested that she, not Eve, broach the subject with Lily.

'She might think it's some sort of punishment if you suggest it.'

This was just what Eve had thought. 'I know, that's what's been worrying me. She might think I'm trying to get rid of her, but she can't go on like this. You know what it's like here. What kind of a job can she get? Everyone just wants to employ the cheapest labour they can and fourteen- and fifteen-year-olds are cheaper than Lily.'

'She hasn't much of a future in Liverpool but if I can make it sound more interesting, even exciting, she might give it a try.'

'I think you might be right, but honestly, Sarah, it doesn't sound very exciting at all – not for a girl like Lily.'

Sarah was optimistic. 'It might be the making of her, Mam.'

'Oh, I'm still not sure.'

'Let her give it a go and if she doesn't like it she can come home and we'll think again.'

Finally Eve agreed. She'd try anything if it would make Lily happy.

Eve was in the bar when Lily arrived home.

'Was it a good film?' Sarah asked brightly.

'Not really, or maybe I just wasn't in the mood. It was quite full and I kept thinking if all those people had gone to the Playhouse I would have had a job,' Lily answered dispiritedly. 'But it was good of Mam to give me the money, I know she spent a lot on Maggie's wedding,' she added.

Sarah was sympathetic. 'You're really down in the dumps, aren't you?'

Lily nodded miserably, throwing herself down on the sofa and clutching a cushion to her chest.

'You know what I'd really like to do if I had the chance?' Sarah confided.

'What? I thought you liked working at the Stork.'

'It's not bad. It's a job and sometimes you do meet nice people, but I'd like to travel, maybe work as a stewardess on one of the big liners.'

This surprised Lily. Sarah had never mentioned this before and she'd always been of the opinion that her sister was rather dull and staid and unimaginative. 'Really? Where would you like to go?'

'Oh, anywhere! I'd love to get away from Liverpool, visit different places, and see how other people live. It would be exciting.'

Lily brightened up. 'It would, wouldn't it? Although I thought London would be different, sort of more glamorous. Yet all I saw were roads and streets like the ones here.'

'You had a bad experience in London, Lily, it's bound to make you think like that.'

'I suppose so. But it would be nice to get away from here.'

This was just the opening Sarah had been hoping for. 'What if Mam gave you the chance of going somewhere?'

This took Lily completely by surprise. 'Me? She'd say I was too young. It would be different if it were you, she thinks you're sensible.'

'I've got a job and I don't feel as though I can leave Mam just yet, but it's different for you.'

'Has she said anything? I do know she's worried about me.'

'She is. She just wants you to be happy. We all do.'

'Has she said anything?' Lily pressed. This certainly sounded promising, although it was something she herself hadn't thought about.

'She was wondering if you'd like to go to Ireland.'

'*Ireland!*'

'She's got cousins there. She thought you might like to go for a bit, to work and see what life's like. You never know who you might meet. It could be really interesting, Lily. You'd have to go on the ferry and then the train.'

It wasn't what Lily had been expecting but she deliberated on it. 'I know that Dublin's a big city and quite fashionable.'

'I don't think she had Dublin in mind, but of course I don't know how far away her cousins live. It might be quite near.'

Lily considered the idea further. She was fed up living in Liverpool and under no illusions about the kind of job she could hope to get. If she was lucky enough to find work at all it would be in a factory and that didn't bear thinking about. This might be just what she needed: to get away from everything, and if she were near a city like Dublin . . . well, who knew?

'I suppose I could think about it. There's nothing for me here,' Lily finally agreed.

Sarah smiled. 'No harm in doing that. Mam could write, it would probably take a bit of time to sort it out, and you can give it more thought.'

Lily felt considerably better. It would be something to look forward to.

Eve was surprised and relieved when Sarah imparted the news that Lily hadn't thrown ten fits and refused to go; in fact she had seemed quite taken with the idea.

'But it's miles from Dublin, Sarah!'

'You don't have to tell her that, Mam.'

'As far as I know, it's way down the country. Quite a few hours by train.'

'Just write to them, Mam, they might not want to have her,' Sarah advised.

The more Lily thought about it the more the idea appealed to her. As she went on hopelessly searching for work she began

to *want* to get away. One morning she wandered down to the
Pier Head and watched the ships moving up and down the
river. It would be great to sail off on one of them to a more
interesting life, and *anything* had to be more interesting than
wandering aimlessly around this city with no money in her
pocket. Yes, she did want to see other places, meet other
people, and live a different kind of life. She wanted to travel,
to have *experiences*! She didn't want to be stuck in a dead-end
job like Sarah, doing the same boring things every day, seeing
the same boring people every day, and coming home to what?
The same four walls.

Eve was pleasantly surprised when a week after she had
written to her cousin Aoife a reply arrived. She was delighted
when she read that Lily would be very welcome, that they
were all very sorry they hadn't been able to come over for
Maggie's wedding and if Lily could get herself over quickly
there might even be a grand job for her at Rahan Lodge, a
big house owned by the Ormonde family, where there were
a rake of servants. The Ormondes, being Anglo-Irish, always
preferred English servants, it was one of their ways of going
on, Aoife wrote, although she didn't say exactly what kind of
a job it was.

Eve replaced the letter in its envelope and put it on the
mantelpiece. Whatever, it was work and Lily was bound to
find the prospect of being in a big house pleasing.

As soon as she came in Lily spotted the letter. 'That was
quick! Can I read it?'

'Of course. It's good news.'

Lily scanned the address. 'Where's Tullamore?'

Eve was evasive. 'I'm not really sure. Doesn't it say County Offaly?'

'Where's that?'

'I'm not sure about that either. I never was much good at geography.'

Lily read the letter quickly. 'How soon is soon? She doesn't say. And she doesn't say what kind of a job it is either.'

'The main thing is that she says you'll be very welcome and that there *is* a job. It sounds like a posh house. "Major Ormonde"!'

Lily was apprehensive. 'It might be a bit too posh.'

'Will I write to her again and ask a few more questions?'

'Will there be time? If it's really a good job I don't want to miss it.'

'Miss what?' Maggie had arrived and had caught the end of the conversation.

'Sit down, luv, there's tea in the pot. It's nice to see you, have you finished for the day?'

'Yes, Billy and I decided that we need one day when we close early, so from now on we're shutting at half past four on Wednesdays. We're open until seven every other night including Saturdays and it's hard work. Poor Billy is up at five to go to the market and we open at half past eight.'

'Heavens, you both work very hard. Mrs McMillan didn't open those hours.'

'We want to make more of a go of it than she did. I've brought you some fruit and eggs, Mam. Now, what's going on?'

'I'm thinking of going to Ireland, to work,' Lily announced.

Maggie raised her eyebrows. She'd heard that it might be a possibility and she had agreed wholeheartedly with Sarah that it might be the making of Lily. This sounded promising. 'Doing what?'

'There's a job going at a big posh house but I have to go over quickly.'

'Oh, my! Won't there be all kinds of entertainments and diversions in a house like that,' Maggie exclaimed encouragingly.

It was just the right thing to say, Eve thought, watching Lily's eyes light up. Obviously she hadn't thought of that.

'Rahan Lodge, it's called,' Lily informed her sister.

'Sounds very grand! So, when do you intend to go?'

Lily looked at Eve. 'Mam was going to write another letter, asking a few more questions, but there might not be time. The job might have gone.'

'If it's any way decent it will have. You don't want to miss out on something like that, Lily!'

'But I don't really know what it is or where Tullamore is.'

'Does it really matter? And it's bound to be a great job. They must have pots of money; you'll be living the life of luxury!' Maggie enthused.

'I suppose I could send a telegram,' Eve suggested.

'It would cost a fortune, Mam!' Maggie protested, knowing her mother would have to find Lily's fare and give her some spending money to tide her over until she was paid.

Lily decided Maggie was right. It was too good an

opportunity to miss out on. 'It will, Mam. Just write back and tell her that I'll be very interested in the job and will come over as soon as we can arrange it.'

Eve looked at Lily's animated face and wondered at the wisdom of sending her off to a place she had never been to, to relations she hadn't seen for years and to an unspecified and perhaps even uncertain job, but how could she put a damper on Lily's enthusiasm and maybe even disappoint her again?

'Do it now and I'll post it on my way home,' Maggie urged.

Lily hovered over Eve's shoulder. 'When do you think I can go, Mam?'

Eve paused. 'Is next week too soon, do you think?'

'I don't think so, I don't want to miss out and if I don't go for a few weeks I might. Ask her how far it is from Dublin?'

'Lily, will you just leave Mam to write it. You can sort things like that out later,' Maggie advised. 'I'd start thinking about your packing. Perhaps you could go and make some enquiries as to the price of the ferry fare and when they sail. I can let you have a bit of money, you'll need it for expenses and things like stockings.'

Lily was delighted. 'That would be great, Maggie! I haven't got anything to speak of.'

'That's very generous of you,' Eve added, sealing the envelope.

'My wedding was a drain on you, Mam.'

'It was a pleasure, and don't you bring me stuff every time you come to see me? It's a big help.'

'A bit of fruit and a few vegetables and half a dozen eggs, it's not all *that* much.

'It's the thought, luv. You never come empty-handed.'

Maggie smiled. 'Right, let's pop this in the post and get Lily off on her travels!'

Chapter Fifteen

————◆————

NEXT MORNING LILY WENT down to the offices of the British and Irish Steamship Company and was told that the ferry sailed for Dublin from the Landing Stage at the Pier Head at half past eleven every night and arrived in Dublin at eight o'clock the following morning. Sometimes it took a little longer if the weather was bad, but as it was now May there should be no delays. The fare was fifteen shillings or a guinea if you required a cabin. Lily thanked the clerk but knew she wouldn't be able to afford the luxury of a cabin.

When she returned home she looked through her meagre wardrobe, thinking there wasn't much to pack. She decided to cut short her bridesmaid's dress, she would get more wear out of it that way and with the extra material she could perhaps make a nice blouse. It would have to be something simple and sleeveless but it would be dressy. She might even be asked to dances and she'd need something smart. She would ask Mam if she could spend some of the money

Maggie was giving her on a couple of lengths of cheap dress material and make two nice summer dresses and a skirt; she didn't want to arrive looking like a drab pauper. She had her good black shoes and the white court shoes for best and her jacket was fairly new. If she put a new ribbon around the crown of her hat she'd look as stylish as anyone. She had to admit that the skills she'd learned were very useful. She couldn't have afforded to have bought all that. She was so glad now that she'd said she'd go next week. It didn't leave her a lot of time to get everything done but that couldn't be helped – she'd make it. She began to feel the stirrings of excited anticipation. She was going to travel. It was quite a long way to go on her own. She would be working in a grand house, mixing with very grand people, seeing at first hand how the wealthy lived and, as Maggie had said, living in luxury herself, because whatever kind of a job it was they would be bound to want her to live in.

Eve was delighted and relieved to see her so happy. She was also surprised when a telegram arrived from Aoife saying that on the following Friday morning Lily should go to Heuston Station in Dublin and get a train to Tullamore and Aoife herself would meet her. Mrs Kavanagh, the housekeeper at Rahan Lodge, had been informed of Lily's impending arrival and an interview had been arranged for Saturday morning.

'I wouldn't have believed everything could have been sorted out so quickly!' Lily enthused.

Eve still thought privately that her cousin could have mentioned just what kind of a job was on offer. 'You're going to be very busy, Lily.'

'Sarah said she'd help me. She's getting quite good at sewing herself,' Lily said happily, deftly cutting out the white cotton piqué she'd bought for a skirt. She was going to trim the hem with rick-rack braid and it would look lovely with her blue jacket and white shoes. She'd got a couple of yards of blue ribbon for her hat too. She'd bought a length of blue and lilac and white flowered cotton and one of red and white gingham, which would look great when made into summer dresses and the white shoes would go with both. There was enough white piqué over to make a short bolero-type jacket with short sleeves, which she could wear with both dresses, and also the skirt and her yellow blouse. She smiled with satisfaction; she would have a very stylish wardrobe fit for all occasions and all for a fraction of what they would have cost in the shops.

She had, on Eve's advice, decided to travel in a navy blue skirt and a white blouse and her old beige jacket.

'You'll be travelling for hours and you'll get creased and grubby, you'd ruin your new things,' Eve had remarked, thinking of the long and tiring journey that lay ahead of Lily.

'Won't you be the envy of the place in all this finery!' Maggie had added, looking with admiration at the new clothes Lily had laid out ready for packing in her small suitcase, proud of her sister's accomplishment. 'Do they know she can sew like this, Mam?'

'I did mention it in my letter.'

Lily looked a little dismayed. 'Oh, I hope the job isn't going to be dressmaking!'

'I shouldn't think it will be. I should imagine they get all their things in Dublin,' Sarah added quickly, frowning at Maggie.

Thursday night couldn't come quickly enough for Lily but finally she was ready. Eve had decided that it was a big enough occasion to close the pub half an hour early so they could all go to see her off. She had given Lily three pounds, which would cover her fare, her train ticket, something for Aoife, and leave her money for additional expenses until she got paid. It had left her very short but she didn't want the girl to go so far with virtually nothing in her purse. Lily still had five shillings left from the money Maggie had given her and Sarah had also given her five shillings, so she felt she was very well off indeed, which in itself was a new experience.

To their collective dismay the weather had turned un-seasonably chilly and damp and as they alighted from the tram and walked across the cobbled expanse of Mann Island a steady drizzle was falling.

'Let's hope this isn't a bad omen,' Maggie muttered to Billy as they followed Eve and Lily, Sarah and Harry towards the Landing Stage where the *Leinster* was tied up. She was very relieved that at last her mam might get some peace of mind and sincerely hoped everything would turn out well for Lily.

'Now, have you got everything? Ticket, money, your case, those sandwiches I made for you, Aoife's address in case something happens and she's not at the station?' Eve fussed, devoutly hoping her cousin would be waiting for Lily.

Harry laughed. 'Eve, she's a big girl now, going off into

the wide world!' He too was relieved that Lily seemed so excited about her future.

'I know, but she's still my baby!'

Lily grimaced. '*Mam!*' she cried, impatient to join the throng at the foot of the gangway.

'Now remember you promised to write and tell me everything,' Eve reminded her. Oh, Lily looked so young, so pretty and so impetuous! Maybe she should have sent Sarah with her, just to see Lily safely installed. But for one thing she couldn't afford Sarah's return fare and for another Sarah had her job to go to. Should she have found out more about the Ormondes and the job? But then Lily was so enthusiastic – she just had to hope she really was doing the right thing.

'I will. I'll write on Sunday night. I should have plenty to tell you,' Lily promised, her eyes shining.

'You'd better get aboard or you'll not get a seat. I didn't think it would be so crowded,' Sarah urged.

Lily hugged them all in turn and then joined the crowd of passengers.

'Oh, please God let her be all right. I hope she's not going to be disappointed again,' Eve said anxiously.

'Mam, stop worrying about her. She'll be fine. She can't wait to go – look at her elbowing her way through that lot.' Maggie laughed, watching Lily determinedly pushing her way forward.

'She will be fine and I'm sure she'll love it,' Sarah added, waving to Lily as she turned at the top of the gangway, raised her hand in a final goodbye and then disappeared from sight.

'Well, let's get back or we'll all be soaked. I've got to get up early in the morning,' Billy grumbled as he took Maggie's arm and Harry shepherded Eve and Sarah up the floating roadway towards the tram stop.

Lily found a seat in the saloon, which was crowded, raucous and smoky. It wasn't very comfortable, being little more than a slatted wooden bench with a high back, but she placed her suitcase on the floor and rested her feet on it and leaned back. At least there was no wind to speak of so it should be a calm crossing. She really should try and get some sleep, although with the noise of the people around the bar and various fretful crying children she doubted she would.

Despite her misgivings, she did sleep, and she was surprised to see that it was daylight when she awoke, cramped and stiff. It was quieter in the saloon now but still stuffy and smoky. Some people were already gathering their belongings together so she decided she would go up on deck to get some fresh air and see what there was to be seen.

The air was tangy with salt and sunlight sparkled on the calm, grey-green waters of Dublin Bay. Blue-tinged, misty mountains ringed the bay and the rocky outcrop of Howth Head could be clearly seen off the starboard side. The city was bathed in sunlight and Lily's spirits rose. She could just make out the docks, which even at this early hour looked busy.

'Could you tell me how far is it to Heuston Station, please? Can I get a tram or a bus?' she asked politely of a man standing next to her.

A Mother's Love

'Sure, you can get a tram there, if you've the fare. It's a fair piece to walk,' he replied genially.

'Oh, I've the fare.'

'Then you'll get one on the Quays. Where is it you're after going?'

'Tullamore. County Offaly.'

'Begod, the bogs!'

Lily looked at him quizzically. 'Is it far?'

'It is that! Way down the country.'

This didn't sound too promising but Lily shrugged it off. What did he know? He only looked to be a labourer judging by his clothes and accent and she'd heard that all Dubliners considered anywhere outside a five-mile radius of the city to be a long way indeed.

She followed the crowd of passengers along the North Wall and out on to the Quays. She crossed the Liffey at Butt Bridge and as she gazed around at the fine buildings her spirits rose again. Dublin was quite a big city and there were certainly many fashionable people on the streets, who made her feel dowdy and grubby in her travel-stained clothes. She caught the tram, paid her fare and settled down to see the sights from the window.

Heuston Station surprised her. It was almost as big as Lime Street and twice as ornate. She bought her ticket and received directions to the platform where she had to wait for half an hour for the train which, the station master informed her, was the Galway Express but she was to alight at Tullamore which was approximately half way.

'And how long will that take, please?' she'd asked.

'About two and a half hours, circumstances permitting,' was the reply, although he hadn't elaborated on the 'circumstances'.

Two and a half hours, she thought with rising excitement. In just two and a half hours she would see what was to be her new home!

The time passed quite quickly as she found her fellow travellers friendly and entertaining, although she had a little difficulty in keeping up with both their accents and the speed at which they conducted their conversations. She was informed that things were not the same here as they were in England. Ireland was a new country – they'd only become totally independent a few years ago – and in the rural areas there wasn't as much progress as there was in Dublin. There would be no trams, for one thing.

'How will I get around?' Lily asked, at a loss, having lived all her life in a city where there were both buses and trams and even trains.

'Walk. Or maybe ye'll be fortunate enough to acquire a bicycle,' came the amused reply.

To her disappointment no one had heard of Rahan Lodge but Tullamore was described as a 'grand town' with shops, churches, a hotel and all kinds of diversions and entertainments, which cheered her up.

When the train at last pulled into the small station she bade her companions goodbye and alighted. She walked to the little stone station house and handed in her ticket, looking around uncertainly at the tree-lined yard. It was very quiet compared to Liverpool and Dublin. There was a small group of people standing a little distance away talking, but she was relieved when a woman detached herself and came towards her smiling.

'Lily, is it yourself? You're very welcome!'

'Cousin Aoife?' Lily enquired, thinking there was no resemblance between her mam and this plump, grey-haired woman dressed in an old-fashioned skirt and blouse with a light shawl draped around her shoulders.

'Thank God ye've arrived safely. It's a desperate long journey. Was it rough? The only time I was ever in it didn't the wind howl all the night long and weren't we tossed around like a cork and I thought my end had come!'

'It was very calm and I managed to sleep for most of the way.'

'Thanks be to God for that! Now, come on and we'll get home. I've the trap over there and the pony is after destroying the bushes and Himself will have my life over it.'

Lily smiled and followed her to where a small brown and white pony was indeed devouring the shrubs beside the gates. Aoife took her case and Lily climbed up. It was an unusual experience for her; she'd never ridden in a trap before and had to hold on to the side with one hand and her hat with the other. As the trap rattled along the country road Lily looked around her with interest.

'Is Tullamore far?'

'A couple of miles down the road in the other direction.'

'Oh, do we not go through it?' Lily was a little disappointed, she'd been looking forward to seeing the town.

Aoife laughed. 'Not today. I've to get you home, they're

all eaten up with curiosity about ye and dying to meet ye! I'd be killed if I took ye off to see the sights of Tullamore first!'

'Is "home" far?' Lily asked, pleased her arrival seemed to be a major event.

'Not at all. Just a piece down the road. Once past the Charleville Demesne we're in the parish of Rahan. Then it's on to Killina and the home place is there, not far from the church and the convent and the school.'

Aoife chatted on about her family, the farm and how long it was since she had seen Eve. She asked Lily all about her sisters and Maggie's wedding and the Wainwrights.

'I really would be grateful if as little as possible could be said about Da,' Lily interjected.

'What is there to say about the eejit at all? Except that he's just that – an eejit! But he isn't the first and he won't be the last, Lily. Men of a certain age often lose the run of themselves altogether and nearly always live to regret it.'

'Well, even if he does, Mam won't have him back.'

'I'm glad to hear it! Now, let's not waste another breath on him!'

Chapter Sixteen

LILY WAS THANKFUL WHEN they finally turned down a narrow lane barely wider than a cart track with high hedges on either side. It was very warm and she was hungry, thirsty and decidedly grubby. The lane opened out into a farmyard flanked on two sides by low, whitewashed outbuildings. The small stone farmhouse was two-storeyed with ivy growing up one gable wall. The front door stood wide open and a figure disappeared quickly inside.

'That's that bold brat Kathleen! She'll have been waiting at the door this past hour instead of doing the chores I left her!'

Lily took her case from Aoife as her cousin passed the reins over to a red-haired lad who had come out from one of the outbuildings to greet them.

'And this is Joe, my eldest lad.'

He nodded and Lily smiled at him.

'Come on in with ye,' Aoife instructed.

Lily was ushered inside the kitchen, which was large and

comfortably furnished. A huge range took up most of one wall and a dresser another. A big rectangular table stood in the middle of the room, surrounded by chairs of various shapes and sizes and there were presses around the walls. A basket of turf stood beside the door.

She was soon greeted by her cousin's five other children, ranging in age from Teresa who was sixteen, Con aged thirteen, Ita at eleven, Kathleen who was nearly nine to Denis, the baby at seven, and she was bombarded with questions and regarded with great curiosity.

'Will ye leave the girl alone! Isn't she worn out entirely after the long hard journey? Teresa, put on the kettle and Kathleen, cut up that soda bread and get the ham out of the press and Ita, see you lay the table while I show Lily where she's to sleep,' Aoife fired instructions to her brood while taking Lily's arm and drawing her towards the stairs.

She was to share a room with Teresa, Kathleen and Ita, she was informed. A narrow bed had been crammed in beside a large double bed. A small wardrobe stood against one wall and a press, on top of which stood a flowered delft bowl and jug, stood under the window.

'This will do ye for the short while you'll be with us. Meself and Carthage have the room beyond and the lads have the other.'

Lily wanted to get the matter of the job sorted out. 'I expect I'll be living in at Rahan Lodge. What kind of a job is it exactly?'

Aoife looked surprised. 'Mrs Kavanagh will tell ye all about it tomorrow, but isn't it a fine thing to be offered work there at all? Oh, there's many around here would think they'd died and gone to heaven to have a job there, I can tell ye. Nor will they have anyone from these parts. It's one of the ways they have of going on, always have done from the days when that auld one, Queen Victoria, was on the English throne. Sure, nothing will do but they have English servants. 'Tis a "tradition", so they do tell everyone!' She cast her eyes to the ceiling.

'Don't you know what the job is? Have you any idea?' Lily pressed.

Aoife was astonished. 'Isn't it sufficient to have one that pays well and be living with the gentry?' she remarked a little curtly.

Lily felt rebuked. She didn't want to seem ungrateful so she decided not to press the matter further. A job was a job, after all.

'Teresa will be up now with some hot water, you wash yourself and then come on down.'

Lily unpacked her things and then pushed the case under the bed. Teresa arrived with the kettle and while Lily washed her face and hands, the girl marvelled at Lily's clothes. Then they both went down to the kitchen where a meal had appeared on the table.

'Sit yourself down, Lily, Carthage and Joe will be in soon from the fields,' Aoife instructed.

Lily was hungry and tucked in eagerly, watched by her younger cousins.

She was on her second cup of tea when Carthage and Joe arrived, followed by a lad a few years older than Lily herself.

'Ah, so she's arrived then. You're very welcome, Lily,' Aoife's husband said, holding out his hand. He was a tall, wiry man with auburn hair, grey-green eyes and a weather-beaten face.

Lily shook hands and thanked him for having her.

'You've met Joe, and this is young Myles Carroll who helps me around the place, when I can get a day's work out of him!'

Lily instantly liked the lad. He was tall with dark curly hair and brown eyes that crinkled at the corners when he smiled.

'Hello, Lily. I hear you've come all the way from Liverpool? It must be a grand big place. I wouldn't mind going there myself someday.'

'Oh, he's a one for the big ideas!' Carthage laughed.

'It is a fine city but there's not much work there, not at the moment. In fact there's hardly any, which is why I'm here.'

'Did you not have a job at all?' the lad asked, taking a mug of tea from Kathleen.

Lily shrugged. 'Yes, but I lost it. They didn't want to pay my wages when they could pay a younger girl less.'

'She's a great one with the sewing. She made her sister's wedding dress!' Aoife informed them.

Myles looked at Lily with admiration and she felt her cheeks redden. 'It wasn't very complicated.'

'Ma, ye should see the style of her clothes. She'll put us all to shame!' Teresa said enviously.

Lily encountered another admiring and slightly

speculative glance from Myles Carroll and to her dismay began to blush in earnest.

'Teresa, will ye stop that, aren't ye embarrassing Lily. When ye've had your meal, take Lily and show her around for I've work to do myself.'

After Lily had helped Teresa and Ita with the dishes she walked with Teresa down the lane to the church and the school and convent. The convent was a fine building with the small stone church set a little way beyond it and the school was on the opposite side of the road.

'You'll come with us to Mass on Sunday, Lily?'

'Oh, yes. What do you do for entertainment here, Teresa?'

'There's a dance sometimes on a Saturday night in Mucklagh and there's all kinds going on in town.'

'Will I be allowed to go and how will I get there?'

Teresa looked doubtful. 'Ma might let ye go but ye'll have to walk or maybe get a lift . . . Myles has got a bicycle, he might take ye on the crossbar – if he's going, that is.'

Lily thought this sounded a rather uncomfortable way to travel and she wondered what kind of a state her clothes would be in when she arrived, but the idea of going to a dance with Myles Carroll was very appealing to her. She'd mention it when she got back. After all, it might be the last Saturday night when she would be able to go out for a while if she started work on Monday.

At first Aoife looked doubtful but after Lily had coaxed and wheedled she agreed, providing Myles Carroll was going and would agree to take Lily and bring her home. Lily fervently hoped he was and made herself as useful as she could until Carthage arrived home and her cousin asked him.

'Oh, he's sure to be quite willing; he's taken with Lily. He's never stopped talking about her.'

Lily was pleased and immediately began mentally deciding which of her new outfits she should wear.

'Ye never let me go, Ma!' Teresa complained.

'Ye haven't the sense ye were born with! Lily's used to living in a big city and meeting all kinds of people!' her mother commented acidly.

'Oh, Ma!'

'Hasn't your da told ye time and again, Teresa Minnock, that ye'll be going to no dances and the like until ye're eighteen! Now take that puss off your face. Ye can go into town tomorrow while I'm above at the Lodge with Lily, I need a rake of things from Boland's in Patrick Street. That will be outing enough for you.'

Teresa didn't look convinced but said nothing more. Lily set about pressing the two outfits she intended to wear the following day, which was now promising to be very interesting indeed.

There had been great exclamations over her appearance the following morning when, dressed in the white skirt and yellow blouse and the matching white bolero jacket, she announced she was ready to go to meet Mrs Kavanagh.

'Are ye intending to walk the roads in those shoes?' Aoife asked, looking with some apprehension at Lily's white high-heeled court shoes.

'It's not that far, is it?'

'Not in the trap but Teresa will need that to go into town.'

Lily bit her lip. She wanted to look smart but she didn't want to ruin the shoes. 'Should I wear my black ones and carry these? I could change when I got there.'

'That might be the best plan,' Aoife agreed.

By the time they reached the main road Lily was very glad she'd made that decision. The laneway was dusty and rutted by the wheels of the farm carts, to say nothing of the manure left by the heavy horses. The sun was very warm so she took off her jacket until they reached the high stone wall and gateway of Rahan Lodge.

Lily was very impressed. 'Is this it?'

'It is so,' Aoife replied, urging her into the drive.

As they walked up the long avenue flanked by its tall trees and the house loomed closer, Lily began to feel apprehensive. The nearer they drew, the more imposing the building looked. It was a large square house with six stone steps leading up to a magnificent porticoed entrance porch, surmounted by an elegant fan-shaped window. Either side of the door were long sash windows. Ornate iron railings flanked the steps and the basement windows were just visible.

When they finally reached the Lodge Aoife didn't go up the stone steps but instead walked around the gravelled area that surrounded the house to the back door, which was reached down a flight of narrow stone steps.

The door was opened by a young girl with a shock of

bright red curls and a rash of freckles across her nose and cheeks.

'Mrs Kavanagh is expecting us,' Aoife informed her.

'So she is, ma'am. Will ye follow me?'

Lily followed them down a long narrow stone passageway, catching a glimpse of an enormous kitchen and several other rooms, which looked like pantries or storerooms, until they reached a door on which the girl knocked sharply.

It was opened by a rather severe-looking woman in her forties, with a pair of spectacles balanced on her nose and wearing a plain black dress from the belt of which hung an assortment of keys.

'Good morning, Mrs Kavanagh, ma'am. This is my cousin's girl, Lily Dobson from Liverpool.'

'How do you do, Mrs Kavanagh,' Lily said politely, feeling rather intimidated by the close scrutiny her outfit was receiving. She had the distinct feeling it wasn't being admired as much as she'd hoped it would be.

'Come in and sit down,' the housekeeper instructed.

It was a very neat and tidy room, Lily noticed, a sort of small parlour or sitting room with a table and two straight-backed chairs, an armchair and a roll-top bureau. She and Aoife sat in the chairs indicated.

'How old are you?' the housekeeper asked. The girl looked rather frivolous to her and was decidedly unsuitably dressed.

'Eighteen, ma'am.'

'And you are a hard worker?'

'Oh, yes, ma'am.' Lily was emphatic.

'You have no formal references?'

Lily looked confused but Aoife spoke. 'If you remember, ma'am, I explained that she was an apprenticed seamstress in a big establishment in Liverpool.'

'Indeed. Your mother's letter explained the circumstances of your dismissal, Miss Dobson, and it seems you are a girl of good character.'

'I can vouch for that, ma'am. She's been well brought up!' Aoife added firmly.

Lily plucked up courage. 'May I ask what kind of a job it is, ma'am?'

'One for which I'm assured you are fitted. You will be required to do some light housework as well as see to the repair of all the linen and furnishings and do any alterations that the ladies may require.'

Lily's heart plummeted. Housework and *mending*! It wasn't what she had hoped for or indeed imagined. She had expected to be more of a sort of dresser or secretary to the young ladies: running errands, posting letters, laying out their clothes, seeing to their wardrobes.

'You do not seem to be very interested?' Mrs Kavanagh observed rather tartly.

'Oh, she is! I'm sure she's just taken aback, ma'am.' Aoife kicked Lily sharply on the ankle.

'Oh, yes. Yes, indeed,' Lily stammered, not knowing what else to say and trying to mask her disappointment.

'Good. Then you will start on Monday. The wages are eight pounds a month. You will live in; a uniform will be provided, for which you will be responsible. It goes without saying that you will be neat and clean at all times and respectful and polite. You will have every other Sunday off, plus one afternoon a week that will be decided upon later and you will be directly responsible to myself. You are a Catholic?'

'Yes, ma'am.'

'Then you have leave to go to Mass on Sunday mornings and to Confession on Saturday evenings. Please present yourself at half past seven on Monday morning.'

Aoife rose. 'She will indeed, ma'am, and thank you.'

Lily got to her feet. 'Thank you, Mrs Kavanagh.'

'Isn't that a grand sum of money to be paid for some housework and a bit of sewing?' Aoife said when they were once more outside.

Lily was trying not to show her dejection. 'I suppose it is. I expected something . . . Oh, I don't know! More exciting.'

Aoife was a little exasperated. 'Won't it be exciting seeing all the fine clothes Herself and those girls have? And living in luxury. They have a bathroom and inside toilets!'

'It's just that I really wanted something different to sewing. I hate sewing!'

'And you so good at it! I wish I'd be paid that much for so little.'

Lily said nothing; suddenly it seemed ungrateful to complain. She was here now, she couldn't go home already. She'd have to give it a try. It wasn't a bad wage, if you took into account your keep. Then she brightened. At least she had the dance tonight to look forward to.

* * *

Lily felt a bit better after her good fortune had been exclaimed upon by everyone and she had washed her hair. She decided to wear the blue and lilac dress and her blue jacket as Aoife said it went very chilly at night.

'You look gorgeous, Lily! You'll have them all green with envy at the style of you!' Teresa exclaimed, full of admiration and not a little envy.

'You mind you keep your skirt out of the spokes of the wheels or it'll be destroyed altogether and you with it,' Aoife advised. 'And don't you stand no shenanigans out of that lad. Carthage has had a word with him about having drink taken, too!'

Lily felt even better when Myles arrived, looking considerably smarter in a suit, shirt and tie and with his dark hair tamed by some sort of hair oil. He announced that he'd have to watch her or she'd be dragged off before his eyes and he wouldn't get a single dance with her all night.

'You mind her, Myles Carroll, or ye'll have me to answer to,' Aoife instructed firmly.

'Oh, please!' Lily cried, mortified, feeling like a fifteen-year-old being allowed out for the first time.

'Oh, get off with the pair of ye,' Carthage laughed.

It was a bit awkward getting herself comfortably settled on the crossbar and keeping her skirt away from the spokes of the wheel but at last they set off amidst some laughter.

'You will go carefully and not tip me off!' she begged.

Myles grinned. 'Would I do that to a beautiful girl like you, Lily?'

'I'm not beautiful!' she protested, laughing, but she was flattered.

'Indeed you are. You're the most beautiful girl I've seen in a long time and the most stylish.'

'Oh, stop it, Myles Carroll!' She laughed again, but she was delighted and very aware of the closeness of him. She liked him. She liked him a lot.

Soon she began to enjoy herself, despite the fact that she found that there was a vast difference between a dance held at a parish hall in rural Ireland and one held in a Liverpool ballroom such as the Grafton. For a start there was no bar, although she of course wasn't old enough to drink officially. In fact it seemed as though the clergy and nuns who were present kept a very strict eye on everyone, to make certain no alcohol whatsoever entered the building. Their presence was something else she found quite astonishing.

'Do they always come to the dances? Do they stay all night?' she asked Myles.

'They do so,' he answered, grimacing.

She, too, pulled a face. 'That must really put the damper on things!'

He laughed. 'Ah, forget about them, Lily, and enjoy yourself. I always do.'

She also noticed that all the girls and young women seemed to remain on one side of the room while the men congregated on the other, but she made up her mind that she wasn't going to conform. She'd come with Myles and she was going to stay with him.

She found herself in great demand and realised that she

must be something of a novelty. Her clothes alone made her stand out and she caught the envious looks from the other girls and the disapproving ones from the clergy. Neither upset her, she just threw back her mane of dark curls and took to the floor enthusiastically with her many partners.

After the interval, during which gallons of tea and soft drinks were consumed, Myles rescued her from a small group of admirers, all insisting she had the next dance with them.

'Right, Lily. Ye've paid enough attention to the gossoons to keep them happy for a lifetime. Now it's my turn!' He laughed, taking her arm and pulling her away.

'You mean you're a gossoon too?' she teased.

'Less of that now! Come over here.'

She submitted to being led towards a less crowded part of the hall.

'Will we leave early, do you think? I'm sick of drinking tea and I know where there's some real drink to be got and a bit more lively company too.'

Lily looked at him coyly from beneath her long dark lashes. 'You know what Carthage said about having "drink taken" and Aoife won't be happy either.'

'Ah, Lily, it's only a bit of fun and ye'll come to no harm, I promise. Aren't ye too . . . sophisticated for this lot? Aren't ye a city girl?'

Lily giggled delightedly. She'd never been called sophisticated before and it made her feel very grown up. He went up in her estimation too for knowing such words. 'And aren't you "sophisticated" too?'

'Will we make a run for it then?' he pressed.

She tossed the cloud of curls and glanced coquettishly up at him. 'We will so,' she replied, mimicking his accent.

They left as surreptitiously as they could and laughed all the way to what he described as a 'shebeen', which to Lily appeared to be a house where an impromptu party was going on and alcohol was freely available. She enjoyed herself enormously, dancing and flirting and not only with Myles, although she had sense enough not to drink too much.

When they finally left he put his arm around her waist as he wheeled the bicycle up the laneway to the road.

All too soon they reached the farm and dismounted. Myles took her in his arms and kissed her.

'Have ye enjoyed the night?'

'Oh, yes! I've loved being out with you, Myles, and I'm glad we left the dance.'

'So am I. You're gorgeous, Lily! Will ye come out with me again?'

'Yes! Yes, I'd really like that and I . . . well, I really like you.' She felt adventurous and a little light-headed.

'And I like you. I like you a lot! You're different. Exciting and so modern.'

She put her arms around his neck and he kissed her again before, eventually and reluctantly, she pulled away and left him, turning to blow him a kiss before she opened the door to the farmhouse. Oh, she was going to enjoy living here, despite the job, she thought happily. She was sure she was falling in love.

* * *

Eddie looked around the room with some annoyance. It was an absolute mess, he thought. Doreen was far from tidy, he had to admit that, although it hadn't bothered him until recently. At first he'd found it a refreshing change from Eve's tidiness, which he'd thought bordered on obsessive, but now! There wasn't a surface that wasn't covered with clothes and cosmetics. The bed was never made and seldom changed. The curtains were never drawn back or the window opened to let in fresh air and he wrinkled his nose at the smell.

'If we're going out, you'd better shift yourself and get changed. Hurry up, I'm starving!' Doreen instructed waspishly from her usual place in front of the dressing table.

'Have I got a clean shirt or even a clean collar? This one is grubby.' He knew he sounded annoyed but he didn't care. He too was hungry and he was getting fed up with always eating out or bringing chips or pies back here to eat.

'I brought your collars back from the laundry, they're on the chest. It cost me two shillings to have them washed and starched. It's a disgrace how much they charge!'

Eddie rummaged around in the clutter that covered the top of the chest of drawers until he found the small brown paper parcel. 'Everything is more expensive here, Doreen, you should know that by now.' And the supply of money was dwindling fast, he thought. 'You know soon I'll have to think seriously about trying to get a pub to run.'

She turned around on the stool and faced him. 'A pub to run! What the hell do you want to do that for? You said you'd had enough of that with the flaming George!'

'Doreen, luv, money doesn't grow on trees!'

'You can say that again! You can get a job, a better job than running a pub.'

'I'm trained for nothing else and I'd sooner be my own boss.'

'Well, I just hope you don't expect me to run it with you! I've had enough of working behind a bar and we'd never get a night off. We'd never get out, Eddie.'

Her words disturbed and disappointed him. 'But, Doreen, luv, we'd be working together – for ourselves – and there'd be plenty of people for you to have a laugh and a joke with. You know how popular you are,' he coaxed. They'd do well running a pub together and he'd thought she'd enjoy it.

'I'd *hate* it, Eddie! Listening to drunks and old bores every night, being on my feet for hours, worrying about the takings and the orders and never getting out to enjoy myself. No, I'd much sooner you got a decent job doing something else. Anything else! Now, will you get a move on, my belly thinks my throat's been cut!'

Eddie hastily changed his collar. He wasn't going to press her on the subject and cause an argument. Maybe she'd change her mind in time. Maybe she'd have to if he couldn't find what she called a 'decent' job.

Chapter Seventeen

----•◦•◦•----

E

VE WAS RELIEVED WHEN Lily's letter arrived at last. She had begun to get worried as there had been no word from her for nearly two weeks and she had written to her daughter twice.

Sarah tried to allay her mother's anxiety. 'She's probably enjoying herself so much that she's forgotten.'

'She can't have! How long does it take to scribble a few lines just to say she arrived safely and she's all right?'

'Mam, you know Lily! Things just go right out of her head.'

'I thought Aoife would have let me know.'

'She probably thought Lily had already done so. You can't blame her, she's got enough on her plate.'

'Well, if I don't hear very soon I'm going to send a telegram. I don't care how much it costs!' Eve had replied determinedly.

Eve read the brief letter and then tucked it into her pocket and went through to the bar. Harry had opened the door wide and the sun streamed in, catching the brass handles of the beer pumps and making them shine like burnished gold.

'You look happier this morning,' Harry commented.

'Lily finally managed to put pen to paper!'

Harry smiled although privately he thought it very thoughtless and irresponsible of Lily not to write a few lines to put Eve out of her misery. 'So, what has she got to say for herself?'

'She's sorry she hasn't written but she hasn't had time.'

'Eve, she's been there weeks!'

'I know, but she's fine, that's the main thing. She only stayed with Aoife for three nights; she had to start work on Monday morning. She went to a dance though on the Saturday night and she enjoyed that but as she only has every other Sunday off she won't be going again.'

'Does she like the job?'

Eve sighed. 'No. She has to do housework which she says she never seems to do to their satisfaction and she has piles of mending to do and alterations.'

'It doesn't sound too bad.' Harry wondered just what Lily had expected. After all, she had never been in service and had very little experience in anything other than sewing. In his opinion she was very fortunate. 'What does she say about the house?'

'It's very big and old and beautifully furnished but she says she has a poky little room in the attic, which is stifling, and has her meals in the kitchen, which is in the basement, with the rest of the staff, and she has to wear a plain grey dress and a white apron and a cap which she says make her look hideous.'

Harry polished a glass, looking thoughtful. 'But she gets paid and gets her bed and board and some time off. What does she do with it?'

'She goes to Mass and sometimes to see Aoife and she's been into Tullamore a couple of times with a lad called Myles Carroll.'

Harry grinned. 'Oh, she's met someone then.'

Eve looked doubtful. 'She doesn't say exactly who he is or what he does. Perhaps I should write to Aoife and ask her about him.'

'But does she sound miserable? I mean really unhappy?'

'No, not really. She's not talking about leaving or coming back home – yet!'

'Tell her to stick it out, give it a proper chance, get to know more people,' Harry advised.

'I will. Oh, I'm sure she'll settle down and get used to it. After all, it's not bad money and she does say things are quite cheap. In fact, she doesn't really need a lot of money as there are no shops the size of the ones we have here, so there's not the same amount of choice.'

'So she should be able to save something then.'

Eve laughed. 'Lily, save something! That'll be the day!'

'She should at least put something by for her fare home, should she need it.'

'Let's hope it doesn't come to that.'

'I agree. Anyway, now that you're feeling happier about her, what about that afternoon out I mentioned?'

Eve was evasive. 'Harry, I don't know if I can spare the time.'

'We could go one afternoon in the week when it's quiet and be back for teatime.'

'I suppose so.'

'Jim Stokes would always stand in for an hour so we could get off early. What about Tuesday? It's always quiet then and the weather is glorious. It would be a shame to miss out, it could break.'

'Where would we go?' It was years since Eve had been on any kind of outing.

'New Brighton? We could get the ferry over. Or what about Southport? We can get the train straight there.'

'I think that would be a bit too far for a couple of hours, although I hear it's very nice – very refined. No, it had better be New Brighton.'

'If we had a whole day we could go to Llandudno or even the Isle of Man. They do day trips to both.' He would have liked a whole day with Eve, it would have been like a holiday for them both, something neither of them had ever had.

'We'd have to close the place up and I couldn't do that! I've only a couple of weeks before I hear whether I've got the licence or not. I honestly thought after the day the man from the brewery called and found me serving fish and chips I'd never get it but when we didn't see him in here again – or anyone else suspicious either – and there was no letter from Mr Harrison, I began to hope again.'

'I'm certain you'll get it! The takings are up, thanks to

you and the food now on offer, which I have to admit goes very well.'

'And to you! You work as hard as I do – harder, as you do all the cellar work – and the pay isn't that good.'

'But it's regular and that counts for a lot, Eve. So, it's New Brighton then?'

'Yes.'

Harry couldn't believe his luck. She had agreed. She'd actually agreed! He was going to do his best to make sure it was the most enjoyable day she'd had for a long time. She deserved it. 'Great! Let's hope the sun keeps shining.'

Eve began to look forward to it herself. It would be good to get out for a whole afternoon, to forget all her worries and just enjoy herself, but she had one nagging doubt and that was to do with Harry. He'd said he was fond of her and she knew it was true; she was fond of him too. But was that all it was? Was she relying on him too much? Was she becoming overly fond of him? He's just a lad, a nice, kind, thoughtful lad, she told herself. But he wasn't a lad, he was a man and, as he'd reminded her, only twelve years younger than herself. And that's far too young for you! she said sternly before realising with a jolt that she had actually, for a second or two, considered she felt far more for him than just affection. 'This has got to stop, Eve Dobson!' she told her reflection in the mirror. She was a married woman even though Eddie had abandoned her. Two wrongs didn't make a right!

The weather held and the following Tuesday, after they'd had a bite to eat and Jim Stokes was installed in the bar, they caught the tram to the Pier Head for the ferry across the Mersey to the seaside resort of New Brighton on the Cheshire side of the river. Eve wore her blue costume but without the matching hat which she felt would have been a bit too ostentatious for the occasion.

'I might as well get some wear out of it and I don't go out much,' she replied, smiling, when Harry said how smart she looked.

They climbed the narrow stairs to the upper deck of the ferry and sat on one of the wooden bench-type seats at the bow. The breeze ruffled Eve's dark curls and the sun was warm on her back and she already felt happy and carefree.

'I've always loved the river. There's so much to see, so much going on,' Harry commented, pointing out the massive bulk of the Cunard liner *Aquitania* making her way towards them from the estuary, inbound from New York. The Canadian Pacific's *Empress of Scotland* was making her way towards the estuary, outbound for Montreal, and the peace of the summer afternoon was suddenly shattered by the deafening blasts of steam whistles as the two ships saluted each other.

'That didn't do my eardrums much good!' Eve laughed when she could make herself heard again.

'A time-honoured tradition; you should be used to it by now. Have you ever been down here on New Year's Eve? Every ship in the river and the docks sounds off at the same time.'

Eve grimaced. 'I'm normally being deafened by a crowd of drunks!'

They sat in companionable silence watching the tower, the Ferris wheel, the lighthouse and the fort at Perch Rock growing ever closer until finally the ferry came alongside and they made their way towards the gangway.

They strolled along the promenade, admiring the fine hotels and shops and restaurants, then they walked along the stretch of sandy beach where Eve took off her shoes and stockings and Harry his socks and shoes; he rolled up his trousers and they paddled in the still chilly and rather turgid water.

'I haven't done this since I was a child!' Eve giggled, holding her skirt up.

'I never even did it then. They didn't go in for outings to the seaside.'

Eve was sympathetic. 'You didn't have much of a childhood, did you?'

'I didn't have much of a life until recently, but let's not spoil the day by being miserable! Come on, I'll race you to the lighthouse!'

'I'm too old for such things!'

'You're not and today you're going to enjoy yourself! Forget about the pub, and the customers and the licence and the girls. Come on, Eve!' Harry grabbed her hand and laughing they ran across the sand to the low rocks that bordered the lighthouse.

'Oh, if anyone could see me now they'd think I'd gone mad,' Eve gasped, out of breath.

'Why?' Harry brushed the sand from his feet.

'Acting like a big kid! Maggie would be scandalised!'

'Maggie's too serious for her age; besides it's doing you good. You look . . . beautiful!' She did, he thought. Her dark curls were windblown, her cheeks were pink and her eyes sparkled. She looked like a young girl.

'Oh, Harry Dempsey, you flatterer!'

'You *are*, Eve. To me you are.'

Eve fell silent, searching for something to say.

Harry took her hand. 'Eve, you must know how I feel about you? I can't hide it any more.'

'Harry, stop! I'm still a married woman.'

'I *know* that, but I can't help it.'

Eve pulled her hand away. 'I don't want to hurt you, Harry, believe me I don't, but I *can't* think like . . . that!'

'But if you could, Eve?' he pleaded.

Eve was totally confused and her heart was thumping. With alarm she realised it wasn't just because of what he'd said. When he'd taken her hand she'd felt something stir in her, something she thought she'd never feel again. Something she'd once felt for Eddie.

Seeing her consternation, Harry plunged on. 'Eve, just, think about it. Can I ever be more to you than just a friend? If I can, I'll wait, no matter how long it takes. I'll wait!'

Eve pressed her hands to her hot cheeks. 'Oh, how can I even *think* about it? I don't *know* how I feel! I've no right to feel anything!'

'You deserve to be happy!'

'I'm happier than I've been for a long time, Harry, I really am. Can't we just leave it like that? I was enjoying the day so

236

much, please, please don't spoil it by asking for answers I can't give?' she begged.

Slowly he nodded. Perhaps he was going too fast. Rushing her, trying to push her into a situation she was finding it hard to cope with. He'd just told her he'd wait and yet he was being so impatient. 'All right. I'm sorry. Let's get on with "enjoying the day"!'

Eve smiled thankfully and got to her feet, but she was shaken, far more than she would admit.

They replaced their shoes and went up to one of the cafés and had tea and scones. Then Harry insisted they go for a ride on the Ferris wheel, which Eve found a little hair-raising, but she admitted that the view across the river to Liverpool from the top was wonderful and well worth it. Then they had ice cream and Harry tried his luck on the rifle range and managed to win Eve a pretty little vase.

'Souvenir of a perfect day,' he said, presenting it to her proudly.

'And it only took you six attempts! But, thanks, it's lovely and it *has* been a perfect day!'

'Really?'

'Really,' she said firmly.

'It's just a pity it has to end. I could stay here for ever.'

'We've a pub to run and we'd better be getting back.'

'We could do it again?' he suggested hopefully.

'Do you think that would be . . . wise?'

'I'll leave it up to you. I don't want to upset you, Eve.'

'Maybe towards the end of the summer, before the days

start getting shorter,' she agreed before she realised just what she'd said.

'I'll hold you to that!'

Oh, God, what have I done? Eve thought, but at the same time she acknowledged that she did want to have another afternoon like this – and with him.

Lily was thoroughly fed up and fuming at the dressing down Mrs Kavanagh had given her. At least she was getting out for a couple of hours and she was meeting Myles. It was time due to her and no one could complain about it.

It was a warm, rather sultry evening and by the time she had walked along the laneway to the stile that gave access to the field where she was meeting him, she felt a little better.

He was waiting for her, leaning against the open doorway of an old ruined cottage sheltered against the hedge of blackthorns. 'I wondered if you'd be let out, Lily.'

'I said I'd come, it's time they owe me. Oh, I hate it there, Myles, I really do!' She felt tears prick her eyes as she clung to him.

'Ah, Lily, is it still as bad? What's she been saying to ye now?'

'Oh, all the usual complaints. I wish I could leave.'

He held her tightly. 'Why don't ye?'

'Where would I go?'

'Why don't ye come with me?'

She leaned back and stared at him, her heart plummeting. He was going away. He was going to leave her here. What would she do without him? She would have nothing,

nothing at all to make life worth living! It would be just an existence. Days and months of just housework and mending and being nagged at. Nowhere to go. No one remotely interesting to talk to. She would go mad; she would lose her mind. 'You're leaving here? You're leaving me?'

'I'm thinking of it, but I don't want to leave you. I love you!'

'I love you too, but where are you going?'

'To Dublin. I'm sick of hanging around here in the bogs. What is there to look forward to? I'm only young, I want to see a bit of life, see different places. All the rest of my family are in America and they say it's a grand country; eventually I might even go there myself, but Dublin would be a start. There's people around here who've never been further than Tullamore in their whole lives. I don't want to be like that, Lily. I want some excitement!'

'Oh, so do I! All this peace and quiet is driving me mad. It's *too* quiet. I hate it, Myles!'

'Then come with me. We'll get jobs, find somewhere to live and have an exciting time. We should do what we want while we're young, Lily!'

Lily was completely swept along by his enthusiasm. Her eyes sparkled, all the restraints of Rahan Lodge, of rural living, seemed to melt away. 'I always wanted to work in a theatre, maybe I could get something in Dublin?'

'I'm certain of it. There's a rake of theatres up there, so I hear. We'll have a great time!'

'I have a bit of money, not much . . .'

'And so have I. Enough for our fares and a couple of weeks' rent.'

'We'll soon get work and wages . . .'

They clung together, caught up in the excitement of the magical future they envisaged.

'I'll look after you, Lily. We'll be together and won't I be the envy of all with you on my arm: the prettiest, smartest girl in Dublin!'

'Oh, Myles! When can we go?'

'Tomorrow. I'll just put together my few bits and pieces this night. There's a train mid-morning, we'll be there by teatime tomorrow.'

'I haven't got much to pack either. I'll leave a note, giving in my notice. Oh, just think, this time tomorrow we'll be in Dublin. I'll be in a big city again. Bright lights, noise, people – excitement! I've really missed all that!'

'I've never experienced it!'

'You'll love it – and I love you!'

He kissed her and held her close. 'Everything's going to be just great, Lily. I know it is.'

Chapter Eighteen

❦

SARAH MADE HER WAY home slowly. It was very hot for July and she was exhausted; she'd had a particularly trying day. The dining room had been stifling and her head had been aching for hours. Mr Stevens had been in a foul mood as there had been a large party of commercial travellers in for lunch; they had been noisy, demanding and awkward. They'd had too much to drink too, which had led to something of an argument over the bill, and then – the final straw – a smarmy-looking, overweight, red-faced man had pinched her behind. She had complained furiously to the head waiter, who had told her sharply to ignore it, that they would be leaving shortly, which wouldn't be too soon for him!

'I've worked here for four years and I've never had to put up with behaviour like that, and I don't intend to start now!' she'd hissed back angrily.

'Miss Dobson, please have a little patience,' had been the unsatisfactory reply: the only one she got.

She was beginning actively to hate working at the Stork but what else could she do? she thought dejectedly. It must be great to be like Maggie and be your own boss. And Maggie was so happy in her marriage. Mam had said only the other day that marriage really suited her, she was positively glowing with happiness and contentment. Even Lily was lucky, living in a lovely big house in the country with well-mannered people and not in an overcrowded, hot, noisy and increasingly stinking, airless city. She kicked some rotting garbage into the gutter, wrinkling her nose in disgust at the cloud of flies that rose from it. It was no wonder people got sick! What wouldn't she give to live somewhere where there were trees and fields and flowers, fresh air, peace and quiet with just some housework and sewing to do? Lily didn't know how lucky she was and yet all she seemed to do was complain – about everything. She wrote that she was always being picked on, it was too quiet, there was too much boring sewing, the young ladies were spoiled brats, Mrs Kavanagh was an old harridan, there was too much praying, no one really approved of her ... and so it went on. In Sarah's opinion Lily was carrying on like a spoiled brat herself, and what's more she was worrying Mam with her list of complaints when Mam had seemed so much happier lately. It had helped that she had been granted the licence for the George and that Harry too had been given the barman's job permanently and the two of them got on so well together. Sometimes it seemed as though Harry had always been there and she wondered if Mam ever thought much about Da now. If she did she certainly didn't mention it.

It was just as hot in the kitchen, she thought as she put the kettle on, and it would probably be in the bar as well. Still, it would be good for business. Men were always thirsty, and more so in hot weather; they always seemed to find the money for a pint or two.

Eve came through looking rather tired. 'Oh, open that back door, luv, it's like an oven in here!'

Sarah frowned. 'The place will be full of flies if I do, Mam. There's that much rubbish in the back entry it's attracting them in droves. It's about time the City Council did something about the state of this city. When I came through Queen's Square it was full of rubbish dropped from carts and muck from the horses that pull them. It's disgusting!'

Eve looked at her closely; Sarah wasn't usually so snappy. 'You're not in a very good mood.'

'I've had a bad day, I've got a headache and I wish we'd have a thunderstorm, it would at least clear the air.'

'Sit down then, I'll make the tea. Our Maggie is coming round, it's their day for finishing early.'

'Oh, I don't think I can take how high the cost of vegetables has gone! It's all she ever goes on about.'

'She's worried that they aren't doing as well as she hoped they would, despite all their hard work.'

'Mam, there's still no work around and if she insists on buying top-quality stuff and charging high prices she *won't* make much.'

'Oh, I know, but I'm saying nothing. It's their business, let them run it the way they want to.' Eve was worried about

Maggie too. She did work long hours and she was looking thinner and a little pale, but this sultry heat did no one any good and it was impossible to get a decent night's sleep. The rooms were so hot and airless, even with the windows open, and then you had to contend with the noise from the street outside too. 'You're right, this heat isn't helping. A good storm will freshen the air.'

Sarah sighed. 'Is Harry still going on about you having another outing? It might do you good. What about August Bank Holiday?'

'I couldn't go then, we'll be busy, and anyway, I don't know, people might start to talk.'

'You sound like our Maggie! What "people"? Why can't you have a bit of time off to enjoy yourselves?'

Eve began to set the table. She *had* promised Harry but ever since that day she'd felt she had to keep her feelings in check. She wouldn't be being fair to him if she gave him reason to think she was in love with him. But was she? That was the question that tormented her.

Maggie arrived, which put paid to both Eve's thoughts and her conversation with Sarah. She was concerned to see that her middle daughter didn't look well.

'You look really tired and washed out, luv.'

'I am, Mam. It's so hot! I think I've caught something too.'

'Why?'

'For the last couple of mornings I've felt really sick. Billy's been very good, he's told me to go back to bed and even brought me a cup of tea but I can't drink it.'

Eve looked at her closely. 'Have you had your curse?'

Maggie looked at her blankly. 'Why?'

'Well, have you?' Eve pressed.

Understanding dawned on Maggie. 'Oh, God! Come to think of it, I haven't!'

'Isn't it a bit soon for anything like that?' Sarah asked, for Maggie had gone very pale.

'I was very quick with you, Sarah, and it's been two months since . . .'

Maggie stared at her in disbelief. 'No! Oh, Mam, no, I can't be! Not yet. I can't be expecting. I didn't want any children for ages. Not until we'd got on our feet and paid some of the money back.'

'Maggie, luv, it's not that easy to plan a family. You *must* have realised. Look at the girls you know who are married, some have two and three children already.'

'But Billy said he'd take care of . . . that.'

'And you believed him? You didn't do anything yourself?'

'No, I trusted him! Oh, I'll kill him!' Maggie cried in despair.

'Maggie, you can't blame him entirely, it takes two.'

'What are we going to do now? You know how hard we work and things haven't been all that good and if I can't work . . . Oh, God, what will we do?'

'Don't get upset, Maggie. Just wait and see, it might not be that. You might just be under the weather or have picked up a germ.'

'There's enough of them going around and it's no wonder!' Sarah tried to console her distraught sister.

'Mam, isn't there something I can do?' Maggie cried.

Eve was shocked. 'In the name of God, Maggie, don't say things like that. Just wait and see what happens.'

'And if I am?'

'And if you are expecting then be thankful and don't fly in the face of God. Children are a blessing and if there's one on the way there is nothing you can do about it except welcome it. You are married, after all, and that's what it's all about! Now calm down and drink this tea and you'll feel better.'

Maggie didn't answer. She felt sick, really sick, at the thought of the money they owed and how little there was coming in, despite the long hours and hard work and the economies she made. They couldn't afford to have a baby now, not for a long time. Oh, she'd give Billy a piece of her mind when she got home, no matter what Mam said! It was the end of all her plans and dreams. She'd wanted a thriving business, a nice house, comfortably furnished, in a good area before she started a family. She'd been a complete fool to leave precautions to Billy. If she was pregnant she could only work for a few months before decency dictated she should retire from the shop and afterwards . . . how would they manage? And she was still so young. She certainly hadn't envisaged having a crowd of children hanging on to her skirts – ever! She only wanted two at the most, for in her opinion that's where the downfall of many families lay. Too many mouths to feed and not enough money to do it with. No, she'd always vowed that wouldn't happen to her and now she was even more determined and she didn't care what Billy said about it. If, by some miracle, she wasn't expecting

246

then she would make damned sure that she didn't get pregnant until she was good and ready – and if Billy didn't like it, he could lump it!

'Do you really think she's expecting?' Sarah asked after Maggie had gone home.

'I don't know but she's obviously not happy. What's to be will be, Sarah, but I wish they hadn't borrowed so much money. It's a terrible responsibility and I'm not in a position to help her.'

'She knows that but I'm sure Billy's granny won't mind waiting a bit – she'll understand, surely? After all, it will be her first great-grandchild and Maggie said she's going to leave Billy her money anyway, so why all the fuss?'

'She obviously didn't bargain on being a mother so soon and she might not be. It could just be the heat or some kind of upset stomach.'

'Do you think if it is she'll . . . well . . . you know?'

Eve shook her head. 'No. She's a sensible girl; she wouldn't take a risk like that. Those women are nothing more than butchers; you run the risk of dying if you go to one of them. I remember a girl I was at school with, she was only twenty-five when she died. She had six kids, he had no steady work and she was at her wits' end. She went to some woman in a court off Scotland Road; a week later she was dead!'

Sarah shuddered. 'Then you'd better tell our Maggie that!'

'Oh, I will, believe me,' Eve said determinedly, but she was certain that Maggie wouldn't do such a terrible thing.

Eve went back into the bar and Sarah began to clear up. Even though Maggie wasn't very happy at the moment at least she had Billy and the shop, and Sarah was sure old Mrs Wainwright wouldn't be awkward about the repaying of the loan; she liked Maggie. Maggie still had a much better life and prospects than Sarah herself had. What did she have? All she faced was that flaming dining room and then home to helping Mam. Even Lily had gone to live somewhere different where she might meet someone, fall in love and settle down, even though it didn't look very probable at the moment. Lily at least was experiencing life, even if that life wasn't living up to her expectations, which Sarah considered to be far too high and fanciful to start with. She'd happily settle for the kind of life her youngest sister had. What was she going to do with *her* life? She was going nowhere, meeting no one, and doing absolutely nothing!

The first clap of thunder made her jump nervously, and then she smiled with relief. An end to this oppressive heat would be some small comfort. She heard the yard gate slam shut and looked up impatiently. Now what? She was surprised to see the telegraph boy coming up the yard; normally they came into the pub. Then she realised it was Tommy Stokes, Mary's youngest son.

'Looks like we're in for a storm. I'll get soaked,' he greeted her cheerily, not being averse to getting wet in such warm weather.

'You've done well for yourself! Since when did you start working for the Post Office?'

'Since last week. It's great, I get to keep the bike, I'm out in the open all day and the money's not bad either.'

Sarah smiled at him. 'I bet your mam's pleased.' Mary wasn't the easiest of women to get on with, but she must be proud to have her boy looking so smart.

'Oh, aye. She always said I was useless and I'd never get a decent job, but I have! Here, this is for your mam.' He held out the small brown envelope.

'Who's it from?' Sarah asked, startled.

He looked at her askance. 'I don't know! I don't open them and read them – it's more than my job's worth!'

Sarah took it hesitantly. No one really liked telegrams, they usually meant bad news. Was it Da? Was he coming home?

'Right then, I'm off. I've only got one more and then I can go home for my tea. I'm starving.'

'When are you ever anything else?' Sarah answered laconically and went to find Eve.

'Tommy Stokes brought this for you. He's got a job with the Post Office.'

Eve took it from her and ripped it open.

'Is it from . . . Da?' Sarah asked tentatively, watching her mother's face tighten.

Eve shook her head. 'No. It's . . . It's about Lily. It's from that housekeeper, Mrs Kavanagh.'

'What's the matter with her?' Harry asked, seeing the anxiety in Eve's eyes. Eve had only just confided in him her worries about Maggie and now it was Lily – again! Was Eve ever going to be free of worry over her girls?

'She's run off! Left her job and . . . gone!' Eve informed them. She could not keep the note of despair from her voice.

Chapter Nineteen

HARRY WAS FURIOUS. BLOODY Lily! Eve's dark eyes had filled with tears and she was biting her lip apprehensively. He hated to see her so agitated. What was wrong with the girl? Didn't she realise just how much pain she caused her mother, or did she simply not care?

Sarah's voice interrupted his thoughts. 'Mam, what will we do?'

Eve caught Harry's arm. 'What am I to do?'

Harry looked grim. '*You're* not going to do anything, Eve. I'll sort this out.'

Sarah had made up her mind. 'Neither of you is going anywhere! *I'm* going to find her and give her a piece of my mind, and if necessary bring her home or drag her back to her job!'

'Sarah, you've got your own job to think of, luv!' Eve protested.

'Mam, I'm sick to death of it, I really am. You can't drop everything and go chasing after her and neither can Harry, you've got a business to run and a roof to keep over your head. But I can. I'll go. Send a telegram to Aoife and tell her I'm on my way.' She meant it. She was thoroughly fed up with work and would be glad to escape the city, even if it was only for a short while and meant having a huge row with Lily.

Harry was thoughtful. Maybe it would be better if Sarah went; she was at least Lily's sister while he was what Lily would view as an outsider. Eve was far too lenient where Lily was concerned and would listen to the girl's excuses. Sarah, he could see, was far more resolute and angry.

'I think Sarah is right, Eve. Lily can't expect you to just up and go running after her.'

'I don't think that's what she wants anyway,' Eve said morosely. She was concerned that yet another of her daughters was ready to pack in her job before there was the prospect of another on the horizon, but she was more worried about Lily.

'Well, it's what she's going to get, Mam, whether she likes it or not!'

'When can you be ready, Sarah? Will you have to work your notice?'

'I suppose I should but I won't and if they don't like it they can lump it! I'll go round in the morning and tell them and then I'll go and get my ticket. Don't worry about the money, I've got a bit saved up. It hasn't been easy on what they pay me at the Stork but you know I've always been careful and I really don't mind spending it.'

'But, luv, where will you start to look for her? You might

need train fares and things; she could be anywhere! Oh, God! What's got into her? I knew she wasn't really happy but . . . this!'

'Mam, don't get upset. She can't have gone far, it's not that big a country.'

'But Dublin is quite a big city and I'm sure that's where she'll have headed – for the bright lights!'

'I'd try the theatres first, Sarah,' Harry advised.

'I'll see what Aoife and Mrs Kavanagh have to say before I go anywhere,' Sarah said firmly. 'Now, I'd better go and start to get my packing done and then organise some kind of a meal.'

'I don't think I could eat a thing,' Eve said distractedly.

'Eve, making yourself ill isn't going to help anyone,' Harry said gently.

'He's right, Mam, and you've the evening ahead of you,' Sarah added.

Reluctantly Eve nodded and began to scribble down the wording of the telegram she would send to her cousin. Why was Lily so difficult to manage? She could see only trouble and heartache ahead, whatever the outcome of Sarah's journey.

Harry worked quietly and thoughtfully at the mundane tasks at the bar. He had been intending to ask Eve if she would like to go out again early next week. He had heard that Thurstaston Common on the Wirral was nice for an afternoon. It would make a change from New Brighton; it was quiet and peaceful, which would have suited his purpose very well. With no distractions and very few people about they could have talked, but Lily's disappearance had put paid to all that. There would be no outings and no tête-à-têtes until it was all sorted out and God alone knew when that would be. But, on the other hand, perhaps it would take Eve's mind off the matter while they were waiting? He would just have to wait and see how things went. At least Sarah was steady and reliable and sensible. Maggie would have ten fits when she heard, but maybe in the light of what Eve had told him earlier, Maggie would be too preoccupied with her own position to upset Eve further.

The heat hadn't improved Maggie's temper and by the time she got home she was seething. She found Billy upstairs in the kitchen.

'I'll put the kettle on, luv, you look worn out! At least that storm has cooled the air down a bit. It didn't do much for custom though,' Billy added morosely.

'It won't matter whether we have any customers or not soon! We'll be having to close and God knows how we'll be able to pay your granny back then and still exist!'

'Maggie! What do you mean? What brought all this on?' Billy looked mystified and concerned. She certainly had a bee in her bonnet about something. 'Is your mam all right?'

'Mam's fine! It's me who isn't and it's all your fault, Billy Wainwright!'

'Now what have I done?' he cried.

'I trusted you! You said I could trust you to "take care of things"! Oh, I should have known better!' Maggie stormed, pacing the kitchen.

Billy caught her by her arms and held her. 'What are you talking about? What things?'

'I'm expecting, that's what I'm talking about, Billy! That's why I've been feeling so sick. It's not the heat or something I've caught. Mam pointed it out to me. Oh, I'm such a fool!'

Billy's worried look disappeared and a smile slowly spread across his face. 'Maggie! Maggie, that's great!'

She exploded. 'It's not! It's not bloody great, Billy! It's a disaster. I don't want a baby yet. How will we manage? I won't be able to work and what will we do then? Oh, all the plans we made! Everything is . . . ruined!' She was so distraught that she burst into tears.

Billy pulled her to him and held her. True, they hadn't planned on starting a family so soon but he couldn't see what all the fuss was over. Why wasn't she pleased? It wouldn't matter that she couldn't work in the shop for much longer, he'd work twice as hard and he knew his gran would be so delighted that she wouldn't pressure them for the money.

'Maggie, luv, don't cry! Don't upset yourself, it can't be good for you,' he soothed.

But Maggie just sobbed harder in rage. He didn't mind! He just didn't understand how she felt – and it was *she* who was going to have to have this baby and all it entailed.

'We'll manage just fine and everyone, especially Gran, will be delighted. And it needn't change all our plans, just alter them a bit.'

Maggie raised a tear-stained face. 'You don't understand, do you? I . . . I'm too young! I don't want babies for years

255

yet. I wanted us to get on our feet, have a nice house, have some time to ourselves . . . but now . . .'

Billy looked at her sadly. 'Oh, Maggie! I'm sorry but there's nothing we can do about it now.' He genuinely felt sorry for her but it was too late. They were going to be parents whether they were ready for it or not.

'Just pray it's a false alarm, Billy. I'm going to and if it is then you can just get yourself a single bed because you're not coming anywhere near me. I'm not going through all this again!'

'Maggie, you don't mean that? Any of it?' Billy pleaded.

'I do! Oh, indeed I do, Billy Wainwright!'

Billy sat down heavily in the wicker armchair, stunned and hurt. He loved her but did she love him? If she did, surely, surely she wouldn't do this to him? Oh, was she just upset and overwrought? Would she get over it? He prayed she would but deep down he knew that Maggie had a will of iron and he did not.

It seemed incredible, Sarah thought, that in such a short space of time she was standing with her suitcase on the deck of the Dublin ferry as it drew away from the Liverpool Landing Stage. Mr Stevens had been far from pleased at her going but she hadn't cared. Mam had received a reply from Aoife saying she would meet her from the train and Sarah was determined to find her errant sister and talk some sense into her.

When the lights of Liverpool began to fade she made her way down to the saloon in search of a seat for the long night ahead. It was warm so she hadn't wanted to go down into the close, stuffy atmosphere right away, but neither could she stay on deck all night. At the foot of the stairway three youths were crowding the door to the saloon and eyed her with interest.

'Do you think you could move yourselves so a person could get through the door?' Sarah said coldly.

'Oh, get 'er!' the tallest and oldest of them remarked mockingly.

Sarah caught the whiff of beer on his breath and her temper rose. 'Get out of the way!'

'An' are yer goin' ter make me?'

'If I have to!'

'Snotty bitch, ain't she?' another sneered.

'I'd like ter see yer try, girl!'

Sarah began to feel a little afraid but she was determined not to show it. 'If you think I'm afraid of overgrown flaming street Arabs like you, you're mistaken! Now move before I call a deck steward!'

The tall lad grabbed her arm. 'Who're yer callin' a street Arab? I'm no bloody beggar!'

Before Sarah could move or cry out a hand shot out from behind her and caught the lad by the throat and he was lifted bodily off his feet with a half-strangled cry.

'Have more respect for the young woman, you black-guard, or it's over the side you'll be after going!'

Sarah turned quickly and saw a big, dark-haired man dressed in a tweed suit towering over them all. Two of the youths fled and when the tall lad was finally released with a contemptuous shove, he followed them.

'Thank you! I . . . I really don't know what I would have done, there doesn't seem to be anyone in charge!'

'There never is and there should be to deal with the scum they carry on these boats. Are you hurt?' The man looked down at her with concern. She was a fine-looking girl and obviously not used to travelling.

'No. No, just a little . . . shaken.'

'Are you travelling alone?'

'Yes. It's such a warm night that I didn't want to come down too soon, I've been told it's very hot and stuffy in there.'

'It is so.'

Sarah remembered her manners. 'Oh, I'm so sorry. I'm Sarah Dobson. Miss Dobson.' She held out her hand.

He took it and shook it slowly. 'Michael Nolan, and it's a pleasure to be of assistance, Miss Dobson. And now I'd better see you settled before I turn in myself.'

'You have a cabin?' Sarah was surprised. He didn't look wealthy.

'I always invest in one. It's worth it.'

'You travel regularly then?'

'Not all that often. I have a sister in Liverpool, and sure I'm fond of her so I come over to see her three or four times a year.'

'I'm going over to see my sister. Well, to see if I can find her really. The little madam has run off from her job and Mam can't leave the pub to go chasing after her.'

He looked at her with interest as he ushered her through the door to the saloon. 'And your da?'

Sarah's eyes became cold. 'He ran off too!'

'Sure, it seems to be a bit of a family trait!'

'Doesn't it just!' she answered tartly, before feeling a little shocked with herself for revealing all this. The feeling didn't last long; she felt oddly relaxed with him, even though he was a stranger. She followed him as he effortlessly moved through the crowded room to the port side where he had spotted an empty seat.

'There now, you're settled. I'll bid you goodnight, Miss Dobson, and safe journey. I hope you find her.'

'I hope so too and thank you again for everything, Mr Nolan, you've been very kind.'

'Ah, 'tis nothing. A gentleman would do as much for any lady.'

'And you are a gentleman, thank you, and goodnight, Mr Nolan.'

'God go with you, Miss Dobson,' he said, tipping his cap respectfully before turning away.

Sarah settled herself as comfortably as she could on the hard wooden seat, envying him the comfort of a cabin but very thankful that he had come to her rescue. She doubted she would see him again but as she began to doze she thought how attractive and kind he had been – and quite gentle too, for such a big man.

She hadn't seen him again despite looking for him as she followed the crowds on deck, down the gangway and along the dock road, but by the time she had finally reached Heuston Station she had forgotten him in the hustle and bustle of buying her ticket, finding the right platform and getting a seat in a third-class compartment.

On the journey down she wondered just what faced her.
What had Lily been up to? Had she given anyone any idea
of what she intended to do? She hoped Aoife could give her
some insight into her sister's behaviour. The one thing she
was determined to do was see Mrs Kavanagh and impress
upon the woman that Lily was in no way the same as either
herself or Maggie and that Mam was not at all to blame for
the way Lily had behaved. She owed her mam that much at
least.

She was tired when she finally arrived at Tullamore
Station and was irritated to find that there was no sign of
Aoife. She walked impatiently to the gate and stood tapping
her foot as the other passengers all departed. Oh, this was
a good start! she thought.

'Ah, Miss Dobson, we meet again!'

The frown disappeared from Sarah's face to be replaced
by a smile of genuine pleasure. 'Mr Nolan! I didn't know
you lived here!'

He smiled down at her. She was lovely when she abandoned that rather serious demeanour. 'And I didn't know your
sister lived here either!'

Sarah laughed. 'Used to live here.'

'Have you no transportation? Where is it you're off to?'

'My cousin was supposed to meet me but she's late.'

'Your cousin?'

'Aoife. Aoife Minnock from Killina.'

'Ah, I know her well enough and Carthage too. So, it's
young Lily you're after coming to find. I heard she left the
Lodge.'

A Mother's Love

Sarah raised her eyes to the sky. 'Oh, God! She has us the talk of the parish!'

'She's a fine-looking girl but, if I might say so, a little bold.'

'More than a little bold, I'd say.' Sarah hesitated a moment then decided to carry on. 'You don't know where she might have gone?' Oh, this was so humiliating, she thought. Where was Aoife?

'All I heard was that she had taken up with Myles Carroll and then she'd up and left the Lodge and Herself up there in high dudgeon over it and giving out about it morning noon and night.'

'And I'll be "giving out" to our Lily when I get my hands on her!' Sarah replied with venom. So, Lily had 'taken up' with this Myles Carroll. She remembered the name from her sister's letters. Then she heaved a sigh of relief as a small brown and white pony clattered into the yard pulling a trap in which a flustered-looking woman with grey hair sat waving.

'Ah, 'tis yourself at last, Aoife! I was about to bring Miss Dobson out to you.'

Aoife yanked the pony to a halt beside them. 'Michael! Thanks be to God ye were here to keep her company. Didn't those blasted bullocks of O'Brien's get out again and run trampling all before them 'til Carthage and himself rounded them up and me waiting to get down the laneway! Sarah, climb up here beside me now and we'll be away home, ye must be desperate for a cup of tea!'

In one swift movement Sarah's case was swung up and

then strong arms swept Sarah herself effortlessly into the trap.

'No doubt I'll see you again, Miss Dobson!'

Sarah felt herself begin to blush and to cover her embarrassment concentrated on adjusting her hat. 'Er, yes, no doubt, Mr Nolan, and thank you again,' she said quietly.

'Did ye meet him on the train?' Aoife asked when they had cleared the station entrance.

'I met him on the boat. He was very kind to me.'

'He would be. He's a grand man and he's not short of a bit of money either.'

'Where does he live?'

'He has a fine place over at Ballincur. He has six men working for him.'

Despite herself Sarah was curious. 'Is he married? He looks . . . older.'

'He's thirty-four and there's many a one in this parish that's set her cap at him, though much good it did them! Ah, he's a confirmed bachelor, that one!'

'Maybe he's just not met the right girl yet,' Sarah mused.

'Or maybe he's not yet met the girl with the right size of a dowry to bring with her!'

'A dowry?' Sarah was puzzled. She'd never heard of such a thing, not in these modern times anyway.

'Money, land.'

'I didn't think that was necessary these days.'

'Oh, ye can see ye're a city girl.'

Sarah pushed all thoughts of Michael Nolan from her mind. 'What can you tell me about Lily? Mam is terribly upset and worried; we all are! And just who is this Myles Carroll that she's "taken up with", according to Mr Nolan?'

'She wasn't happy, Sarah, the Lord alone knows why. She had a grand job with a good wage and living in that fine house with the gentry and all the luxuries.'

'We gathered that from her letters, yet they were full of complaints.'

'She was seeing quite a lot of Myles Carroll but we really didn't think it was serious. He's a lad who used to work for Carthage until he up and left a few weeks ago. He wasn't a bad lad, but full of the big ideas about travelling and making a rake of money and nonsense like that. He used to take Lily out whenever he could. They got on well together.'

'If he was full of "nonsense" they would have got on well together – Lily's head was permanently filled with rubbish like that. It was the reason Mam sent her over here in the first place. Has she gone off with him, do you think?'

'She might have done. She doesn't really know anyone else very well. All I know is what Herself up at the Lodge told me. That there was a row and Lily left and that she's a bold strap if ever there was one!'

'Oh, no! Didn't Lily even come to see you before she left?'

'She did not for she knew I'd give her the lash of my tongue. Wouldn't our Teresa give her right arm for a job like that and the money and the clothes Lily had?'

'She's spoilt. That's always been Lily's trouble. Well, I intend to go and see Mrs Kavanagh.'

'What for?'

'I won't have us all tarred with the same brush as Lily. Despite everything, she has been well brought up. Mam's done her best and it's not her fault and I won't have people thinking it is!'

'Well, go if ye must but ye won't get much of a warm welcome, I can tell ye. Now, let's hope those damned bullocks are all safely penned and we can get our tea in peace.'

After meeting Aoife's family and hearing from Carthage much in the same vein concerning her sister, Sarah was taken up to the room she would share with her cousins. She decided that she would have a talk with Teresa who was nearest Lily's age and might have been her confidante.

'Teresa, did Lily talk to you much?' she asked as she unpacked.

'Sometimes,' the girl answered cautiously. Sarah was very businesslike and made her a little nervous.

'I know she wasn't happy up at the Lodge and that she saw a lot of Myles Carroll.'

'Oh, she did so. Lily used to escape with him whenever she could.'

'Escape?'

'That's what she called it. She hated it above at the Lodge, Sarah, really hated it.'

'I didn't realise that. Would you hate it?'

Teresa looked astounded. 'I would not! It's a grand place to work, so I hear tell, but they won't have us local girls.'

'Why ever not? I bet you would work far harder and with less complaints than our Lily!'

Teresa shrugged. 'It's their way of going on, always has been.'

'So, she escaped with Myles Carroll. What kind of a lad was he?'

'Handsome and funny and generous and daft, so me da says. He was quite often getting into fights, he had a temper on him, so he did. He liked Lily, he really did. Lots of the young fellers liked Lily. She was so different. So . . . beautiful and stylish and clever!' Teresa said enviously.

'She's far from clever, Teresa. She's just downright stupid – or, as your da says, "daft".'

'Do ye not like her much, Sarah?'

'Of course I do! She's my sister! But she's infuriating and spoiled and it's about time she grew up and stopped causing so much trouble and heartache.'

'I think she was in love with him and I know he was in love with her. Sure, ye could see by the way he looked at her,' Teresa confided, dewy-eyed.

This was far worse than she had expected, Sarah thought. 'She didn't give you any idea what she was planning or where she was going or who with? Do you think she's gone to Dublin?'

'She could have. She loved the theatre.'

'Tell me something I don't know! Could she have gone off to Dublin with him? Does anyone know where he's gone?'

'No. He's no family here now, they're all off in America.'

Sarah devoutly hoped he hadn't decided to join them and taken Lily with him. If he had, they'd never find her. There was obviously no point in trying to pursue the matter further with Teresa, but Mrs Kavanagh was a different matter.

* * *

Next morning Sarah dressed with care in a plain navy dress with a neat white collar and cuffs. She brushed her hair up into a pleat and carefully placed her wide-brimmed navy hat over it. She looked tidy and respectable, she thought, certainly in no way flashy or even what Lily would call 'stylish'. It was the effect she desired.

Aoife accompanied her to the Lodge but told her to expect a wait as they had no appointment and the housekeeper was not going to be readily disposed to see them. Sarah replied that she would wait all day if necessary.

They were kept waiting for an hour and then ushered into Mrs Kavanagh's office.

'Thank you for seeing me at such short notice, Mrs Kavanagh,' Sarah began calmly, not attempting to offer her hand or take a seat.

'You are not what I expected,' the woman stated bluntly.

'No. I am not like Lily and neither is my sister Maggie who is married and runs her own business. I have no excuses to make for Lily, what she has done is unpardonable, ungracious and ungrateful. She wasn't brought up to be like that.'

'Indeed!' came the cold reply.

'No indeed!' Sarah was quietly emphatic. 'My mother tried extremely hard with us all but particularly Lily. She is sick with worry over the girl. Did she give you any indication at all as to where she was going, ma'am?'

'She did not! She was impertinent in the extreme that morning and I gave her a final warning. She had had others,

266

particularly about the company she was keeping. She then had the temerity to tell me that she would no longer stay here, that she was leaving that very minute and with that she stormed out, packed her things and left while I was informing Mrs Ormonde of the situation. Madam was extremely annoyed and it left me in a very poor situation indeed, I can tell you! Julia had leave to visit her mother in Belfast who is ill, so we were short-handed and there was company expected for the weekend and the young ladies both had gowns that needed some alterations. A most unfortunate and exasperating situation.'

Sarah nodded. 'I can understand that and all I can say is that I am extremely sorry and impress upon you that my other sister and I are not like Lily.'

'It does not resolve the situation, Miss Dobson!' the housekeeper snapped. The whole situation reflected badly upon her and her judgement in taking Lily on in the first place – something her employer had pointed out very coldly indeed.

Sarah looked confused. 'I'm sorry, ma'am, I don't understand?'

'Julia is still absent and I have no one capable of even taking up a hem! Madam is decidedly put out!'

'I can only repeat that I am very sorry, ma'am.'

'No, Miss Dobson, you can help to resolve the situation if you are as steady and reliable and accommodating as you would have us believe. Do you sew?'

Sarah was completely taken aback. The woman seemed to have dismissed Lily completely from her mind and with it her worries about her sister. 'I do, ma'am. Not as well as Lily but—'

'Do you have a job?'

'I . . . I work— worked in a hotel, in the dining room, but I had to give in my notice to come to find Lily. Mam couldn't leave the . . . er . . . business.'

'Then you can rectify some of the damage your sister has done. Rectify the situation she has left us in.' And restore my reputation with Madam, Eliza Kavanagh added to herself. Even if the girl only stayed until she could find a suitable replacement. She had no intention of having to face Olivia Ormonde's acid comments for a day longer than necessary.

Sarah glanced at Aoife, who had remained silent. Her cousin shrugged.

'Do I understand you to mean that you are offering me Lily's job? That's not why I came here, ma'am.'

'I'm aware of that, Miss Dobson, but your sister has gone and I still have a household to run!'

Sarah was lost for words. The woman seemed heartless and yet . . .

'How will she find Lily, Mrs Kavanagh, ma'am?' Aoife asked, quite shaken herself.

'I'm sure she can pursue her enquiries by post to the newspapers and such publications. The girl might even come to her senses and either return to Liverpool or to yourself, Mrs Minnock. Well, Miss Dobson?'

Despite the circumstances forcing her visit to Ireland, from what little she had seen of the country, Sarah thought it was a lovely, peaceful place. When she'd woken that morning the warmth of the slight breeze wafting in through the open window had held the perfume of wild flowers, newly harvested crops and baking bread. Birdsong and the distant lowing of cattle had drifted to her ears, not the cacophony of traffic noise and shouting and yelling, which was what she usually woke to. Everyone had been very friendly and helpful, except Mrs Kavanagh, but she couldn't blame the woman. Why not take the post? She supposed she could still try to find Lily by putting advertisements in the newspapers, writing to the Dublin theatres or any other place Lily might have been attracted to. On her days off she could go and speak to people who had known this Myles Carroll.

'Well, Miss Dobson?' The brisk tone interrupted her deliberations.

'Yes. I would like to work here, ma'am, and I will try to give every satisfaction,' she heard herself say.

'Good. Your duties will be the same as those of your sister, as will your salary. You will live in, a uniform will be provided and I would be obliged if you could start immediately. The situation has been extremely vexing to me – to us all!'

'May I return to my cousin's home to collect my things, ma'am?'

'Of course, but I would be obliged if you could be back here before lunch. Twelve-thirty?'

'Of course. I can assure you I will be punctual.'

Neither she nor Aoife spoke until they were outside the gates of the Lodge then Sarah pressed her hands to her cheeks.

'I can't believe that that has just happened! I went there to find out about Lily, not to get the job myself!'

'Ye could have knocked me down with a feather too! Sure, all that woman thinks about is her position! Though I have heard that she's fair and has a soft spot for those she likes and gets on well with. I'm beginning to have some sympathy with Lily – not that I'm saying what she did was right,' she added, seeing Sarah's brow furrow in a frown.

'Maybe I shouldn't have gone on about Maggie and me not being like Lily.'

'Now ye've the chance to prove it!'

'That won't be hard, but what am I going to tell Mam?'

Aoife shook her head, thinking Sarah had been rather rash in her decision. 'I don't know but ye'd better get a letter off to her soon or the poor woman will be demented altogether. I will say this, Sarah, looking for Lily will be like seeking a needle in a haystack. Sure, they could be anywhere in Ireland or England or even America, though please God she hasn't run off across the whole width of the Atlantic Ocean! No, it will be nigh on impossible but I realise that you do have to try.'

'If I get a chance I'll write tonight and perhaps someone will post it for me in the morning,' Sarah answered a little weakly.

She remained deep in thought as they drove home until just beyond the church the sound of cartwheels came to her ears. Aoife nudged her.

'Look, 'tis himself!'

Sarah looked up to see a laden farm cart coming towards

them with the shirt-sleeved figure of Michael Nolan driving it.

'Another fine morning, Aoife! And how are you, Miss Dobson?' he called as they drew closer.

'Oh, she's grand altogether! Hasn't she just got the job up at the Lodge that Lily up and left! Left them in the lurch altogether did Lily, so much so that Herself offered Sarah the position. She's to be back above by half past twelve.'

Sarah could have killed Aoife as she watched his dark eyes fill with mirth. She sincerely hoped her cousin's words hadn't put her in a bad light. It looked so mean for her to take her sister's job.

'She must have been quite taken with you, Sarah!' There was laughter in his voice but admiration too.

'I . . . I really didn't intend to do anything like that! I don't know what it must look like!' Sarah managed to stammer, embarrassed.

'Well, I'm glad you're staying. I hope it will be a longer visit than Lily's was. I'd best get on, I've the lads to pay today. Tell Carthage I'll be down at the Thatch tonight. Harvesting is thirsty work!'

'He'll be down there himself later on. We'd best get on ourselves. Good day to ye, Michael.'

'Good luck, Sarah,' he said sincerely.

'Thanks,' she managed to reply and then looked down at her tightly clasped hands. Had he been one of the reasons she had decided to stay? He'd said he was glad she had taken the job and he had called her 'Sarah' . . .

Chapter Twenty

————

A WEEK LATER MAGGIE AWOKE to the familiar dragging cramps in her abdomen. She could have cried with relief. It had been a long, terrible week. She had prayed and prayed that she wasn't pregnant but there had been times when she'd felt guilty about it. Was it right to pray for such a thing? She didn't know if Billy was praying too. They hadn't spoken much but she'd caught him looking at her with sadness in his eyes, which had made her feel worse. She hadn't banished him from their bed but she'd slept as far away from him as she possibly could without actually falling on to the floor. Oh, never had she welcomed pain as she did now. She felt she could get on with her life, look forward again.

As she lay in bed alone – Billy had been up for hours to get to the market – she wondered why she had felt only despair. There had been no joy, no excitement and no maternal feelings at all. Was that right? Was there something wrong with her? You were supposed to feel loving and

273

protective and all kinds of things towards your children. She'd ask Mam. She'd go round later and tell Mam the news and ask her if she was unnatural. She was truly bothered by this. She did want children – some day.

She threw back the bedclothes. Well, cramps or no cramps, she had to get up. She had work to do and she was very thankful she could continue to do it.

Billy noticed the change in her but said nothing. He was very confused and he was tired. He hadn't slept much lately. When, mid-afternoon, she announced she was going to see her mam he just nodded affably. She hadn't been round to see Eve since the day she'd come home in such a state. Maybe Eve could sort Maggie out; he had a lot of faith in Eve. In fact, perhaps he should go and have a private word with his mother-in-law himself?

Maggie found Harry alone in the bar.

'Your mam's upstairs. She's got a headache so I told her to have a rest.'

'Poor Mam, she always seems to have so much on her plate. Well, I've got some good news.'

'Thank God for that, she could do with something to cheer her up. She had a letter from Sarah in the post today.'

'Our Sarah? Where is she? I didn't know she was going anywhere!'

'I'm saying nothing. Let your mam tell you everything, but, Maggie, see if you can persuade her to agree to an afternoon out. She needs a break.'

Maggie nodded and went quickly upstairs, wondering what was going on now.

'Mam? Harry said you were up here and you've had a letter from our Sarah!' she called.

'In here, luv,' Eve called from the bedroom.

'What's going on now? Where's Sarah?'

Eve sat up; her head was still very muzzy. 'She's gone to Ireland to try to find Lily.'

Maggie's eyes widened. 'Where the hell has Lily gone?'

'I wish I knew! We had a telegram saying she'd run off and so Sarah insisted she go over to try to find her – and now Sarah informs me she's staying there.'

Maggie sat down on the bed. All this was news to her. 'Why didn't you tell me all this? Why didn't our Sarah come round and tell me?'

Eve patted her hand. 'You had enough on your plate; we didn't want to worry you. Anyway it all happened so fast. I thought Sarah would be back soon, with or without Lily.'

'Oh, Mam!' Suddenly Maggie's news seemed very unimportant, even trivial.

'How are you, Maggie?' Eve pressed.

'I'm fine. I got my curse this morning, so that's the end of that little drama,' Maggie said briskly.

Eve smiled thankfully. It was one less worry.

'Just what's wrong with our Lily now? Wasn't she happy? Does no one over there know where she's run off to? Oh, honestly Mam, she's the living end!'

'No, she wasn't happy and apparently she's taken up with some lad and everyone seems to think she's run off with him.'

'I could kill her – has she no sense at all in that stupid head of hers? She'll end up in trouble!'

'That's what really worries me, Maggie. She's still so young and so trusting.'

'And what's our Sarah doing? Has she any idea at all where she's gone?'

'No. She's written to all the newspapers – she's put advertisements in the local ones – and to most of the theatres in Dublin.'

'Does this lad have any family or friends who might know?'

'Apparently not. He used to work for Carthage and Aoife says he's not a bad sort of a lad, but—'

'He can't be that responsible if he's encouraged her to run off with him!' Maggie interrupted.

'I know. Oh, I know I should have gone myself but Harry agreed with Sarah and she was adamant.'

'So what's she doing? Why isn't she coming back?' Maggie was still mystified on this point.

'She's doing the job Lily left. The housekeeper was so mad with Lily leaving her in the lurch that Sarah said she more or less had no choice but to accept, but I think there's more to it than that.'

'What?' Maggie demanded.

'I had a letter from Aoife too and she said that Sarah loved living in the country and that she thinks a local farmer, a Mr Nolan, has taken a shine to Sarah.'

Maggie looked astounded. Sarah had always seemed to be quite happy here in Liverpool and had never shown much interest in men. 'So the pair of them have left us in the lurch!'

Eve managed a wry smile. 'It would seem so. Oh, I really don't mind Sarah staying if she's happy, and if she's met a decent man, I'll be even happier. It's Lily who's the real worry.'

'She always damned well is! Well, I don't suppose there's much more we can do – except wait until either Sarah gets some news or Lily decides to get in touch with you.'

'Except worry about her.'

'You worry too much about her, Mam. She's got to learn to stand on her own two feet at some stage in her life and take responsibility for her actions *and* her mistakes. Let's just hope she really does have some sense at the end of the day.'

Eve nodded. It was very easy for Maggie to say she worried too much; she wasn't a mother, for heaven's sake! 'You wait until you *are* a mother, Maggie. Then you'll realise it's not easy; it's not easy at all.'

Maggie plucked at the bedspread. 'Well, I'm not going to be one yet.'

'I hope you didn't give Billy too hard a time? It wasn't all his fault, you know.'

Maggie sighed. 'I did. I said he had to get a single bed for himself.'

Eve was horrified. 'Oh, you didn't? You don't mean it, do you?'

'I don't know, Mam. I don't want to have to go through all this again.'

'You do love him, Maggie?'

'Yes! Yes, I do love him, but . . .'

277

'Then you listen to me, girl. Don't push him out of your bed or sure as eggs are eggs he'll find another bed where he *is* welcome! He's young, Maggie, you can't expect him to stay chaste until you decide you're ready to have children. Marriage doesn't work like that! It's give and take, in *all* things!'

'Is . . . is that what happened . . . with you and . . .' Maggie hesitated.

'No! No, it most certainly was not. If it's any of your business at all, I never denied your da . . . anything!'

Maggie was contrite. 'Mam, I'm sorry! I shouldn't have said that.'

'No, you shouldn't,' Eve said wearily.

'But just what can I do? I feel I'm too young yet and I do want other things.'

'Don't put a nice house and money in the bank before your feelings for Billy or his for you, because you might even find that when eventually you have all those things and want babies, babies might not appear!'

Maggie nodded slowly. Her mother's words made sense. She didn't want to lose Billy to someone else. She did love him and she did want babies at some stage and she'd never even thought about the fact that she might not be able to have them. It was all very sobering.

'I haven't been much of a help or a comfort to you, have I? I've just brought you more worries,' she said sadly.

Eve put her arm around her. 'If you can't come to me with your troubles, Maggie, who can you go to? I'd sooner know about problems; at least then I can try to help.'

'You have. You really have.'

Eve got to her feet. 'Let's go down and have a cup of tea before I go and give Harry a hand.'

'You were supposed to be having a rest and Harry said I was to try to persuade you to have an afternoon off. You should, Mam. It really would do you good. Take your mind off everything – off all of us! Think of yourself for a change.'

'I might just do that.'

'Go this week, before the Bank Holiday. I'll come in and cover for you – both of you. I presume you will be going with Harry?'

'You presume right. I'd feel a fool going off on my own and I don't know anyone else.'

Harry was relieved and delighted that Eve had agreed and they decided to go on Wednesday afternoon, which was convenent for Maggie, it being half-day closing in the shop.

Eve hadn't wanted to go as far as the Wirral, nor had she wanted to go to New Brighton again, so they decided on a trip to Southport, which was easily accessible by train.

'I feel like going somewhere smart for a change and it will be very pleasant on the promenade. I hear they have a marine lake and lovely floral displays,' she'd said. 'And we can check out some of the pubs there. They're bound to have some good ideas for bringing in extra custom.'

Harry had been hoping for somewhere a bit quieter and was concerned the place would be too crowded. He'd heard that there was a fun fair but he intended to stay away from that. He cheered up when Maggie told him that Hilda had said there was a lovely park quite near the seafront, called Victoria Park, which was usually quite peaceful.

Eve again wore the suit she'd had for Maggie's wedding, but as it was a warm day she carried the jacket over her arm.

'I expect I'll look very dowdy compared to all those smart women and expensive shops,' she laughed as they changed trains at Seaforth Sands.

'I bet you won't. Lots of people go there for days out and even holidays and they can't all be wealthy.'

'If they go there for holidays they can't be short of a few bob! Wouldn't it be heaven to stay in an hotel and be waited on?'

'You might one day, Eve!'

'And pigs might fly!' she retorted, smiling.

When they reached Southport they left the station and walked across Chapel Street, down London Street and into Lord Street, the town's main thoroughfare with its elegant Edwardian buildings. Harry decided that they would make for Victoria Park as soon as possible. Lord Street was very crowded. Eve was delighted with the shops in the Wayfarers Arcade, although she could only afford to look at the goods displayed. Then they crossed the road and sat and listened to the brass band playing on the wrought-iron bandstand near the town hall.

'Will we try and find this park? It might be nice and cool,' Harry suggested, not wanting to waste precious time.

'I wouldn't mind a cup of tea first,' Eve said, looking longingly at the little open-air café almost beside them. She sighed. 'I suppose we really should go and check out some pubs but it's so hot and that'd make this a sort of "busman's holiday" when it's supposed to be our day off.'

'Right, tea and scones first, then the park,' Harry agreed.

It wasn't too far and on the way they admired the huge houses with their vast gardens and speculated just how much money you would have to have to own one of them. Eventually they arrived at Rotten Row and the park entrance. Through the open wrought-iron gates they could see vast expanses of lawn and flower beds, which were a riot of colour, and beyond them shady trees and shrubberies.

'It looks lovely,' Eve remarked.

'Let's head for those trees, it will be cooler,' Harry suggested.

Eve nodded. Her feet were getting hot and tired, although she noticed with a little apprehension that there were fewer people in that direction.

When they had settled themselves on a bench under a huge spreading oak bordered by a screen of large shrubs, Harry took out his handkerchief and mopped his forehead.

'Are you glad you came, Eve?'

'Of course. It really does do me good to get away from the pub.'

'Well, Maggie is fine and Sarah seems happy enough over there, it's only Lily you have to worry about now.'

'I know. I do wish she'd write! A postcard would do, just to say she's all right.'

'You know Lily!'

'Oh, I do! But she must know I'm worried to death.'

'You have to stop fretting about them some time, Eve. They're all growing up – even Lily.'

Eve sighed. 'I don't suppose I will until I see both Sarah and Lily married and settled.'

'Sarah might surprise you in that respect.'

'I hope she does.'

'And what about us, Eve?' Harry asked quietly. 'Is there going to be an "us"?'

Eve picked at the edge of her jacket, which she had laid across her knee. 'I . . . I've been thinking about that, I really have, despite everything else and . . .'

He looked hopefully at her. 'And what?'

'I . . . I do care for you – a lot.'

Harry took her hand. 'I love you, Eve!'

'I know and I think . . . I think I love you, Harry, but it doesn't change things.'

'It does!'

'No! I'm still a married woman. I can't commit myself.'

'You can't help how you feel and it's not your fault!'

'I know all that, but what I'm saying is, I can't . . . well, I can't . . .'

'You mean you'll never let me make love to you.'

Eve nodded. Oh, she wanted him to. There had been nights lately when she'd lain alone in bed and wondered what it would be like to have him lying beside her, holding her, caressing her, loving her, and she had wanted him – desperately. But in the cold light of day she knew it could never be. She was still tied by her vows to another man.

'Eve, I won't say I don't want to because I do, more than

anything else in the world, but we don't have to. It will be enough to just hold you and kiss you and know you love me.'

'Oh, Harry, will it? You're young and healthy and virile and I . . . well, I've experienced being made love to and I wonder if just holding and kissing and even fondling will be enough for me? Is it fair on either of us? Is it just going to lead to disappointment, resentment, arguments and worse?'

'Don't say that . . . please,' he begged. 'And you never know what the future holds, he . . . he might . . .'

'Don't say *that*, Harry! I wouldn't wish harm on him, it would bring neither of us any luck!'

'I'm not wishing harm on him but if . . .'

'Then things would be different but until then . . .'

'Until then don't deny us both some happiness, Eve?'

She looked into his eyes and gently touched his cheek. It was all Harry needed. He took her in his arms and kissed her and she clung to his lips, wishing with all her heart that things were different and that the afternoon would never end.

When finally they left the park Harry knew just how hard it would be for him to keep his promise. For her part, Eve was fearful of the future and of what her girls would think, for it was something that couldn't be kept from them. Yet with Sarah away and Lily missing, it was only Maggie she had to worry about immediately.

Lily was a little disappointed to be leaving Dublin. She'd quite enjoyed the work in the Paragon Theatre. It was very small and not one of the well-known theatres and she had really been nothing more than a general dogsbody, doing every job imaginable, but it had been a hundred times better than working at Rahan Lodge even though the wages had been terrible.

'Ah, won't ye get work in a better theatre, now ye've some experience at least? That place is a kip: ye deserve better, Lily!' had been Myles's reply to her complaints. She had to agree that he was right but she still wasn't totally clear on why they had to leave Dublin. He'd said there were lads at the pub where he worked who had taken a 'down on him' and they weren't lads to be crossed, not if you wanted to walk upright on your two legs for the rest of your life.

'What did you do to upset them? Who are they? Can't you go to the Guards?' she'd demanded fearfully.

He'd laughed at her naivety. 'Lily, ye don't go to the Guards about these lads! Ye'd end up in the Liffey! Now, don't be worrying and upsetting yourself. Sure, I'm the first to admit I've a bit of a temper and sometimes it gets me into trouble, but it's time we moved on anyway, we can both do better.'

'Where are we going?' she'd asked.

'Belfast. There's plenty of work up there and good money too. We'll earn more than we do now.'

She sighed as she leaned back in her seat, waiting for the train to pull out of the station. Her small suitcase was stowed on the rack above her head and Myles was lighting a cigarette. She slipped her hand into the crook of his arm. She still loved him. In fact she loved him even more now. A slight flush crept into her cheeks. Mam would kill her if she knew that they shared the same bed. Sometimes it did worry her, but she trusted him and she loved him and it felt *right* even if most people would say it wasn't right at all. It hadn't seemed to matter in the neighbourhood where they'd had their one room. A lot of girls weren't married to the men they lived with. She wondered, would it be different in Belfast? She smiled up at him. Maybe she would get work in a bigger, grander theatre. She *did* have experience now.

Chapter Twenty-One

To Eve's GREAT RELIEF a postcard had arrived from Lily in the middle of August. It was of a rural scene but the postmark was Belfast.

'How the hell did she get up there? That's in the north. No wonder Sarah's had no luck with her enquiries,' Harry had exclaimed. 'What does she say?'

' "Don't worry I'm fine and doing well. Myles is taking care of me and we're both working and I might have a job in a theatre," ' Eve had read aloud. 'Don't worry! She must know how worried I've been – how worried we've all been. Oh, the thoughtless little madam!'

'Nothing about where she's living or how? Is it with this Myles, do you think?'

'I hope not! At least, not in the way you mean. She doesn't mention anything like that. Not even what she's doing for a job now.'

'If she's not given an address she obviously doesn't want you to land on the doorstep and drag her home,' Harry surmised.

'Obviously not.'

'Then I suppose we'll have to be satisfied with just knowing she's all right, she's got work and has some kind of a roof over her head.'

'And hasn't got herself into trouble.'

Harry refrained from saying that there was plenty of time for that, especially if she was living with this lad. Still, if that did happen, if he was halfway decent he'd marry Lily. Privately he thought the lad wouldn't be getting much of a bargain. Lily would always be trouble with a capital T. He doubted she'd ever settle down. Eve was relieved to know that Lily was all right but she was far from happy about the situation. If Lily thought she was in love with this lad then she was certain it would only be a matter of time before the inevitable happened and Lily lost her virginity – and then what? Oh, it really didn't bear thinking about! She had tried desperately hard to bring her girls up with decent morals; with Maggie safely married and Sarah so sensible, she had felt she had succeeded. Would Lily be the one to let her down? Would Lily be the one to bring shame on her, on them all? All she could do was pray she wouldn't.

Harry and Eve had slipped into an easy relationship but they both made sure that in public and in front of Maggie it wasn't obvious that they were all but lovers. There were times when they both became frustrated with the situation and there had been rows, but nothing that had led to serious trouble between them. Harry still boarded with Ma Flanagan so their time alone was fairly limited, and thus far Maggie hadn't hit the roof, although Eve wondered just how much her daughter really knew or even suspected about the time she and Harry spent together, for they often went out – when they could get some obliging soul to keep his eye on the bar.

Sometimes Eve worried about Maggie. She worked so hard and seemed so determined to be successful and there was no sign of her becoming pregnant, but Eve refused to pry into her private life. She just hoped that if things were going wrong Maggie would come to her for advice.

She wasn't worried about Sarah. As the summer slipped into autumn and finally winter all the letters from Sarah were cheerful and confident. She had settled very well at the Lodge; Mrs Kavanagh was very pleased with her work and she got on well with the woman. She also got on well with Madam and the two young ladies, which was no small thing, so Mrs Kavanagh often said. She loved the life in the country. It was so peaceful. She loved the changing seasons, the traditions and customs and people, and she saw quite a lot of Michael Nolan. Eve was not to worry on that score. It was all proper and above board. Sarah would never do anything to cause scandal or jeopardise her position.

Aoife had written that if Sarah could get the fairly well-off Mr Nolan up the aisle it would be nothing short of a minor miracle, she having no dowry. This had amused Eve until Sarah had explained that the custom was still very much alive in rural Ireland, even in this day and age.

'I'd be more than happy if she did marry him, that's if she truly loves him and he's good to her,' she confided to Harry.

'I just hope she doesn't get hurt, Eve, if he takes the custom very seriously. She's no money or land.'

'Or the chance of any either! We'll just have to wait and see, I suppose,' she answered, hoping Harry was wrong.

There had been another letter from Lily, again with no address, and this time from Londonderry. Harry had looked it up in an atlas in the public library. 'It looks to be a town much smaller than Belfast,' he'd announced.

'She does move around! She doesn't say what happened in Belfast but she appears to be doing all right. She's back at the sewing again. She says work is not that easy to find. Sometimes Myles has work and sometimes he doesn't.'

'It's not that easy to find here either, but at least she's not complaining,' Harry had commented.

'If I had an address I could send her a bit of money from time to time. And it will be Christmas next month, where am I supposed to send her card and her present?'

'I know, Eve. But if she wanted you to know she'd tell you.'

Eve nodded sadly. She didn't understand Lily, she really didn't. And she still worried about her. She couldn't help it.

By the end of August Eddie had reluctantly decided that he would have to find a job. They were broke and Doreen had said she had no intention of looking for work yet. He had also decided that Doreen was extravagant. He still idolised her, of course, but she did seem to get through the money.

He hadn't found it difficult to find work in a pub but of course it meant that he had to work almost every evening and lunchtimes too, which hadn't pleased Doreen.

'You can't expect me to sit in every night staring at the four walls!' she'd exclaimed. 'I didn't come here to do that! I'm young, I like going out, and I like company! It's not *fair* to ask me, Eddie!'

Of course he'd agreed, he could see her point, but it hadn't made him very happy. And as the weeks turned into months and she spent hardly any time drinking in the pub where he worked, as she had promised to do so they could at least have some time together, he began to get worried and afraid that she was seeing someone else. The friends she had occasionally brought into the Fox and Goose were all of her age group, and he did not like them very much. When he'd remonstrated with her over them she'd laughed and called him 'a jealous old fool', and that had really upset him. He needed no reminding that he was forty-one.

She hadn't been in tonight although she'd promised faithfully she would. She had said she was going to the cinema with 'the gang', as she called them, carefully avoiding his questions as to exactly who would be going and to which cinema. Eventually, after an argument, she'd said it was the Gaiety just up the road and that she was going with Joan and Freda and Millie. There was a musical on that was supposed to be good and the 'lads' had decided they'd sooner go for a pint but would meet them afterwards.

At half past ten Eddie made a decision. 'Fred, do you think I could go off a bit early tonight? I'll make up the time tomorrow. There's something I've got to do. It's really important or I wouldn't ask and it's a bit quiet.'

Eddie was a good worker and he was trustworthy, so the

licensee nodded. 'Right. Get off with you, Eddie, but don't make a habit of it.'

'Thanks, Fred, I won't!' Eddie shrugged on his jacket and reached for his hat.

It was cold and windy and he shivered as he walked down the road. His overcoat was so shabby that Doreen had said it was fit only for the rag-and-bone man, but there wasn't the money for a new one. He wished now he'd worn it. He'd only been going to work, after all. He bent his head against the chilly blasts and walked on until he came to the main road at the furthest end of which was the cinema. He was thankful to see that it hadn't let out yet, so he sheltered from the weather in a shop doorway.

He didn't like spying on her but he hadn't really believed her. He wanted to believe her, he did! But he had to know. He simply had to know if she was seeing someone else. He hunched his shoulders and dug his hands deep into the pockets of his jacket. It was freezing cold. He began to shiver, thinking that, whatever happened, he would be glad to get home. There was still a drop of whiskey left in the bottle. It would warm him up.

Eventually to his relief people started to leave the cinema and he noticed that they were indeed mainly women and girls, though there were a few fellers too. He stepped out on to the pavement to get a better view and caught sight of Joan and Freda, both of whom he knew well, and searched for Doreen and the other girl, Millie, whom he'd seen once or twice. There appeared to be no sign of either of them.

'Eddie! Eddie, what are you doing here? Skiving off work then?' Joan had seen him and was waving and calling.

Eddie crossed the road. 'Got a bit of time off, so I thought I'd come and meet Doreen.'

'Oh.' Joan shot a warning glance at Freda.

'Er, she decided at the last minute she really didn't want to sit in a stuffy, smoky fleapit all night. Said she had a bit of a headache, so she'd go for a drink instead,' Freda lied.

'It's just as stuffy and smoky in a pub!' Eddie said suspiciously.

'Not all of them,' Joan added.

'Which one? Has she gone with Millie?' Eddie demanded.

'Yes! But she didn't say which pub,' Freda answered quickly. Too quickly.

Eddie didn't believe her. He didn't trust either of them but he couldn't call them liars to their faces. His suspicions had deepened but there was nothing he could do.

'Well, we'll be off, Eddie. It's freezing standing here. We're going for some chips.'

Eddie nodded and turned away. What could he do? He couldn't search every pub for her and she might not have gone to a pub at all. She could have gone anywhere. A dance, a club, even another cinema. There were hundreds and hundreds of them in London. Dejectedly he realised there was nothing he could do except go home and wait for her to come in.

He felt really miserable as he walked down the cold, dark streets. He was jealous and it was a horrible feeling. And he was afraid. Afraid he would lose her. That she'd pack her bags and leave him for someone else. It didn't bear thinking about. His life would be in complete ruins. There would be nothing left for him to live for, he thought morosely.

As he reached the junction of Westmoreland Street and the main road he looked across and stopped dead. Getting off the bus on the corner was Doreen with Jack Whiteside whom he particularly disliked. A real Cockney wide boy that one, all flash suits and hair oil. So, she *had* lied! She'd been out with him! And he didn't like the way she was gazing at the feller. Well, he was going to have it out with her – with them both!

Doreen had been enjoying herself and was a little tipsy. It was great to go out with someone young and handsome. Eddie was getting to be a real pain in the neck: always fussing about something, like an old woman.

' 'Ere, Dor, isn't that your old man?' Jack said, catching sight of Eddie.

Doreen frowned. 'Oh, hell!'

'I thought you said he was working?'

'He was! Oh, now there'll be a row. He'll make a holy show of me!'

'He bloody well won't,' Jack said grimly.

Doreen grinned. 'Let's make a run for it!' she urged.

Jack laughed. 'OK. He'll be out of breath by the time he reaches the next corner!' He grabbed her hand and they turned and ran up the road.

Eddie let out a yell of rage and dashed forward. So, they were running away from him, were they? He'd seen them both smirking. They didn't think he could catch them. Well, they weren't making a fool out of *him*.

As Doreen and Jack reached the corner they stopped and turned.

'I told you we'd outrun him, Dor!' Jack laughed.

Doreen was peering down the road. 'What's all the commotion going on down there? Why are people running and shouting?'

' 'Ere, mate! What's up?' Jack yelled at a passer-by.

'Some feller ran out in front of a bus – just come hurtlin' off the pavement. Poor bloody bus driver couldn't do a thing about it!' the man replied.

'Is he hurt?' Doreen asked, her stomach turning over.

' 'E's more than that, girl, 'e's brown bread – dead!'

'Oh, God! Eddie!' Doreen cried, the colour draining from her cheeks.

Eve didn't cry. She felt cold and numb but she didn't cry. She'd cried all her tears for Eddie in the days after he'd left her.

It had been Mr Travis who'd come with the news to the saloon bar of the pub.

'Is there somewhere we can 'ave a private word, Mrs Dobson?' he'd said, looking furtive.

'Why?' Harry had demanded, recognising him instantly.

'It's about 'er 'usband and it's not . . . er . . . good, I'm afraid.'

'Come into the snug. There's no one in there,' Eve had said, her heart sinking. She had hoped he wasn't here to tell her that Eddie was coming home or that Doreen was pregnant. 'What's the matter with him?'

'I got a message from a mate I know what 'as a telephone. That our Doreen was goin' ter ring me. She was dead upset about somethin',' he said. 'Well, I told 'im, she's never bothered 'er 'ead about 'er mam an' me up 'til now—'

'What's wrong with Eddie?' Eve interrupted.

'Well, ter cut a long story short, luv, 'e's 'ad an accident, an' I 'ate ter be the one ter tell yer, but 'e's . . . 'e's dead. Run out in the road and in front of a bus.'

Eve said nothing. She just sat staring down at her hands.

Mr Travis hadn't expected this. He'd expected tears, hysterics even, not this utter silence. It unnerved him. He got to his feet. 'Well, I'm sorry fer yer loss, luv. I'll be off now. I told the missus I wouldn't be long.'

When Eve didn't reply he shrugged and left.

Harry saw him leave and went quickly into the snug. 'What is it?'

Eve looked up at him. She felt quite calm. 'Eddie's dead. Apparently he . . . he was in an accident with a bus. That's all he said. *She* contacted him.'

Harry sat down beside her and put his arm around her. 'Are you all right?'

Eve nodded. 'Yes. I . . . I feel sort of numb. He was my husband for all those years and all I feel is numb. Not sad, not sorry, just cold.'

'It's the shock, Eve. Look, go into the kitchen and put the kettle on. I'll close up and then come through. I won't be long. There's only Jim Stokes and Uncle Uk in the bar and I'll tell them what's happened. They'll understand about me closing up early.' He gently pulled Eve to her feet and guided her to the kitchen door and opened it. Then he went back into the bar.

'A right bloody waste of a life!' Jim Stokes said sadly after Harry had imparted the news.

'If he'd stayed here with Eve and his girls instead of chasing off with that little tart he'd be alive today!' Uncle Uk added.

Harry nodded. If Eddie Dobson had stayed he would never have had the opportunity to love Eve himself and now the absent Eddie no longer stood between them.

Eve had made the tea and was sitting at the table with a mug clasped between her hands when Harry came into the room.

'Have you put plenty of sugar in it?'

'I can't drink tea that's too sweet,' she answered vaguely.

'It's good for shock, Eve.' Harry sat down and took her hands. 'I should say I'm sorry but . . . but I'd be a hypocrite if I did.'

She managed a smile. 'I *am* sorry. No one should have his or her life cut short and his was, but I'm not heart-broken. Is that wrong of me?'

'No, Eve! He broke your heart when he walked out on you. When he chose *her* instead of you.'

Eve nodded. 'I cried for him then.'

'You'll have to tell the girls. How do you think they'll take it?'

'I don't know. It was one thing for him to leave them; it's another for them to accept that he's dead. You know the way Lily carried on.'

297

'She's grown up a bit since then, and she has a life of her own now.'

'I know.'

'I don't suppose he said anything about . . . arrangements?'

Eve looked at him in dawning horror 'Oh, God! What am I supposed to do about that?'

'Do you think *she*'ll take care of everything?'

'I don't know. I . . . I . . . suppose she should but I don't think she will.' She covered her face with her hands. What should she do? If Doreen did nothing then he would be buried in a pauper's grave, in some cemetery in London with not a single soul to mourn him. She couldn't do that! She couldn't do that to her girls. He had been their father when all was said and done. 'I suppose it will be left to me to have him brought back and see him buried decently. It's all I can do – for the girls' sake, if nothing else.'

Harry nodded. 'I suppose you're right, but let me help? You can't do it all on your own and I'm not letting you have anything to do with *her*! If she's got to be contacted, then I'll do it.'

Eve reached for his hand. 'Oh, Harry! What would I do without you?'

Chapter Twenty-Two

S ARAH PATTED THE SHEET she had been hemming with satisfaction. Her sewing had improved. She'd never have Lily's expertise, she'd never really be able to make something as complicated as a wedding dress, but now she could at least do alterations and make herself simple garments. The winter dusk was falling rapidly; she got up and switched on the light and went to the window of the small linen room, which overlooked the back of the house. The trees and hedges in the distance were black and bare against a duck-egg-blue sky, tinged with the last pinkish rays of a frosty sunset. She could smell the aromatic turf smoke from the fire. She was as happy as she'd ever been in her life. She loved living here. She enjoyed her job, she got on very well with Mrs Kavanagh and the other servants – and then there was Michael.

At first when he'd taken her on an outing he had been pleasant and considerate and she'd enjoyed his company as an amusing friend, but gradually they had become closer.

Finally the evening had come when he took her in his arms and kissed her and she had known that she loved him. The only thing that spoiled her complete contentment was the fact that she didn't know exactly where she stood with him. She wanted to get married, have a house of her own and children, but so far he'd not mentioned anything along those lines. Oh, she told herself he was a cautious man, set in his ways even. That it was early days yet. She'd heard of couples who had been engaged for years and years but she sincerely hoped that a lengthy engagement wasn't what he planned. If he was actually planning anything. Aoife often said he was a confirmed bachelor and warned her not to get her hopes up. Then there was the matter of the dowry. She'd plucked up courage once to ask him just how important a dowry was in this day and age.

'Ah, now, Sarah, there's many who consider it very important – imperative – even in this modern day. It helps to increase a man's land and wealth and the standard of living for the whole family.'

'I see. And . . . and are you one who considers it imperative?'

'I wouldn't say it was imperative to me, but a nice sum or a parcel of land is always very welcome,' had been his answer.

She'd said nothing further, not wishing to remind him that she had neither.

She sighed and drew the curtains across the window. She'd go along to the kitchen and help Cook; she wouldn't mind a cup of tea if there was one going.

Cook and young Bernie, the kitchen maid, were up to

their elbows in flour and Mrs Kavanagh and Maureen, the parlourmaid, were engaged in making a list of cleaning supplies that would be needed from town for the complete overhaul of the house in preparation for the Christmas season.

'Sarah, there's a letter for you. The post was extremely late today. I often think that if Paddy Conway spent less time chatting he'd get his deliveries done far quicker.' Eliza Kavanagh didn't approve of what she considered idle gossiping, although in such rural areas the postman's round not only allowed him to keep abreast of everything that was going on in the parish, it also allowed him to keep a watchful eye on the elderly and the sick and needy.

Sarah smiled at her. 'I'm always happy to get a letter from home no matter what time of the day it arrives. There wouldn't be a cup of tea by any chance?'

'Isn't there always one in the pot at this time of day! Help yourself, Sarah,' Cook instructed, looking pointedly at the cups on the table beside the housekeeper and the parlourmaid.

Sarah poured herself a cup and then sat down beside the range and opened her letter. She didn't cry out. She just dropped her head and stared into the depths of the blazing turf fire. Her da was dead! Killed in a road accident, so Mam said. She was stunned. Oh, she had got used to him not being there. Some of her anger at his desertion had diminished but the hurt had never gone away and now . . . now he'd gone for ever. She realised that at the back of her mind there had always been the belief that one day she would see him again, although just how she would feel and behave she hadn't envisaged. And how did Mam feel? She'd written that she was very sorry his life had been cut short and that she assumed it had been happy but she wasn't devastated. She was going to have him buried in Liverpool, Harry was attending to it, as apparently Doreen Travis had washed her hands of the whole thing and gone off with a new boyfriend.

'Sarah, is anything wrong? You've gone very quiet and pale?' Eliza Kavanagh's voice broke into her thoughts.

'It's Father. I . . . I'm afraid he's . . . dead,' she said sadly.

'Oh, the Lord have mercy on his soul!' Cook cried, crossing herself, and Bernie and Maureen followed suit.

'I'm so sorry, Sarah. When? Had he been ill? He can't have been very old.' Eliza's tone was sympathetic.

'It was a road accident. A bus, apparently. He . . . he lived in London, I think you knew that.'

'Aren't these huge cities desperate places to live? Sure, you take your life in your hands whenever you cross the road!' Cook said knowingly. She had spent time in both Dublin and London in her younger days.

'You did mention it once or twice, Sarah.'

'Is he to be buried in London?' Cook asked.

'No, Mam's having him brought to Liverpool.'

'So, you'll be wanting time to go over?'

Sarah hadn't thought that far ahead. 'I . . . I suppose so. If it's not going to be too inconvenient.'

Cook and Eliza Kavanagh exchanged glances. After next week things would become very busy, not to say hectic, but

A Mother's Love

death and funerals were taken very seriously in this country and it would be unheard of if Eddie Dobson's eldest daughter were not to go home for his funeral.

'Not at all. I'm sure Madam will give you three or four days' leave to go home. Of course it would be very helpful if you could be back by Sunday week at the latest.' Eliza was businesslike. 'Do you wish me to see her?'

'Oh, please, if you don't mind!' Sarah was grateful. 'And if I may get word to Mr Nolan? He is expecting to take me into town tomorrow evening, there's a recital in the ballroom of the courthouse he thinks we would enjoy.'

'Does he have a telephone?' Eliza asked.

'Yes, he does.'

'Then I'll ask Madam if you might telephone him. I don't think she will object, this once.'

Sarah was still in a daze when Olivia Ormonde herself showed her how to use the telephone, after having first engaged the services of the operator.

'Just speak in your normal tone of voice, Sarah, there is no need to shout into the instrument as many people do. And just replace the receiver on the cradle when you've finished,' she instructed kindly, handing the mouthpiece over.

'Michael, it's Sarah. I'm afraid I won't be able to see you tomorrow, I . . . I've had some bad news.'

'What kind of bad news, Sarah?'

His voice sounded somehow different, she thought. A little tinny.

'My da has died, in London.' There was silence and she

303

panicked a little. 'Michael! Michael, are you still there? Can you hear me?'

'I can, Sarah. Look, I'll come over tonight. Sure, they can't complain at a time like this and I expect you'll be going over to England for the funeral? They *are* going to let you go?'

'Oh, yes! But I don't know when. I only got the letter half an hour ago.'

'Then tell Herself I'll come to the back door at about half past eight and I won't keep you up all night!'

The phone went dead and after a couple of tentative hellos Sarah replaced the receiver and went back to the kitchen.

Four pairs of eyes turned expectantly towards her.

'If you don't mind, ma'am, he said he would come over tonight, about half past eight.'

Eliza Kavanagh nodded. He was a respected man and not without means. She didn't want to lose Sarah but if the chance arose the girl would be foolish not to accept him.

Sarah had been kept busy with her duties and with making arrangements so she had only time to tidy her hair and change her dress before young Bernie ushered him into the kitchen.

'Mr Nolan to see Sarah, ma'am,' she announced.

'Good evening to you, ma'am,' he greeted the house-keeper affably.

'Bernadette, go and inform Sarah that Mr Nolan is here and will be waiting for her in my sitting room. You can have a little privacy there and Sarah can inform you of the arrangements.'

His eyebrows rose. The woman was being very considerate.

Young Bernie exchanged a startled glance with Maureen but on intercepting a warning look from Cook, hastily left without making a comment. Sarah was certainly in favour. All Herself ever did was give out to her about 'not making herself cheap or losing the run of herself with the lads'.

Sarah found him standing in front of the fire. 'She must like you. This is most unusual.'

'Begod, don't they have some strange ways of going on! You'd think we were living in the last century! I'm sorry to hear about your da, Sarah.'

She sat down in the small armchair. 'It's still a shock, even though . . . well, you know all about him.'

He took her hands. 'I do so and it still can't be easy for you. How is your mam taking it?'

'She sounds all right. She's being practical, as usual.'

'When are you going?'

'Tomorrow night. On the night ferry from Dublin. I'll get the train up in the afternoon.'

'I'll come up with you, see you off. Matty Cleary is quite capable of managing for a day.'

'You don't have to, Michael.'

'I want to, Sarah. When will you be coming back? You *will* be coming back?' It was a question he'd been wondering about ever since her telephone call. Would she feel obliged to stay and support her mother? Would she find she had missed the bright lights of the city? Would she build a life

for herself over there in Liverpool as the weeks lengthened
into months and years?

'Do you want me to come back?'

'Sure, you know I do!'

'Really? Sometimes I wonder . . . exactly what you do
want.' She fell silent. Was she pushing him?

He drew her to her feet and took her in his arms. He
knew what she was getting at and if he did nothing,
said nothing, he might drive her into staying in Liverpool
and he didn't want that. She was so very special to him.
It was as if he had waited all his life just for her. When
he'd been younger there had been other girls but none of
them had made him feel as though he wanted to spend his
life with them. Sarah was so different. He'd felt it almost
from the minute he'd met her. She was *meant* for him and
he wasn't going to risk losing her because of his own
tardiness.

'Sarah, don't you know that I love you? I want you to
come back and we'll get engaged – if you'll have me! Oh, I
know it's a dreadful time to be asking you to marry me, but
I've no choice. I can't wait! I can't take the chance that you
won't come back!'

She felt tears sting her eyes and she clung to him. 'Oh, of
course I'll have you – I love you! I didn't think you wanted
me because I've no dowry!'

'Ah, to hell with the dowry! If it's a choice between a
dowry and you, I'll take you any day! So, you'll come back to
me and we'll go and choose a ring?'

'Oh, Michael, I will and we will and I know it's really not

the right thing to say what with Da and everything, but I'm so happy! So very happy!'

'Do you think Herself would mind if you came home with me for an hour?'

'I can ask her.' Sarah had been to his house on a couple of occasions but she felt that this would be very different. Previously she had just been merely a visitor, now she was going as his bride-to-be.

'No, I'll ask her. She's less likely to refuse me,' he said with determination.

Sarah smiled at him and nodded.

Mrs Kavanagh agreed, providing Sarah wasn't going to be very late back. If she thought it a strange time to be visiting, she said nothing. It did cross her mind that, despite her family tragedy, Sarah looked happy and excited.

The doors to the sheds and barns were all tightly closed and the house was enveloped in darkness, except for the light burning in the kitchen. It was a well-built stone house with thick walls; a small wooden porch painted green and white kept the worst of the winter weather off the front door. In summer the stonework on the front of the house was softened by the green leaves of the Boston ivy that covered it and in autumn those leaves turned to vibrant shades of red and orange and gold before they fell. It was such a pretty house, Sarah thought. Secure, homely and welcoming – and that's just what it would be: her home and her refuge. As Michael helped her down from the trap she breathed deeply of the clean, night air, which was sharp with frost and pungent with the unmistakable aroma of turf burning in the kitchen range. A plume of blueish smoke spiralled from the chimney towards the dark sky where tonight there seemed to be thousands of stars. It was so quiet, so tranquil; she loved it.

'Come on inside before you freeze,' he instructed, his arm around her waist.

'Oh, I'm not at all cold! It's such a beautiful night!'

'I'll put down some more turf. Sit yourself down while I see to the pony.' Effortlessly he emptied half a basket of turf into the range.

Sarah smiled at him as she took off her coat and hat. 'I'll put on the kettle, there'll be tea ready by the time you get back.'

She continued to smile to herself as she went about the everyday task. Soon this would be her kitchen. It was a lovely room – the real heart of the home – with good, solid furniture, lovely delftware on the dresser, a serviceable rug in front of the fire. The brass ornaments shone and on the wall above the range the red glow from the little lamp fell softly on the features of Christ as the Sacred Heart, a traditional feature of every Irish Catholic home.

It was a substantial home too. Oh, a lot of people thought he was very wealthy indeed but he wasn't. He'd explained to her that he had nearly two hundred acres, some set to barley and maize, the rest to grazing and silage. He was building up his dairy herd and that took time. Yes, he did employ six men to do the heavy work but wages weren't high and yes, he did have a bit of money put by but agriculture was always a precarious occupation, dependent as it was on the elements and so many other influences beyond his control. There were indeed many farmers who had less land and fewer beasts, so he was considered by many to be well off, but it was nothing on the scale of Rahan Lodge. Yet that wasn't what she wanted: high society and servants. She was more than content to be the wife of a country farmer.

'There, that's him settled until I'm ready to take you back. There's a fierce frost settling out there!' He stretched his hands out to the fire.

She handed him his tea. 'Drink this, it will warm you. I couldn't find a biscuit or a bun to go with it, I'm afraid.'

'There's never many of either in this house, Sarah,' he said apologetically.

She laid her hand on his arm. 'There will be plenty of both, Michael, when I come back.'

'Ah, this house will be all the better for a woman's touch, something it hasn't had for many a year. Although Biddy Brady does her best to keep it clean and halfway decent.'

'It's a grand house and it will be a lovely home.'

He set down his cup and put his arms around her. 'It will be your home, Sarah.'

'It will be *our* home, Michael! I'm so lucky! So very, very lucky!'

'You'll really enjoy living here? You won't feel isolated? Biddy will still come in if you want her to.'

'No, I won't want that and I love the peace and quiet. I will love looking out of my windows to the fields and woods and the Slieve Bloom Mountains. I'll love cleaning and polishing and cooking and seeing to the hens and maybe

Lyn Andrews

even trying my hand at making butter and cheese, but most of all I'll love being your wife!'

'Oh, Sarah! Whatever made you think I'd not marry you without a dowry? You mean more to me than any land or money. You're my real treasure!'

She put her arms around him. How could she ever have thought herself even a little bit in love with Harry Dempsey, even though that silly girlish crush was so long ago? Now she knew what real love was and it was far more exciting and fulfilling.

Lily kicked disconsolately at the small pebbles on the laneway and pulled her coat closer to her body. The cold wind on which there was a promise of sleet whipped tendrils of her hair against her cheeks. She was cold, hungry, tired and utterly fed up, walking down the dark, narrow streets of the Creggan from the shirt factory where she worked. She hadn't wanted to come to Londonderry – or Derry as most of the people she knew called it – in the first place, but as usual Myles had persuaded her. She hated working in the factory. It was boring and tiring but it was all the work she could get and they needed the money. They always seemed to need money; there was never enough of it although lately Myles seemed to have plenty for drink.

Oh, this wasn't the life she'd envisaged when she'd left Rahan Lodge. He'd promised they would see places, do exciting things. Get on in the world. They were in love and the world was a bright, sunny place full of promise. And they had enjoyed themselves in Dublin. They'd had a bit of money and Myles had got a job in a pub and she'd even got a job in a small theatre. She was only a general dogsbody but she hadn't minded. But then there had been some trouble at the pub – she'd never got to the bottom of it – and they'd moved north, to Belfast. She'd been lucky enough again to find work in a theatre but it hadn't even been as big a place as the one in Dublin and it had been there that her dreams had started to crumble. As a career, being on the stage didn't seem all it was cracked up to be. Often there was no work and when there was the pay was usually pitifully small and late in being handed over. Conditions were sometimes grim: cold, damp and dirty theatres; faded, grubby costumes that were seldom laundered; people who were self-centred, unreliable and frequently took to drowning their sorrows in a bottle. It wasn't glamorous at all.

Again there had been some trouble where Myles worked and they'd ended up here. The only work she could get was machining the backs of shirts to the fronts before they were passed along to someone else who put in the sleeves, then yet another machinist attached cuffs and collar bands. Tears of self-pity stung her eyes. Was this how they were going to spend the rest of their lives? Always moving on, always living in one cramped, dingy room, never enough money, slaving in dingy pubs or dismal, soul-destroying factories for a pittance? Well, she had had enough of it and when she got home she was going to tell him so – and she was going to be impervious to that charm of his. Did she still love him? If she was really truthful the answer was that she just didn't know. But if he loved her, as he said he did, then he could just try and find a decent job for himself and a decent home for them. He could make some plans for the future. A proper future. He could just think about her for a change and spend less time drinking with his mates.

The room was cold for there was little in the way of a fire, which depressed her further. He was shrugging on his jacket and that didn't please her one bit. He was going out already.

'Where are you going? It's not even half past six yet and I thought you said you had no money?' she snapped, kicking the spluttering coals to try to liven them up.

'I haven't! Aren't I going to work and isn't it a nice mood ye're in – again, Lily!'

'Haven't I a right to be in a mood? I'm tired and cold and hungry and look at the state of this place! It's a pigsty!'

'Am I supposed to be a housewife as well as a breadwinner now? There's no pleasing you!'

Lily lost her temper entirely. 'I'm fed up with *everything*, Myles! This isn't what you promised me! This isn't how you said we'd live!'

'Ah, for Jaysus' sake, grow up! Life is never how ye expect it to be. We've just had a run of bad luck, that's all.'

'Bad luck! You seem to pick fights and get on the wrong side of half the men in the entire country, north and south! How long will it be before we have to move on again? Well, I'm sick of it and I'm sick of you!'

'Great! And do ye know something, Lily? I'm bloody sick of ye and your big ideas! All ye ever wanted to do was work in a theatre, ye told me and when ye do it's not what ye wanted at all. Just what do ye want, Lily?'

'I . . . I . . . Oh, something better than this!'

'Ye don't even know what ye want!' he mocked.

'I know this much: I don't want you, Myles Carroll! I . . . I'm going home! I'm going back to Liverpool!'

He threw some coins on the floor at her feet. 'Good! Here's the fare! Go back where ye belong, Lily! Go back to the mammy!'

He nearly took the door off its hinges as he slammed out and Lily sank down on the stool by the fire and began to cry. She hadn't intended to say that. She hadn't intended to go home but what was there here for her now? She couldn't, *wouldn't* go back to Rahan Lodge. She hadn't been happy there and she couldn't face the humiliation. She'd go back to Mam and Sarah and Maggie. Things were bound to have improved, she'd get work and it wouldn't be in a factory. She'd have a decent home again, clean, comfortable, warm and with good food. She knew Mam wouldn't be too hard on her. She dashed away the tears on her cheeks with the back of her hand. She'd go tonight, before she changed her mind and before he got home. She had no idea how she was going to get to Belfast. Was there a train? Well, she could ask, and if there wasn't, she'd wait in the station all night and get the first train in the morning. She bent and picked up the coins, then stood up. She didn't have much to pack and she'd take whatever food there was to keep her going. Let him find his own supper!

Chapter Twenty-Three

S ARAH ARRIVED HOME TIRED and still feeling queasy. It had been a bad crossing and she had been sick: so sick that she felt she was going to die. Never had she been so glad to feel solid ground beneath her feet as when she'd made her way down the gangway on to the cobbles of the Landing Stage and trudged, head bent against the icy wind, towards the line of waiting trams and buses.

Eve had been up early and a good fire was roaring in the kitchen range and the kettle was boiling.

'Oh, Mam! It's lovely and warm in here! It's freezing out there!'

'Sarah, luv, sit down, you don't look well!' Eve was a little worried by Sarah's pasty cheeks and fussed around her eldest daughter.

'It's a long journey and the crossing was terrible. I was so ill! I just don't want to think about going back. I won't care how cold it is as long as there's no wind.'

Eve placed a mug of tea in her cold hands. 'Drink this

quickly now. After you've had a bit of toast, go and have a lie down. You'll feel much better then. I've heard that those crossings in winter can be really awful!'

Sarah felt better as she sipped the tea. 'Are you all right, Mam?'

'Yes. It was a shock but I'm over it now. Harry has been really great and Maggie's been a support too. She's coming round a bit later on. What about you, luv?'

'I'm very sad for him, Mam, and I suppose in my way I will miss him, but he'd gone – and so had I, to Ireland. It would have been different if he'd still been here with us.'

'If he had he would still be alive. Harry heard from Mr Travis that that little madam was playing fast and loose with him. Seeing someone else, running around with a bit of a wild gang, but I suppose it was only a matter of time before she got fed up with Eddie. He was working in a pub, just as a barman. Not even his own boss.'

'Poor Da! He was such a fool!' Sarah said sadly.

Eve nodded. 'He was, but we shouldn't speak ill of the dead.'

'Is everything arranged?' Sarah wanted to change the subject. She didn't want to think about her da being made a fool of by Doreen Travis.

'Yes. It's tomorrow. He's being taken to the Chapel of Rest after he arrives at Lime Street today. He's coming by train. They – the undertakers – will meet the train. I know it's usually the custom to have the deceased at home but . . . but I just couldn't, Sarah!'

'No one would expect it! Not in the circumstances.'

A Mother's Love

'The Mass is at ten o'clock and then I've said I'll have a few drinks here.'

'Does Lily know? Have you been able to contact her?'

'How? I've no address. The last letter was postmarked Londonderry but there was nothing at all to indicate exactly where she was. She might even have moved again.'

Sarah shook her head sadly, wondering how Lily would take it when she eventually found out. The way things stood Da would be long buried before she did.

'How long are you staying?' Eve asked.

'I promised to be back on Saturday next. There's so much to be done to prepare for Christmas and . . . and I've something to tell you, Mam!'

Eve looked curious.

'Michael and I, well, when I get back we're going for the engagement ring.'

A smile spread across Eve's face and she hugged Sarah tightly. 'Oh, I'm so happy for you! I really am! I mean, I've never met him but from what you've said and what Aoife's told me, he sounds very nice and not short of a bob or two either!'

'Oh, Mam! He *is* very nice and he has a nice house and he's comfortable but I love him. I was worried that I had nothing to bring to him but he said he doesn't care.'

'You might not have material things to bring with you, Sarah, but you have love and loyalty, thriftiness and diligence and lots more qualities that make a good wife. He should be thankful he's getting you.'

'We're both happy, Mam.'

317

'Then so am I! Now, get upstairs and have a sleep. I still have work to do; Harry will be here soon.' Eve had decided not to say anything to Sarah about herself and Harry until after the funeral was over.

Sarah did feel much better when she came downstairs later in the morning and found Eve and Maggie in the kitchen.

Maggie got up and hugged her sister. 'Mam's told me your news and I'm delighted for you, I really am.'

'Thanks. You look well, Maggie. A bit thinner but—'

'She works too hard,' Eve said worriedly.

'No harder than anyone else. So, when is the wedding going to be? Will you come back here or get married over there?'

'Oh, Maggie, I've not even got the engagement ring yet! I haven't thought that far ahead. I was hoping that when the funeral is over, Mam would come back with me to meet Michael and everyone.'

'Why don't you, Mam? It would do you good,' Maggie urged.

'I've a pub to run, in case you'd forgotten!'

'Harry can do that! Things are not particularly hectic, except on Saturdays, and I'm sure he can cope.'

Eve said nothing. Of course she would like to go to see everyone and meet her future son-in-law but . . .

'Well, Mam?' Sarah urged.

'Let's just wait and see. Let's just get the next few days over with.'

* * *

318

A Mother's Love

Coyne's the undertakers had taken care of everything and Eve announced in the bar and to her neighbours that if anyone wanted to go and pay their respects they were welcome to go to their Chapel of Rest.

'We'll go to the Mass and the burial, Eve, but I've no wish to see him, not after what he did to you and the girls,' Mary Stokes replied curtly, she being of an unforgiving nature (as Jim, her husband, remarked to Harry later on).

'What about you two?' Eve asked of Maggie and Sarah. 'You won't offend me if you want to go but you won't think me hard-hearted for not going myself?'

'Of course not, Mam. I don't think I want to go either. I'd sooner remember him the way he looked before he left us,' Maggie said thoughtfully.

'Was he . . . did he look different? You know, after the accident?' Sarah was hesitant.

'No. They said his injuries were internal. He wasn't disfigured,' Eve replied. 'You don't *have* to go, Sarah. People will understand.'

Sarah wasn't sure what to do. 'I'll think about it.'

It was quiet in the bar that afternoon. It was a dark, dismal late November day and few people were out and about. The regulars had all been in during the previous days to mutter their condolences to Eve. Some were embarrassed, not knowing quite what to say; others were outspoken in their opinions, but at least they had come in, Harry thought as he stacked bottles of stout under the bar counter. Eve was polishing glasses and looking thoughtful, wondering just how many people would come back after the funeral and how much food she should provide. Sarah and Maggie had gone to Blackler's to buy suitable mourning clothes.

'Eve, I know this is not the best time, but it's the first time we seem to have had any time alone and, well, this does change the situation for us,' Harry said tentatively.

Eve put down the glass cloth. 'I know, Harry, but . . . but just give me a bit of time, please? Let's get tomorrow over with. I haven't said anything to Sarah yet about . . . us.'

Harry nodded. She wasn't being unreasonable; it was just that he supposed he was being impatient. 'We'll all be better once tomorrow is over. Oh, a customer at last! Someone's braved the elements!'

They both looked expectantly towards the door, hoping for someone to lift the atmosphere a little.

'My God! Lily!' Eve cried as Lily pushed open the door, dumped her case on the floor and burst into tears.

Eve rushed to her. 'Thank God you've come home!'

'Oh, Mam! I'm so fed up! I'm so tired and cold and I was so sick! I've been travelling for hours and hours and I've no money and . . .' she sobbed into Eve's shoulder.

Harry looked sadly at the dishevelled, shabbily dressed girl who was clinging to her mother. Just how would she react to the news that her father was dead? She hadn't even noticed that the curtains were closed, that Eve was wearing a black dress and there was a black armband on the sleeve of his jacket. Lily was too wrapped up in herself.

'Come on into the kitchen. Stop crying now, you're home and we'll sort everything out,' Eve soothed and Lily let herself be led from the bar. Eve was so thankful to see her but wondered fearfully what kind of trouble the girl was in now.

Eve made a pot of tea and hastily put a meal together while Lily pulled herself together. She looked different. She was pale and tired but she looked older, dejected and decidedly bedraggled.

'Eat that up, you'll feel better, then you can tell me all about it.'

'Is our Sarah at work? How's Maggie? I'm sorry I didn't keep in touch,' Lily said through a mouthful of food.

'They're both fine. They'll be in soon. And I have something to tell you.'

'But I want to tell you everything before they come in and start going on at me!' Lily cried, wanting at least to enlist her mother's support and understanding before having to face her sisters and their comments.

Eve took her hand. 'Lily, I think I'd better get this over with first. It's not good news, luv, I'm afraid. Your da . . . your da's dead. He was killed in a road accident in London. He was brought back today. He's being buried tomorrow. Sarah and Maggie have gone into town for clothes for the funeral. I'm glad you've come home, luv, I had no way of letting you know. I'm so sorry, Lily, I really am.'

Tears welled up again in Lily's eyes. She hadn't expected *this*! 'Oh, Mam!'

Eve squeezed her hand. 'I know, it's been a terrible shock for us all.'

'Was it *her* fault? Oh, *she's* not coming, is she, Mam?'

'No! No, she's not. I don't know if she had any part in it

and I don't want to know. Harry just said she didn't know what to do but that she had no intention of coming back to Liverpool.'

Lily remained silent, her emotions in turmoil.

'I *am* sorry he's dead, Lily. He was still only a young man really, but we have to remember that he'd chosen that life. We . . . we'd all had to get on with our lives without him, and we *did*.'

Lily nodded miserably. She hadn't done much with hers.

'If you want to go and see him for the last time, Lily, he's at Coyne's Chapel of Rest. Maggie doesn't want to go but Sarah hasn't made up her mind yet.'

Lily shrugged. It hadn't sunk in yet. She didn't know what she wanted to do.

Eve smiled at her sadly. 'You're home, Lily, and I thank God for it, and I have to say you look almost as bad as our Sarah did when she got off the Dublin ferry this morning. I presume you came in on the one from Belfast?'

Lily was startled out of her reverie. 'What was she doing there?'

'I'll pour you another cup of tea and then I'll tell you,' Eve said wearily.

Maggie and Sarah were both astonished to see Lily sitting by the kitchen fire when they returned. Of Eve there was no sign.

'Holy Mother of God! When did you turn up?' Maggie exclaimed.

'Did you hear? Did someone manage to contact you?' Sarah asked.

Lily shook her head. She was still trying to take in everything Eve had told her about what had happened since she'd left Rahan Lodge. 'No. I . . . I got home a couple of hours ago.'

Maggie put down the bags and parcels. 'But you do know about Da?'

'Yes. Mam told me. She . . . she doesn't seem very upset.'

'Why should she be? She's sorry, we all are, but I'm not heart-broken either, Lily.'

'You always were hard on him, Maggie.'

'No more than he deserved!'

'Oh, let's not go down that road, please!' Sarah begged.

'Mam said I could go and see him, if I wanted to, and she said you hadn't made up your mind, Sarah.'

'I have. I'm going. I'm going to have a cup of tea and then . . . I'll go.'

Maggie said nothing.

'Can I come with you?' Lily asked.

'Of course. Are you all right, Lily? What happened? Where's Myles?'

'Mam will tell you; I don't really want to talk about it now, but it . . . it's all over. Nothing was as I expected it to be.'

Maggie glanced at Sarah, raising her eyebrows. A look that said: 'We've heard all this before.'

Sarah gave a brief nod in reply. 'Well, things will be better for everyone after tomorrow. I'm glad you're home, Lily, and I know Mam will be too. We were all worried about you, weren't we, Maggie?'

Maggie sighed. 'I expect we'll always worry about you, Lily, you're such a flighty little scatterbrain.'

The weather the following morning hadn't improved. It was bitterly cold and damp. The beginnings of a fog hung over the city; they all hoped it wouldn't develop into one of the dense, choking yellow blankets that often brought the city to a halt at this time of year: fogs that made day almost indistinguishable from night, when traffic crawled and the constant mournful sound of the foghorns on the river depressed you further.

Sarah and Lily had gone to see Eddie and both had wished they hadn't.

'It just didn't look like him! He looked so old and sort of . . . waxy,' Lily had sobbed as they'd left.

'I know. Mam was right, we should have remembered him the way he was when we last saw him,' Sarah had replied sadly.

'And he didn't look even a bit happy.'

'Maybe he wasn't, Lily.'

'Oh, I *hate* her! I hope she ends up broke and in the gutter!' Lily had cried venomously, remembering her encounter with Doreen Travis and the fact that her da hadn't looked happy then either.

Sarah had put her arm around her and nodded her agreement. It was what Doreen Travis deserved but she doubted it would come to that. Doreen's sort would always find someone willing to spend money on her.

'Wrap up warm, it's horrible out there,' Harry advised when he arrived that morning.

'It's a miserable enough occasion as it is without the weather adding to it,' Eve agreed.

'How many are coming back, do you know?' Maggie asked her mother, pulling on her black gloves and turning the collar of her coat up around her ears. Billy was standing warming his hands in front of the fire. They hadn't closed the shop; his mam was standing in for them. He'd wanted to but Maggie had been firm. They couldn't afford it.

'About a dozen. Mostly regulars,' Eve replied.

'Then they shouldn't stay all that long. Billy, would you move yourself, you're blocking the heat!' Maggie remarked.

Lily felt it keenly that she was the only one who had no proper mourning clothes but there hadn't been time to get any so she just had a black hat that Mam had lent her and a black armband that she'd sewn around the sleeve of her tweed coat. She wasn't looking forward to the next few hours but then, judging by the looks on everyone's faces, neither were they. She'd had some time to think last night as she'd lain in bed. Maggie and Billy seemed to be doing all right, Sarah was going back to Ireland to get engaged to a boring farmer and Mam looked happy enough. She seemed to rely an awful lot on Harry Dempsey, who also appeared to be around most of the time.

She'd made up her mind that once her da's funeral was over, she'd have a long hard look at her life. Think about what she really wanted to do with the rest of it. Maybe try for some kind of decent job – a career even. *She* wasn't going back to Ireland but she would still like to travel, doing something rewarding and interesting and fairly well paid –

but *what*? It had been then that she had remembered the conversation she'd had with Sarah when Sarah had persuaded her that it was a great idea to go and work in Ireland. Sarah had said she'd thought about going away to sea as a stewardess. Why couldn't she do that herself? On the big liners you got to see really exciting places, met all kinds of people, got paid, got your keep and even tips! What was wrong with all that? It was rewarding, interesting, stimulating and respectable. You had to work hard and of course she had been sick on the ferry crossing but she supposed you got used to it – or maybe on a really big ship you didn't get sick. And if companies like Cunard employed the likes of that common little ferret of a man Mr Travis, why wouldn't they employ her? It was certainly something to think about – once today was over.

It was on these thoughts and plans that she focused her mind during the long morning. She resolved to have a talk with Mam about it soon. As she glanced around at the faces of her family she realised she wasn't the only one who would be glad when tomorrow came.

Chapter Twenty-Four

THE MORNING AFTER EDDIE's funeral both Lily and Harry planned to have a serious talk with Eve but Maggie's arrival thwarted them both.

'Maggie, what's the matter? It's half past nine, shouldn't you be in the shop?' Eve asked.

Maggie sat down. 'Oh, Mam, more bad news, I'm afraid.'

'Now what?' Lily demanded.

'It's Billy's gran. She was taken very ill in the night. Hilda and Jack went round and sent for an ambulance but . . . but she died on the way to Walton Hospital. It was a heart attack, they said.'

'I'm so sorry, Maggie! Is Billy very upset?' Eve was sympathetic. Nothing seemed to be going very well at the moment.

Maggie poured herself a cup of tea. 'He is. He was very fond of her. Oh, I know she could be a bit of a tartar and she was often very blunt but I liked her.'

'So did I,' Eve agreed. 'You knew where you stood with her. She called a spade a spade.'

'So there'll be another funeral. It's a good job I did buy that new black coat and hat.'

'Well, you won't be out of pocket, will you? Didn't you say she was going to leave all her money to Billy?' Lily remarked.

'Lily! What a thing to say!' Eve cried.

'Trust you to say something like that. But yes, she did say that, and I suppose I *am* relieved that we won't be in debt for ever.'

'Don't get your hopes up, Maggie. The debt might be cancelled but you never know, she might not have left *everything* to Billy. Did she leave a will?'

'Billy said she did.'

'And you said she was worth hundreds!' Lily added. It looked as if Maggie was really going to be well off.

'Lily! This is neither the time nor the place! And, as I've said before, wills can be contested,' Eve remonstrated.

'What?' Sarah asked, catching the end of the conversation.

'Old Mrs Wainwright has died, God rest her soul,' Eve informed her.

'Oh, I'm so sorry, Maggie. That was very sudden.'

'A heart attack, but she was seventy-seven.'

'A good age,' Eve agreed.

Maggie got to her feet. 'Well, I just came around with the news. Billy's gone to his mam's and I said I'd follow him.'

'I'll send them a Mass card. Will you let us know when the funeral is, Maggie? I'll go. As I said, I liked her,' Eve informed them.

'I will and thanks, Mam.'

'I hate this time of year, it's so miserable,' Sarah said, shivering.

'Well, I don't know what either you or our Maggie have got to be miserable about!'

'Lily! How can you say that about Maggie?' Sarah demanded.

'She and Billy will come into a fortune now and you're going to marry Michael Nolan and he's certainly not short of a bob or two! It's only me who's got no job and no money,' Lily answered morosely.

Sarah compressed her lips tightly to stop herself from remarking that Lily had only herself to blame for that.

'Lily, that's enough! No one knows for certain what Mrs Wainwright has put in her will. Now, I want to hear no more about Maggie coming into a fortune or Sarah marrying money either. It's about time you started to think about just what you are going to do now. And, young lady, I intend to have a serious talk to you later about the way you've been living your life because I'm not happy about it, not one little bit! Well, I have work to do even if you two have not!' Eve finished, going through into the saloon bar to start the cleaning.

'You and your big mouth, Lily!' Sarah snapped.

Lily shrugged. 'I do know what I'm going to do now but I want to make some enquiries first.'

'I just hope it's something sensible for a change!' Sarah muttered. It never seemed to take Lily long to recover from the disasters in her life, she thought, and privately she admitted her youngest sister was very shallow, thoughtless and selfish.

Maggie couldn't get Lily's words out of her head as she walked to the tram stop. Billy had always insisted that his gran was leaving everything to him. She didn't like Charlie or his parents very much, nor her other daughter and her family, but she had got on well with Hilda and Jack was her only son. She really wouldn't mind if the old lady had left the others something, it was only fair after all. Just as long as it wasn't too much. Billy had said she had to have a thousand pounds and that was an awful lot of money. Just a third of it would be enough to buy a really lovely house in a nice part of the city and to furnish it well. They still had quite a bit of the money his gran had given them as a wedding present. They could buy another shop and pay a manager to run it. She smiled to herself. They might even be able to afford a car! Wouldn't that be really something? They could go for drives out to the country on a Sunday. They could take Mam on outings, and then she wouldn't be so reliant on Harry. Oh, they would be very well to do and so respectable. And she could think about starting a family. That would keep everyone happy. She could buy a really nice outfit for Sarah's wedding. They could afford a cabin on the ferry over and perhaps stay in an hotel instead of being crowded in with Aoife. She felt a little guilty as she thought about the rosy future that seemed to lie ahead. It was sad that Mrs Wainwright had died, but she'd been seventy-seven and, as Mam had said, it was a great age. She frowned. The only fly in the ointment seemed to be Lily, for her sister was so unpredictable. You just never knew what she was going to do next and whether or not it would make a holy show of you!

* * *

Eve managed to get a word with Lily half an hour later while Sarah had nipped along to the corner shop.

'Now sit there, Lily, and don't interrupt me,' she instructed.

Lily said nothing but fiddled with her hair. She had a good idea of what was coming next.

'I've said nothing until now about you and that Myles, I wanted to wait until after the funeral, but were you living together as man and wife?'

Lily cringed at the thought of what Eve would say if she told the truth.

'Mam!' she cried.

'I did my best to bring you all up to know right from wrong. I know your da didn't set a good example, running off with *her*, but that's not the issue here. You know it's wrong, very wrong, to live like that before you're married. You *know* that, Lily! I drummed it into you often enough.'

Lily gathered all her courage. 'Mam, I *didn't*! I swear I didn't! How can you think such a thing? I . . . I thought I loved him, I admit that, but . . . but I always had my own bed, my own bit of the room curtained off!'

'You don't necessarily need a bed!' Eve shot back.

'There was never anything like that going on! We did kiss and . . . and do some other things but . . .' Lily wasn't fool enough to think that Eve would imagine that she hadn't let Myles lay a finger on her. 'I swear it, Mam!'

Eve didn't know what to believe. Lily was very vehement in her denials and yet was she being entirely truthful? She'd

331

admitted to 'other things' and that seemed plausible, but Lily and this lad had shared their lives, away from parental control or censure.

'Anyway, it's all over now. I want to put it behind me. I want to get a decent job – a career! Do you believe me?' Lily pressed.

Eve bit her lip. She couldn't call Lily a bare-faced liar; she had no definite proof. Lily had never told her such an outrageous lie before, if she was indeed lying now.

'I don't know, Lily, and that's the truth. But I have to give you the benefit of the doubt. Just you remember everything I've told you or you'll make a terrible mess of your life.'

Inwardly Lily breathed a sigh of relief. She couldn't have told the truth. She just *couldn't* have. It would have broken her mother's heart. 'I won't, Mam and I am going to do something with my life. I promise.'

Eve shook her head then nodded, hearing the back-yard door slam, which heralded Sarah's return.

To Eve's relief, Lily took herself off into town. Sarah announced that she also was going to have a look in the shops for Christmas presents and maybe something new to wear, as she had saved quite a bit of money and there was far more to choose from in the shops in Liverpool than there was in Tullamore.

'I've put the towel on for half an hour, Eve. There's no one in,' Harry informed her, closing the kitchen door after him.

'I'll put the kettle on while we've got a bit of peace. Those two have gone into town although what Lily is up to I don't know. I know she's broke; Sarah gave her a pound.'

'Maybe she's gone to see if she can find herself a job,' Harry said hopefully.

Eve sighed. 'I'll have to rig her out before she can go for interviews. You should see the state of the clothes she has! She's been living hand to mouth for months.'

'Eve, I want to talk to you.'

Eve sighed but smiled at him. 'I know.'

'Things have changed now and you know how much I love you! Will you marry me now?'

She reached up and gently stroked his cheek. 'Oh, Harry, I love you too.'

'Then say you will?' he begged. 'There's nothing in our way now.'

'There's Lily to think of and I haven't told either Sarah or Maggie about us.'

'I don't think Maggie is blind, and Sarah's getting married herself and you can't always think of Lily! Besides, it's not as if we're going to go off and leave her.'

'I know but . . . just give me a little more time?'

'I love you and you love me! We've waited long enough. It's not as if people will say you aren't showing Eddie the proper respect. He showed you none at all!'

'I know all that. Just let me get Lily settled in a job first, then—'

'Eve, do you love me?'

Eve was stricken. 'Oh, you know I do! You know how much I . . . want you!'

Harry took her in his arms. 'Then say you'll marry me.'

'I will! I will, but just let me tell them in my own time.'

'But not too long a time, promise?'

She kissed him. 'Not too long, I promise.'

Maggie had called back with Billy just after Sarah and Lily had returned from town and after they'd all had supper – Harry included – Eve had determined that she would confide in Sarah first. She had always been the most sensible.

When Harry had closed up and gone to Ma Flanagan's and Lily had announced her intention of going to bed, Eve had told Sarah she wanted to talk to her.

Sarah assumed it was something to do with her wedding. 'You will come to Ireland to meet Michael?'

'I've said I will,' Eve replied, placing a bottle of sherry and two glasses on the table.

'God, Mam, what is it you want to talk to me about?' Sarah joked, although she was a little fearful if it needed the sherry bottle. 'He really *is* a lovely man and he'll be good to me. You've no reason to worry. Is it our Lily?'

'No, it . . . it's me.'

Sarah was concerned. 'What's the matter? You're not ill, are you?'

Eve smiled. 'No. No, I'm very well and I'm happier than I've been for a long time.'

'So?' Sarah was mystified.

'So, I . . . I'm going to get remarried.'

Sarah choked on the sherry. 'Remarried! Who to?' she spluttered.

Eve took a deep breath. 'To Harry. We've been seeing a lot of each other and I love him and he asked me and I said yes. Oh, I know he's younger than me but . . .'

Sarah put down her glass. Why wasn't she really surprised? In the short time that she'd been home she'd noticed that there seemed to be a certain intimacy between them. Oh, Harry had been such a help and a great support too in the days after Da had left and it was only natural that he spent so much time here, but she hadn't realised that it had grown into more than friendship between him and her mam. She liked Harry, she always had. She smiled.

'I'm glad. I'm really glad and I'm happy for you – both! Age doesn't matter; Michael's more than ten years older than me.'

Eve frowned. 'It does when the woman is older.'

'Oh, Mam, it doesn't! He's not *that* much younger! Ten, eleven years?'

'Twelve.'

'So what? You've a right to be happy. Why shouldn't you get married again, you've years ahead of you and you shouldn't be expected to spend them on your own. Maggie's married, I will be too and who knows what our Lily will do in the future?'

'So you really don't mind? You don't think I'm making a fool of myself?'

'No, I don't! You marry him, Mam!'

Eve was so relieved. 'You don't know just how you've set my mind at rest.'

'Good. Let's drink a toast. To you and Harry. Mr and Mrs Dempsey!'

Eve smiled. 'It sounds a bit odd.'

'You'll get used to it. I take it you haven't told Maggie or Lily yet?'

'No, I wanted to tell you first. To sort of test it out.'

'I can't see why either of them would have a problem with it.'

'I can.'

'Now stop that! I know Lily is selfish and thoughtless and Maggie is inclined to be a bit snobbish but what can they object to? It's perfectly respectable. I suppose you'll carry on running the pub and our Lily will live here until she goes off at a tangent again. Will you get the licence put in his name?'

'It should be, he does most of the work, but whether Mr Harrison will be agreeable is another matter.'

Sarah was practical. 'I would have thought it better to have a husband and wife running the place. More stable for business.'

'It wasn't the last time!'

'Mam! This is different!'

'*I* know that and *you* know that but Mr Harrison doesn't.'

'Well, let's not worry about that now. When are you going to tell my dear sisters?'

'Let Maggie get this funeral over with first.'

'You will tell them before I have to go back home?'

'I will.' Eve smiled. Sarah had said 'home'. She obviously no longer thought of Liverpool as home, but Eve supposed that as the man she loved was in another country it was only

336

right. After all, home was where the heart was, so the saying went.

Mrs Wainwright's funeral passed without incident and two days later the family assembled for the reading of the will. It was an occasion that was to divide the Wainwright family for many years. To Jack and Hilda the old lady had left three hundred pounds, and the rest of her estate, which was nine hundred and twenty pounds and her house in Claudia Street, was left entirely to Billy.

Maggie had sat in seething silence while Jack's two sisters and their husbands, beside themselves with fury, had threatened to contest the will. They had ranted and raved about the sheer unfairness and humiliation of it, and the utter bloody-mindedness of the old tartar, and the conniving ways of Billy, who had obviously been such a creep and had played in all manner of ways on her affections, no doubt aided and abetted by Jack, Hilda and Maggie.

'I didn't! I didn't! I loved Gran!' Billy had cried bitterly after they'd departed in high dudgeon.

'Of course you did! We all know that! It was her money to do with what she wanted. Take no notice of them,' Maggie had soothed.

'She still could have left them *something*!' Jack said a little sadly. He hated to see the family at odds like this.

'They can of course contest it but I doubt it will be overturned and it would take time and money. You could make them a gift from what has been apportioned to you,' the family solicitor suggested.

'Why? It's not what she wanted! If she'd *wanted* to she would have left them something!' Maggie had snapped. Billy's da could do what he liked but that lot were not getting their hands on a penny of Billy's money.

'Oh, dear, what a mess!' Eve said after Maggie had imparted the news.

'I don't care, Mam! I don't like either of them.'

'It doesn't sound as though she did much either,' Sarah added.

Eve shook her head. 'It's a shame.'

'Not for us, Mam.'

'It's an awful lot of money, Maggie. Has Billy any plans?' Eve asked.

'*I* have. I want us to buy another business and a house in a nice area.'

'What's wrong with the house in Claudia Street? The old lady's house?' Sarah asked.

'That's just it. It was *her* house. *Her* choice. It's not mine,' Maggie replied firmly.

'So, you'll sell it?'

'Yes.'

'Billy might want his mam and da to have it,' Eve suggested.

Maggie hadn't thought of that. She shrugged. 'He might, I don't mind as long as I get one of my own – although we could rent it out.'

'Don't be so mercenary,' Sarah warned.

Maggie shrugged again. She wasn't going to make an issue out of it.

A Mother's Love

'Harry, come in here and see my millionaire of a daughter,' Eve called, catching sight of Harry in the doorway.

'Oh, Mam, I'm not!' Maggie protested.

'But if she has her way in ten years' time she might well be!' Sarah laughed. 'Two businesses, her own house—'

'And maybe now a family?' Eve interrupted, looking meaningfully at Maggie.

Maggie pursed her lips. She didn't want to discuss things like this in front of Harry Dempsey. 'We might even get a little car. We could take you out on Sundays, Mam.'

'A *car*! There's no end to her ambitions!' Sarah cried.

Eve pealed with laughter. 'Maggie, you make me sound like an old granny to be taken out for an airing once a week!'

'You'll never be that, Eve.' Harry laughed too.

'I hope one day I'll be a granny and then you'll be a granddad!'

Sarah grinned. 'Don't you think you'd better tell her? She's looking very confused.'

'Tell me what?' Maggie demanded.

'I've some good news myself, Maggie. Harry and me, we're getting married.'

Maggie felt as though she'd been punched in the stomach. She opened her mouth and gasped for air. No! No! Mam must be joking!

'Well, say something, Maggie!' Sarah urged.

Maggie found her voice. 'You can't! You can't marry *him*!'

'Maggie!' Eve cried, stricken.

'He's years younger than you – he's the hired help – he was brought up in an orphanage! What will people say? Oh,

339

Mam, say it's not true!' How was she to tell Billy this? What indeed would people say? They would be sniggering behind their hands at all of them. Calling Mam names. 'Cradle-snatcher' came to mind for one. Oh, it just wasn't *respectable*!

Sarah was on her feet, her cheeks scarlet. 'How dare you! How *dare* you!'

Eve had gone pale and was clutching Harry's hand tightly. 'Maggie, that's enough!' she choked.

'No, it's not! How could you? How *could* you . . . disgrace me like this!'

Eve caught the hurt and humiliation in Harry's eyes and rage filled her. She jumped to her feet and the sound of the slap she gave Maggie seemed to echo around the room.

'You asked for that! You really did!' Sarah shouted at her sister. 'You little snob! Have you no thought for Mam's happiness or Harry's?'

Eve was still shaking with temper. 'He's as good as Billy Wainwright any day – with or without money! With or without a family! Oh, I never thought I'd see the day when a daughter of mine would act like this. That money will do you no good at all, if this is the way you're going to carry on!'

'I'm not staying here another minute!' Maggie yelled, tears of shock, rage and shame stinging her eyes. What was the matter with Mam? Had she lost her reason? She'd never slapped her before, not even when she'd been a child.

'Then go. And don't come back until you're ready to apologise!' Eve stormed.

With tears streaming down her cheeks, Maggie slammed out.

'Oh, Mam! I'm so sorry!' Sarah cried, near to tears herself.

Harry was shaken himself. 'Eve, are you all right?'

'I'm fine, and I meant it. I won't have her here until she says sorry!'

'Eve, if it's going to cause so much trouble—' Harry began.

'No! Don't even *think* it, Harry!'

'I don't want to tear the family apart, and if Lily acts the same way – and she might, you know how she carried on about me giving Maggie away—'

'Leave Lily to me,' Eve said grimly, realising he had a point.

'But, Eve, if Lily turns against us, you won't be happy.'

Sarah was beginning to calm down. There was a very strong possibility that Lily would react in the same way as Maggie. 'Perhaps they both need time. Time to get used to it. I'll tell Lily if you like, Mam, and maybe it would help if you came back to Ireland with me. Give them both time to calm down and get used to the idea.'

Harry seized on the suggestion. 'Sarah might be right, Eve. Go back with her, have a break, let them get used to the idea.'

Eve was very doubtful. 'Oh, I don't know about the wisdom of leaving you and Lily together, you know what she's like.'

'I'll talk to her, Mam. Make her promise not to do anything stupid. I'll go and talk to our Maggie too.'

'Thanks, Sarah,' Harry said, relieved. He was thankful for some support – he had been so over the moon when Eve had agreed to marry him that he had not really anticipated any of this. Eve had been right to be wary.

'I'll think about going to Ireland, Sarah,' Eve said sadly, still very distressed. Oh, how had their family come to this?

Chapter Twenty-Five

E VE WAS BITTERLY HURT by Maggie's disapproval and especially the cruel things she had said about Harry. Had Maggie so far forgotten her own humble background? Had her marriage to Billy and now the money he had inherited changed her so much?

'Oh, Harry, I'm so very sorry about the things she said! It's not as if she had been brought up like that. I never taught her to be such a little snob.'

Harry put his arms around her. He had been deeply wounded by Maggie's outburst too. 'I know, but she's upset.'

'I just didn't think she would feel so strongly against it! I know we did try to keep our relationship a secret from them but I often thought she must have had some idea, she's not stupid or blind.'

'They say there's none so blind as those who don't want to see, Eve, and I really am sorry that it's caused so much trouble.'

'It's not your fault!'

'It's not yours either. I just hope Sarah can keep Lily from going off the deep end too.'

'So do I. At least Sarah's happy for us.'

'I always did think Sarah was the nicest of your girls, Eve. I think she takes after you.'

Eve nodded sadly. It did seem as though both Maggie and Lily had inherited more of Eddie's traits than her own. Lily was inconsiderate and Maggie was stubborn and both were selfishly single-minded in pursuing their dreams. They did of course have their good points too though, she added firmly to herself, and she did love them both. 'We'll just have to wait and see, Harry.'

'I think Sarah is right though. You should go back with her. Give things time to settle down. A break would do you good, you've been through a lot lately and you've got to meet your prospective son-in-law sooner or later. I'm sure you'd like to see your cousins too.'

'I will think about it, I promise,' Eve said, still wondering about Lily and the wisdom of leaving her and Harry together.

Sarah was furious with Maggie and resolved to go and tell her just what she thought of her. She was determined too that she would do everything in her power to stop Lily from making matters worse.

She broached the subject early next morning when Eve had gone to do the grocery shopping and Harry was out in the yard with the brewery deliveryman.

'Lily, sit down. I want to talk to you and I don't want any

344

interruptions until I've finished, is that clear?' she said with grim purpose.

'I suppose you're going to give me a long lecture about . . . everything. Well, I can tell you—'

'Lily, shut up! I'm not going to give you a lecture. It's your life and you can make a mess of it if you want to. It's about Mam. Mam and Harry to be exact. They're going to get married. They love each other and there's no reason why they can't get married now, it's perfectly respectable. I suppose you loved Myles, so you should at least be able to understand. Mam has a right to be happy after all she's been through. And Harry is a decent, thoughtful, steady person who won't run off and leave her!'

Lily gazed at her, stunned. 'Mam and . . . and . . . Harry!' she finally managed to get out.

'Yes. So just you think about Mam for a change and don't go having hysterics!'

Lily said nothing. She'd never thought much about Mam *loving* anyone. She was *old*! She realised that she must have fallen in love with Da, that she had loved Da, but . . . 'You . . . approve?' she asked at last.

'Of course I do. I've always liked Harry and, as I said, Mam deserves to be happy. And now that I know what it's like to really love someone and want to spend your life with them, I'm happy for her.'

'Does Maggie know?' Lily was still trying to take it in.

'She does and she certainly doesn't approve. There was a terrible row over it, she said some awful things and Mam slapped her.'

'Mam *slapped* Maggie!' Lily was incredulous.

'She deserved it. She was acting like a spoiled child. A spoiled, snobbish little brat. She said Harry was only the hired help, that he had been brought up in an orphanage – as if that mattered! Now that Billy's got all that money she thinks she's the landed gentry. Oh, you should hear the plans! A fancy house, another business, even a car! Well, I intend to go and see her and give her a piece of my mind, the stuck-up, selfish little madam! She's really upset Mam and Mam told her not to come here again until she's apologised.'

'Will she?' Lily asked fearfully. It must have been a terrible row indeed.

'If she doesn't, she's a fool! Well, what have you got to say?'

'I . . . I don't really know. I can't say I'm as happy as you are about it but . . . but I'll think about it.'

'Just as long as you don't start giving out to Mam or making nasty remarks to Harry. I've asked Mam to come back to Ireland with me; she needs a break, I want her to meet Michael and it will give our Maggie time to cool down.'

'And is she going to?'

'Harry wants her to so I think she might, so I don't want you and Harry at each other's throats while she's gone!'

'You've got awfully bossy!' Lily said, but with a wry smile.

Sarah relaxed a little; it didn't look as if Lily was going to be difficult. 'I haven't. And I'm not going to start giving out to you about anything you've done.'

'I was stupid, Sarah. I mean about running off like that. I

hated it at the Lodge but . . . but I've put it all behind me now. I've got plans for the future.'

Sarah fervently hoped they were more sensible than anything Lily had done in the past. 'What are you going to do now?'

'I've decided that I want a career, so I'm going to try all the big shipping lines to see if I can become a stewardess. It's steady, not badly paid and you get to see the world.'

Sarah sighed with relief. Lily was at last being sensible. 'It's also hard work.'

'I don't mind that. It can't be any worse than working twelve hours a day in a flaming shirt factory!'

'No, I don't suppose it can.'

'I was going to start today but I really haven't got anything decent to wear and I at least want to look respectable.'

'You can borrow my new tweed costume and hat and my good shoes and bag. I'll give you the money for gloves and stockings. Have you a decent blouse or jumper?'

'Not really, but I'm sure Mam has. Oh, it's really good of you, Sarah! You've only just bought that costume and hat, you haven't worn them yourself yet.'

Sarah smiled at her. It was a small price to pay to keep Lily happy. With any luck, she would get a job and be away from Liverpool for long periods of time and wouldn't be a source of worry for Mam. 'Go and get yourself washed and changed and make a start. I'd try Cunard and Canadian Pacific first, then White Star, Elder Dempster and the Blue Funnel Line,' she advised. That would keep Lily busy for a few days.

Sarah's visit to Maggie later that morning wasn't a success. In vain did she plead, cajole and finally yell at her sister. Maggie wouldn't budge. It was a disgrace, an out-and-out disgrace, she insisted, and Billy agreed with her.

'Billy Wainwright hasn't got the guts to argue with you,' Sarah'd snapped.

'And I suppose this Michael Nolan has the guts to argue with you?' Maggie had fired back. 'Oh, a fine marriage yours is going to be. You'll be fighting all the time!'

'Well, at least I will have some respect for him. He has a mind of his own.'

'And what has Lily got to say? Surely she isn't all in favour of Mam making a show of us?'

'Lily isn't having hysterics and that's just what I think you are doing – being hysterical! And downright selfish.'

'I don't care what you think! You're taking yourself off to Ireland. It's not you who is going to be a laughing stock. I *won't* apologise! She's *mad*!'

Sarah could see it was useless. 'No, she's not, it's you who are mad, Maggie. You're going to lose Mam and most of your family because until you come to your senses I'm not going to speak to you either and for what? Pride! That's all it is. Stupid bloody pride!'

She'd left after that, feeling thoroughly miserable but praying that her threat might force Maggie at least to think about her position.

Dressed in Sarah's new outfit and a stylish heather-coloured jumper she'd borrowed from her mam, Lily felt very smart.

She'd bought a nice pair of gloves and new stockings from Mrs Atkinson, who had a small drapery shop in Clayton Square, and as she headed towards the tram stop she knew she looked good and felt her confidence rising. She'd go to the Pier Head first, to the Cunard Building. Then if she had no luck she'd go on to Canadian Pacific and the others whose addresses she'd written down.

It was a cold, blustery day but at least it was sunny and bright, she thought as she walked across from the tram terminus towards the three most imposing buildings on the Liverpool waterfront. Buildings known to seafarers the world over, she thought. The Liver Building, the Cunard Building and the classical domed edifice that housed the offices of the Mersey Docks and Harbour Board. As she went up the steps of the Cunard Building some of her confidence left her. It was very grand indeed. There was a uniformed commission- aire sitting at a polished wooden desk in the foyer. She took a deep breath and went towards him.

'Good morning, miss. Can I help you?' he asked pleasantly.

Lily was very thankful she looked so smart and chose her words carefully. 'Yes, please. Could you tell me who do I see about going away to sea – er . . . about a career in the Merchant Navy?' she amended hastily.

He smiled. She was very attractive. 'You need to go up to the third floor, miss, and ask for Mr Parsons. That's the Personnel Office, they'll be able to advise you.'

She gave him a dazzling smile. 'Thank you, you've been very helpful.'

'Mr Parsons,' she repeated to herself as she took the lift. 'Personnel Office' sounded very grand and a bit daunting. It was quite a daunting place, she thought as she entered and looked around. There was a long, highly polished counter behind which were desks where half a dozen clerks were working diligently. The walls were covered with huge posters advertising the ships and their destinations. They were very colourful, stylish and modern. Sunlight streamed in through the huge ornate windows that overlooked the Pier Head and the river, filling the room with brightness and cheering her enormously. There was a small brass bell at one end of the counter and she pressed it twice.

A middle-aged man with grey hair and a clipped grey moustache looked up and then got up from his desk. He wore a sombre dark grey suit and a very white shirt. Lily squared her shoulders and summoned up every ounce of confidence she possessed.

'I'd like to see Mr Parsons, if I may?'

'I'm Mr Parsons. How can I help you, Miss . . . ?'

'Dobson. Lillian Dobson.' Lily held out her hand and smiled.

He looked a little surprised but shook her hand. She seemed very confident. 'Well, Miss Dobson?'

'I'd like to enquire about a career in the Merchant Navy, please.'

She went up in his estimation. They usually came in asking: 'How do you go about getting a job going away to sea?' 'How old are you, Miss Dobson?'

Lily was ready for this. 'Twenty-one, last birthday,' she

lied, knowing she did look older than her eighteen years.

'Then would you like to come through?' He lifted a flap in the long counter and ushered her through.

Oh, this was very promising, she thought, her confidence soaring as she followed him into a small, sparsely furnished room.

He indicated that she sit down. 'You will have to fill in this application form but I would like to ask you a few questions first.' A quite lengthy form was passed across the desk.

Lily glanced at it, nodded and then smoothed down the skirt of Sarah's new costume.

'I presume it's the position of stewardess you're interested in? Have you any previous experience?'

'It is and I'm afraid I haven't. I served my time as a seamstress and I have worked in service in a country house in Ireland. I also worked for a short time in the theatre, both in Dublin and Belfast, so I am used to dealing with all kinds of people, and I'm not afraid of hard work.' She had rehearsed all that over and over and thought it sounded impressive.

'You certainly seem to have packed quite a lot into your life already.'

'I enjoy travelling and meeting people but now I want more of an interesting and rewarding career.'

She did have potential, he thought, and ambition, and it wasn't uncommon for a young woman to rise from steerage to first class stewardess and finally Chief Stewardess. 'So, it's a career and not just a job you want?'

'It is indeed, sir! I can get a job anywhere.'

'Your parents are quite happy with your choice?'

'My . . . my father died very recently and my mother is quite happy about me coming here today. She runs a business herself, as does one of my sisters.'

'My condolences on your loss, Miss Dobson. What business is your mother in?'

Lily had anticipated this too. 'The brewers' and vintners'.' She'd seen that on some brewery stationery.

A pub, he thought. So, she must be used to dealing with the public in that area as well. He stood up. 'I'll leave you to fill in the form and then I'd like you to see Mr Hayes, our Personnel Manager.'

Lily beamed up at him. 'Thank you, you're most kind.' She really wanted to ask if there was indeed a vacancy but she didn't dare.

The form wasn't too difficult; she just hoped they wouldn't write to Mrs Ormonde although she'd had the good sense to make the address a little obscure. She doubted that the managers of either theatre would even remember her, let alone bother to reply. She was apprehensive about giving the wrong age but she'd worry about that when she really needed to.

The Personnel Manager proved to be a different kettle of fish entirely. He was much older and barked questions at her, scanning her form as he did so. She didn't feel very confident at all at the end of the interview when she was asked to wait in the outer office. She fiddled nervously with the cuffs of her gloves. Oh, if she just got this chance she could really make something of her life. She didn't want to have to traipse around dozens of shipping offices and have to go through all this again.

Eventually Mr Parsons came towards her and indicated that she follow him. She clasped her bag tightly and tried not to bite her lip.

'Well, Miss Dobson, you seem to have made a favourable impression and it so happens that we do have a vacancy for a stewardess in the *Berengaria*. Steerage class to start with, but if a vacancy occurs and you prove satisfactory you would be considered for first class. The *Berengaria* is sailing out of Southampton for New York and then a cruise around the West Indies, which will mean you will be away for approximately six weeks. I have here a list of the uniform you will require – it can be obtained from Greenberg's, the naval outfitters – and your Articles, which you must sign. These set out your terms of employment and pay and the company's rules and regulations. You will need to obtain a Discharge Book, a sort of passport, from the shipping pool; your birth certificate will be required. Can you be ready to leave for Southampton to join your ship by Monday next?'

Lily was so excited she could hardly speak. Her eyes shone and her cheeks flushed pink. Join *her ship*! 'Oh, yes, indeed, sir! Oh, thank you!'

His smile was genuine. She was a very pretty girl. He doubted it would be long before she was swept off her feet by some well-off American passenger. He'd seen it happen often enough.

Lily could have kissed him. Life was *wonderful*! However,

she shook his hand instead, very warmly, after folding all the papers and putting them in her bag. Wait until she told Mam and Maggie about this! New York and the West Indies!

When she was once more out in the fresh air she decided to walk down to the Landing Stage to try to calm down a little and take a good look at the shipping. She'd never really taken much notice of it, it had always been there, a backdrop to her life, but now it was going to *be* her life.

The Isle of Man ferry was tied up, as were two vessels of the Coast Lines, but what really drew her attention was the white-hulled *Empress of France* of the Canadian Pacific Line, preparing to leave for Canada.

She watched the preparations excitedly: the crowds of passengers on deck waving to relatives and friends on the Landing Stage; the shore gang preparing to cast off the heavy hawsers and the officers high up on the bridge watching the proceedings attentively. Oh, soon she would be a part of that world! Getting ready to sail across the wide ocean to New York! Not just a few hours on a cramped old ferry to Dublin or Belfast, but days and nights on a floating hotel!

She turned away. She had to think of the practicalities now. She had to get home and tell them of her astonishing good fortune.

Chapter Twenty-Six

BOTH EVE AND SARAH were astounded. Sarah hadn't thought she would get a job so easily and Eve had known nothing at all about Lily's plans.

'When did you decide all this?' Eve asked, dazed.

'I've been thinking about it ever since I got home. I told Sarah and she lent me her new outfit and I'm sure it helped to get me the job. Oh, I can't believe it! I'm sailing for *New York* next week, and then the West Indies! Look, I've to get all these things: my uniform, and I'll get my keep and I'll get paid! I have to leave you something called an allotment, Mam. A bit of money so that if anything awful happens to me you'll get some kind of a pension. It says that here in my Articles.'

'Oh, Lily!' Eve cried fearfully.

'It's probably just a precaution or something.'

'Don't you have to have my permission?' Eve pressed.

Lily had thought all this out on the tram coming home. 'No. No, I'm old enough. I'm eighteen. If you're under eighteen you have to have permission,' she lied. She'd already decided to alter the year on her birth certificate; not even realising it was a crime.

Eve looked uncertain but then shrugged. She supposed it was right. She really didn't know all that much about going away to sea.

'I can let you have a few pounds towards the uniform; it's going to cost quite a bit, Lily. Don't they give you anything for it? I'm surprised they don't supply it,' Sarah offered. This just might be the making of Lily and at least it would keep her out of Mam's hair.

'No, but just think: I won't need as many ordinary clothes so I'll save that way.'

'But you'll still need underclothes and stockings and I dread to think what state yours are in.'

Lily shrugged.

'You're going to have a busy few days ahead of you, Lily. If I were you I'd go through what you do have and see what is in any way reasonable,' Eve suggested.

'And you can take off that suit while you're up there,' Sarah called as Lily virtually danced up the stairs.

'Do you think she really will like a life at sea?' Eve asked, doubtfully.

'She seems to think she will – she's as high as a kite about it. She really is lucky, Mam. I didn't think she'd get something without trailing around half the shipping offices in the city, and then I thought she'd have to wait.'

'She was terribly sick on the Belfast ferry. What's she going to be like on the Atlantic Ocean at this time of year?'

'It might not be so bad on a big ship. I suppose the *Berengaria* is a big one?'

'I saw her once or twice before they moved her home port to Southampton,' Harry interrupted. He had got a garbled version of the news from Lily herself whom he'd met in the hallway.

'And?' Eve enquired.

'She's huge! In fact she's one of the biggest in the world. And it's not a picnic, so I've heard. Those girls work really long hours. It's hard, back-breaking work but they have to be pleasant and helpful at all times.'

'It doesn't sound very glamorous at all,' Sarah mused, knowing that Lily was viewing her trip through rose-tinted glasses.

'I would say it's far from that. Even if she's seasick she'll still have to work, looking after and cleaning up after seasick passengers. And I've heard the Atlantic is unpredictable at any time of year but especially in winter. I remember a feller telling me that he worked on the old *Lusitania* before she was sunk in the last war, and he said they went through three blizzards in one day on one trip in February!'

'Oh, God, she won't like that!' Eve cried.

'Well, like it or not, she's signed on for six weeks. It said so in those Article things *and* she's signed them,' Sarah informed them grimly. This time Lily really had let her enthusiasm carry her away and, unlike her job at Rahan Lodge, she couldn't up and run away from it. This was a binding contract and she would be on a ship in the middle of a vast ocean. There was nowhere to run *to*.

* * *

Lily was rummaging through her meagre selection of underwear, thinking that she would definitely have to buy some more, when she suddenly sat down on the bed, the colour draining from her face. In all the upheaval and upset of moving from town to town and her final quarrel with Myles, her journey home and Da's death, then the news of Mam and Harry's marriage and the excitement of today, she had completely forgotten about her curse! Now, feeling quite sick, she realised that she had seen nothing for over three months! 'Oh, no! I'm pregnant!' she gasped.

She collapsed on the bed, still clutching a faded and creased underslip in her hands, and began to shiver. All the excitement had gone. No! Not now! Not when she'd just got the most wonderful chance she'd ever been offered! It couldn't be! It just *couldn't* be! She went over and over the dates again on her fingers. There was no mistake. It was three months. Oh, what was she going to do now? How could she tell them all about ... this? Mam would be horrified – and after she'd told her a barefaced lie! They all would be. Lily, the disgrace of the family. Lily, the little fool. She didn't even want to think about how Maggie would carry on. Oh, this was all Myles's fault! She hated him. He'd *ruined* her life. Why had she ever taken up with him? What had she ever seen in him? How could she have thought she *loved* him? She *was* a fool. What was she going to do now? She thought about all her dreams that now lay in utter ruins and she began to cry.

She lay there for what seemed to her hours, only pulling

herself together when she heard Sarah shouting up to her. She managed to reply but realised she would either have to tell them or bluff it out – for now. They would have to be told eventually. She had even thought about still going to Southampton and working until it became too obvious what kind of condition she was in but she'd eventually abandoned that idea. But, oh, how she wanted to go to New York!

'Well, why shouldn't I? Why should I have to have this baby?' She didn't realise she'd said the words aloud. The thought amazed her but suddenly she became determined. She *wouldn't* have it. She *wouldn't* have her life ruined. You didn't have to suffer unwanted pregnancies. There were women who knew about these things and could help you – for a price. It wouldn't be cheap but it would be worth it to have her future back – her life back!

She tidied her hair and washed her face in the bowl on the dresser and put on some lipstick. The determination was growing stronger and stronger. Maggie had money. She couldn't tell her what she wanted it for, she'd ask her to lend it to her for . . . for her uniform. She'd tell Maggie she wouldn't ask Mam or Sarah, because she didn't approve of Mam getting married to Harry Dempsey. Maggie would understand that and think she was siding with her. Maggie'd give her the money and then she'd go and get it done and then she could look forward again. She smiled grimly at her reflection in the mirror. She'd do it! She most certainly would and no one need ever know.

* * *

That evening after Lily had gone out, Sarah again broached the subject of Eve returning with her.

'You don't have to worry about Lily being left here with Harry now, Mam.'

'No, but you said you'd be back on Saturday, luv; we'll have to go on Friday night and she won't be leaving for Southampton until Monday.'

'So?'

'So how can I leave her to go off halfway across the world without being there to wave her off at Lime Street?'

'Oh, Mam, she's not a child! She's traipsed halfway across Ireland and she made her way back here alone. She'll be fine. By Friday she should have everything sorted out and she'll see it as a big adventure, you know she will. And all you can do is see her to the train. You're not going down to Southampton to the ship with her.'

'I know but I just feel I should at least be here when she goes.'

'Let Harry see her off, he won't mind, or even Maggie. That's where she's gone now – to tell her.'

'Let's hope Maggie doesn't try to talk her out of it.'

'Why should she? It's a very *respectable* career. She can't have any objections. Let Lily stand on her own two feet. Make sure she's got everything she needs and let her go, Mam.'

Eve sighed. 'You're right. She won't mind me not being there, she's just so delighted about it she probably won't notice who sees her off.'

'Good. I'll send a telegram to Michael and one to Aoife, she'll be delighted to see you – they both will.'

Eve smiled. 'We'll have an awful lot to do.'

'We will so.'

'You're becoming more Irish by the day, Sarah.'

Maggie was looking tired, Lily thought as she sat down in Maggie's small but comfortably furnished living room.

'If you've come to go on at me about Mam and *him* getting married, then you're wasting your time,' Maggie said firmly, thinking that Lily looked sort of distracted.

'I haven't. I don't approve either.'

'Well, I'm glad you're seeing sense for once. I just don't understand her – or our Sarah either. He's years younger than her and he's so . . . common!'

Lily bit back the retort that came to her lips. Harry wasn't common! She too liked him – but not particularly as Mam's husband and her stepfather.

'I don't suppose he's that bad – in his place, I mean,' she added, seeing the frown that crossed her sister's face. She couldn't afford to alienate Maggie now. 'But there's nothing we can do about it. Mam is supposed to be going to Ireland with Sarah, for a break.'

'Let's hope she comes to her senses while she's there.'

'I don't think she will.'

'Then I'm having nothing more to do with them. I mean it!'

Lily sighed. This wasn't going to be easy.

'So, what do you intend to do? Go to the wedding? Live with them?' Maggie demanded.

'No! I've no intention of doing either and anyway I won't be here.'

Maggie looked at her with suspicion. Just what mad plan did she have in her empty head now? If Lily was going to embarrass her even further she would just show her the door, even if she too was against this awful misalliance.

'What do you mean you won't be here?'

'I'm going to Southampton on Monday. I've got a job – the chance of a career at sea as a stewardess with Cunard. I went this morning and was interviewed. I was so lucky!'

Maggie stared at her in astonishment. 'What on earth made you decide to do that?'

'Oh, just something our Sarah said when she persuaded me that going to Ireland was a great idea – which it wasn't. She said it was something she'd thought about doing.'

Maggie raised her eyebrows. She couldn't imagine her staid sister doing anything so adventurous.

'It won't be a bed of roses, Lily.'

'I don't expect it to be. I don't mind hard work and it's a very respectable career.' She stressed the word *respectable*.

'It is. Didn't we know someone from school whose aunt ended up a Chief Stewardess?'

Lily shrugged.

'So, which ship is it? Where are you going and why Southampton?'

'It's the *Berengaria*, on the Atlantic run to New York and then on to the West Indies to go cruising. I don't know why Southampton. The thing is, Maggie, I've got a list of things I've got to have. You should see it. Dresses, two different types, shoes, again two different styles, a bridge coat – whatever that is – caps, a hat, underwear: the list is endless and I'm not asking Mam or our Sarah for money and I haven't got any. I really am broke. I was wondering if you'd lend me enough to get everything. I'd pay you back, of course. The pay's good and I hope I'll get tips too and I won't be spending money on food or lodgings.'

Maggie looked thoughtful. She could see Lily's point. If she was so upset at the carry-on of Mam and Sarah she naturally wouldn't want to ask them for money and she did have to have all these things. But Cunard was a big company: 'Don't they provide anything?'

'No. Just your keep and your train fares.'

'How much will you need?'

Inwardly Lily relaxed. 'I don't really know.' She was telling the truth. She had no idea how much an abortion would cost. And, of course, if all went well, she would still need her uniform.

'Will fifteen pounds be enough?'

'Do you think you could manage twenty?' It sounded an awful lot but she didn't want to have to come back and ask for more. 'I don't know how much all those clothes will come to.'

'All right. Twenty it is. I suppose it is specialised stuff, you can't get it in any of the ordinary shops.'

'No, you have to go to a naval outfitters.'

'Even for the underwear?'

'No. You can get that anywhere.'

Maggie got up and went to a drawer in the sideboard and handed Lily four white five pound notes.

'I will pay it all back, I promise.'

'Oh, keep it. You heard Billy got all his gran's money. That's where he is now, out looking at another business.'

'Thank you, it's really good of you!' Lily pocketed the money thankfully. 'Is it another shop?'

'Yes. Grocer's on the corner of Commutation Row; it's supposed to be a little goldmine. He's going to run it and I'll see to the greengrocer's until we get a new house, then we'll get someone to manage the greengrocer's. I'm sick of it. It's always freezing cold at this time of year and you get filthy.'

'I'm really glad for you, Maggie. You'll do well, I know you will.'

Maggie smiled. 'You have to keep behind Billy all the time.' She had taken Mam's advice about not banishing Billy from her bed to heart, that would be asking for trouble, but she had taken it upon herself to see that she didn't get pregnant. She'd spoken confidentially to a couple of girls she knew who were married and as yet had no children and while there wasn't actually much she could do, she'd had a long talk to Billy about it. They had come to what she liked to call 'an arrangement' and what he referred to very vulgarly as 'getting off at Edge Hill'. 'What I really want to do is invest in property to let. You can really make money from that. Now, let's have a cup of tea and a chat. You don't have to get back early, do you?' Maggie wouldn't admit it even to herself, but she was already missing her chats with her mam.

'No. I do what I want,' Lily answered.

When she left Maggie's an hour and a half later she breathed a sigh of relief. She had the money and, best of all,

A Mother's Love

Maggie didn't want it repaid. She would make some discreet enquiries and then by next Monday all this would be over and she would be on her way to a new life.

Chapter Twenty-Seven

E**VE HAD LITTLE TIME** to worry about either Lily or Maggie for the rest of that week. Things became very hectic as she and Sarah packed and Lily spent her time running between shops, naval outfitters and various official buildings.

'Our Lily seems to have quietened down a bit,' Sarah remarked, checking over the pile of small gifts she had bought in preparation for Christmas.

'Thank goodness! I couldn't have stood her being so up in the air with excitement day after day. Do you think I'll need more than one decent costume?'

Sarah looked slightly bemused. 'Do you have more than one?' Mam looked as if she was intending to take her entire wardrobe.

'No, but I think I could stretch to one now I don't have to rig Lily out. It was very good of Maggie to give her the money for her uniform.'

Sarah said nothing, wondering just what sort of a tale

Lily had told her sister. Maggie wasn't known for her generosity.

'I've got my blue suit but I think it's a bit light for this time of year,' Eve said dubiously.

'It is. Just your good dark grey costume, a couple of blouses and jumpers, your best coat and maybe a warm dress are plenty to take. No one gets really dressed up, except to go to Mass, and of course Madam and the girls but they're the gentry so I suppose it's expected. And, apart from visiting, there's not that much to do. I think we're too old for the local dances.'

'You're not!'

'I'm about to become an engaged woman or had you forgotten? Unless I go to a dance with my fiancé I'll be the talk of the parish!'

'It really is different, isn't it?'

Sarah nodded. 'But very nice.'

'I hope it's not going to be rough. I've only ever been on the Mersey ferry so I don't know how I'll be on a longer trip.'

Thinking of her journey to Liverpool, Sarah shuddered. 'I'm praying it's not going to be!' she said fervently.

They were both extremely thankful when on Friday they drew back the bedroom curtains to bright sunshine and a heavy frost but not a breath of wind.

'Oh, thank God for that!' Sarah sighed, shivering. There was ice on the inside of the window pane, it was so cold.

'Sarah, make up that fire, it's absolutely freezing. I don't know about blouses, I think I'm going to need heavy jumpers and scarves.'

'We will, but it's lovely to see the frost in the countryside, Mam. It's so pretty.'

'I hope Aoife keeps a decent fire going,' Eve mused.

'She does. Everyone does and it's turf and smells lovely.'

'I bet it's not so lovely to clean out though.' Eve was beginning to think that Sarah was glorifying everything a bit too much.

'No worse than coal,' Sarah said firmly.

'And you say Michael is going to meet us at the station tomorrow?'

'He is so.'

Lily appeared, yawning and pulling her old dressing gown tightly around her. 'Oh, it's so cold!'

'There's tea in the pot. What are you doing today?' Eve asked.

Lily poured out a mug although she didn't feel like tea. She felt a bit queasy. 'More packing and this afternoon I've to go and see someone.'

Eve raised her eyes to the ceiling. 'Does this someone have a name?'

'Ginny Bennet. You remember, she was in my class.'

'You haven't seen her for years and as far as I can remember you were never the best of friends even then,' Sarah remarked.

Lily was evasive. 'I . . . I met her the other day in town. She's changed. She's married now and I said I'd go and see her before I sail.' It wasn't a bad cover story and was half

369

true. She changed the subject. 'What time are you two leaving?'

'The ferry sails at half past eleven and we have to be on board by eleven at the latest, so we'd better be down there for half past ten to get a seat. We'll leave here at about a quarter past ten.'

'I'll come down with Harry to see you off,' Lily offered. If everything went well she wouldn't see either of them again for quite a while.

'You don't have to, luv, it'll be bitterly cold standing around down there and you're looking a bit peaky.'

Lily was feeling very nauseous but was trying desperately hard to conceal it. 'It's just all the excitement and running around.'

Eve was concerned. 'Can't you have a bit of a rest this morning? Sit by the fire for a while. You really don't look very well.'

Lily lost her battle and dashed from the kitchen into the yard where she was sick in the grid.

'Oh, Lord! She really isn't well. Maybe I should stay, Sarah.'

'She's just got herself over-excited and I saw a packet of Woodbines in her bag. They're enough to make anyone throw up and I bet she's smoked one already. Cigarettes on an empty stomach and over-excitement, that's all that's wrong with her.'

Eve shook her head. 'I expect you're right. Oh, I do wish she hadn't taken up smoking.'

'She probably thinks it's very smart and grown up. Don't

worry, I can't see her being allowed to smoke when she's working.'

Lily leaned against the wall, feeling faint but a little better. Oh, God! It was a good job Mam and Sarah were leaving tonight. She was going to see this woman that Ginny knew this afternoon and she prayed that the woman could 'fix her up', as Ginny put it, tomorrow afternoon or Sunday afternoon. It hadn't been as easy as she'd expected to find someone who would 'help her'. Ginny had been to this woman herself and said it was nothing to worry about. Just a bit of pain, a bit of bleeding and that was it. You were as right as rain next day. She was to be sure to have the money with her and it cost eight guineas, which was a small fortune, but this woman was better than a lot of the others. She'd been a nurse of some sort. Oh, the sooner it was all over the better, Lily thought, and at least she did have the money: she'd kept enough back. In the end her uniform hadn't cost as much as she'd anticipated so she'd have enough to buy some stylish things in New York for the warm weather of the West Indies. That cheered her up no end.

She was tired but relieved when that night she accompanied Harry, Eve and Sarah to the Pier Head. The woman had looked all right and had said she was to present herself at two o'clock on Sunday afternoon when her husband would be out and that there was nothing to worry about. Of course the house was in a slum but at least by this time on Sunday it would all be over.

Eve hugged her, after glancing around at the crowds on

the Landing Stage, hoping against hope that Maggie would have changed her mind.

'Lily, you take care of yourself. Work hard and be polite and don't go getting into bad company!'

'Oh, Mam! I've learned my lesson, I really have. I'm going to make a success of this and I'm looking forward to it.'

'You will write? Even if it's just a few lines on a card?'

'I've said I will.'

'You said you had a quick turnaround and that you might not be able to write long letters.'

'I know and I might not, we'll just have to see. But I'll definitely send cards. Now, go and enjoy yourself and stop worrying about me. Harry is going to see me off.' She turned quickly to Sarah before Eve could fuss further. 'Bye, Sarah and good luck.'

Sarah hugged her sister. 'Good luck to you, Lily. I really do hope you'll find it's everything you want it to be.'

'Thanks and don't forget to let me know when the wedding is and I'll try and be home.'

'I will.'

Eve turned to Harry and kissed him on the cheek. Their goodbyes had been carried out in private. 'Make sure she gets off all right and you take care of yourself. You're sure Alf will give you a hand if you need it?'

'I'm sure and I'll see milady here safely on the train and I'll take care of myself. Now, off you go, Eve, and enjoy yourself. You're not going for months, it's only two weeks,' Harry laughed.

'He's right. Now let's get aboard and find ourselves a

decent seat. It always gets crowded. It certainly was when I went the first time,' Sarah urged.

As Sarah guided her towards the gangway Eve began to feel a little excited. The only thing that overshadowed her happiness was the rift with Maggie but she pushed that to the back of her mind. This was the first holiday she had ever had and she was going to enjoy it. Aoife had written that she was delighted Eve was coming and the whole family was dying to see her. All Aoife's friends wanted to meet her; she would get to know Michael and his family; she was even invited to tea with Mrs Kavanagh up at the Lodge. She'd have a grand time altogether. So now she would put both Lily and Maggie firmly out of her mind and concentrate on Sarah and the new life her eldest daughter had made for herself, she thought.

It was a long journey and she was very tired as at last the train pulled into Tullamore station. She hadn't got much sleep on the crossing and the railway carriage had been full so she hadn't even managed to have a doze. As the train had travelled across Ireland towards the midlands she'd begun to see what Sarah found so pleasant. It really was a lovely country and even in the depths of winter it was so green.

Sarah had smiled when she'd remarked on it. 'That's because it rains a lot.'

She liked Michael Nolan from the minute she was introduced to him as he came forward, smiling, and kissed Sarah and then held out his hand to her.

'Mrs Dobson, it's very pleased I am to meet you and I hope we'll get along well together,' he said sincerely.

'I know we will, if everything Sarah's told me about you is true.'

'It is!' Sarah laughed.

'All good, I hope?'

'Very good!'

'Then let's get your bags and yourselves in the trap. I promised Aoife I wouldn't stand chatting but would bring you to her directly and I'll be killed if I don't!'

'Will you be staying a while?' Sarah asked him.

'I will so, and then I'll take you on up to the Lodge. Was it before or after supper you told them you'd be back?'

'After.'

'Then we'll have a bit of time to ourselves. I've missed you, Sarah.'

She smiled at him shyly. 'I've missed you too, Michael.'

'And we've plans to make.'

'I expect you have and I expect Aoife has lots of plans for me,' Eve said, settling back contentedly.

Aoife had indeed. After Eve had unpacked and met the entire family and they'd had some tea, she chased Sarah and Michael off on their own and her various offspring to do their chores and her husband away to his milking.

'Now, Eve, tell me all the news! All about poor Eddie, and what that bold strap Lily got up to, and this new man in your life, and what Maggie is doing and what plans Sarah has? We're all so delighted about Sarah; sure she's a lovely girl, a credit to ye. She's well thought of up at the Lodge, I can tell ye. Herself is fierce snobbish and doesn't take to many the way she's taken to Sarah. Aren't ye invited up there to take tea? Sure, that's the first time that's happened!'

Eve smiled. She could see she wasn't going to get away with a single detail but she didn't mind. It might help to unburden herself to her cousin. She didn't have any female friends close enough to bare her soul to.

Michael took Sarah home and once inside the warm, comfortable farmhouse kitchen that would one day be hers, Sarah finally relaxed.

'Oh, it's so good to be home at last!' she said sincerely, holding her hands out to the welcoming turf fire that burned in the range.

He took her in his arms. 'I really did miss you, Sarah.'

She leaned her head against his shoulder. 'I wish you had been with me; it would have helped.'

'It must have been hard on you.'

'It was. Not so much Da's funeral although I do miss him. I can't help thinking about him and wondering if he really was happy with *her*. But there was a terrible row between Mam and Maggie over Mam marrying Harry. Mam's very upset about it, that's why I brought her here.'

'Maggie doesn't approve?'

'No. She and Billy have come into quite a lot of money and it's given her all kinds of airs and graces.'

'Ah, it often happens, but families do fall out. Sometimes for years.'

She sighed and held him closer. 'I know but I hope Maggie will get over it. And then Lily finally arrived home. She'd left that Myles. He was always getting into fights and having to move around.'

'He had a temper on him, so he did, and a knack of upsetting people. A nice enough lad, just . . . restless.'

'You never seem to see the bad side of anyone, do you?'

'I'm an optimist. There's a bit of good in everyone, I think.'

'That's one of the reasons I love you so much! Well, anyway, now Lily has got herself a decent job as a stewardess with Cunard and she's off to New York on Monday. Well, to Southampton first. I hope it works out for her as she isn't too happy about Mam and Harry either but I managed to talk her out of creating more trouble.'

'Always the peacemaker, Sarah. That's one of the reasons why I love *you* so much. Now, let's forget about families and concentrate on us. Sure, you've to be above at the Lodge in a couple of hours. I don't have you to myself for very long.' He bent his head and kissed her and the only sound in the kitchen for a long time was the sound of the grandfather clock in the corner and the occasional falling of the turf in the range.

Lily felt very nervous as she got off the tram on Scotland Road. She had been sick again that morning but fortunately she was over it before Harry had arrived. She'd told him she was going to see a friend before she left tomorrow and would be back late that afternoon.

She hated this part of the city. It was a festering slum with a pub on the corner of every narrow, dirty street; slatternly

A Mother's Love

women stood on their doorsteps gossiping and barefoot, ragged children played in the gutters. If this woman made so much money why didn't she live in a better neighbourhood? she'd asked Ginny.

'Because people would get suspicious of all the coming and going and someone would take it on themselves to inform the police. They don't do things like that round here. They hate the scuffers and, besides, they know she'll lend them a few bob when they're desperate – which is most of the time!' Ginny had replied.

Lily turned into the damp and dismal court, ducking her head to avoid the soot-blackened bricks of the archway that led into it. There were hundreds of these cramped, crumbling courts where hardly any daylight penetrated and where a row of ashcans stood on one side and a couple of privies at the far end served all the houses. Even in winter they stank and she wrinkled her nose in disgust. Number five was in the corner; at least the windows were cleaner than the rest of the houses and the paint on the door wasn't peeling quite so badly. She clenched her bag tightly to her. In her purse she had eight guineas and her tram fare home. The rest of the money she had left in the top drawer of the chest in her bedroom. It wasn't safe to bring too much money to a place like this.

The thin, bony woman with the severe hairdo and rather abrupt manner, whom she'd already met, opened the door to her.

'Come inside quickly. Now, upstairs to the back bedroom with you. Take off your coat and hat and skirt, underclothes

and stockings. There's a bed up there. Lie down on it and I'll
be up in a few minutes.'

Lily just nodded. She felt sick with fear. The room was
almost completely bare. There were damp patches on the
wall by the window, which was covered with a heavy cotton
lace curtain. There was a narrow bed covered with newspapers, no pillows or linen of any kind, and a rickety old
bentwood chair and a small wooden table.

She got undressed and put her clothes on the chair and
then gingerly sat on the bed. It was freezing cold and she
began to shiver. Just concentrate on the fact that it will soon
be over and you can start again! she told herself firmly. Think
of all the wonderful places you're going to see and the things
you're going to do and the people you're going to meet. She
lay down and stared at the ceiling but she couldn't stop
trembling.

The woman came in carrying a tray and Lily forced herself
not to look at what lay on it.

'Now just lie still and try to relax. Take deep breaths. It
doesn't take long. I've done this so often I could almost do it
blindfold. Have you got the money?'

'It . . . It's on the table,' Lily said between teeth that
chattered. Oh, let it be over soon and not hurt too much!

'Good. You're young and healthy and this is the first time
so there should be no problems. I refuse to do this for women
who've had it done more than three times before. Now,
bend your knees and pull your legs up.'

Oh, how did women go through this more than once?
They must be mad! Lily thought in panic.

Chapter Twenty-Eight

L
ILY LEFT THE HOUSE in number sixteen court an hour later and walked slowly towards the tram stop. She was still shaking. It had hurt terribly and she had screamed until a rag had been pushed into her mouth to stifle her cries. Then she had been covered with a threadbare grey blanket and left to 'recover'. Oh, she never wanted to go through that again! When the woman had returned she had been handed some more newspaper and told to clean herself up, get dressed and go. Never had she been more relieved to get out of a house.

'I didn't expect you back so early, Lily,' Harry said when she came in. She looked very pale and exhausted, he thought. 'Are you all right?'

'I've got a shocking headache, Harry. That's why I'm back so soon. I think I'll go and lie down.'

'I'd do that, Lily. You've a long day ahead of you tomorrow.'

'I know,' Lily replied and went upstairs.

She must have dozed off, she thought later; she hadn't drawn the curtains and now it was dusk and the streetlights were on. She'd better get up; she still had things to do for tomorrow. She felt groggy and feverish and as she swung her legs over the side of the bed an agonising pain ripped through her abdomen. She fell to her knees, gasping. It was as though red-hot knives were being thrust into her. She gripped the bedcover tightly and stuffed it into her mouth, stifling the screams. Oh, God! What was happening to her? Why was there so much pain? She hadn't felt this bad on her way home.

Wave after wave of agony washed over her; she was sweating and shivering. She tried to pull herself up but couldn't, the pain was too intense. She managed to crawl back on to the bed, her knees drawn up almost to her chest. Oh, please God, let it pass! Let it pass! she prayed, before realising that it wasn't much use appealing to God; what she'd done was a heinous sin for which there would be no forgiveness.

She lay there shaking and moaning. Terrified, sobbing, she cried for her mam or Sarah or Maggie. Someone, just someone to help her. Then to her horror she felt the hot blood begin to flow. She was haemorrhaging. Oh, what had that woman done to her? She knew she had to get help now.

Holding the sheet as tightly to her as she could she dragged herself to the door and began to shout. Her panic increased as she realised that Harry was in the bar, which would probably be half full, and couldn't hear her. With a huge effort that made the sweat stand out on her forehead, she dragged herself down the stairs.

Harry thought he'd heard her calling him but had had to finish serving two dockers who were having an argument. The drink might pacify them; if not he'd have to get rid of them. Then he heard her again, this time more clearly.

'Be back in a second, lads. Don't kill each other in the meantime!' he quipped, going into the kitchen.

Lily was managing to hold herself upright by clinging to the doorpost.

'Lily! God in heaven! What's the matter?' he cried as she slowly slid to her knees. Then he saw the bright scarlet stain on the sheet she was clutching to her. 'Jesus! Lily!'

Lily was feeling very faint. 'Harry, help me. Get . . . get Maggie!'

Harry faced a terrible dilemma. She was in a bad way: if he left her, what would happen? Yet it was obviously some women's problem and Maggie would be the best person for that. He managed to get her to her feet and half dragged, half carried her to the sofa and lifted her on to it. She was losing a terrible amount of blood. He made up his mind.

'Will you be all right while I go for Maggie?'

She nodded and he ran back into the bar. 'Alf, do me a favour, get behind this bar. I've got to go for Maggie. It's an emergency!' He didn't wait for an answer but ran back through the kitchen and into the yard.

Billy was startled on opening the door to the insistent hammering to find a breathless and sweating Harry Dempsey in his shirt sleeves and with no hat or cap on his head.

'Billy! Where's Maggie? It's Lily! She's got to come right now!' Harry gasped.

'What's happened?' Billy knew Maggie wouldn't be pleased to see Harry Dempsey.

'For God's sake, Billy! Where's Maggie?'

'I'm here. What do you want?' Maggie snapped, appearing behind Billy.

'It's Lily. She's in a terrible state. She's losing blood, pints of it! You've got to come, Maggie. Eve and Sarah went to Ireland on Friday night.'

'Did she cut herself? Did she fall?' Maggie was worried now.

'No. She went out, and when she came back she said she had a headache and went to bed, then I heard her calling me and . . . Maggie, for the love of God, please come!'

'You'd better go, luv,' Billy urged. There was something very wrong here.

Maggie grabbed her coat.

'Harry, take my bicycle, you'll be quicker. I'll bring Maggie,' Billy added.

'Thanks. I've left a pub full of people and only Alf in charge.'

Billy shrugged on his coat and Maggie snatched up her bag. 'Maybe we'll be lucky enough to catch a cab,' he said, slamming the door behind them.

They caught one on the corner and arrived a few minutes after Harry. Billy's bicycle lay abandoned in the yard. As soon as she saw the state of Lily, Maggie knew it was something very serious.

'Oh, God, what happened? Billy, you'd better go to the emergency police telephone in Williamson Square and tell them we need an ambulance quickly.'

Lily grabbed Maggie's hand as both Billy and Harry disappeared. 'No, Maggie, stop him! Please, no ambulance! No police!'

'Why?' Maggie's eyes widened as an awful thought struck her. 'You weren't pregnant? You ... you haven't done ... something?'

Lily nodded weakly. 'I was and I ... I *had* to! There was no other way, my new job ...'

'Mary, Mother of God, you little fool. When? Was it today?'

Lily nodded. 'This afternoon. I was all right at first, then ... pain, terrible pain and then the blood. Maggie, I'm scared! I want Mam!'

Maggie dropped to her knees and gathered her in her arms. She too was scared. So many girls and women died after visiting these back-street butchers, she knew that – and Mam had warned her against it. Lily must have been to one of them. 'Hush, Lily, it's going to be all right now,' she soothed, holding her sister tightly in her arms until Billy returned and informed her that an ambulance was on its way.

'Billy, she's been to an abortionist. It's a crime. What are we going to do?' Maggie pleaded.

Billy looked shocked and helpless. 'Oh, no! I ... I don't know what we'll do.'

'Can't you do better than that, Billy?' Maggie almost screamed at him.

'What's wrong now?' Harry asked. He'd cleared the bar and put the towel on.

'She's gone and had an abortion! Jesus, what are we going to do?' Maggie wailed.

'The idiot! But it can't be helped now, Maggie. She'll have to go to hospital and then take the consequences.'

'It will destroy us all,' Maggie snapped at him.

'Where did she get the money?' Harry asked. 'She was broke and those women charge the earth.'

Maggie uttered a stricken cry. 'Oh, heavens! It . . . it was me! I gave it to her, but she said it was for her uniform!'

Billy stared at her in horror. 'You gave it to her!'

'What was I supposed to do? I didn't know . . .' Maggie was near to tears.

'That doesn't matter now, Maggie, it wasn't your fault. How were you to know she'd use it for something like this?' Harry said. 'Thank God, there's the ambulance now. Maggie, you go with her. I'll come too. Eve would never forgive me if I didn't. I was supposed to be keeping my eye on her.'

'What shall I do, Maggie?' Billy asked helplessly.

Maggie looked at him impatiently. Could he never make a decision on his own? 'You'd better try and get word to Mam. Send a telegram.'

'But don't, for God's sake, say what's wrong with Lily. Just say she's had to go to hospital,' Harry added.

On the way to the hospital Lily lost consciousness. Maggie held her hand tightly, her face as white and drawn as Lily's own, while Harry looked anxiously at the ambulance man whose expression was very serious indeed. Lily was rushed into the Casualty Department and Maggie and Harry were told to wait.

A Mother's Love

Maggie sank down on the wooden bench, shaking, and Harry put his arm around her. 'She'll be all right, Maggie,' he said comfortingly, but he doubted his own words. Lily had looked ghastly and she'd lost so much blood.

Maggie was sobbing quietly on Harry's shoulder when half an hour later the doctor came through and told them that, despite all their efforts, Lily was dead. Maggie's sobbing became uncontrollable and a terrible feeling of grief and loss descended on Harry. Poor Lily. Poor foolish little Lily. She'd had so much to live for and now . . . He gently drew Maggie to her feet.

'I'm afraid the police will have to interview you both to see if you have any idea who did this to her. These women should be strung up by the neck!' the doctor said angrily.

'I agree but we don't know who did it. We didn't know she'd been to see anyone – we didn't even know she was pregnant,' Harry replied.

'You're not the husband?'

'No, just a family friend. This is her sister.'

The doctor shook his head.

Billy appeared in the doorway and looked with shock at his weeping wife, a dazed and grieving Harry and the grim-faced doctor.

'Lily's dead,' Harry announced flatly.

'Oh, Maggie, I'm so sorry!' Billy took Maggie in his arms. 'I'll take her home.'

'We should all go back to the George, Billy. We've got to decide what to do now,' Harry said sadly.

Maggie had calmed down a little by the time they reached

the pub. She still couldn't believe it. Harry brought a bottle of brandy in from the bar and made her drink a glass. Both he and Billy had a glass too.

'Did you send the telegram, Billy?' Harry asked.

'Yes. I just said Lily had been taken to hospital. I didn't say what was wrong with her.'

'Then we're going to have to send another.'

'No!' Maggie cried. 'You can't put something like that in a telegram. Just think what it would do to poor Mam!'

'Don't get upset, Maggie. I'm going to send the telegram to Sarah's fiancé, Mr Nolan. Sarah gave me his address in case I should need it. Someone over there should know exactly what has happened and from what I've heard of him, he sounds like an understanding man and one who can keep his mouth shut. He's not going to want the circumstances of his poor sister-in-law's death broadcast all over the parish, is he? I'll go over myself tomorrow.'

Maggie's opinion of Harry Dempsey had undergone a radical change in the last few hours. 'I'll come with you. We were both with her almost to the last and Mam will want to know . . .' Maggie broke down again and sobbed on Billy's shoulder.

'What about Lily?' Billy asked.

'Can you go and see them at Coyne's, Billy? Explain. Ask them to take care of Lily until Eve and Maggie and I get home.'

Billy nodded miserably. There had been so much death lately. It was terrible. Eddie, then his gran and now poor Lily. And both Eddie and Lily tragically. 'But what about

Aoife? Shouldn't she know? Shouldn't she be told?' he pressed.

'She might get into such a state herself about Lily that she blurts something out to Eve and that would be disastrous. No, I'm certain I can trust Michael Nolan. I'm confident he'll know how to handle it all.'

Billy nodded.

'Maggie, do you think you can be ready for the ferry tomorrow morning? Will you be up to it?' Harry asked gently.

Maggie could only nod. She wasn't up to it, she couldn't even think straight, but there was nothing else she could do.

'Is there one?' Billy asked.

'Yes. It sails at ten. Sarah got the timetable when she was toying with the idea of going on Friday morning. I don't know what time we'll get to Tullamore. It will be very late. I just hope there's a train. If not we'll have to stay in Dublin for the night.'

'Then I'll get Maggie home now. She'll have to try to get some rest. I'll see you in the morning. You'll close up the pub until you come back?'

Harry nodded. There was nothing else he could do and if the brewery didn't like it they could lump it!

Chapter Twenty-Nine

I CAN SEE WHY SARAH loves living here, Eve thought as she walked back from Mass on Sunday morning. Everyone was friendly and she had been made to feel very welcome. It *was* so peaceful and quiet compared to Liverpool and especially Upper Dawson Street. She'd spent a pleasant evening with Aoife and Carthage and had slept very well last night.

It was another crisp, sunny morning and the hedgerows sparkled with a silver tracery of frost. The air was so fresh and clear that it almost made you feel light-headed. She said as much to Sarah who was walking beside her with Michael.

Sarah laughed. 'I think it's probably more to do with the fact that you've been fasting for Communion, Mam.'

Eve smiled. 'That too but it certainly gives you an appetite—'

'Ah, it won't take me long to put a good plate of rashers and eggs on the table,' Aoife interrupted, having heard the exchange from a pace behind. 'Kathleen, run on ahead and

389

put on the kettle. Ita, go with her and put down a fire if it's died on us!'

'Michael, are you going to the Thatch before your dinner?' Carthage asked.

'I am so and I was thinking of taking Sarah and Eve too.'

'God have mercy on us! Ye can't take them to that place! Sure, it's only fit for farmers and the like,' Aoife said, disparagingly.

'Oh, I don't mind. I'm well used to dealing with working men and have been all my life. The George is far from a posh pub, Aoife,' Eve laughed.

'Well, I don't think Sarah should be seen in there. Herself above at the Lodge won't like it one bit.'

'I'm not going to have to consider "Herself above" for very much longer,' Sarah informed them, smiling at Michael. They were going for the ring on Monday and intended to get married after Christmas.

'Then that's settled. I'll see you all at about one o'clock. You're very welcome to come too, Aoife. Make it a sort of celebration.'

'And who is going to put the meal on the table for half past two, Michael Nolan, will ye tell me that?' Aoife demanded.

'What's wrong with Teresa? Isn't she a fine strap of a girl and you've taught her to cook? And you never get out much,' Carthage stated.

'Look, you and I will get everything prepared and then I'm sure Teresa can finish off,' Eve suggested.

'I'm just sorry I have to go back to the Lodge. I only have

a few hours off this afternoon and that's only because Mam's here,' Sarah said wistfully.

'That can't be helped and we can manage,' Eve said firmly.

Aoife had finally consented to join them and they'd spent a pleasant hour in the rather dismal bar of the local pub. Eve had to agree with her cousin that a good clean wouldn't do the place any harm.

'But it's not a bad little place. It could be made quite nice.'

Carthage looked at her askance. 'Not too fancy, Eve! You'd not get a working man over the doorstep if it was all lace curtains and carpets.'

'You could have two separate rooms. One for the workers – a saloon bar – and a nice parlour where they could take their wives.'

'If they take their wives at all 'tis only on high days and holy days!' Aoife remarked cuttingly.

'Well, that's what I'd do if I had the place,' Eve said.

'Would ye consider taking it, Eve?' Aoife asked curiously.

'Would you, Mam?' Sarah asked.

'I've the experience and it might make a nice change from a city pub. Why, is there a chance the licensee would sell?'

'Ah, hasn't he been saying he'd get rid of it for years and hasn't he done nothing about it?' Carthage commented.

'I don't have the money anyway. I just rent my pub from the brewery,' Eve said. A little sadly, Sarah thought.

'But Maggie does,' Aoife put in before remembering that Eve and Maggie were at daggers drawn.

'I can't see our Maggie giving you and Harry the money to buy this place,' Sarah said. 'Unless of course she would look on it as money well spent to get you out of Liverpool and not be offending her notions of *respectability*.' She was joking but there was a grain of truth in her words, she thought.

'Oh, let's not spoil the day by thinking along those lines. We're here to celebrate you two going for the ring tomorrow,' Eve said firmly, closing the subject.

Sarah had gone back to the Lodge reluctantly but thankful that she would very shortly be giving in her notice. She was sitting talking to Cook after dinner was over and the kitchen tidied when Michael arrived at the back door.

'What's wrong? It's nearly ten o'clock!'

'Paddy Conway came out to me not half an hour ago with two telegrams. One is for your mam and one for me, so he thought he'd save himself the journey to Aoife's and asked me to take them both.'

'Telegrams! At this time of night on a Sunday! Oh, Michael, what's wrong?'

He looked quickly at Cook and took Sarah's hands.

Cook left the room instantly.

'Sarah, sit down. I'm terribly afraid it's shocking news, my love, the worst. Maggie and Harry will be on the morning ferry. Lily . . . poor Lily is dead. It seems she was expecting and went to a woman to . . . to get rid of it.'

Sarah just stared at him and then suddenly everything went very black.

When she came to Cook was chafing her hands, Michael

had his arm around her and Mrs Kavanagh was standing over her, looking very concerned.

She struggled to rise from the chair. 'Oh, I'm so sorry, I don't know what happened. Michael, why are you here?' She was confused.

'Sarah, don't you remember?' he asked, helping her to her feet.

And then she did. She collapsed against him. Maggie and Harry would be here tomorrow and Lily . . . Lily was dead! She sobbed broken-heartedly in Michael's arms.

'I think it would be best if you took her to her mother, Mr Nolan.'

'Her mother doesn't know yet, ma'am.'

'Oh, dear! Well, take her to my sitting room and try to calm her while I go to see Madam. This is very distressing – for everyone.'

Michael Nolan guided Sarah towards the door whilst thinking that Eliza Kavanagh was being very considerate.

'What do *you* want to do, Sarah?' he asked when she had calmed down a little. He had made her drink a small glass of the sherry he had found in a cupboard.

'I don't know. I want to see Mam, but how am I to tell her this? Oh, Lily! Lily! You poor little fool!'

'You need to be with your family, my love. I'll take you to Aoife's and I'll tell her if you'd prefer that.'

Sarah nodded. She didn't want to stay here now, and she knew her mam would need her. They would need each other.

'It's going to be very hard on you all, but I want you to know that I'll be by your side through everything, Sarah. I'll come to Liverpool with you and when it's all over we'll come back together. And you're not coming back here. Just put a few things together for now, I'll send for the rest.'

Sarah was in a complete daze as they drove over to Aoife's but never had she been so thankful for Michael's complete love and support. She knew she could always trust and rely on him in any emergency.

Carthage opened the door to them and Michael pulled him outside and they had a quiet, hurried conversation. Then Michael helped Sarah down.

'Carthage is going to get Aoife out here. She'll take care of you while I go and tell Eve. If Eve sees you, she'll know something is wrong.'

Sarah nodded and pulled her coat closer around her. In a few seconds Aoife was out, a shawl wrapped around her shoulders.

'Ah, Sarah, come here to me. God have mercy on her soul. What made her do something so terrible as that?'

Sarah couldn't answer her. It was a question that would always haunt her.

When Michael finally came back outside Sarah was leaning against Aoife's shoulder. It was strange, she thought, there were no more tears. She just felt numb. Cold and numb.

Michael helped her down. 'Come on in to the fire now.'

'How is she?'

'Shocked. But she needs you and she's so thankful that Harry is coming and, of course, Maggie.'

Eve was sitting beside the range and Sarah was horrified

to see how pale her mother looked. 'Oh, Mam! Mam!' she cried softly.

Eve turned and Sarah saw the raw and bitter grief in her eyes. Within seconds she was in her mother's arms and Eve was holding her tightly.

'Oh, Sarah, I blame myself. I should have been there. If I had this would never have happened. I let her down. I let her down when she needed me.'

'No, Mam. I . . . I shouldn't have talked you into coming,' Sarah choked.

Aoife took them both in hand. 'Stop that, both of ye. How were ye to know? She didn't *want* ye to know – either of ye. Eve, if ye'd been at home ye still wouldn't have known until it was too late. Ye can't blame yourselves. Ye *can't*!'

'She's right. Lily kept it from you both. From everyone,' Michael added. There was no point in either of them tearing themselves apart with guilt. 'Aoife, have you a drop of something in the house? I think they both need it.'

An hour later, when Michael left, both women were calmer and had agreed to try to get some sleep. Sarah was staying. Aoife had hastily informed two of her daughters that they were sleeping in the kitchen for tonight. Eve and Sarah needed some peace and quiet.

They both lay awake for a long time, clinging to each other, Sarah quietly sobbing while Eve stared into the darkness, silent tears sliding down her cheeks.

The next day was miserable. Utterly depressing. Heavy clouds poured forth an unceasing torrent of icy cold rain and it never really got light. Both Sarah and Eve just sat holding on to each other, staring out of the window. Even the skies were weeping, Eve thought. Oh, Lily! So young, so pretty, so headstrong, so thoughtless. Looking no further ahead than tomorrow. Lily's tomorrows were always brighter and more promising than her todays had ever been. Lily was a dreamer, always had been. She'd dreamed of being 'famous', then of 'travelling'. She'd always wanted life to be 'exciting'. And now her short life was over. Would she ever get over the loss of her youngest daughter?

It was almost ten o'clock that night when Harry and Maggie arrived, tired and grief-stricken. Michael had been at the station to meet them.

Maggie fell into her mother's arms. 'Mam, I'm so sorry for everything I said! It's my fault. I gave her the money. I didn't know what she was going to do with it, I swear to God, I didn't.'

Eve tried to soothe her. 'Of course you didn't. It's not your fault, Maggie. It's . . . it's no one's fault. How were we to know, although I should have guessed. She was so sick the other morning.' Eve looked pitifully at Harry. How she longed to throw herself into his arms and sob out her grief, but she was a mother first and foremost.

'Harry's been so good, Mam. I don't know how I would have managed without him.' Maggie meant it. Now she could see why her mother loved him.

'Sit down, luv. Aoife's got a meal ready and after that you and Sarah must try and get some sleep. It's been a terrible day for us too.'

Maggie tried to pull herself together. 'Billy's going to make arrangements with Coyne's. They'll look after Lily until we all get home.'

'That's good of him. I wondered what . . .' Eve couldn't go on. She hadn't been able to bear thinking about poor Lily lying alone and deserted on a hospital mortuary slab.

Maggie wanted to be fair. 'It was Harry's idea.'

Eve's heart went out to Harry. She should have known. Billy would have been lost and confused and Harry was far more thoughtful than Eddie had ever been.

Maggie disentangled herself from her mother's arms. Mam needed time with Harry. She needed comforting too. Maggie knew she would never disregard her mother's feelings so utterly again. 'Come on, Sarah, you'd better show me where we're going to sleep. I'm dead on my feet.'

Aoife had lit a fire in her small parlour and when the girls had gone up she told Eve to go and sit in there with Harry. 'If ye need me, just shout,' she said.

When they were alone Harry took Eve in his arms. 'I'd have done anything, Eve, to have spared you this. I *had* to come. I couldn't let Maggie come on her own and Billy's not much use.'

'Did she . . . suffer?'

'Not a great deal. She came back about three, went to bed and then I heard her calling at about five. We sent for the ambulance right away, after I went for Maggie. She'd lost a lot of blood and she slipped into unconsciousness in the ambulance. The hospital did everything they could to save her but . . . but it wasn't to be.'

'Did she say anything?'

'No, but I know she was sorry.'

'But she had so much to look forward to, so many years ahead of her . . . If only she'd told me. I wouldn't have turned her out! She could have had the baby; I would have cared for it. She could have had a life! Oh, Lily . . . She had so many dreams, Harry.'

'I know. A handful of dreams and the love of a good mother and two caring sisters. It should have been enough, but it wasn't. She always wanted life to be full of excitement and life's not like that. Maybe she would have had a life full of disappointments and never really have been happy. We'll all go home tomorrow, Eve.'

'I don't think I will ever be happy there again. Everything will remind me of her – *everything*!'

Harry said nothing. There was nothing to say. He just held her and stroked her hair.

Epilogue

Spring

'MAM, ARE YOU SURE these colours go together?' Maggie looked doubtfully at her outfit in the long mirror in Eve's bedroom.

'You look lovely. You can take bright colours.'

Maggie smoothed down the skirt of the green and cream check suit and turned her head to get the best effect from the primrose-coloured, large-brimmed straw hat, which was trimmed with the same green as her suit.

'And they're real spring colours,' Eve added, thinking how striking her dark-haired daughter looked.

'And it was extremely expensive. From Cripps in Bold Street, no less! I must have been mad to let our Sarah talk me into buying it – I paid a small fortune.'

'Well, she's only getting married once, please God, and she wanted you to look like the successful young woman you are.'

Maggie smiled. She and Billy *were* going to be successful. They had two businesses, a nice house in Walton-on-the-Hill, two houses rented out in Everton and the part share in Mam and Harry's pub. She had been quite relieved when Hilda had said she had no wish to live in her deceased mother-in-law's home, but was quite happy where she was. She'd lived there for twenty years and knew all her neighbours and was too settled to move now. It had meant that they could sell the house in Claudia Street, which had given them more capital, and she intended to buy cheaper property to rent out. It brought in a good income. She was also thankful that Billy's family had decided it would be too expensive to contest the will. They had calmed down considerably after she had agreed to Billy's suggestion that they give them a small share of the profits from the sale of Claudia Street.

'You look really nice too, Mam. It's going to be a "grand" occasion, as they say over here.'

'Well, it didn't come from Cripps but I must say that nice little dress shop in Harbour Street did have quite a good selection.' Eve had chosen a mauve dress and jacket trimmed with pale lilac and her hat was pale lilac trimmed with mauve. It suited her and she would get quite a lot of wear out of it, she told Harry; she could wear the dress when she served in the lounge bar on Sundays. Her shoes were a little tight but she was ignoring the fact. The heels were quite high but Sarah said they made her look taller and more elegant.

She reflected for a minute on her own wedding to Harry. She'd had nothing like this outfit for it had been a very quiet affair with just Maggie and Billy, Sarah and Michael and a couple of her close neighbours present. It had taken place two days after Christmas and two weeks later she and Harry had left the George and come to Ireland. Maggie had insisted on giving them the money to buy the Thatch, which was now called 'Dempsey's Bar' or just 'Dempsey's'. In his turn Harry had insisted that Maggie and Billy have a share in the place, for, as he'd said, although Maggie had changed he never wanted to be totally beholden to her or Billy.

'I just hope those kids of Aoife's behave when we get to the Bridge House Hotel for the wedding breakfast. They'll be all right in church but they can be a bit wild.'

'Oh, Maggie, they're not bad. They're just excited. They've never been anywhere so grand before.'

'That's what I mean!'

'Eve, the flowers have arrived and that fancy carriage Sarah's having will be here in less than half an hour.' Harry's voice came up to them from the bar where he and Billy were giving the Pearce brothers their instructions, they being in charge for the day.

'Run down and bring them up, Maggie luv, while I find my gloves and then we'd better see how Sarah's doing. Teresa's supposed to be helping her but she's in such a state of nerves herself about being chief bridesmaid that I doubt she'll be much use.'

Eve located her gloves and put them beside her bag on the dressing table while Maggie went down for the flowers.

She returned with her arms full and shooing four young

girls ahead of her. 'In there and sit down on the bed and don't move. You'll have your dresses creased to bits. Kathleen, fix Ita's head-dress, it's slipped to one side and looks a mess,' she instructed.

Aoife's young daughter did as she was bid and then sat with her sister and Michael's two nieces on Eve's bed. They were all delighted with themselves and very excited. It was going to be a very fancy wedding and they all had lovely pale pink taffeta dresses with wide white sashes and long rustling skirts, small frilled puff sleeves and little white silk flowers around the necklines. Kathleen examined her white buckskin shoes with the ankle straps and thought they were the most gorgeous shoes she'd ever seen. Ita fiddled with the clips that fastened the wreath of pink and white artificial apple blossom to her mop of thick auburn curls.

'Ita, my love, leave it alone or it will slip again,' Eve said kindly while Maggie raised her eyes to the ceiling in irritation. 'Now, I'm going to put your posies on the window ledge; don't touch them until we're ready to go. Then we're going to see how Sarah and Teresa are getting on.'

Maggie gave them all one quelling look before following her mother out.

Sarah was dressed and Teresa was quite expertly fixing the small Juliet cap of stiffened white lace sewn with seed pearls over Sarah's shining blonde hair, which had been swept up in a chignon. The yards and yards of silk tulle veiling had been expertly attached to the cap by Liverpool's foremost milliner herself.

Catching sight of her mother and sister through the

mirror Sarah stood up, helped by Teresa. 'How do I look, Mam?'

'Oh, Sarah! You look . . . you look like a princess!' Tears pricked Eve's eyes. Sarah *did*. She looked so beautiful, so tall and slim and elegant.

'Aren't you glad I made you go to Miss Drinkwater and not buy a ready-made wedding dress?' Maggie said softly. Miss Drinkwater's Dressmaking Emporium was considered a little old-fashioned now but it was still the best Liverpool could boast.

'I am and it's the most beautiful wedding present I could have had!' Sarah replied smiling, for the dress had been a gift from Maggie and Billy.

'I've never seen anything so gorgeous! Ye wouldn't have got the like in any of the places above in Dublin. It'll be the talk of the parish and Tullamore too, so it will!' Teresa added, spreading out the skirt for full effect.

Eve dreaded to think what it had cost. The whole of the tight-fitting bodice and long sleeves had been embroidered with tiny seed pearls and silver bugle beads in an intricate design of flowers and leaves and the small stand-up collar was edged with drop pearls. The front of the skirt was of plain white duchesse satin but the back and the long train were embroidered with tiny clusters of roses and shamrocks.

Maggie laid Sarah's bouquet down on the bed. It was a glorious confection of pink and white roses and carnations, entwined with dark green foliage and small sprigs of silver-green rosemary and feathery smilax down. 'Will we ruin the effect entirely by hugging you?'

Sarah held out her arms to her mother and sister. 'Of course not! Come here to me, both of you!' She put an arm around each of them.

'If Lily was here she'd be too excited to keep still,' Maggie said sadly.

'She *is* here – in spirit. I *know* she is,' Eve said firmly, wiping a tear from her own eye. 'And she'd want us all to be happy. Only tears of joy will be shed today.'

'I . . . I like to think she's with Da and that now they're both happy,' Sarah said a little unsteadily.

'Eve, the cars Harry's hired are after pulling up outside,' Teresa informed them, glancing quickly out of the window and then into the mirror to check her appearance. It was going to be a grand day for her too. She had a very stylish deep rose-pink taffeta dress and Juliet cap, to set her apart from the little bridesmaids, a new hairstyle and her first pair of high-heeled shoes – thanks to Sarah's persistence in overcoming her ma's objections. And she would be riding in a big black shiny car, instead of being jolted around in the trap.

Eve pulled herself together. Harry was giving Sarah away and they would go to church in the open carriage. Maggie and Billy and the four small bridesmaids would go in one car, while she and Teresa would go in the other. 'Right, let's get those four organised. Teresa, you go with Maggie and I'll go and send Harry up.'

Maggie handed Sarah her bouquet. She was certain Sarah would be happy with Michael. As happy as she was with Billy. 'Good luck. He'll think he's getting an angel when he sees you – and he is!' She kissed Sarah on the cheek and then took Teresa by the arm and went back to Eve's bedroom to hand out the posies and shepherd the other four downstairs.

'She's right, Sarah. I wish you so much happiness and every blessing!' Eve hugged her again.

'Oh, Mam, go and get Harry before I ruin my make-up by bursting into tears,' Sarah choked, although she managed to smile.

Harry was standing at the foot of the stairs and Eve thought how handsome he looked in his new suit from Farrell's. These days he was more confident too and she knew she could always rely on him for he'd been her rock through the darkest days of her life.

'Is everyone ready?'

'Yes. Maggie and Teresa will be down with the girls in a few seconds and Sarah . . . well, I know Maggie looked lovely on her wedding day but Sarah looks *radiant*! She looks like a princess and an angel rolled into one.'

'Then he'll be delighted with her!' He put his arm around Eve. 'I hope they'll be as happy as we are. We have each other, we have a new life and new friends.'

Eve looked at him sadly. 'If only . . .'

'I know. Lily will be in everyone's thoughts, it's only natural. It will be a bittersweet day, but one we'll always remember – as we will Lily. She'll never grow old in our memories, Eve, and we've not left her. Maggie's over there building her business empire, she'll watch over her.'

Eve smiled a little tearfully. 'I know she will.'

'No tears today, Mrs Dempsey!' he chided, kissing her gently.

'Just tears of joy, Harry. Just tears of joy for Sarah and Michael and Maggie and Billy.'

'And us, Eve. I love you!'

'I love you too, Harry Dempsey!'

When Daylight Comes

Lyn Andrews

Jessica Brennan is just nineteen years old when her world falls apart. Losing her father at sea was devastating enough, but the death of her mother is almost too much to bear. The grieving has barely begun when Jess learns that the family business is in ruins, but there are further blows to come. Jess's brother Patrick is determined to gamble with what little they have left . . .

Suddenly a young woman who has known only comfort and security finds herself alone and friendless. But Jess is a fighter and in her darkest hour she finds the strength she needs to start again. From buying and selling dyed feathers as hat trimmings, Jess gradually establishes a business that can support not only herself and Tilly, a little girl she rescues from the streets, but also Patrick. Tragedy, however, is just around the corner, leaving Jess more determined than ever to regain the happiness and security she once had . . .

Praise for Lyn Andrews

'Gutsy . . . A vivid picture of a hard-up, hard-working community . . . will keep the pages turning' *Express*

'An outstanding storyteller' *Woman's Weekly*

'The Catherine Cookson of Liverpool' *Northern Echo*

0 7472 6712 X

headline

Now you can buy any of these other bestselling books by **Lyn Andrews** from your bookshop or *direct from her publisher*.

FREE P&P AND UK DELIVERY
(Overseas and Ireland £3.50 per book)